For all carers, everywhere.

THE IMPERFECT ART OF CARING

JESSICA RYN

ONE PLACE. MANY STORIES

HQ
An imprint of HarperCollins*Publishers* Ltd
1 London Bridge Street
London SE1 9GF

www.harpercollins.co.uk

HarperCollins*Publishers*
1st Floor, Watermarque Building, Ringsend Road
Dublin 4, Ireland

This edition 2022

1
First published in Great Britain by
HQ, an imprint of HarperCollins*Publishers* Ltd 2021

ISBN 978-0-00-836470-0

MIX
Paper from
responsible sources
FSC™ C007454

This book is produced from independently certified FSC™ paper
to ensure responsible forest management.

For more information visit: www.harpercollins.co.uk/green

This book is set in 11.5/15.5 pt. Bembo

Printed and Bound in the UK using 100% Renewable Electricity at
CPI Group (UK) Ltd, Croydon, CR0 4YY

Praise for Jessica Ryn

'Warm and entertaining ... shines a light
on a sector of society that is mostly overlooked'
Katie Fforde, *A Springtime Affair*

'The perfect warm-hearted novel for our
current moment − a book full of hope, love
and kindness, with a powerful message'
Kirsty Capes, *Careless*

'Dealing with heartbreaking issues with
humour, this will uplift your soul'
Heat

'I absolutely adored it! A joyful, uplifting novel that
made me laugh and ugly-cry in the best possible way'
Freya Sampson, *The Last Library*

'A poignant reminder about the importance of
connection and community, written with such heart'
Nicola Gill, *The Neighbours*

'So good I read it in one sitting.
Warm-hearted, moving and funny'
Frances Quinn, *The Smallest Man*

'Oozing warmth and compassion, it will make your heart melt'
Closer

'Speaks for so many who aren't heard. I absolutely loved it'
Anstey Harris, *The Truths and Triumphs of Grace Atherton*

'Completely beguiling − a messy, loveable cast of characters'
Beth Morrey, *Saving Missy*

Jessica Ryn is a former midwife and homeless resettlement worker. She has recently completed her MA in Creative Writing at Canterbury Christ Church University, and her stories have been shortlisted for the Kimberley Chambers Kickstart Prize, Wordsmag and the Val Wood Prize for Creative Writing. When she's not scribbling away, Jessica can be found meandering through the woods, reading stories that pull on the feel-strings and eating yoghurt-covered Skittles. Jessica lives in Dover with her husband, two children and their high-spirited springer spaniel. You can find out more about Jessica on her website www.jessicaryn.com or follow her on Twitter @Jessryn1.

Also by Jessica Ryn
The Extraordinary Hope of Dawn Brightside

CHAPTER I

Violet

A PERSON'S HOME IS their castle. It doesn't matter how tiny it is, or how messy. The important thing is that its defences are properly maintained.

Violet Strong's bedsit is her sanctuary, a small piece of the world that's just for her. She can walk its perimeter in thirty-two steps, one for every year of her life. She hasn't washed up her breakfast things and her bed looks like something from a Tracey Emin exhibition.

Usually, this wouldn't matter; she wouldn't care very much about the piles of laundry and dirty crockery, not when there's a soft rug beneath her bare toes and stacks of beautiful books lining the walls. She's in her happy place after all. Her very own castle that's just the right distance from work and bursting with the delicious smell of chicken chow mein from the takeaway downstairs.

Now everything's changed. The defences have been breached. The door buzzer is sounding its warning alarm.

Violet runs through the names of people who have her address. It's a short list and there's only one way to know for sure. She balances on the very tips of her toes to peer through the peephole. Her feet catch on the hem of her purple dungarees, making it even harder not to topple over when she sees who it is.

Jodie.

Now Violet's eyes won't be the only ones she has to view her surroundings with. Now she has her sister's.

Jodie's eyes won't have the same filter.

It's been fourteen years since they last saw each other, and her sister still looks the same. Impossibly neat as if she's been stitched together by a home economics teacher.

With a hammering heart, Violet lets down the drawbridge and puts the kettle on. Of course she does, what other choice does she have? She wrestles Jodie's dusky pink jacket onto a hook by the door with trembling hands, covering a bulge of old cardigans as she whips out a welcoming smile and forces it onto her face.

Turns out the smile is too heavy. It keeps slipping up and down and Violet wishes she could stuff it back in a drawer, like she should have done with the shirt that's digging into her elbows, making her arms look like bulging sausages.

'This is … a surprise.' Violet looks to her left to avoid catching Jodie's eye, and tries to focus on the fact that the sun has ripped a hole in the grey clouds outside and is beaming through her grimy windows, kissing her face with warmth. 'Nice to finally see some sunshine.' Stick to small talk, Violet. Safer that way.

'Nice place.' Jodie cranes her neck in every possible direction as if she's trying to find something to compliment. She perches on the only corner of the sofa that isn't covered with fluffy cushions or chocolate wrappers, and picks up Violet's new book, *Reasons to be Happy,* before leafing through it. The bookmark falls out. Violet's place is lost.

'We need to have a chat about Mum,' Jodie says.

Violet tries hard not to clench her teeth, her fists, or her toes. Her afternoon had been set aside for reading, chocolate, and solitude. *Just breathe.*

'I'll make us a drink.' Violet's voice still carries her usual tune. It's the one that sings happy, happy, happy. It's hard sometimes to make it sound like anything else. 'Milk? Sugar?' Violet expects most sisters know such things about each other – they make each other's beverages without a second thought. But most other siblings don't go quite so long before remembering to speak to each other. She just needs to get through this conversation without unravelling like the corner of the blanket on her futon.

'Mum's gone downhill. Further downhill. Worse.' Jodie shakes her head as she stands up and her perfect bob stays in place like Lego hair, a far cry from Violet's unbrushed mop that she'd shoved into two thick red braids. 'I just can't do it anymore. I really think it's time …'

'Cake. I have cake. Three different sorts.' Violet takes two steps towards the kitchenette and yanks open a cupboard, wishing her home has more than one room so she can close a door between her and Jodie, just for a moment. Long enough to slow down the thud, thud of her heart. To take a breath, poke her tongue out or flick a defiant middle finger. 'Ginger, chocolate or a Victoria slice.' She hauls herself onto the worktop and balances her knees on it as she reaches up to the top shelf. She pulls at a Tupperware box and a bottle of soy sauce dives to the floor, cracking and seeping its contents onto the off-white lino.

'I thought you were a cleaner?' Jodie is beside her staring into the cupboard. She's a foot taller than Violet and has an unobstructed view of the sheer amount of crap crammed into it. She'll be able to see the spilled grains of rice on the surfaces of the top shelf and the sticky gloop of honey that coats the bottom one.

'Yep. All the same, us cleaners.' Violet nudges out a laugh. 'Spend all day making other places nice and can't be bothered to do our own.' It's not true. Most of the others on her team keep their places spotless. Why work hard making the offices gleam and then come home to a cesspit, they'd say.

This is why she never has visitors.

17B, Harper's Court, is Violet's safe place. It's warm and fully stocked with smelly candles, soft throws, and comfy cushions. Piles of books, head-high, line two of the four walls. One wall is kept clear except for the bright yellow canvas that sits above a spotless white shelf holding a vase of ornamental daffodils, a buddha and a colour-coordinated row of paperbacks in size order. That's her Instagram corner. No one needs to see the rest.

'So, about Mum. I know it's been a long time since you've been home,' Jodie starts again.

'Fourteen years.'

Jodie's mouth stays ajar, unsure whether to let any more words out.

Violet makes the most of the pause and turns around to make the coffees. All her spoons are submerged in the washing-up bowl. She doesn't fancy dipping her hand in the cold water with all those floating cornflakes, so she tips the contents straight from the coffee jar.

'You really do need to come and see her. You can't stay away forever.'

'Last time I saw Mum, I was eighteen years old. Eighteen.' Violet keeps her voice gentle as she pours the kettle. None of this is Jodie's fault and it wouldn't be fair to spew her own guilt and agony in the wrong direction, her sister's had enough to deal with. Violet should be the one to pick up the slack, but she's the last person on this shiny round Earth her mum would ever want to see.

Violet picks up both mugs and carries them to the table, slopping unstirred coffee onto the tablecloth. Good thing it's waterproof, otherwise the books at the top of the pile beneath it would've got wet. Violet bets her sister has never seen a table made entirely of novels and a plastic sheet.

Jodie picks up her mug and peers inside before putting it back down. 'It's been a long time.' She nods. 'But the past is the past. Time we all moved on.'

A door slams somewhere in the flat next door. Footsteps clatter down the main stairs and above her, kebab shop Chris is listening to 'One Love' on a loop. Sounds of people living their lives.

'I've already done that.' Violet gulps her drink, wincing as it burns the back of her throat. 'Moving on is my thing. I'm pretty good at it.' She points a daft grin she doesn't really mean in Jodie's direction and braces herself for the rest.

'The truth is, I … we need your help. Mum too. I'm not getting any younger,' Jodie says.

'You're only three years older than me.'

'Exactly. There are things I need to do in life. Travel. Maybe a baby. Dave and I have been married two years now and it's not fair to expect him to just … well, he's been offered a new job. Amazing money. Too much to turn down.'

'Wonderful,' Violet says in her brightest voice. She hasn't met Dave, she's only seen the photo of him, the one stuck to the front of Jodie's wedding invitation somewhere in her bottom drawer, but it all sounds very jolly. Her sister deserves some happiness. Most people do.

'It's in New Zealand. He starts in four weeks.'

'One Love' comes to an abrupt finish. Kebab shop Chris must be on his way out to open up. Violet's tummy rumbles. She could eat a chicken doner.

'Mum can't manage at home on her own. I've taken her to visit some residential places – one of them in particular looks wonderful.'

'Did Mum … did she like it?' The words come out as a whisper.

Jodie screws up her face and turns her attention towards the window. 'As much as Mum can like anything. She didn't say she hated it.'

'Great.' There aren't any other words to fit in the gap.

'The only problem is the money. Costs a fortune to stay in those places. The house will need to be sold first and these things take time.'

Violet's mouth fills with the sour taste of guilt. Poor Jodie having to be apart from her husband all that time until Mum's house sells. And poor Dave, having to move to a whole new country on his own.

'I can spread the word about the house, if that would help,' Violet says. 'I don't know anyone around here who wants to move all the way down south, but I can pop it on my Insta.

I've got a lot of followers, one of them is bound to know someone who fancies living in a pretty little village in the middle of nowhere.'

Not Violet, though. Never again.

Jodie snaps her gaze away from the window. 'That's not what I'm asking. The estate agents will find a buyer. But the place will need valuing first and surveying. Possibly some minor repairs.'

'Sounds like a lot of work.' Violet's heart is tapping fast again, she can hear its echo all the way inside her ears.

'And obviously, Mum will need someone with her at all times until she moves.'

'Uh huh. Mmm.' Violet nods. She pulls at the neckline of her jumper, and wafts it up and down to let the air in. It's so hot. She wants to open the window but Jodie's standing in the way. She stumbles back to the sink and runs the cold tap, splashing her cheeks with water.

'I mean, surely you'd jump at the chance to get away from here?' Jodie's peering through the glass again and sweeping her hand towards the street outside.

Violet joins her at the window. Dickson Avenue, the street sign across the road used to say before the 'son' had been sprayed over with red and replaced with 'head'. A car speeds around the corner and stops, brakes squealing, on the other side of the road. Faces appear at windows opposite as the over-egged car speakers almost vibrate themselves out of the alloyed, dragging-its-body-along-the-floor Golf GTI. There's music somewhere underneath the rumbles, but Violet can't tell what's playing.

Teenagers flood to the driver's side and lean in through the windows, talking fast and looking over their shoulders. One of them lobs a can into someone's garden. The car screeches off again, its horn blaring out one continuous roar. A bit like the tinkle of an ice cream van, except this one says, *Come and get your crack, kids, it's the school holidays after all.*

'I like it here, actually.' Violet folds her arms. 'There's a great sense of community.'

Jodie laughs and it's not a nice sound. 'What – that lot out there? You must have to hold on tight to your handbag every time you walk up the road.'

'I don't carry a handbag. And for your information, those three boys out there are brothers. They don't have parents – they got killed whilst on holiday last year – they do what they have to just to put food on the table. The older one, Hamish, he's saving up for university. He wants to become a social worker.'

'Oh.'

Yes, *oh*. Violet's never actually spoken to them, but the oldest one seems like a Hamish. And they do look as if they could do with a bit more parental input, so she's probably not far off.

'You seem to be missing the point, so I'm going to have to sharpen it for you.' Jodie stands up straight and tugs at the curtains, so they're open an even amount. 'I need you to stay with Mum until the sale's gone through and until she's got somewhere to go where she can be properly taken care of.'

The food smell from downstairs that had been making Violet feel so hungry is now thickening at the back of her throat. She grabs the handle on the sash window and pushes it upwards, gulping on the burst of cooler air.

'She won't want that. She won't want to see me.' Violet

scrunches her eyes, blinking away the picture inside them. If she lets herself see that one, others will follow, and she can't have that. 'Too much has happened. It's been too long.'

'Yes, Violet, it has. Way too long. I've looked after Mum on my own for fourteen years – longer than that if you count those years when everything happened. I've barely left that bloody house. Dave has made so many sacrifices living with Mum and me and this job is a great opportunity. I'm going to support him and put us first for a change. Four weeks.' Jodie puts four fingers up in front of Violet's face – two lots of swearing fingers, pointed in the sweary direction. 'You have four weeks to get your shit together, then Dave and I are off to New Zealand. It's time you came home.'

CHAPTER 2

Violet

IF VIOLET HAD BEEN able to sleep even a little bit, she might have been able to hold onto some hope that Jodie's visit had been nothing more than an unwelcome dream. Before yesterday, her only contact with her sister in the last fourteen years was Jodie's signature at the bottom of a Christmas card and a birthday text each April. The wedding invitation had been the hardest to ignore – what kind of person makes excuses not to go to her sister's wedding?

The same kind of person who refuses to look after her own mother it turns out.

Violet screws up her face as she throws off her duvet, causing an avalanche of cushions to fall from her futon. The soothing tones of Ed Sheeran from her phone alarm tells her it's 5 a.m. Too early for most people, but Violet always opts for the early shifts: that way, the few who are up and about outside are still bleary-eyed, content with a *Good morning* or an *Isn't it warm already?* and less likely to want to stop and chat. Or ask awkward questions.

She would drive to work in Pat-the-Fiat if it didn't take twice as long to park than it does to walk.

It takes Violet thirty-eight minutes and twenty seconds of her audiobook to stroll to the office. It's a historical romance, right up Violet's street.

It's always better to keep the mind focussed on a story, especially when your own takes a tricky turn. The narrator is good company. Being alone is wonderful, but not so good after a shock or a visit from an estranged relative.

This morning, the Regency Building is resplendent in the early sunshine. Its glass panels bathe Violet in light as she walks towards the entrance. She takes the lift to the sixteenth floor where the *Salford and Manchester Times* offices are. The muscles in her shoulders start to untangle as she enters the air-conditioned, open-plan haven and breathes in the smell of furniture polish and good coffee. After her bedsit, this is her favourite place to be.

Desks are arranged to face the front of the room so that staff can look through the windows across Media City, home to many buildings just like this one. Most chairs are empty as it's still so early, but some bums are already perched on seats, typing away as they begin the race towards their deadlines.

Violet makes her way to the kitchen and fills a kettle before scurrying towards the cleaning cupboard so she can prep her trolley whilst it boils. Time efficiency is key.

'There she is,' Violet's colleagues say as they grin at her from inside the walk-in cupboard. Dusters are plucked from shelves, and curls are pulled into ponytails as the group launches back into their conversation about *What Happened Last Night*. This is always the most important topic for the Saturday morning shift. Friday nights in The Pink Pig are a key part of their team's week. Violet usually goes along, of course – rude not to, and a properly constructed life ought to include an appropriate amount of socialising. Otherwise, it wouldn't be a real life at all. Work, play, home, and a hobby. Four corner posts that hold up her existence, so it doesn't come crashing down on top of her.

Though of course she always leaves The Pink Pig before nine fifteen. Plenty of time before discussions begin about sharing cabs or whose houses to go back to afterwards, and *way* before people want to start deep and meaningfuls in the ladies loos.

Violet doesn't do deep and meaningfuls, at least not ones she's expected to contribute to. She's more of a listener than a talker. There are several benefits of being a good listener and she loves to hear a good story she can get lost in when she's outside of her books. Of course, the biggest plus of all is that when you're listening, you don't have to talk.

She walks towards Jenny Jones, the *Salford and Manchester Times'* most dedicated journalist. She always says hello to Jenny because Jenny is her favourite for three reasons:

1. Jenny writes the very best articles
2. She's the only person in the world who knows about Violet's secret wish to be a journalist
3. Jenny is the closest anyone has come to being an actual friend of Violet's since she left home

A growl emanates from Jenny's throat as Violet approaches her desk.

Violet keeps her distance. 'Can I get you anything – coffee? Chocolate Hobnob?' she whispers. Sometimes Jenny will show her what she's working on or regale her with tales about her early days on the job. A coffee and a biscuit every now and again seems only fair.

Jenny's pointy glasses slip down her nose as she keeps pressing the same key on her laptop over and over again, with ever-increasing vigour, whilst letting out a string of words that would never be allowed on a Scrabble board.

'It's you,' Jenny says when she looks up from her screen. 'That's good. That's ... good. Maybe you can help me. Forget the coffee. Right now, I need you to read over this for me and tell me what you think. I can't quite get the angle right and you were a huge help last time – you really do have an eye for this sort of thing.' Her red nails flash brightly against her mass of dark curls as she scrunches them between her fingers.

A thrill travels through Violet's every vessel as it does every time Jenny asks her opinion on an actual story. That's what she loves about this office. A whole room holding so many tales within it. They zap from screen to screen, getting framed and reframed, edited and embellished. But the real stories can be found inside the people who write them.

If Violet could, she'd be a journalist. Hearing stories, considering the angles, passing them on ... it would be heaven. It would be a life worth living out loud in every possible colour.

But things haven't quite worked out that way.

'Of course.' Violet slides into the chair next to Jenny. Not many journalists would show their work to a cleaner, but ever since the day Violet found her sobbing in the cleaning cupboard and listened as she spilled her guts about her husband running off with his life coach, they've become something close to friends.

Usually, other people's problems happen *after* they meet Violet, and it had been nice to offer a shoulder for something that wasn't her fault.

The article Jenny is working on is a sad one. The photo of the woman in the middle of the words is even sadder. No one should die alone and not be missed by another soul for that length of time.

Violet pulls her sleeves down to cover the goosebumps that have pricked up on her arms. 'Write it as if she were your own mum or someone you love. Think about how you'd feel if it were your story – what would you want to include?'

The words must have hit the right note somewhere on Jenny's keyboard as she lets out an 'ah-ha' and punches the desk. 'Violet, you're amazing. You'd make such a great journalist.' Jenny squeezes her arm. 'I bet you still haven't looked into that NCTJ course I told you about, have you? I really wish you would just go for it. What's stopping you?'

'Maybe one day.' Violet manages a quick smile. 'I'd better get on. Good luck with the article.'

Jenny reaches into the middle drawer of her desk. 'And before I forget – I've got three for you today – for your blog.' She hands Violet a small pile of books.

Violet picks one up, a frisson of excitement dancing in the front of her mind. Jenny gets given upcoming titles from the person who writes book reviews for the *Salford and Manchester Times*, and she's been passing them on so Violet can write about them on her book blog. The top one is a romance title she's desperate to read. Keeping people at a respectable distance in real life is one thing, but there's nothing quite like living vicariously through the characters in a good love story. It's the safest way of experiencing what it might be like to find a soulmate.

'Thank you,' says Violet with a grin.

Life is good. It's comfortable and nice. A job she loves with people who tell her their stories and notice when she's around. Plenty of people to pop to The Pink Pig with for a quick half after work once a week but who've learned not to ask questions or expect invites to her flat.

Her flat. Her home. Her safe space. A hiss of air leaks out of her bubble of joy as she pictures her sister standing next to her futon, smudging the lines she'd so carefully drawn between past and present: before and after.

She pictures her mum, alone in her chair, her face frozen in place like the woman in Jenny J's article.

A face that says one thing. *It's all your fault.*

By the time Violet arrives back at her flat after work, the bubble has burst. As she walked, the joy continued to seep out onto the pavements, the zebra crossings and the urine-scented public steps up to her flat.

She hadn't been able to stop thinking about the poor woman in Jenny's article. Which then meant she couldn't stop thinking about her mum. It was one thing to stay away all these years, and even to miss her own sister's wedding. She had solid reasons not to go back inside that village hall. But it's another thing entirely to ignore a call for help. Her mum can't be left alone, and Jodie can't stay there forever.

Violet has a myriad of mess-ups in her back pocket and she's spent so many years trying to keep them there. Returning to her past is likely to make them all tumble back out again, rolling across the floor for everyone to see. She doesn't have room for any more mistakes and nothing she does now can ever come close to mopping them up.

At times like this, Violet needs to channel her literary soulmate, Anne Shirley from *Anne of Green Gables*: 'You can nearly always enjoy things if you make up your mind firmly that you will.'

As soon as she's back in her flat she scribbles a to-do list on the back of her council tax bill which includes:

1. Look into subletting the flat (there's no way she wants to give up her very own palace for good)
2. Get a storage quote (she should probably make a little bit of room amongst the clutter for the lucky subletter)
3. Start packing
4. Hand in notice at work

Number one does not go well. Subletting is an absolute no-no according to her contract and her landlord's barking voice on the other end of Violet's pleading phone call. Which means the storage quotes rise considerably on account of Violet needing to store everything she owns.

Before she starts on number three, Violet whips her phone from her pocket and strategically arranges her new paperbacks from Jenny across the pretty shelves in her Instagram corner before taking photos from every conceivable angle.

The likes she'll get on this book post will be just what she needs to perk herself up. A way to be alone without being alone. Connection is key when life gets scary.

She uploads the photos, book titles, and sentences such as *Look what I'll be reading this evening! Reviews to follow!* before furnishing them with book-related hashtags and waiting for the likes to flood in. Not likes for her, obviously, but for @BookWorm1908. 1908 was the publication year of *Anne of Green Gables*, so it felt only right to honour it with her username. Her profile photo is a beautifully ornate shelving display from a Swedish bookshop. Completely anonymous, just the way Violet likes it.

Highlighting wonderful books is a way to bring people joy. She directs them to other worlds and introduces them to characters who can't hurt them.

She does this to redress the balance, to bring some good news, because for most of her life, Violet herself has been *Bad News*.

Sitting at the table, Violet starts writing a new post next to a photo of her laptop with a pair of glasses perched on top. She doesn't wear glasses, but she thinks they add a certain something.

Excellent news! Looks like I'm taking this blog on tour all the way to the rolling hills of beautiful Sussex. 😊😊 Packing up now for my next adventure – keep your eyes peeled for my books-on-the-road posts 📕 🚚

What are some of your favourite books about new starts or travel – any recommendations?

#blogger #adventure #sussex #freshstart #cantwait #excited

There's temporary comfort to be found in digitally indulging your own bullshit, even just for a little while. It takes the edge off the thought of having to squeeze her carefully constructed life into dusty cardboard boxes.

Violet's notifications make satisfying ding sounds. Comments and emojis galore.

Congratulations and all the best for your new adventure.

How wonderful, Sussex is beautiful.

Can I come?

People she's never met. People who don't know what she's done or that she's *Bad News*. They may not know the real her, but those little hearts on her screen are what keep her going. They make her feel like people care; like she's part of something bigger than just herself.

Violet scrolls through the comments and replies to each one and then turns to sorting her bottom drawer with one hand and making a call to Jenny with the other.

'Violet?' Jenny sounds surprised. Which is understandable: Violet never calls anyone *Just For A Chat*. But she doesn't want Jenny to hear about her resignation from anyone else.

After all, she's an almost-friend.

'You'll be missed.' Jenny seems sad. 'But it sounds like you're really excited. I'm happy for you.'

Violet's hand finds something at the bottom of the drawer. Something squidgy, something she'd forgotten about. A photo inside a plastic inflatable frame that's oh-so-very 1990s. Most of the air has leaked from it.

'Thank you.' Violet's voice stays bright and clear, showing

no trace of the tear that's escaped down her cheek. She runs a finger over the face next to hers in the photo in front of her.

'Bye, Jenny. See you Wednesday.'

Another tear falls, splashing onto the photo in the tiny space between Adam's laughing face and Violet's smiling one.

Adam was always laughing – until he wasn't.

Violet does what she always does when she's reminded of Adam; it's a well-practised reflex now. She scrolls to the five text messages he sent her; one every New Year's Eve for the past five years – every year since he'd asked Jodie for Violet's number. She knows them by heart, every single word. Her fingers hover over the reply button. Should she tell him she's coming back?

Violet hates clichés and despises platitudes because most of them are lies. But she knows one thing to be true. You never forget your first love.

CHAPTER 3

Violet

VIOLET'S FIAT 500 HAS surprised her. She's called Pat – a reliable kind of name. Violet had read that people tend to live up to their names, but this clearly doesn't translate to cars. She spends more time in the garage than on the road and there's a Pat-shaped hole in Violet's wallet that half her wages seem to fall through. On this occasion though, Pat's done her proud. She's transported Violet two hundred and sixty-one miles and listened to her incessant monologuing for four and a half hours whilst she shifted from home to there. Or from there to home, depending on how you look at it.

The back seat is piled high with as many treasures as Violet could cram in and her suitcase is wedged between the passenger seat and the footwell, squashing all the crisp packets and chocolate wrappers.

At least her car still feels like home. 17B, Harper's Court is an empty shell now most of Violet's possessions are stored away in a huge metal box, paid for by her returned rental deposit. Choosing which books to bring had felt like picking which of her children to leave behind. Ebooks and audiobooks are wonderful, but she'll miss holding her beautiful paperbacks.

Violet shakes her shoulders out and loosens her grip on the steering wheel, only for her fingers to tighten around it once again when she sees the sign she's been looking out for. It's the same as it had been all those years ago, and the words on it make Violet's heart beat faster. *Welcome to Lowerstone: Sussex Village of the Year.* The prestigious title had been awarded on Violet's tenth birthday; she remembers this because there had been a party at the village hall that upstaged her own, meaning half of Violet's party bags were left untouched on the sideboard.

She slows Pat down to a near stop as she passes the sign, reluctant to cross the threshold of the village. Violet doesn't blame her one bit and allows her to inch up the winding road at the pace of a sedated sloth. She opens a window, welcoming the warm sun on her arm as the birds blast out their songs.

Violet glances up at windows as she passes the first row of houses. She wonders who they are now, the people behind the glass panes. Will they be the same faces, the accusing ones who always wore their disapproval on the contours of their faces, or have they been replaced by new bodies, ones who have no clue who Violet Strong is or which family she belongs to?

Flint walls frame the narrow pavements, throwing glimmers of light that bounce across the pond by the chemist and the sweet shop. Violet always called it the sweet shop but now she comes to think of it, it was always so much more than that – it sold everything from bath plugs to butter. The signage has had a lick of paint and is now a deep purple rather than the blue it used to be, but it still carries the same name.

Next to the sweet shop is the cottage she's longed to peek

at since she passed the *Welcome to Sussex* sign. The front garden is full of weeds, nothing like the neat lawn Violet spent so many of her childhood summers lounging across with her very best friend. Adam's cottage was a fraction of the size of Violet's house, but his mum made the best snacks and never moaned about how much noise they made, so his place was the obvious choice to hang out in when they weren't running through the multicoloured fields of the South Downs that surround the village.

Thinking of Adam and his boisterous laugh brings a smile to Violet's tired face. She really should have let him know she was coming back, but then he'd know she'd kept his number and that she'd read his messages.

Violet's tummy starts to spin and her legs wobble as she changes gear. Pat takes her past the telephone box with half its glass missing and the tiny stone chapel where the end of school services used to be. The playground is to her left, but Violet won't look in that direction, not yet.

Some things need working up to.

Next comes the bakery. It still looks exactly the same. Violet can almost taste the freshly made doughnuts her dad used to buy her as a Saturday morning treat. She lets out a long breath before carrying on past The Swan Inn. Every window is boarded up and thick bars sit across the doors. Violet swallows the scratchiness in her throat. It's probably the rapeseed, it always used to prod at her allergies. Nothing to do with the memory gremlin that likes to visit whenever she thinks about that pub. It was number four in the top five times where Violet was *Bad News*.

Over the tiny bridge, three former shops have morphed into

houses. The hairdresser's, the florist and the video shop are no more. If Violet wants to hire *The Wizard of Oz* for a pound every Friday, she'll no longer be able to. Everything's familiar, yet so different. Fourteen years dissolve behind her as past and present collide in a mess of disorientation and unwelcome feelings, leaving her dizzy and breathless.

She pushes her foot further to the floor to help Pat chug to the top of the steepest hill in the world – the one that leaves the village shops behind and leads right to Malvern House.

Malvern House is almost hidden by a huge circle of trees. The gate is not only open, but missing, so Violet is able to steer Pat straight through the gap between the flint walls and park on the gravel next to the crumbling fountain. She switches the engine off, her heart thudding in her ears. She clicks off her seatbelt and sits still, closing her eyes and wishing she could transport herself back to the safety of her bedsit.

Tap, tap, tap. Jodie's looming over the car.

'You made it.' Relief drowns out any other emotion that might be hiding inside Jodie's voice. 'Mum's inside – she's umm, expecting you. I've just got to pop to the shop – we've run out of gravy. Kettle's just boiled though if you want to make yourself a cuppa.'

Violet winds up the window and waits for Jodie to step back so she can open the door.

'We've been watching out for you all morning,' Jodie says. 'Mum's looking forward to seeing you.'

'She is?'

Jodie looks down at the gravel. 'Well, you know Mum. She shows her feelings differently to most of us.'

The birds are deafening; they're trying to peck right inside Violet's ears. Her fingers graze the wing mirror as she feels for something to touch to keep herself anchored against the dizziness.

'You aren't coming in with me?' Violet's eyes flick between each of the ground-floor windows. Mum will be staring through one of them, she always was. Mum kept to the ground floor after what happened. The stairs were no longer an easy option.

The sun is bouncing off the windows, making it impossible to see through them. Something is different. The front door looks wider, Violet realises, as the sun falls behind a cloud, leaving a chill on her arms. Only the ground-floor windows have net curtains across them.

'You'll notice a few changes inside.' Jodie's eyes follow Violet's gaze. 'But I guess that's what happens when adaptions have to be made. You wouldn't believe how much red tape we had to wade through to get this place turned into flats.'

'Flats?'

'Well, yes. How else could we have kept this place going?' Jodie's mouth moves itself into a strange shape that's supposed to be a smile, but it makes her look a bit like a hyena. Her handbag jingles as she starts walking down the driveway. 'Flat two is on the ground floor opposite Mum's, then three and four are upstairs. I'll be back in twenty. Door's open, just go right in. Mum's flat is the first on the right.'

Violet glances around for a *For Sale* sign as Jodie crunches her way down the gravel and disappears. There doesn't appear to be one – perhaps the estate agents haven't got around to it yet. She'll have to ask Jodie when they're coming to put it up. Her legs stiffen beneath her as she moves towards the entrance.

Most people say that everything feels smaller when they return to their childhood home but Malvern House has never looked bigger or less welcoming to Violet. After easing herself through the heavy front door, her knock-off Nikes meet the parquet flooring and send echoes through the cavernous hallway.

She's outside the first door on the right. It's already ajar so all she needs to do is push it and walk in. It should be simple, but it isn't.

Come on, Violet. What would Anne Shirley say? 'Next to trying and winning, the best thing is trying and failing.'

Be more Anne.

The building is silent; the only noises Violet can hear are the ones from inside her. The pulse in her ear, the sloshing of a nervous belly with too much coffee in it. That inner voice that tells her to turn around, climb back into Pat and pretend to herself she'd taken a wrong turn.

Violet's mum is on the other side of the door. They're no longer separated by over two hundred miles, but by several strips of reinforced wood. Violet takes a long breath to steel herself as she nudges it open, hoping to shake off that feeling of being summoned to the head teacher's office.

'Jodie?' The voice has a creak in it. It's coming from the armchair facing away from the door. Thin grey spirals of hair hang limply over the back of it, threaded with the same shade of red as Violet's messy braids.

Violet takes a wobbly step forward. The furniture is the same. The mustard sofa still points towards the huge bay window. Matching velvet drapes. The tall marble mantelpiece with the brass-framed mirror above it.

The mirror. Oh hell, the mirror. Violet glances at it before she can stop herself and her heart judders. She doesn't see her own reflection; her eyes are drawn to the face in the armchair.

Sunken eyes staring nowhere, surrounded by deep lines on pale skin.

Violet's mum needs colouring back in. She's moving her mouth as if she's going to say something else, perhaps Jodie's name again, but no sound comes out and her mouth goes slack.

Violet prises her feet from the invisible quicksand and forces them to work together until she's standing in the middle of the room facing the woman whose life she ruined.

All the practised words from the car journey have evaporated. They've scarpered up the chimney, escaped through the gaps in the draughty windows. The sentence that falls out holds all the truth she can manage.

'Hi, Mum. Sorry I'm not Jodie.'

The unseeing eyes are unseeing no longer. They flash towards Violet's, blacker than they'd ever been.

'She's just popped out.' The dryness in Violet's mouth makes the words come out in a whispered growl.

Shoulders stiff, Violet's mum reaches her fingers towards her walking frame.

'Mum …'

'It's Glenys.' She doesn't snap or say it like she's angry. More like she's half-heartedly introducing herself to a new staff member, not expecting to be remembered in an hour's time. 'Where's Jodie gone?'

Violet remembers her sister's nervous smile. Glenys hasn't been expecting Violet at all. 'She's gone to get gravy – she's making us a family meal.' The word *family* sticks in her throat.

'My frame,' Glenys whispers, shuffling forward and reaching her hands out so far Violet worries she might topple out of the chair.

Violet fetches the walking frame and parks it in front of the armchair without taking her gaze away from Glenys' face. Eye contact is all that's needed. If her mum will just look at her – properly look at her – some of the wall might come down. Not all of it, obviously, but enough for them both to peep across.

It takes a long time for Glenys to stand. She moves her frame and walks with practised precision towards the door on the far side of the room. It leads to what used to be the dining room but had become Glenys' bedroom two years before Violet left home.

Violet is an adult. She's spent years living alone and supporting herself. She's been back in this house for a matter of minutes and already she's a child again, small, helpless and unable to stop her mum walking away from her.

'Do you want me to get you anything – I'll make us a drink?' Violet's voice is like weak tea.

Glenys clearly thinks so too as she doesn't pause, doesn't turn around. Doesn't even answer, just disappears behind the door, leaving Violet alone in a room that has haunted her dreams for fourteen years.

CHAPTER 4

Violet

'BEEF CASSEROLE OKAY? DIDN'T think to check if you were a veggie.' Jodie's out of breath when she enters the room armed with a tub of gravy and a bag of potatoes. 'Mum in her room?'

Violet follows Jodie to the kitchen. 'She doesn't want me here,' she says. 'I really don't think this is going to work.'

Jodie throws the shopping on the worktop and pulls a packet of diced meat from the fridge. 'She just needs time, that's all. She wasn't keen when Dave first moved in either.'

'Where is Dave?' Violet looks around the room. Another person around the dinner table might help defuse the tension.

'He went on ahead – he's already in New Zealand. Couldn't put off his start date with work any longer.'

A pang of guilt tugs at Violet. It had taken longer than it should have to hand her notice in at work. Every time she looked at the resignation letter in her handbag, flashes of the past had stopped her from handing it over.

'Can I help with anything?' Violet says.

Jodie passes her a potato peeler from the drawer. 'My taxi's coming at seven to take me to the airport.'

'Gosh, that's early. Early night for you, then.' Violet sounds brighter than she feels. The thought of being left alone in the house with Glenys first thing the next morning makes her insides curdle. 'I didn't realise you'd be leaving as soon as tomorrow. That only leaves us tonight to talk everything through. I'll need to know what needs doing, what Mum needs …'

'Not seven tomorrow. Tonight,' Jodie says. 'That's why I'm getting started on dinner already.'

A potato slips out of Violet's hand and bounces across the worktop. 'But we have so much to talk about first. The house, the care home … and why isn't the *For Sale* sign outside yet?'

Jodie picks up the half-peeled potato and passes it back to Violet with an unblinking smile. 'Plenty of time to discuss all that, give yourself time to settle in. Spend some time with Mum. Ah. Here she is.'

Violet follows her sister's gaze. Glenys is moving slowly past the doorway, clinging onto her frame.

'Here, take these.' Jodie holds out a pile of dinner mats. 'Shove these on the table and get Mum settled in front of the telly while I pop the stew on.'

Glenys is lowering herself into a dining chair and doesn't look up at Violet as she arranges the placemats.

'Dinner won't be ready for a while,' Violet ventures.

Glenys sniffs and studies the placemat in front of her. It has a picture of Lulworth Cove on it.

Violet swallows. 'Can't believe you still have these. I remember when you bought them in that little shop on the beach front when we were there on holiday.'

Glenys' eyes remain rooted to the picture.

'It was raining,' Violet carries on, a hint of desperation in her voice. 'Remember?'

Not even a flicker of acknowledgement. Violet had grown used to it before she left for Manchester, but she must be out of practice. Glenys' refusal to look her way is like salt on a papercut. Feels worse than it looks.

'Let's get you onto a comfier seat, shall we? Surely you don't want to sit on a hard chair all the way until dinner time?'

Glenys moves her eyes towards Violet. 'My house. I'll sit where I like.'

Violet grips the side of the table and lets out a long breath before something brushes past her.

'Violet, why have you sat Mum at the table already? She can't sit very long on those hard chairs, remember, and dinner won't be ready for ages yet. Come with me, Mum, I'll get you comfy. You're missing *Tipping Point*. Shall I put it on?' Jodie's words come wrapped in confidence. She knows what to say, what to do. Violet's sister is perfect, Little Miss Right, and she's still *Violet Wrong*.

Glenys slowly stands, smiling at her eldest daughter. 'Yes, please. Thanks, love.' She sits herself down on the armchair in front of the TV as Ben Shephard's cheery voice fills the room.

It seems to take a long time for the woman on the telly from Shrewsbury to win her three thousand pounds to put towards her loft conversion. Violet tries several times to make conversation with Glenys, but her mother's gaze is not for moving.

'Do you want to get your suitcases from the car and pop them in your room and then I'll show you how Mum's bed works – it's a bit temperamental,' Jodie whispers in Violet's ear.

After Violet's chucked her cases in the bottom of her wardrobe, she ventures into her mum's new room, followed by her sister. The door opens onto what used to be the spare room and is now utterly unfamiliar. It has a hospital bed, a wardrobe, and a chest of drawers. No photos, no ornaments, no clutter. The remote control for the bed has a thousand different buttons carrying logos that give nothing away about their functions. Violet listens as her sister explains how it works, but her words just keep swimming around on their own in Violet's brain, rather than staying together in their sentences.

By the time the three of them are back at the dinner table, Violet feels like a frayed old tea towel after a hot wash cycle. 'This is lovely,' she manages to say to Jodie after her first mouthful. 'Isn't it lovely, Mu— Glenys? Didn't realise Jodie had become such a good cook.'

Glenys continues to chew, staring straight ahead.

'Would you like some water?' Violet picks up the jug and holds it close to Glenys' glass.

Glenys covers the glass with her hand and shakes her head.

'You should drink something, Mum. You'll need water for your tablets – I'll grab them for you.' Jodie drops her fork and disappears into the kitchen, reappearing with a tiny cup of colourful pills.

'Fill me up, love.' Glenys holds her glass out towards Jodie, even though Violet's fingers are hovering around the jug handle.

Swallowing food is tricky when your throat is closed for business.

Violet is fourteen again, sitting at the same table, holding the same tears behind her eyes as her mum sits next to her but stays a million miles away at the same time, as her sister rises to the challenge, pushing Violet away with her pointy elbows at every opportunity.

She can't do this again. The past is for glimpsing at in your rearview mirror – just to check you're heading in the right direction. It's not somewhere to keep circling back to and it's certainly not a place to rent a room and hunker down in.

Forward is what matters. Or at least getting through the present as quickly as possible until the future arrives.

'We need a plan,' Violet announces. 'I know you'd rather I wasn't here, Mum. And I know Jodie needs to go. We need to get everything sorted as quickly as possible so we can all get on with our new lives.'

Jodie stares at her empty plate and Glenys purses her lips so tightly the surrounding skin pales to match the tablecloth.

'Let's talk after dinner,' says Jodie.

'We've already finished.' Violet picks up her sister's plate and puts it underneath her own.

'After – you know. *After.*' Jodie nods her head towards Glenys. 'Mum, do you want me to help you back to your room? Violet and I need a bit of a catch-up.'

By the time Jodie returns from Glenys' room, Violet is halfway through the washing up.

'Can't you make more of an effort with Mum? And why do you keep banging on about making plans in front of her – she already thinks you don't want to be here. Look, I know you're worried.' Jodie pulls a tea towel from the cupboard. 'But she'll come around. She needs proper care, and she'll be far better off in the residential home. You only need to be here until everything's in place.'

The casserole dish slips from Violet's hands and falls back into the water, splashing suds all over the front of her T-shirt. 'I'm just not sure where to start with everything. How are things going with the house sale? And does Mum have a confirmed place at the home? I need to know what needs doing.'

Jodie glances at the clock. 'Uh-huh. Right. Of course you do. That's why I've left you step-by-step instructions in the folder in the sideboard. Everything's going fine, just a few bits and pieces to tie up. Don't look so worried, I've every faith in you.'

Violet looks at the sideboard. The same sideboard that used to be bursting with letters from school, old drawings and dried-up pens that no one ever threw away.

'No need to get bogged down with all that boring paperwork now. Let's have a cuppa. Might be years before we see each other again.' The lines around Jodie's face soften and her eyes glisten.

Violet pulls her face into a smile. 'You're right. Sorry – you've a long journey ahead. Guess I can always ring you if I have any questions.'

Jodie turns around and coughs into the crook of her elbow. 'Pop the kettle on. I'm just going to … going to … oh, shit. How am I going to do it? How am I going to say goodbye to her?' Her voice cracks.

Violet drops her sponge into the washing-up bowl and wipes her hands on her jeans as she turns around.

Mascara-stained tears are trickling down the sides of Jodie's nose.

Violet reaches out and places her hand awkwardly on Jodie's shoulder. 'She'll be okay. You've looked after her for so long

– this is your time now. I'll take care of her – I'll do my best. I promise.' The words pick up truth as they leave her mouth. Glenys despises Violet as much as she ever did. Who could blame her, Violet is *Bad News*. But Violet owes this to all of them.

And it won't be forever. Then she can start all over again. Again.

Jodie closes the door to Glenys' room behind her, leaving Violet alone with her thoughts and the rest of the washing up.

Violet pictures her sister and her mum sitting next to each other on the bed, holding each other and crying. It had always been Mum and Jodie, and she used to be okay with that. Violet had Dad. Dependable Dad, solid-as-a-bunker-Dad, but now he's not here. She digs her fingernails into her palms until her eyes water.

Because she's sad for them, obviously. It must be hard to say goodbye. It's an image she's used to, it's exactly how it was after what happened with Dad. Jodie and her mum. Just the two of them, holding their pain between them and scooping it up and away from Violet so she couldn't reach it.

'Mum's got her nightie on.' Jodie appears in the kitchen, dragging two hot-pink suitcases behind her. 'She usually has her evening cup of hot chocolate in about half an hour but wait for her to ask you – she doesn't like to be rushed.'

Violet feels a bit sick. She wants to lie down in a dark room with a thick duvet.

Gravel crunches from outside and Jodie runs to the window. 'Oh, there's my taxi.' She leans forward and air kisses the spaces between them on each side, choking Violet with Anais-Anais. 'You'll be just fine. Now remember, Mum's paperwork is on the sideboard. Make sure you read it carefully.'

Violet nods and attempts a smile. It's taken fourteen years just to get to this point and this could be the last time she sees her sister for another long stretch – maybe ever. Their last encounter ought to be a pleasant one. She places her arms once again around Jodie's stiff shoulders before following her sister onto the driveway.

Jodie looks from Violet to the house and back again. She opens her mouth to speak and closes it again, grabbing at the handles of her suitcases.

'You need a hand getting them in the taxi?' Violet asks. Both cases are bulging, straining the material around the zips.

'I'll be fine. You'd better go in – you don't want to keep Mum waiting.' Jodie yanks the suitcases across the gravel towards the taxi. 'Oh, and Violet?' Jodie calls out through the cab window after climbing in. 'You might want to send a letter to the other three tenants – just to explain the situation. They'll need some notice; it's a legal thing and only fair I suppose to give them a chance to find somewhere else to live.'

That sick feeling is definitely getting worse. Violet feels like she's just got off the teacups at a fairground. 'You mean they don't know yet?' she stage whispers across the driveway.

Jodie grins as she tucks her hair behind her neat little ears. 'Well, they will once you tell them.'

Violet's handwave stays frozen for a few seconds after the taxi has gone. She looks up at the huge stone building she once called home, glancing at each of the twelve windows, wondering what – or who – is standing behind them.

The birds stop singing and the leaves from the surrounding trees cease their rustling as the breeze comes to a standstill. Everything around her is holding its breath and waiting.

Waiting to see what Violet's made of.

There's only one place she can go to that will make this new, temporary life feel just perfect. Somewhere she's successful, just for a little while. She goes back inside, unpacks her laptop, and opens it before clicking on her blog.

@BookWorm1908

Arrived at my destination. Sussex is just as beautiful as I remembered it 🖤☺ The perfect countryside getaway for getting lost in books and updating you all about my latest reads.

The Return of Jade Blair by Jennifer Taby (see photo) is a beautifully written gothic romance about a woman who is reunited with her first love but has only six days to earn his forgiveness for her past mistakes …

CHAPTER 5

Violet

VIOLET'S LIMBS ARE COLD when she wakes after her first night in her new bedroom.

Her old one had been on the floor above, and now someone else is living in it. So many rooms are in the wrong place. Her childhood home has become a stranger she needs to get to know all over again.

The room she's in now was once her dad's study. The wardrobe, the desk and the bookshelves were Violet's though; the marks are still visible from where her Green Day stickers used to be. The sleigh bed she's climbing out of was hers too, but the functional, slightly scratchy bedding is a far cry from the soft throws and fluffy cushions that once adorned it.

Violet shivers as she reaches into her suitcase for some clothes. She really should unpack properly, then all this might feel like real life again instead of a dream she'd rather wake up from.

Once her clothes are hanging up and her dream catcher is pinned to the wall, Violet turns her attention to the shelving unit next to her bed. It had once been bursting with books. Books that used to take her anywhere she wanted from Neverland to Sweet Valley. From Avonlea to Narnia.

Now the shelves are empty except for Bournemouth Bear. He's sitting on the middle shelf, staring. Violet swallows as she reaches for the dusty teddy. Dad had won Bournemouth Bear on the last day of their Dorset holiday. *Waste of money,* Violet's mum had tutted as Dad fished a ticket from the basket on the stall for the tenth time that week. Jodie had already walked off towards the slot machines; she was far too old for teddies. Dad's eyes had lit up when he checked the numbers and lifted Violet up in the air to choose a prize. She didn't let go of Bournemouth Bear for the rest of the summer.

Why hadn't she taken him with her to Manchester? She already knows the answer to that question – too painful. And she'd left in such a hurry. He wouldn't have fitted in her suitcase and she couldn't take much with her anyway, not when she was gate-crashing someone else's student digs.

Dark clouds fill Violet's mind, the way they always do when she thinks about Megan.

Number two on Violet's list of times when she was *Bad News.* On anyone else's list, it probably would have been their number one, but anyone else isn't Violet, and anyone else hasn't done the terrible things that she's done.

Violet leaves the boxes she brought with her unopened. They contain her favourite blankets, her fluffiest cushions and as many scented candles as she could fit into them without the cardboard collapsing. Leaving them in storage would have felt all kinds of wrong but unpacking them wouldn't be right either. They are her home things, and she isn't at home.

She dresses quickly and throws a thick cardigan around her

before venturing out of her room. It may be a sunny day in May, but in Malvern House with its draughts and stone walls, it's always winter.

The silence here is louder than home. Noisier than the traffic of Dickhead Avenue or the bustle from the takeaway below her bedsit. She'd do anything to hear the heavy feet and crackly music of kebab shop Chris upstairs.

Footsteps sound from above as if summoned by her thoughts, and Violet remembers again that she and Glenys are not alone in the building. An envelope catches her eye from the top of the sideboard. It has her name blasted across it, propped up on the dining table against an empty vase. She hadn't noticed it last night.

Later. She'll read it later.

First, she's going to need more coffee.

The same stable-style wooden door that Jodie and Violet always loved vaulting over to get to the kitchen is wedged open with an ancient *Yellow Pages*.

The kitchen looks bigger now that Jodie's gone. It's just as Violet remembered it. Same sagging cupboards, shabby tiles and double Aga against the back wall. The badly drawn pictures brought home by Violet and her sister have been stripped from the walls, leaving them bare and grey except for the whiteboard with a medication schedule scrawled across it.

It's eight thirty. No sight or sound from Glenys – what time does she normally get up? Anxiety simmers in Violet's stomach as she rummages in the cupboards for breakfast. She knows nothing about being a carer. She'd never been allowed close enough to help her mum with much before she left home. Helping another person get from one day to the next feels like a responsibility better held by stronger hands than hers.

As the kettle gurgles to a boil, four sharp knocks sound from the living-room door that leads to the communal hallway.

Violet's stomach lurches and she stands as still as she can, holding her breath and closing her eyes as if it will make it all go away. Maybe they'll give up if she doesn't answer.

Four more knocks, louder than the last lot. Violet tiptoes forward and reaches for the door handle.

A round woman with a bowl-shaped haircut looks over her glasses at Violet from the threshold. She's wearing beige trousers and a brown knitted jumper with a small sunflower embroidered onto the shoulder – it looks out of place on its own, as if its creator had run out of wool or patience before adding the rest.

'I'm Mrs Robson. From upstairs. Flat three,' she adds as she sticks her hand out. She looks around Violet as if hoping for an invitation. Her voice is a pointy one, just like Glenys' had been before it came apart at the edges. 'You must be the other daughter. Jodie said you might be coming.'

Violet swallows hard. 'I'd invite you in, only I need to jump in the shower. Not had breakfast yet and already it's been one of those days …'

'That would be great,' she says side-stepping Violet and entering the living room, bringing the smell of onions and gravy with her. 'Tea, milk and no sugar, just two sweeteners. Just been told I've got type two.'

Violet's mouth is still waiting for words as she turns to flick the kettle back on.

'I'll cut right to the point,' Mrs Robson says after ten minutes of telling Violet about her bunions and new dietary requirements. 'The young woman on the top floor. She's trouble. I've come to get you on board.'

'On board what?'

'Lowerstone's Neighbourhood Watch group. We're not happy, not at all.' She tuts. 'There's a load of riff-raff moved into the village over the past few years. Kids joining gangs and drinking on the street, people selling drugs from their cars at all hours. But the biggest disturbances lately are from *her*.' She points up at the ceiling. 'Loud music, yelling, screaming, she gets ever so aggressive. Frightening it is, what this village is coming to. Wasn't like this when I moved here ten years ago – it used to be a nice place. Neighbourly. You could go out and leave your front door open and still be perfectly safe.'

Violet wants to tell her she lived here fourteen years ago and that village or no village, there was no way in hell anyone would have left their door open.

'A few of us meet up every week in my flat – just us *decent* people, anyway, and we strategise. We want to get this village back to how it used to be. Starting with getting the likes of *her* out.'

'How do you know I'm one of the decent ones?' Violet asks.

Mrs Robson looks her up and down before sighing and perching her teacup on the corner of the dining table. 'Hope or wishful thinking I suppose. Your sister didn't seem bothered about our nightmare neighbour – claimed she couldn't even hear the noise. I don't think she cares who lives here as long as they pay the rent. So, as I was saying,' she carries on, 'we're making progress. I've got on to the council several times this week and they were woefully unhelpful. So, I thought we could draw up some paperwork ourselves and then perhaps you could serve her with one of those ASBOs – of sorts. All of us in the building could keep a diary of each incident, and she's bound to break her conditions. And then she will be *out*.'

Violet watches Mrs Robson sip her tea, willing her to get to the bottom of her cup and leave. It's been a weird, stressful, confusing morning and all she wants is her duvet and the bar of white chocolate she's got stashed in her holdall. Caring for Glenys and getting the house sorted will take up every available space on the plate in front of her. There won't be any room left on it for troublesome tenants.

'Just you remember,' Mrs Robson places a warning hand on Violet's arm before she leaves, 'steer clear of the woman on the top floor. She's trouble.'

CHAPTER 6

Tammy

TAMMY CLOSES THE DOOR on the only visitor she'd had since she moved in. The woman from across the hall just told Tammy she might be getting a letter from the new landlord. She said the words really loudly, as if she thought Tammy might have a problem with her hearing.

She said the letter would have lots of rules in it that Tammy has to stick to. It will be just like something that's called an ASBO, the woman who just left said. It's what people get when they upset the neighbours.

Tammy doesn't really know the neighbours. It's weird to think they would know who she is. She's never said hi or asked for cups of sugar like they do on the telly. Noise levels aren't supposed to make the loud metre go up too high, the woman across the hall said, and sometimes Tammy makes it happen when it's late at night and the other people in the building are trying to sleep.

She never wants them to stay awake, that's not why she does it. It's just the darker it gets, the quieter it gets, and Tammy doesn't like it quiet.

Quiet is like the thickest duvet there is. It's full of stones instead of feathers and it covers the whole room. It makes her suck in the same hot air she's just breathed out. It makes everything too close. Too thick. It lets the pictures in, the ones only she can see, and they get brighter and louder if she lets them. The quiet can get right inside. There are loads of different ways it can get in – ears, nose, mouth. It finds its own way to Tammy's bones and just sits on them, making them stay still so she can't move, only scream. So, she does. Too loud. Too late. And now she might be getting this letter.

She'd wanted to ask the woman from across the hall if she thought Tammy's mum had got into heaven, but she didn't stay long enough. Tammy hasn't seen anyone else to ask since it happened and she's not always good at making the right words come out. Her mum used to help with stuff like that but she's not there today. Wasn't there yesterday or the day before that and never would be again.

This flat was supposed to be Tammy's *first step to independence*, according to her mum.

'I won't be around forever,' she said a few weeks earlier whilst they were unpacking Tammy's suitcase into her new wardrobe. 'And you're getting so grown up now – I can't believe you're nineteen.'

Mum had promised to start teaching Tammy how to do all the things she'd never been allowed to do before. All of Tammy's life, Mum had tried extra hard to keep her safe because of those things written on her medical notes – the ones in the drawer that explain that she has a *General Learning Disability*. Mum always worried something bad might happen to Tammy if she did things for herself – and they both had

44

to take extra special care of each other because it was just the two of them. Just the two of them because it was *safer that way*. That's why they had moved flats so many times since leaving the house they lived in with Dad when Tammy was very little.

Tammy's tummy feels empty like the cupboards in the kitchen. There was lots of food a few weeks ago. Mum had just done Tammy's weekly shop like she always did on Tuesdays. She forgot the milk though. Said she'd be back with it later, but Tammy's eaten almost all the cereal without it now. Tastes like cardboard on its own but apart from sandwiches, it's the only thing she can eat without cooking, and Mum doesn't like Tammy using the cooker. Or the kettle.

Because Mum always comes over to her flat and she does all that for her.

Usually.

Tammy could eat the beans cold, but she's run out of the ring-pull ones and the other tins need the tin opener. She's not supposed to use the tin opener, she might cut her fingers.

The birds have stopped chirping outside and it's coming now, the quiet.

Tammy opens the glass door at the bottom of the hi-fi. There are lots of records behind it. They all used to be Mum's, but she'd said they were Tammy's now.

The ASBO letter might say, 'No loud music,' the woman from across the hall said.

She pulls out her favourite three. *The Dark Side of the Moon*. *The Muppet's Christmas Carol*. 'Especially for You'. Settling on Pink Floyd, she slips the vinyl from its sleeve, balancing the edge against her fingertips like Mum had shown her.

Once scratched, they're never the same again.

She lifts the stylus and lowers it down, pushing the voices into the room.

The volume is only halfway up. Not enough to set off the loud metre the woman across the hall was talking about.

Tammy closes her eyes and lets the words travel all the way through her. The quiet may get in through her ears but the music doesn't. It starts in her tummy and rises from there. The sound of it fills her and dances against the corners of her mind. Tammy's fists unclench. Her shoulders relax and a long breath sails from her into the room in one long train.

There's a pop. A zing. The light clicks off and the music stops. Silence.

Tammy pushes at the buttons, twiddles the knobs on the hi-fi. Nothing. She runs to the light switch and switches it on and off seven times.

The silence is getting thicker. Closer.

Tammy bashes the hi-fi again and again. Nothing.

She knows it's because the electricity needs a top-up from the corner shop. She *knows* this much.

Still, she kicks the glass door on the front of the hi-fi. The shattering of glass keeps the silence away for a few seconds. There are shards on the carpet. Tammy doesn't have her slippers on. *Don't move,* Mum would say if she was there. *Stay exactly where you are while I get the dustpan.* But the glass is guarding the path between her feet and the kitchen.

Footsteps come from the stairs outside. For a moment, Tammy hopes it's Mum with the milk, but it can't be. It never will be again.

The footsteps stop and the quiet creeps up on her. Tammy

hums to keep it away. She wants to sing the words, but they stay in her head.

Her Manchester City duvet is on the sofa; she'd slept on it since Mum stopped being there. Tammy swipes the bedcover and uses it to cover the floor in front of her. She walks over it and fetches the dustpan and brush from the cleaning cupboard.

There. Easy. Somehow the shards have stuck to the bobbles on the cover. She won't be able to pull it over her when she goes to sleep now. By then it will be dark. Then the quiet will get her.

The skin between Tammy's toes throbs with a dull pain. She shifts her foot sideways to look at it and a sharp jab makes her jump. It's the glass, it's in her foot and the blood is pouring out onto the floor.

'Ahgh,' she says. She means, *shit, that hurts*. She says it again, louder this time. The room starts to fill with the sound, her voice bouncing back off the walls and into her ears, keeping her company.

The echoes don't last long enough. The quiet is getting in and bringing the pictures with it. The hallway cupboard in the old house. The ironing board, the hoover and the smell of old coats. The dust that always made her sneeze. *It's the safest place to leave her. She can't do herself any damage in there. She has to learn somehow.* Dad's words. Firm, calm and not for moving.

The air's getting thicker. Tammy runs to the window and shouts through it. No one answers but the quiet has gone.

Then there's a knock at the door.

CHAPTER 7

Violet

VIOLET KNOCKS ON SHOUTING-WOMAN'S door. It had taken half an hour to get rid of Mrs Robson, and even then, she had to promise to go and speak to the ASBO lady upstairs this morning.

Curiosity begins to override Violet's nerves. No one answers, so she knocks again.

The door swings open and behind it is a young woman draped in mismatched, oversized clothes, bearing criss-cross patterns and farm animals. *Cow, horse, chicken. Cow, horse, chicken*, says her T-shirt. She has long, unbrushed hair, a smatter of freckles and a baseball cap that's too small for her head. Large brown eyes stare down at Violet through thick lenses. The woman says nothing but she's quietly humming a tune Violet recognises.

'Hello,' Violet whispers. 'I just moved in with my mum downstairs.'

She peers at the space behind Violet as if to check she's arrived alone before nodding and beckoning for her to come in.

Carnage lies behind the door. Biscuit packets, putrefied

banana skins and dirty washing litters the floor and the smell hits Violet's nostrils as soon as she steps inside.

Violet hesitates. This woman is technically her neighbour. Apart from the stark warnings from Mrs Robson, she doesn't know anything about her except her address, that she has kind eyes and that she's crap at housework. And she still hasn't spoken.

Perhaps she's unable to. Or she could just be shy.

'Tammy.' The woman's voice booms in Violet's ear and she jumps. 'I'm called Tammy. Who are you?'

'Sorry? Oh, um … I'm Violet.'

'What are you doing here?'

'Oh. I don't know what I'm doing to be honest. Not even a little bit. I'm just – just *here* really. I'm your new neighbour … so, well, hello.' Violet's voice sounds like it's getting higher and higher in pitch and the words are all falling out on top of each other. She keeps talking as she walks towards the sofa. Maybe she's fooling herself that speaking will prevent her from smelling the stench of the overflowing bin in the corner. Violet only stops when the door bangs shut, and she realises they're alone. An unfortunate time to wonder about one thing:

What the hell is all that blood doing all over the floor?

Actual footprints of blood trail from the sofa to the kitchen and back again. There's also a duvet bundled on the sofa that's covered with crimson stains. What if there's a body in it? Is that what Violet can smell? And why, oh why didn't she listen to that nosy old bag?

Violet looks at the door, but Tammy is standing in the way. What would she do if Violet charged towards her – would she move out of the way and let her pass? Or would Violet end up joining whoever is inside the duvet? Her heart starts to thud in that special way it only ever does right before she vomits. Violet's not good with smells and she's not good with being trapped.

And before she can stop herself, she's sick all over the lino.

Tammy rushes to the kitchen area and starts frantically opening and closing the cupboards.

There's space for Violet to reach the door now, but Tammy's kind smile from before falls into her mind. She can hardly just leave after being sick on the floor – what sort of neighbour would that make her?

Tammy hasn't opened a drawer yet, so she doesn't appear to be looking for a knife. The sound of rushing water fills the room, and a half-filled dirty mug is thrust in front of Violet's face. She stares at it, weighing up the options and decides to chance it in the end. She couldn't feel much sicker than she already does.

After dashing backwards and forwards from the sink, Tammy holds out a musty tea towel for Violet to wipe her mouth with. There's a good chance she isn't planning to murder her, given her obvious compassion in the face of adversity, but it is quite likely that Violet might catch at least one strain of a bacterial infection before she leaves.

'How did the blood get there?' Violet tries to ask as casually as possible, but it definitely sounds like she's a forensics team member on a crime show.

'Oh,' Tammy says. She lifts up her foot and shows Violet the underside of a blood-soaked sock. 'Glass. Cut my foot.' She peels off the sock to reveal a series of grubby-looking cuts that have fluffy sock fibres stuck to them.

'That needs cleaning up. It will get infected otherwise. Where's the glass now?'

Tammy points to a pile of glass in the far corner behind a dead yucca plant. 'Used a newspaper. Couldn't find the broom.'

A green first aid box is attached to the wall behind the kettle, and Violet manages to clean and bandage Tammy's foot with the supplies she finds inside.

Tammy starts humming that same tune again from outside and it finally comes to Violet – Belinda Carlisle's 'Heaven is a Place on Earth'.

'I'm sorry about vomming all over your floor. I'll clean it up. Do you have any bleach?'

Tammy looks out of the front window, chewing her lip. Of course she doesn't have any bleach. Surely, she'd have cleaned up all that blood by now, wouldn't she? It looks pretty congealed.

'Um, the blood on the floor. Did you want me to clean that at the same time? I mean, I'd need gloves, obviously. Do you have gloves?'

Tammy turns away from the window and looks at the cupboard under the sink.

Violet opens it slowly, dreading what she might find, but she's surprised to see clean shelves lined with neat rows of various cleaning products. Bottles for everything including bleach. There's also a pair of Marigolds, a pack of cloths and a whole carton of disposable gloves.

Once Violet has scrubbed the carpet and the lino, she keeps going until the flat is gleaming. Habits of a cleaner outside her own home. Tammy empties the bin and makes her bed after Violet shows her how.

'Thank you. Mum usually does that for me,' says Tammy. 'She was going to start teaching me how to do some of it by myself now that I have my own flat.'

'How often does she come here?' Violet's nose wrinkles. Tammy's mum can't have been doing very much for the place to have got this bad.

'She's gone.' Tammy shakes her head. 'She went out to get milk. Semi-skimmed. Then her heart ran out of power and wouldn't charge back up.'

Damn. Way to put her foot in it. No wonder the poor woman has got herself in such a state at home. 'I'm so sorry. How long ago did it happen?'

'*Songs of Praise* has been on three times since. I watch it every week. I won't watch it this week because nothing's working – that's why I cut my foot. I kicked the glass in my hi-fi because it went off. That wouldn't come back on again either.'

Bugger. How is Violet supposed to have a go at her for noise disturbance now, after all she's been through?

'I'd better get back to my mum. If you like, I can pop back and take a look at your TV and hi-fi another time? See if we can see what the problem is?' The words fall out of Violet's mouth before she can look at them properly in her mind.

Don't get involved, Violet. The poor girl's clearly had enough bad news without you piling in and bringing more with you.

Tammy nods, grins, and opens her door, closing it after Violet walks through it without saying goodbye.

Three other flats in this building. Violet's met two of the tenants.

Which means there's one more to go.

CHAPTER 8

Violet

VIOLET'S COFFEE IS LUKEWARM. Probably because she's been sitting at the dining table cradling her Peter Rabbit mug for the past twenty minutes whilst staring at that damn envelope.

It was nice of her sister to take the time to leave her so many instructions. At least Violet will have no doubt at any given second between 7 a.m. and 9 p.m. each day as to what she should be doing. A significant number of tasks relating to the sale of Malvern House need ticking off. Apparently, Jodie's kindly left everything for Violet to do.

1. Get house valued – ask three estate agents and pick the one who gives you the middle number.

Violet pictures people in suits holding clipboards and traipsing through the tired rooms, searching for the right price to put on her childhood history. She gives herself a sharp shake – she hadn't even wanted to come here, why should she care about losing a house that had seen so much misery?

Better this way. Better for Violet. Better for Jodie. Mum

would get proper care from someone she doesn't despise, and the walls of the house might be fed some joy by another owner. One that's less cursed, perhaps. Someone who doesn't have a Violet in it to come along and ruin everything.

Just for a second, she feels a longing for her childhood bedroom at the top of the building with the window that looks across the rolling hills and the whole of the village all at once. The room that's now part of Tammy's flat.

2. You may need to get a temporary loan to get the place spruced up if it doesn't sell. The building isn't as mortgage-free as it used to be – the adaptions cost a fair bit. Not much left in Mum's bank account (statements in the blue folder). She was getting disability payments every Wednesday but hasn't received any this month. This will need looking into.

The blue folder on the sideboard holds lots of bits of paper that don't tell a reassuring story. Glenys' finances are in an absolute mess and selling the building is not going to be an overnight task. Lots of letters have red at the top of them. Never a good sign in Violet's experience.

At the front of the folder in a plastic wallet is a glossy leaflet for Rossendale Residential Home. The photo on the front is bursting with smiles. Perhaps Glenys might find hers there; it's been missing since Violet was fourteen.

The rest of Jodie's letter of instructions contains a lengthy explanation about how selling the house to pay for Rossendale is the only way. That they've tried home carers popping in, but it wasn't enough, and Mum didn't like it. That Violet is likely to be needed for at least six months (probably longer) to get everything put into place.

'Six months. Probably longer,' Violet whispers. She'd reckoned it might take about three months when she ended the tenancy on her beloved bedsit and used the deposit to put her stuff into storage. Six months just seems – well, long. An especially long time to live somewhere you're not wanted.

The folder beneath the blue one holds the details of the current Malvern House tenants according to the label on the front. Violet slips it back into the sideboard drawer. Too much information at once is not always a good thing.

Her fingers grasp for the phone in her pocket. The urge to call or text someone for help is getting stronger by the second, but there's no one in her contacts list, no one who will understand how terrifying it is to be smack bang in the middle of her past again.

There is one person.

Should she?

Just one message? It's probably only fair to warn him – be weird to just bump into each other in the village after all this time, and if Jodie hadn't bothered telling their mum that Violet was coming back, she sure as hell wouldn't have got around to mentioning it to Adam.

The cursor on her phone screen pulls Violet's mind into a semi-hypnotic state. Words refuse to move from her brain to the fingers on the keypad. She closes her phone case and shoves it back in her pocket. Seeing someone in person is different to receiving a message once a year and being back in Lowerstone doesn't change the past. It certainly hasn't erased the memory of that awful darkness falling across Adam's fourteen-year-old face. A cloud that still hadn't lifted by the time Violet left the village four years later.

Violet needs to remember she's not in a story book. She's not Anne Shirley and Adam isn't her Gilbert Blythe. Avoidance will be key to surviving this unexpected interruption to life, and she's not planning any trips into the village if she can help it. Lewes and Brighton are both a short drive away if she needs anything. No one from her old life needs to know she's here.

Deciding to stay hemmed up in the house doesn't calm her as much as she thought it might. She thinks about her mum on the other side of her bedroom door, probably waiting for her daughter to leave before she re-emerges. She pictures Mrs Robson and Tammy above her and the tenant she has yet to meet, and all the air in the room seems to want to get into her lungs at once, choking her as it forces its way down her throat.

Out. She needs to get out *and* she must steer clear of the village. She shoots across the room and bangs on her mum's bedroom door.

'I'll just be a few minutes, erm … Glenys. Just going to get some fresh air. Will you be okay on your own?'

Silence. Could Mum be left alone? Violet returns to her Instructions binder. According to point number seven, Glenys is fine at home for short periods of time as long as she's dressed, and it doesn't clash with mealtimes, bedtime, or bath times.

'Fine.' Glenys' tight voice sounds from behind her door.

She's not fine, neither of them are. Violet's not sure if they ever will be again.

Fortunately for Violet, Lowerstone's most scenic walking spots can be accessed without going through the village. All she has to do is walk around the left side of Malvern House and through the back gate. Her feet greet the footpath like an old friend and a familiar thrill runs through her as she looks across the brilliant yellow fields of rapeseed towards the river.

Dear old world, Anne Shirley whispers from her pages in Violet's mind. *You are very lovely and I'm glad to be alive.*

The water is sending sparkles of sunlight in every direction and Violet's pace quickens as she's pulled towards the happiest place on earth. Surrounded by blossom trees of every shade is the widest part of Lower Lake. A flint bridge leads across it and into the woods. Woods that have at least seven great climbing trees and plenty of places to make the most impressive of dens. Adam and Violet had turned den-making into a competitive sport during every one of their school holidays.

Four benches are perched at the lake's edge. Violet knows the inscriptions on them by heart; the names of those they're dedicated to, who they're remembered by and the dates they died. She shivers as she walks beneath the shade of the trees, wishing she'd pulled a hoody from her suitcase before leaving the house.

The bench on the far left next to the bridge has a person on it. A person whose hair sits in tight curls like springs. She's wearing an immaculate tracksuit and the backs of her trainers are white and shiny, possibly enjoying their first ever experience of the outside world.

Violet hasn't got time to formulate a backstory for this mysterious woman, especially as it could be someone who knew her from *before.* Violet will walk the longer way around to the woods. She takes a step backwards, ready to turn around and a twig snaps beneath her feet.

The woman swivels around and smiles. The story's over before it can begin. Violet can't rewrite a narrative that's already been lived. Not for someone she knows so well. *Knew*, she corrects herself. Mrs Goode probably won't recognise her.

Violet spins herself around and moves her wobbling legs back down the path she has just walked.

'Excuse me? Hello? Is that you?'

Just keep walking, Violet. You haven't heard a thing. She thinks you're someone else, anyway. She wouldn't want to see someone who's *Bad News*. No one in this village would.

The sound of hurried footsteps on dried mud gets louder and then she's overtaken.

'Is that ... Oh it is, my goodness, it *is* Violet Strong. Well, I never.' Mrs Goode shields her eyes from the blazing sun, beaming as she leans against a tree to catch her breath.

Violet's heart thuds hard and her eyes start to sting. Probably the pollen from all that rapeseed.

There's still time to run. Why won't her feet move?

'That's me.' Violet does a weird mock-salute, feeling immediately silly. 'Hi, Mrs G.'

'I think you're fine to call me Chrissie now you're no longer a pupil.' Chrissie laughs and pulls Violet into an unexpected hug.

The sudden physical contact with another human makes the breath catch inside her. Violet nudges herself out of the embrace, clears her throat and manages a smile. It even feels like quite a bright one.

'Fair enough. How are you, Chrissie? It's wonderful to see you, actually.' The surprise in Violet's voice when she says 'actually' makes Chrissie laugh, but it's true. It is good to see her kind grey eyes. They have a few new lines around them, but they're still the same ones that twinkled at Violet on her first day at secondary school. The same ones that peered over thick glasses to read her first ever English assignment. *A plus. You have such talent. See me after class.* It had been written on the top in blue ink and Violet's heart had skipped all the way home. It was Mrs G who helped her believe she could write. Mrs G who encouraged her to start up the school newspaper that had become such a success.

'Me? Oh, I'm fine. Fine,' Chrissie repeats. She's holding the handle of a dog lead that's trailing along the sun-hardened ground.

'Your dog having a run about?' Violet peers around, catching a glimpse of a brown and white spaniel running between the trees. Perhaps if they stay on safe subjects, they won't have to make any awkward shuffles down memory lane.

Chrissie smiles but her eyes stay focussed on the river. She's gripping the lead hard enough to turn her knuckles white and Violet realises there's something different about her former teacher. She's older, obviously, and Violet is looking at her through different eyes, but there's something else. A sadness, perhaps, that means she doesn't stand up quite as straight as she used to.

Chrissie's voice is almost a whisper. 'Luna loves to run. She likes it here. Probably because Fred did. It was his favourite place.'

Violet nods and searches for comforting words to say. It *was* Fred's favourite place. Past tense usually only means one thing and it's one of the many things Violet isn't good at talking about. Usually, she'd be looking for an excuse to leave but she realises she doesn't really want to. Having someone smile at her despite knowing who she is and what she's done feels like eating a bacon sandwich in the sunshine.

'Coffee,' Chrissie bursts out. 'I have a flask in my rucksack. Would you like to share? I always like to have my mid-morning cuppa up here. It was Fred's favourite place,' she repeats.

Violet follows Chrissie back to the bench and perches next to her, watching as she pours the steaming drink into a cup.

'Here. You have this. I'll drink from the flask.' Chrissie hands her the plastic mug and taps it with her flask. 'Cheers.'

Violet takes a deep breath. 'Was?'

Chrissie shuffles backwards on the bench and takes a big swig of her drink.

'You said this *was* Fred's favourite place,' Violet says in her quietest voice.

The leaves from the trees on the other side of the river rustle as the breeze picks up. Chrissie fiddles with the lead she still has wound around her wrist. 'Three months ago, yesterday. Cancer.'

'Oh, Chrissie. I'm so …'

'It's OK, it's fine. I'm fine.' Chrissie waves away the rest of Violet's words. 'It's you I want to hear about. It must be what – thirteen years?'

'Fourteen.'

'Fourteen years.' Chrissie shakes her head. 'Doesn't seem possible.'

People always do that, they seem surprised that time passes. Surely, it would be weirder if it didn't. 'I'm here to take care of Mum for a bit. Jodie's gone away.' Violet leaves out the details about the house sale and the care home. Not fair to the other tenants to be the last to know.

'How lovely. Bet your mum's thrilled to have you back.'

A snort falls out of Violet. 'Thrilled isn't quite the word. She hates me as much as she ever did.' Strange how her voice can sound so bitter even through her laughter.

Chrissie frowns. She tilts her head as if Violet has told a joke she doesn't quite get and then goes back to frowning again. 'I'm sure she doesn't hate you. What happened to your mum – what happened to all of you – was a tragedy. One you will find your way through together.'

Violet stops laughing.

'Anyway. Enough about that. What have you been doing with yourself – Jodie said you were living up north?'

'Yup. I mean, I was up there anyway with … with Megan.' Saying her name out loud feels wrong, she shouldn't be allowed to use it.

Chrissie presses her lips lightly together and looks down at the weeds in front of the bench.

Megan hadn't even made it past Freshers week. One party, one pill, shared between her and Violet. Snapped in half. It wasn't fair that only one of them made it home that night.

'Are her family still in the village?' Violet's voice is small, the size of a thimble.

'No, love.' Chrissie leans over and pats her hand. 'They moved away soon after she died. Too many memories, probably.'

It takes several attempts to swallow. Too much air, too much guilt. And then still more guilt for the overwhelming relief that Megan's family no longer live there. Bumping into them after everything, she can't even imagine how that would go.

The last time she'd seen them had been the day Megan and

Violet left for Manchester Uni. Megan's parents had waved them off from the platform at Brighton train station, pride leaking from their faces.

Violet had no such send-off from her own family, what was left of it. Violet wasn't going to uni in the strictest sense of the word, it was a last-minute escape route from the village. She'd bunk in with Megan in her room in a shared student house until she could save enough for a rental deposit of her own. After three years of being inseparable, they were going to have The Time of Their Lives.

Violet had been fifteen when Megan pulled her out of a puddle of White Lightning behind the bakery in the village and took her back to her parents' house. They'd stuck together like chewing gum after that, drinking together, tearing up the village with their antics. It had been the distraction Violet needed after everything that had happened in her family. But she should have known better. She shouldn't have got so close to Megan. Why hadn't she learned her lesson from the other people in her life? When Violet's around, bad things happen. She takes her bad news wherever she goes.

What did she think she was doing, coming back to Lowerstone and dragging it all back with her? The village doesn't deserve any more bad luck, it's had more than its fill already.

'I assumed you'd come back sooner or later,' says Chrissie. 'Just didn't think it would be so many years before you came home.'

A duck glides to the edge of the river and hops out, wandering so close to them that Violet wonders if it's on first-name terms with Chrissie.

'Didn't seem much point coming back at the time.' Violet

watches as Chrissie takes a handful of bird feed from her pocket and flicks it towards the duck's waiting beak. 'I thought about it when Megan died. But Mum and Jodie wouldn't have wanted me back – they could barely look me in the face before I left, let alone after. A fresh start felt like the best way.'

'And did you get one, make a good life for yourself?'

'Rented a bedsit. Plenty of cleaning jobs – I always had work. Kept myself to myself and that's it really. Oh, and I started a blog – a book blog. That kept me busy.'

Chrissie's face breaks into a smile. 'You always did love your stories. Such an imagination – I always thought you'd end up working with stories in some way. Writing, publishing – something like that.'

Violet chews her lip, remembering the look on Chrissie's – Mrs Goode's – face when Violet told her she was dropping out, halfway through her A levels. The disappointment in the air had been thick enough to chew on and Violet had stormed out of the classroom, hackles raised to the roof.

'I was planning to go back to my A levels up north, then start uni the year after. But as soon as Megan died, the landlord kicked me out.'

'Blimey, what a wanker,' Chrissie says.

Violet manages a smile. It's funny when your teacher swears, even when you're an adult. 'Never did get around to applying, but there you go. Life gets in the way, doesn't it?' She lets out a laugh she doesn't mean, and Chrissie leans forward.

'Do you remember when you started up the school newspaper? That was such a success and those pieces you wrote were wonderful.' Chrissie's eyes are shining. 'Perhaps this is your chance. A new start. You could start your life all over again and do something you love – all the things you wished you could have done.'

Violet's chest tightens. She's had so many fresh starts, the phrase has lost all meaning to her. All those Mondays full of starting diets, gym classes, evening classes, distance learning courses. Most things tended to take up time and money she never had. She's two years past turning thirty now – everything should be neatly arranged for the next 'grown up' phase of her life. If she doesn't have it sorted by now, she's unlikely to change much of it – what would be the point? As Anne Shirley would say, her life is a 'perfect graveyard of buried hopes'.

'I probably won't be around here for long. I will keep going with my blog though – it'll give me something to do when Mum's napping.'

'Good idea. The library in the village is open every day except Wednesday if you get short of books,' says Chrissie. 'And there is something else you could do – why don't you write some freelance articles and send them off to magazines? Have a look online – you've got nothing to lose.'

Violet's heart swells. It's good to have her old teacher advising her again. It makes her feel safer somehow. It's been so long since she's allowed herself to think about her hopes and dreams, let alone say them out loud. 'Thank you,' she says. And she means it. 'I'll have a think about it. If Mrs Robson upstairs has anything to do with it, I'll have my hands full with Neighbourhood Watch meetings.'

Chrissie chuckles as she replaces the lid on her flask and tucks it back into her bag. 'Good luck with that. I've been to one or two of them – I think everyone in the village has at one point or other – very few go back for a return visit, mind.'

The duck has started to waddle hopefully around Violet's ankles. Violet remembers her mum, alone at Malvern House, probably waiting for lunch. Instruction number seven had been explicit about sticking to mealtimes. 'I'd better get going – don't want to keep Mum waiting – although I'm sure she'd rather I stay out of the way as much as possible. Thanks for the heads-up about the Neighbourhood Watch.'

Chrissie stands up and pats Violet on the back. 'I'm sure Mrs Robson's heart's in the right place. The village needs something to bring people together. It's certainly not the place it used to be.'

Violet forces down the lump of guilt that's always ready and willing to rise to the surface at any given opportunity. She knows Lowerstone isn't the same. It never will be again thanks to her.

'Perhaps you should start up another newspaper – worked a treat for your school. Maybe a village newspaper would give everyone something to do.'

'Maybe.' Violet manages a polite smile. 'As I said, though, I don't plan on being around for too long. Just until I've got some stuff sorted for Mum.' She says goodbye to Chrissie and starts making her way towards the fields.

Chrissie calls some parting words from the lakeside that freeze Violet's trainers to the ground. 'I bet Adam's thrilled to have you back. Must be funny living in the same building after all those years apart.'

It feels like nails are being hammered through Violet's heart when she reaches the back gate of Malvern House. Hearing Adam's name like that, well, it caught her off guard. Speaking to Chrissie had made her feel less alone for five minutes – she'd even decided to write a plan after dinner, a map for how to move forward and in what order so she can get out of here and move on. Chrissie could be right – now could be the time to take control of her life – make those changes she'd dreamed of for so long. But she can't be thinking about all that now. Thriving is a luxury. Survival is what matters.

Violet rushes through the front door, fumbling with her keys. The old door had a special knack, she's not used to this shiny new one with the intercom system down the side. She jiggles the keys in the lock and pulls the door handle up and down, muttering at it in an attempt to make it open. As soon as she's through the inside door to the flat, Violet calls out to her mum and goes straight to the drawer in the sideboard.

Her hands shake as she pulls out the *Malvern House Tenants* folder.

The document she wants is at the bottom of the pile. The paper slips a little underneath Violet's sweaty hands and she grips it tight, peering at the names on it, ignoring the way her tummy has turned into a washing machine on fast spin. Of course, there are two names. Mr and Mrs Croft. One of Adam's messages had said that he and his wife had just bought a house, but couples move all the time and people downsize for all sorts of reasons.

Violet puts the folder back in the drawer. She just has to get on with everything, that's all. No more musing, or thinking, or what–ifs. If she's going to get through the next few months, she has no time for daydreaming, she needs to focus and take everything one step at a time. She'll make lunch. She'll drag Mum out of her room to sit and eat with her. Maybe her mum might even talk to her today. She'll call the estate agents and set up some valuations to make a start on selling the house.

Once it's sold, they'll have the money to pay for Glenys's residential care. Then, when she's done all that, she'll update her blog and look into this freelancing malarkey. She'll be strong and courageous like Jo March or Lizzie Bennet or Katniss Everdeen. She's got this.

According to the third page of Jodie's instructions, Saturday's lunch should consist of toasted tuna and cucumber sandwiches and fruit salad. Violet chops and toasts and plates up before knocking on her mum's bedroom door with a confidence she doesn't feel.

Fake it 'til you make it is always a handy motto to live by when you're all out of choices.

Her mum doesn't speak, but she does emerge from the door with her walking frame, making her way towards the table without so much as looking in Violet's direction.

'Nice?' Violet asks after they've both taken a mouthful. If she keeps smiling, keeps injecting as much joy into her voice as possible, it's sure to be infectious. It's what everyone at work always said about Violet. *You always seem so happy – and that laugh of yours, that smile – it's just so contagious.*

Little did they know.

Glenys keeps munching away. Her eyes don't move from the blank screen of the TV.

'Do you want me to switch it on? What do you usually watch?'

Nothing.

Violet clenches and unclenches her fists under the table. 'I know this must be out of the blue – Jodie going away and me turning up. But I'm here now, and I'd really like it if we could get to know each other. I mean, we obviously know each other, you're my mum, but it's been a long time. And I know lots has happened in that time to both of us. Now we're here, it would be nice if we could reconnect and make the best of it.'

Glenys pulls apart the second half of her sandwich, pulls the tuna out of it and drops it on her plate. After stuffing all the remaining toast in her mouth until she looks like a hamster, she holds the plate in the air and tips it upside down, sending the rest of its contents to the floor.

'Mum, what on earth are you doing? It's fine. I'll clear it up. You only had to say if you don't like it. Jodie seems to think you do.' Violet jumps up from the table and crouches on the floor, picking flakes of fish from the carpet with her fingernails. Her head spins from getting up and down again too quickly, and the smell of tuna hits the back of her throat.

Glenys swallows her toast and peers down at Violet with eyes of cold, hard steel. 'Jodie's not here. You are. You shouldn't have come.' She shuffles her seat backwards and stands up, gripping hold of her frame. She makes her way to the armchair and lowers herself into it before turning her face back towards the blank TV screen. 'You shouldn't have come,' she repeats.

Violet inches herself back up from the floor. She picks up both plates without a sound and creeps towards the kitchen. The problem with having both your hands full is it's tricky to wipe the tears from your eyes.

She goes to the sink, drops the plates in and runs the hot tap, keeping her back to the living room and her gaze fixed to the unwieldy weeds in the back garden. She takes five deliberate breaths and forces her shoulders back down.

Starting again isn't always a new adventure. Sometimes it's just falling back down a steep hill you've spent years climbing, only to find yourself right at the bottom again.

CHAPTER 9

Violet

CALLING THE ESTATE AGENTS is at the very top of Violet's list for the day. Breakfast had been a silent affair; her mum's words from the night before had clung to the room like a bad smell. The frosty atmosphere is seeping inside Violet's bones, weighing her down and trapping her inside her own sense of inadequacy.

The TV's blaring behind Violet as she sits at the dining-room table, hunched over her laptop. Glenys is watching *Escape to the Country*. Violet would rather like to escape *from* the country. She can't control how Glenys feels towards her. She needs to focus on the things she can change, starting with the house sale.

She does a Google search for local agencies. Getting the house sold and her mum into Rossendale has to be her priority. She can't live like this – neither of them can. Mum had made it 4K, Ultra HD clear that she doesn't want Violet around. She dials the first number she sees, Mullens' Estate Agents.

'We can get someone out to view the building next Thursday?' the voice says on the other end of the line once she's explained about Malvern House. 'As it's flats though, you'll need to give notice to all of the tenants that our agent will need access.'

'Thanks. I'll get back to you about Thursday.'

Bugger.

There's nothing Violet can do until she writes those damn letters to the tenants of Malvern House.

She types a letter, deletes it, and types it again, printing three copies. She's usually good with words, but ones that tell people their lives are about to be spun around are curiously tricky to find.

Guilt prickles the back of her neck as she checks the printed version for errors. She leaves them on the printer for now. One thing at a time.

'Can I get you anything, Mum?'

Glenys picks up the remote and turns up the volume. 'We need food. I'm still hungry and there's sod all in the cupboards.'

'I'm sure Jodie said—'

'Nothing I like eating. We need jam – it's all I can eat with bread. Make sure it's raspberry.'

Violet's tummy churns as she turns around and looks through the living-room window. The village at the bottom of the hill is a blurred blob between the gap in the front wall where the gate should be.

It's not that far away, the village shop. Three minutes' walk, and they're bound to have jam. All Violet needs to do is pop her shoes on, grab her keys and walk through the door.

Easy-peasy.

The heat hits Violet's face as she steps outside, blinking as the glare from the sun bores into her eyes.

Why hadn't she packed sunglasses? Protection and anonymity

should be in order right now. Would they recognise her in the village? Probably. Violet hasn't changed much in fourteen years. Few extra pounds and wrinkles, but still the same flame-red braided hair and green eyes. And she's wearing her favourite purple dungarees – totally wrong for the hot weather and upholding her own obscurity.

She takes three steps forward. *Keep walking, enter shop, look at shelves.*

Same shelves she used to stare up into as a child. Same shop where they all stared at Violet the first day she left the house after it all happened. The last time Violet went in there, they wouldn't even serve her. We don't need your money in here, the shopkeeper had said.

Four more steps and she's at the top of the road. Violet's heart becomes a thudding drum, bashing out a chaotic rhythm without a sound screen around it to soften the blows.

Pick up jam, pay at counter, walk home.

Violet's legs won't work. Turns out they could only manage the eight steps forward. It's those pictures in her mind, the words swimming in her ears. *That's her – that's that Violet Strong. She's Bad News, that girl, Bad News.* Then will come the pointing, the stiffened shoulders, and the turned-up noses.

Sweat trickles down her back as she forces her feet back to the front door, gulping air into her lungs with those long, slow breaths the internet always tells her to take.

She'll go tomorrow, first thing. Might be quieter, less likely to bump into anyone.

Nothing worse than looking into the eyes of someone whose life you've ruined, and Violet should know, she's had plenty of practice.

There is one thing she should be doing – she promised Tammy she'd pop back to see her. Violet's been going back and forth in her head about it. She's already got to kick the poor woman out of her home, why risk making things even worse by hanging around her? But there'd been such sadness in Tammy's eyes when she told her about her mum dying, and she no longer even has her hi-fi or telly for company. Violet might as well be of some use to someone.

An overwhelming smell of furniture polish hits Violet as she walks up the stairs to Tammy's flat.

'So sorry I didn't come back yesterday – I had a bit of a day,' Violet says when Tammy answers the door. 'Mum's watching TV, so I've got an hour or so to look at your hi-fi and TV if you like?'

Tammy's glasses slip down her nose when she smiles. 'Come in.' She keeps talking as Violet follows her into the flat. 'Thank you. I already know what's wrong with my hi-fi though, and my telly. It's because of the electricity. It's all gone.'

A tin of Pledge and a soaking wet dusting cloth are sitting on the coffee table.

Violet plonks herself on the sofa. 'Do you have a card to top it back up? You could probably do it at the village shop?'

Tammy shows Violet a jar labelled *Money* that holds nothing but a bank card and an electric card. 'Don't know how, though. Mum does it. Did it. She gets me the money.'

'Do you know the number for your bank card?'

Tammy's blank look tells Violet enough to know she needs to dig back into her handbag.

Violet forces the words out before they can find excuses to stay safely in her mouth. 'I'll come with you to the shop, I need to go anyway. I'll buy you some electric and bread and milk and stuff. It's not a problem, pay me back whenever.' Violet reaches for her breeziest voice as she does sums in her head from her own dwindling bank balance.

Tammy stares at Violet without blinking. 'You're one of the kind people. Mum said there were some kind people. Most people aren't, though.'

Violet pulls her bag over her shoulder. 'When you look hard enough, there are probably more than you think.'

The buzzing in her ears starts before she's even opened the front door of the building.

Once again, the bottoms of Violet's trainers are made of superglue. She needs to unstick them.

But moving forwards and leaving through the front door of Malvern House is a task she's still not sure she's up to.

'You look funny. Don't you want to go?' says Tammy. 'I don't want to either. My tummy goes weird when I go outside. Mum said it was a good thing; it's how your body tells you you're in danger. And being outside can be dangerous.'

Violet swallows. 'We'll be absolutely fine. It's just the village. One shop, that's all we need. And we'll have each other.' She smiles. One foot frees itself from the floor, followed by the other.

Be more Anne.

Dread draws tight circles around Violet as she walks through the gap in the front wall and steps onto the pavement. She closes her eyes for a moment, pulling out her Anne-thoughts to erase the invisible lines with.

This is for Tammy. She needs this. She has *no one*.

Violet knows what that's like.

Tammy gives Violet a nervous grin before linking a hand into the crook of Violet's arm. 'There's two of us. A kidnapper wouldn't be able to get both of us. We'd be too heavy.'

Right now, Violet might prefer to face a kidnapper over the locals of Lowerstone. Shame holds its own special kind of hostage.

Violet pats Tammy's hand and moves slowly forward, shedding small flecks of anxiety as she moves until she feels light enough to pick up speed.

Tammy's hand disappears from Violet's arm. 'I don't want to, actually. I'm going home. Sorry.' Her face has paled, and her light green eyes fill with water.

'It's fine.' Violet calls to the back of Tammy's already retreating body. 'I'll come straight up when I get back.'

Should she have tried harder to encourage Tammy to walk with her? Violet would hate it if someone attempted to get her out against her will.

Not that anyone would bother.

She squeezes her eyes tight before moving on, picturing Tammy's face when she told Violet about her mum dying on her way back with the milk.

She can do this.

Next to trying and winning, the best thing is trying and failing.
Be more Anne.

As she walks, she's a thousand different Violets all at once as the memories seep into her consciousness. She's nine-year-old Violet, walking to the village shops on her own for the first time with the sun on her arms and the breeze sending her messy red hair in all directions. She's the Violet skipping down towards Adam's house to spend Saturday afternoon in his mum's garden. She's other Violets too, but she doesn't want to remember all of them.

As she nears the bottom of the hill, Violet slows her breathing to calm her rising heart rate. She focuses on the chirps of the birds and the sweetness of the honeysuckle in the air. It's been so many years. Lots of people would have moved away and those that hadn't, might not recognise her.

Nothing to fear.

The shop is tinier than Violet remembered, and the chocolate bars are on the wrong side. It smells the same though: nutmeg and unread magazines. She scoops up a loaf of bread, a tin of beans, a carton of milk and jars of coffee and raspberry jam.

'Five pounds electric on this please.' Violet hands Tammy's card over the counter, avoiding the eyes of the cashier.

A seething male voice behind Violet makes her jump. 'Dad didn't get his newspaper again this morning. Third time in three weeks. You really need to be having a word with the kid who does your paper round.'

Violet keeps her eyes in front of her as irritation creeps across her skin. Nothing worse than entitled men who think nothing of snapping at shopkeepers and ignoring the queue.

'Do you mind at least waiting until I've finished being served before shouting across me like that?' Violet says without turning around. Not drawing attention to herself was the first self-imposed rule she'd decided on before venturing into the village.

The shop fills with silence. Violet smiles and thanks the woman behind the till as she retrieves Tammy's card. She keeps her head down and away from the man as she slinks past him.

'Violet.'

Violet turns to find a familiar face standing in front of her. He's taller than her – he always had been. His hair is long, dark, and scraped up into a messy bun. It turns out a man's voice changes quite a bit from the age of eighteen to thirty-two, but she'd recognise those hazel eyes and wide mouth anywhere, although both have new creases next to them.

Adam Croft.

CHAPTER 10

Violet

VIOLET RUSHES TOWARDS THE door to the corner shop, making herself as small as possible so she can pass through the queue of people without touching them, and the heat hits her as soon as she's through the door and onto the street.

'Violet! Wait!' Adam's voice is behind her.

She runs to the kerb, but there's a tractor coming up the hill. She's trapped between the road and Adam. The red glint of the phone box catches her eye, and she dives inside.

Adam is just a few strides away; she can't just stand there. She picks up the receiver and presses some buttons. She just didn't recognise him, she'll say, it's been so long. Violet only needs a minute or two, that's all. Just to get rid of that image of him from the last time they were together, fourteen years ago.

That last night before she left Lowerstone for Manchester.

It had all started when Violet saw Kirsty Waters in The Swan on the last day of the summer holidays. Kirsty was the class bitch. She sat in front of Megan and Violet for all of year eleven and was always grassing them up for messing about.

Violet had never seen her drinking alcohol until that night. Violet and Megan were there, in The Swan, their shiny new ID cards tucked inside their purses as they sipped their half-pints of cider.

'What's the matter with her?' Megan nodded towards the bar where Kirsty was sitting alone, her head resting in her hands, both elbows on the table.

Violet got up out of her rickety stool and made her way through the smoky haze of the almost empty pub. It was always almost empty by then, that's why the last owners had to sell. Most of the village couldn't afford nights out after what happened, another reason they all called Violet *Bad News*.

Kirsty's bronzed cheeks were stained with tears and cheap mascara. 'Come to gloat? You've got a fucking nerve, Violet *Wrong*, coming over here after what you've done to my family.'

Even after combing through every inch of her memories, Violet couldn't work out what Kirsty was talking about.

'Mum's been fired.'

'Why's that my fault?' For once, that's not because of me, Violet thought.

'Erm, last month? You've actually, seriously forgotten?' Kirsty jumped up from her seat and stepped towards Violet until they were almost forehead-to-forehead.

Oh *that*. Of course, she hadn't forgotten that, Violet still had about a million bruises. She'd almost died trying to cross the road just outside the pub. She might have been hurt far worse, someone had said, had she not been so bladdered on cheap alcopops from the corner shop. Something to do with having relaxed limbs. Of course, if she'd been sober, she wouldn't have run blindly into the road, so there was that ...

78

'Mum drives a minibus for work, you idiot. Since she hit you with her car, she hasn't been able to get behind the wheel without almost having a flippin' heart attack. They gave her some time off, but it wasn't enough. They've got someone else in her place now and she's got to go to therapy. So, thanks for that.' Kirsty balled her hand into a fist. 'Why don't you get the fuck away from this village — no one wants you here. You're bad news.'

'Let's go,' Megan pulled Violet out of the pub.

They bought more alcopops from the corner shop. Blue, pink, orange.

'Sorry to ruin your last night,' Violet mumbled into her second orange one, as they sat on the bench outside the bakery. 'I can't believe you're really going.' She didn't even want to think about what life in the village would be like without Megan. It wasn't as if she really had her family anymore, or Adam.

Violet shook his name from her mind. 'Kirsty's right. I need to get away from here. I've caused everyone so much shit. Mum and Jodie have barely spoken to me since what happened with Dad, and without you here …'

'Come with me.'

'Eh?'

'Come with me,' Megan repeated. 'You can stay in my student place, we'll top and tail. You can come out every night with me, we'll do Freshers week together. It will be amazing.'

'That *would* be amazing.' Violet's heart inched a little higher as something close to hope entered it. She stared at the cottage next to the sweet shop and shook her head when Megan held out another drink towards her. 'No, ta. If we're going to do this, there's someone I need to say goodbye to first. He deserves that much.'

Adam's bedroom was at the back of his parents' cottage on the ground floor. His sash window was slightly open just as it always had been when they were younger.

As her heart thumped out a rhythm of terror, Violet tapped on the glass, using their very own secret code from years ago.

Four seconds passed, five, ten, twenty.

Then his face was at the window, that beautiful face.

'I've come to say goodbye.' She couldn't take her eyes away from him. His mouth, his too-long hair that was always in his eyes.

His face stayed the same. No smile, no frown or look of surprise.

'You'd better come in, then.' He opened the window wide enough for her to climb through.

His room was different: fewer football posters and a stronger smell of socks and Lynx Africa.

'Tomorrow,' she whispered. 'I'm leaving tomorrow, and before I go, I just wanted to say …' She never got to say what she wanted to say. Adam's mouth arrived on hers, his arms around her waist.

He was the one she sat next to in primary school. The one she climbed trees with. He'd been the first boy she kissed when they were thirteen and she couldn't remember a single time in her life when she hadn't been in love with Adam Croft. So, despite the fact they'd barely spoken in four years, and even though she'd gone there to say how sorry she was for her part in what happened to his mum, she let the words melt away and she lost herself in the urgency of his kiss.

The kiss led to Violet waking up the next morning with his arm on her waist and doubts in her mind. She could stay. She could try to make up for the past. He might one day be able to forgive her.

No, Violet. No, no, no.

She climbed out of bed as slowly and as quietly as she could and got dressed. She didn't deserve Adam. And Adam deserved someone who wasn't *Bad News* – he'd had more than enough of that already.

The window didn't make a sound when she closed it behind her.

She hadn't even considered that she could end up being Bad News for Megan.

Violet starts talking into the receiver in the phone box. She'd planned to pretend to be in deep conversation in the hope that Adam would think it was an important call and walk away. But then she'd remembered the missing glass. He'll know she's faking if she doesn't speak.

'Yes, erm, Jenny. It's in the purple folder and it's very important. I need you to read page nineteen, paragraph three to me please.' Violet uses her phone voice and blinks fast, trying to dispel the vividness of those pesky memories.

Adam is peering through the hole in the glass. It's too late to look away, their eyes have met, and Violet's stomach is plummeting towards her toes.

He clears his throat and points a finger towards the phone. The wire's been cut and the receiver isn't even attached to anything.

Bollocks.

'Adam.' A whisper/squeak hybrid. She hangs up the phone and swings the door open in feigned surprise.

Smooth.

'It's amazing to see … I can't believe it's really you.' The soft lines next to Adam's mouth deepen when he smiles.

'Neither can I. I mean, I know it's me, obviously, but I can't believe I'm here – or that you are. You being here isn't that weird, I suppose. I already knew you lived here but – you know. Still weird.' Violet's tongue needs holding down.

'Very weird. And sorry about before – with the newspaper. It's just Dad, that's all. He looks forward to getting his paper. I'm sure he wasn't missed out on purpose; I shouldn't have had a go at them. I'll go back and apologise when the queue's gone down.'

Violet can't find anything else to say. Her face feels as red as the telephone box that Adam's still staring at.

'Remember when we were tiny, and we said we were going to sleep in that telephone box one night?' He turns to face Violet and chuckles, holding his arms out for a hug.

Violet swallows and steps forward, patting the backs of his shoulders with her fingertips. She doesn't deserve Adam's arms or his smiles. She remembers how he looked the last time she saw him. His pale face pulled tight around red eyes with sunken shadows beneath them. She steps back. 'I, erm … it was lovely getting your messages. Nice to catch up on your news each year.'

It had been. Seeing that first message five years ago had been like having her soul cuddled by something warm and furry. She'd been shocked to see his name and even more shocked that Jodie had bothered to give him Violet's number.

'What are you doing back here? Staying at your mum's? Not sure if you know already, but I'm living right across the hall from her in flat two.' He grins and pauses, as if waiting for Violet to jump up and down with excitement.

Violet puts her thoughts on fast forward. She can't tell him she's only staying until the building's sold – wouldn't be fair to dump that on him as soon as she sees him. She'll work up to it. 'Just looking after Mum whilst Jodie's away.'

A car trundles past, scattering the birds in the trees over the road. Adam's eyes are entirely focused on Violet. She fiddles with the button on her purple dungarees.

'How long's Jodie away for?' asks Adam.

'Not sure – few months, maybe.'

Another smile crawls across Adam's face and he shakes her head, chuckling. 'I still can't believe you're here. You walking home?'

Strolling back up the hill next to Adam is like going back in time. She wants to enjoy being in close proximity to him again, but a very important point keeps jabbing at her, and it is sabre-tooth sharp. Eighteen years ago, Adam had his whole world yanked from underneath his Adidas–clad feet and it was all Violet's fault. She can't just rock up all these years later and go back to running around the village and climbing trees with him. Too much has happened. Plus, he's married now – he'll be too busy to want to hang out with some kid he used to play with – especially one who's about to have him evicted.

'How's your dad? Apart from not getting his newspaper, obviously. Lovely that he still lives in the village.'

Adam slows his pace. 'Still in the village, yes. He lives with me now. He has Parkinson's like Grandad. I've been his carer since his health got worse.'

'Oh, Adam, I'm sorry.' Knots bunch up across Violet's shoulders. Adam's dad was always the active, cheery type. Always jogging or riding his bike. If Adam's mum was still alive, he'd have more support – he probably wouldn't have had to leave his home and move in with his son.

Another thing to add to Violet's list of regrets.

Adam shrugs. "S'okay. He has good days as well as bad ones and we like living together.'

'Must be a bit of squeeze though, three of you living in one flat,' says Violet.

Adam increases his walking speed. 'Only two of us.' His words sound like they've been snipped off at the ends.

'Oh, sorry. I was just going off your tenancy agreement – I thought it said Mr and Mrs Croft. And after your message about getting married, I just assumed ...'

'So, you did know I was living there?' A tinge of amusement covers some of the sadness in Adam's voice. 'If you look closely, you'll see it's Mr and Mr Croft – Kelly left way before we moved out of the old house. She wasn't keen on us being a three. Dad being there all the time was too much for her – she said I had to choose.'

Violet turns her face towards the blossom trees on her left to hide the shock. She searches for some good words to say, but there don't appear to be any handy for something so shitty. 'Sorry,' is all she manages. Again. Violet's word of the day.

'Not your fault.' Adam sounds bright and cheery, but his face doesn't match.

Their footsteps align and echo on the silent street. Violet

had forgotten the quiet moments of the village. Bursts of time where no cars drove through, no one opened their doors and even the birds pause for breath. The absolute peace of it stills her mind as she walks.

'Do you see much of the others? Mum's other tenants?' Violet asks.

'Mrs Robson upstairs – she's quite a character.' Adam raises an eyebrow and just for a second, he looks exactly like he did as a kid sitting next to her at school and gossiping about the teachers. 'Has she invited you to her Neighbourhood Watch group yet?'

'She did mention something about that. Didn't sound much like my cup of cocoa to be honest.' Violet laughs.

'I don't think it's anybody's. Everyone in the village has been once, but no one has ever returned. Most people probably only went out of boredom. Not much to do in Lowerstone since the pub and the community hall closed.'

'Have you met Tammy? The woman who lives above you?' Violet asks.

'Only once when she first moved in. She didn't want to talk to me. I definitely hear her, though. She likes to shout a lot.'

'That's why I was at the shop – getting her some bits. Think she's struggling on her own. Her mum's just died.'

The silence creeps back but this time it's thicker. Adam and Violet both know what it's like to lose a parent.

'You should come in and see Dad. He'd love to see you again,' Adam says once they reach the front door of Malvern House.

Violet's chests squeezes as if a belt has been fastened too tightly around it. 'He wouldn't want to see me, I'm sure. Not after … everything. It wouldn't be fair.'

Adam gets his keys out of his pocket and turns to face Violet. 'People aren't always thinking what you think they're thinking. Sometimes people would rather let you know for themselves – don't they deserve that chance?'

Violet swallows. 'I'll come and see him soon. I promise. I just need to get these back to Tammy.'

Adam places a warm hand on Violet's shoulder. 'Okay. No pressure. It's just so good to see you again.' Adam leans over and kisses Violet's forehead. 'Don't be a stranger – you know where I live.'

Violet smiles as she walks into the hallway and up the steps.

'Oh, and Violet?' Adam calls up the stairway. 'I'm always around if you need any help with your mum – us carers need to stick together.'

Violet replays Adam's last sentence in her head as she knocks on the door to Tammy's flat. She still can't get over the fact that he lives in the same building, let alone all his other news. It's a lot to process in one day.

'Thank you.' Tammy's face lights up when Violet shows her how to put the electric card in after popping her shopping on the kitchen worktop. 'And I'm sorry I didn't make it all the way to the shop. It's been a long time since …' She runs out of words and stares at the numbers on the electricity meter.

'No problem. I'm pleased we've met properly. I'd better get back to Mum – she'll be awake by now. Just remember I'm only downstairs if you need anything.'

A flicker of panic travels across Tammy's eyes when Violet says goodbye. The lost look on her face stays imprinted on Violet's mind as she gets dinner ready for her mum. She thinks about Adam, caring alone for his dad in the flat across the hall. She thinks about lonely Mrs Robson above her, putting the kettle on for Neighbourhood Watch meetings that no one ever goes to.

How can she ask any of them to leave? Violet plucks the eviction letters from the printer, folds them up and shoves them into her handbag. They'll all have to know eventually, but she'll give them more time – she'll wait until she knows there are other places in the village for them to go to first. No one should have to leave their hometown unless they want to, and they all clearly have things going on that she might be able to help with in the meantime. There are other things she can be getting on with: clearing the driveway of all those weeds, having the upstairs windows repainted and looking into getting those loose tiles on the front wall fixed.

The quicker she can help the tenants to find somewhere to live, the faster she can sell the building and get Glenys safely tucked up at Rossendale Residential. Then she can move on and start again with life. Another fresh start. Perhaps this time she could change her name – Lisbeth or Hermione, something elegant. As Anne Shirley would say, 'tomorrow is a day with no mistakes in it yet'. Violet needs to be more like Anne.

But first things first, Violet needs to get some money coming in. The tiny amount she has left from her rental deposit won't last forever and Glenys' finances appear to be in a dire state – not that she'd dream of taking a penny from her mum.

She somehow needs to find a job – a local one with hours that fit around her mum's routines and close enough that she can nip back quickly in an emergency. Either that or she needs to find something she can do from home.

Violet takes out her phone and finds the number for the nearest Jobcentre. She might need to make a benefit claim in the meantime. Who knows how long it might take to find a job that she can fit around Glenys?

She makes the call. Tomorrow, two-thirty.

One step at a time, and everything will be fine.

CHAPTER 11

Violet

THE JOBCENTRE IS SQUARE and brown with small windows and a long queue of people outside it smoking roll-ups and looking at the floor.

'Violet Strong. I have an appointment,' she says to the woman behind the desk who has perfect hair, perfect nails and perfect teeth.

'What time?' she says, glancing down at Violet's trainers.

'Nine twenty with Sangit Chadha.' Violet peers at the woman, recognising the sneer in her voice.

'That's it! I know where I know you from. You don't remember who I am, do you?' the woman says.

Violet puts the sound of her voice and the smug smile together and comes up with her answer. The penny does so much more than just drop. It sinks and plummets to the bottom of her soul. 'Kirsty Waters.'

'Yes! I can't believe you recognised me – though everyone does tell me I haven't aged much. I don't think I'd have known who you were without you telling me your name. Sangit.

Violet *Wrong* is here to see you,' Kirsty calls across the room, swinging her highlighted hair over her shoulder.

Violet shuffles across the floor, aware that embarrassment has painted her face a bright shade of pink. She studies the worn carpet as she walks, avoiding all eye contact.

Sangit gives Violet a big smile when she reaches his desk. A professional one. Empty and stretched from being pulled out for the many people who had been in front of her in the queue.

Be more Anne, Violet tells herself, taking a breath and holding her hand out towards him. 'Violet Strong.' She even manages to match his smile. Sangit asks a million questions. Qualifications, experience. Hours available for work. When it's clear how tricky it would be for Violet to find work that fits around caring for her mother, Sangit wheels himself away from his computer screen.

'I think you're going to need to claim Carer's Allowance. I can give you the forms or you can go home and do it online. Up to you.' He hands Violet an information leaflet for carers. On the front is a beaming woman leaning over an elderly person who is smiling just as widely. Whoever designed the leaflet has obviously never cared for anyone like Violet's mum.

Violet glances at the people waiting in seats and in queues. Two teenagers are fiddling with their piercings and chewing gum as loudly as possible.

'Carer's Allowance can take around six weeks to put in place,' Sangit says without looking away from his screen. 'Hopefully, it won't be as long as that. If you get stuck in the meantime, I can give you some vouchers for the food bank.' He smiles over Violet's left shoulder at the next person in the queue.

'But … six weeks?' Violet has very little left from her rental deposit and her mum's account has next to no cash available either. The electric is running low and the council tax still hasn't been paid for this month.

'Perhaps you could ask family?'

'Yeah … yeah, I'll do that. Thanks for all your help.' Violet smiles, shakes Sangit's hand and holds her head up high as she stalks past Kirsty in reception.

Through tear-filled eyes, Violet sees the blur of office blocks, houses and cars around her as she runs towards the car park.

How is it possible for life to change so much within the space of less than a week? Her old life might not look like much from the outside, but she had a job she liked, her own money and a cosy bedsit. Now she's trapped with a mum who doesn't want her and next to nothing to live on. How are they going to buy food or pay that TV licence bill that slid through the letterbox this morning?

Kirsty's jeering voice plays in surround sound in Violet's head. *Violet Wrong. She's Bad News.* Kirsty's probably right. Violet's still getting it wrong; she's fallen at the first hurdle. All she had to do today was to get some income sorted for Glenys. The most basic level of support, and she hasn't even managed that.

A lorry booms past, sending a dirty puddle into the air and back down onto her thinnest trousers. The icing on top of a very stale cake.

'Come on, Jodie,' Violet mutters to herself as she waits for her sister to answer the phone.

'Ah. Yes. The Carer's Allowance. Just apply online – it's

easy.' Jodie sounds tired on the other end of the line. Jetlag, she mumbles when Violet tries to ask how she is. 'You don't need to call me about every little thing. All you need to do is go on to the Gov website and date your claim from last week. Mum's benefits might need another look at too – just check everything's up to date. I got a bit behind with things before I left, what with arranging everything for Dave and I and the move. It's not that easy to pack up and move to New Zealand – you wouldn't believe the amount of paperwork and phone calls.'

'Mmm.'

'How's Mum? Hope the two of you are getting on okay?'

'Great. Mmm. Great.' Violet remembers why she hates talking on the phone. It's so hard to get off the damn thing again. She can never think of a good enough excuse to hang up, she just gets trapped in a loop of endless murmuring.

'Anyway – I'd better be going. Nearly time to get out of bed. Still early over here – must be time for Mum's dinner, isn't it?' Exaggerated yawning sounds come from Jodie's end. 'Speak to you soon.'

The line goes silent. Jodie has gone. The house is even quieter after hearing her sister's voice. She puts the radio on whilst she boils the pasta.

Dinner is another uncomfortable affair, eaten in silence while Glenys stares at her plate, the window and anywhere that isn't in Violet's direction to avoid having to acknowledge her daughter – the wrong daughter. Once Glenys has gone back to her room, Violet distracts herself from the loneliness by replaying every word and every look from Adam on their walk yesterday as she stares at the bubbles in the sink. So strange to be doing that again. She remembers her diary, the one with the pony on the front and the tiny padlock on the side – one word dominated every one of her entries: Adam.

A delicious wave of nostalgia laps at her feet – it feels good to remember happier times, and the longing to return to *before* almost knocks the air from her. She may not be able to go back, but she can do the next best thing.

Violet shoves on her shoes and picks up her handbag before letting Glenys know she's going for a walk.

The breeze is laced with honeysuckle and Violet inhales deeply as she skips through the field towards the woods, enjoying the coolness of the air against her warm skin.

She finds the tree she's looking for immediately. It's the biggest tree in the woods, fourth from the left of the bridge with the clearest view of the lake. The branches are thick and strong and perfect for climbing, and for making dens beneath as it's surrounded by tall bushes to drape blankets over.

Violet pulls herself up to the widest branch and swings her legs over each side, her muscles remembering exactly how to navigate the tree until she finds the comfiest spot. She leans back against the trunk and looks out across the shimmering lake surrounded by an array of blossom trees, smiling as she remembers how she'd emulated Anne Shirley, and renamed it The Lake of Shining Waters.

She pulls her notebook and pen from her handbag and starts to scribble away. She underlines the date and draws a tiny heart next to it before describing every detail of her encounter with Adam. The childishness of it feels thrilling.

The first diary entry she'd ever written was on New Year's Eve, 1999 and it had been co-created with Adam underneath the very tree she's sitting on right now.

'Do you think they'll notice we sneaked out?' ten-year-old Adam said, frowning as he added his signature to the bottom of the page.

'Doubt it – they all had a lot of wine and they think we're in bed.' Violet giggled. Adam's and Violet's parents always saw the new year in together at Malvern House. Adam and Violet had planned all day to sneak out before midnight and watch the new year arrive by torchlight in the den – why should the grown-ups get to have all the fun? They decided to write a message to their future selves on New Year's Eve, 2000, to remind them of all the things they wanted to do that year, and bury it beneath the tree. Violet wanted to swim the whole way across the lake without stopping and Adam vowed to climb the trickiest tree on the far side of the woods.

The following year when the two of them dug up the diary, they crossed off their pledged tasks with a proud flourish before adding new ones for next time.

Then there was the New Year's when they were thirteen. Violet grins to herself as she remembers and wiggles her toes to get the blood running through them – she's been sitting still for far too long on this branch and the bark is beginning to prickle her back.

Adam had written something in the diary, blushed and then crossed it out again, giggling as Violet begged him to tell her what it was.

'Very well,' he sighed in the end. 'I'll write it again – but you're not allowed to laugh.' His blush deepened as he turned the diary around with two words underlined: *Kiss Violet*.

And kiss Violet, he did, right there and then. Violet had glided home with a smile that took up her whole face. Little did she know she'd be spending the following New Year's Eve in that den all alone. She'd still dug up the diary. She wrote two words, addressed to Adam even though she knew it would never be unearthed again. *I'm sorry.*

Is the diary still there now, all these years later? Violet peers over the branch at the ground below. Maybe, maybe not. Being back here is bound to dredge up the past and tempt her to think about what might have been.

But some things are better left buried.

CHAPTER 12

Violet

'MUM, PLEASE COME AND sit on the shower seat.' Violet fights to keep the impatience from her voice, but she's been running the water for over five minutes and Glenys is still standing naked in the corner of the bathroom, shivering, and holding onto her walking frame.

Violet's been back at Malvern House for five days and her mum has so far refused a shower on every one of them.

Glenys looks at the shower and back down at the floor again without speaking. Getting Mum out of her nightie had been one of the hardest things Violet had ever done. She'd never undressed another person. Jodie's instructions stated that Glenys is physically able to change in and out of her clothes but on her bad days she doesn't have the energy. Violet's fingers had fumbled with the buttons and it had taken ages to pull the damn nightdress up and over Glenys' dimpled arms. She tried too hard to be gentle; she'd been scared of hurting her, but awkwardness and clammy hands caused her to get Glenys' arm stuck inside the sleeve.

Then when she finally wrangled the garment away from

her mother, Violet garbled on too fast, too loud and for too long, trying to show her mum just how normal and okay she was about seeing her naked body. It should be normal. It's the same body she grew inside, was born out of and fed from as an infant.

Nurses and carers do this all day for complete strangers. Why is she shaking in her size sixes over showering her own mother? Perhaps it's easier with strangers. Or maybe it's harder because her mum *is* a stranger.

'Mum, just – please. You're getting cold. The water's nice and warm. At least come and check the temperature's okay for you.'

Glenys glances in Violet's direction for the first time since entering the bathroom. She moves slowly towards the seat and turns herself around, shrugging off Violet's hands and offers of help.

'Erm. How do you normally do this?' Violet plucks a flannel and a bottle of lavender shower gel from the shelf. 'Do you – does Jodie – should *I*?'

The room is stifling, and the floor keeps slipping beneath Violet's damp feet. The mirror and the walls are thick with steam and Violet's head is spinning.

'I can do it.' Glenys puts her hands out for the flannel. She dabs at herself whilst Violet stands and counts the wall tiles.

'You can wash my hair, though. Please.' Glenys looks up at Violet with the smallest glimmer of a smile. She places a gentle hand on Violet's wrist. 'Your hair's grown long again. Like when you were little. I always liked it long.'

A bubble of joy dances across Violet's skin. It's her mum's touch and the way Glenys is looking at her as if seeing her for the first time. She remembers sitting next to the old gas fire in the living room whilst her mum brushed out her tangles after a bath. She never pulled her hair, she was always gentle. Afterwards, she'd make hot chocolate for Violet and Jodie and read to them whilst they waited for Dad to come home from work.

Hope. Perhaps there's still some left. 'Of course,' Violet says, a smile leaking into her voice. She leans across to pull the shampoo from the shelf and her elbow catches on the metal dial, shifting it anti-clockwise.

Glenys screams. The sound reverberates off the walls and rattles Violet's eardrums.

'It's freezing. You're freezing me solid. Turn the water off, you useless, *useless* excuse of a girl.' Glenys spits the words out between gasps.

Violet stares at the dial and the coloured arrows around it blur into one. She doesn't want to turn in the wrong way and scald her, that would be much worse. Which way is off?

'Are you trying to give me bloody pneumonia?' Glenys slaps Violet's hand away from the dial and replaces it with her own, twisting it towards the wall until the water stops.

The shower seat vibrates beneath Glenys' violently shivering body and the chattering of her teeth punctures the silence.

'Mum, I'm so sorry, I didn't—'

'Just pass me my towel and get out. Get *out*. I don't need you in here. I don't need you at all, you do nothing but ruin things,' Glenys says through clenched teeth, holding her arms tightly around herself.

Violet slips the towel from the rail and hands it to her,

tipping her head back slightly so the tears don't fall from her eyes. 'Okay,' she says. 'I'll just be outside if you need anything.'

Once in the living room, Violet sinks down on the armchair next to the bathroom. She stares at the front door, wishing she could storm out and slam it behind her, but she can't. Her mum might slip, hit her head. Then that will be Violet's fault too. She sits in silence until Glenys moves slowly past her, clothed in the clean trousers and blouse that Violet had hung on the towel rail for her. She doesn't look in Violet's direction, just disappears into her bedroom after mumbling that she'd be back out at lunchtime.

Violet makes a coffee and plonks herself down at the table with her laptop. She'll write a blogpost, immerse herself in writing a review of the last book she read and escape for a while. It was a story about love and overcoming the odds, a far cry from the mess of Violet's life. Whilst Violet was living inside its pages, she didn't have to worry about overdue bills, empty cupboards or a mum who didn't want her. Books are safe places where you can become someone else for a little while.

As soon as she's finished, she logs onto a rental website. She does a search for flats to let in Lowerstone and the surrounding villages. Be easier to tell the tenants about the sale if she can point them towards some local flats. Nothing at the moment.

Bugger.

Before she moves to another lettings site, a notification flashes in the corner of the screen. As she opens it and begins reading the email, she tries to suppress the urge to pull out all her hairs, one by one. It's from the Carer's Allowance department, informing Violet that she cannot be awarded the benefit, because her mother's Personal Independence Payments have been suspended due to non-attendance of a face-to-face assessment.

No wonder Glenys' finances are in a mess – why hadn't Jodie taken Glenys to her PIP assessment? It was bad enough finding out how much needed doing with the sale of the building, and now Violet has to clear up the mess from missed appointments and suspended benefit payments. All those digs her sister had made about Violet not being around, and it turns out Jodie wasn't so perfect after all.

Violet pictures the stubborn line of Glenys' pursed mouth when she was refusing to get in the shower. Violet's been doing this for less than a week, and already she wants to run for the green hills of the Sussex Downs. Jodie had been at it for years; maybe Violet needs to cut her sister some slack.

She reads the email over and over, her mind whirling. She knows nothing about disability benefits, PIP assessments or forms. Jodie has left the country and Violet can't keep bugging her about every little thing, not while her sister is trying to settle into a new life.

There is one other person who might be able to help her. *Us carers have to stick together.*

Violet closes her laptop, grabs her keys from the sideboard and rushes out of the flat, letting Glenys know she'll be back before lunch.

Violet's heart is beating so loudly, she's surprised she even has to bother to knock on the door; Adam and his dad can probably hear it from the other side.

The door clicks and for a split second, Violet pictures Adam's mum welcoming her in like she always used to, long black hair straddling her shoulders and a kind smile that always preceded the offer of lemonade or a homemade scone – she was one of those types of mums. A feeder, Adam used to call her.

'You're here.' Adam's grin helps Violet let some of her breath out.

'I am,' she says.

It's strange crossing the threshold into what used to be her dining room. Now it's an open-plan room with a kitchenette in one corner and a hospital bed in the other. Two other open doors lead into a bathroom and a smaller bedroom. A well-worn sofa sits in the middle, facing a TV that looks two decades old.

On the left-hand side of the sofa sits a man whose eyes Violet has been avoiding ever since his world was ripped to pieces.

'Hello, Bill,' she manages to say.

Bill may have shrunk in height, but the energy behind his smile still takes up the entire room. 'Young Violet,' he cries out. He pats the space beside him on the sofa.

Violet sits down as gently as she can, not wanting to jolt him.

He reaches out and grabs one of her hands in both of his with a surprising strength. 'Adam said you were back. How wonderful.' His pleasure at seeing her is genuine, same as it always had been whenever she came over to play with Adam at the weekends.

How he can still want to be in the same room as her, Violet has no idea.

'How are you?' she croaks before cringing hard. Anyone can see how much his health has deteriorated and that's without acknowledging that this is the first time she's spoken to him since his wife died.

'Good days and bad days. Main thing is, I've got my boy with me.' Bill's pale eyes mist over. 'Most important thing, is family.'

Violet swallows. 'Bill, I'm so sorry, I—'

'I'm sure your mum's pleased you're back too.'

Violet wishes everyone would stop saying that. It's like a sharp shard of ice turning inside her, a reminder that most mothers *would* be pleased to have their daughter back.

'I know it might not seem that way. Jodie told me she can be a little … difficult nowadays.' Bill's eyes get their twinkle back. 'Not that I've seen much of her, she hardly comes out of her flat.'

'Is everything okay?' Adam crouches down in front of Violet, just as the water begins to pool in her eyes.

No one has asked Violet if she's okay for such a long time. She blinks fast, but the kindness in Adam's voice sends the tears cascading down her cheeks.

'I might go and have a lie down in your room, son.' Bill shuffles forward and slowly stands up, leaning a liver-spotted hand on Adam's shoulder to steady himself. 'For goodness' sake, make the lass a cuppa, she looks like she needs one.'

Once Bill has disappeared behind the bedroom door and Adam is holding a steaming mug of coffee towards her, Violet opens her mouth. 'I just don't know where to start. The whole caring thing – I'm pretty shit at it.'

'Give yourself a chance. You've only been back a few days.' Adam laughs. 'Seriously though, it's not as easy as people think and it's always harder when it's family. I've lost count of the amount of people who say, "Wow, it must be lovely not having to go to work every day – you must get so much done!"

They just don't get it.' Adam shakes his head and glances at the closed bedroom door before lowering his voice. 'Don't get me wrong, I love supporting Dad, and I'm happy to do it, but some days … And it was much harder to begin with, for both of us. Dad hated me doing things for him that he had done for me when I was just a baby. He likes his independence and getting that balance right is hard. Really hard.'

Violet counts the swirls inside the triangles in the carpet beneath her. 'She hates me. Her benefits have lapsed, she's barely speaking to me and I can't even shower her properly without it turning into a disaster.' She takes a huge swig of coffee and forces her shoulders back down. 'Sorry to be a big whinger, it just feels so overwhelming.'

He really is the last person she should be off-loading to. It's Violet's fault Adam has so much to juggle, and she shouldn't be throwing in her own problems for him to catch.

'Has your mum had a shower today?' he asks.

'Yes – eventually.'

'So that part's fine and that will only get easier once you both get used to each other's ways of doing things. And I'm sure she doesn't hate you, but if she does, there's not much you can do about whether she wants to speak to you or not. That just leaves the benefits, and that's something you *can* do something about.'

Violet had forgotten about Adam's methodical brain. Even when they'd built dens, he'd always write a list of required materials and sketch an outline of their plans before starting.

'I wouldn't even know where to start,' says Violet.

Adam jumps up from the sofa and grabs his phone from the TV stand. 'I know someone who'd be great to talk to. Do you remember Mrs Goode from school?'

'I bumped into her the other day.' Violet smiles. Chrissie is one of those people who can make you feel happy just by thinking about them.

'Chrissie's next-door neighbour, Claire, is a carer for her husband. She's great at filling out the forms, she helped me with Dad's. Plus, she had to fight an appeal for her husband when he had his disability benefits dropped to a lower band. She really knows her stuff. Shall I call her and arrange a meet-up for you? Might have to be at her house, I don't think she can get out very often.'

Violet ignores the bubbling in her tummy. Speaking to anyone else in the village is not high on her wish list, but she needs all the help she can get. 'Yes please. And thank you for helping, you really don't have to,' she says in a low voice.

The knots in her muscles slowly untie themselves as Adam makes the phone call.

'Sorted. She can't do today – her husband's having a difficult day. She should be able to do tomorrow at two thirty, and she's happy to meet us at the library as she's dropping books off. That okay with you?'

Stupid, flippin' tears again. It's as if her eyes are allergic to kindness. 'I'm so grateful, honest. I wouldn't have blamed you if you'd told me to take a hike, turning up here like this.'

'Oh pssh.' Adam waves his hand away. 'It was only a bloody phone call, didn't take me thirty seconds. Now I want to hear about you. Fourteen years of your life since leaving Lowerstone. Go.'

Adam's smiling at her as if this is a normal conversation. Nothing about the last fourteen years has been normal.

'I assume you know about what happened to Megan?' Violet fiddles with the ring on her middle finger.

'Yes. I was so sorry to hear. Must've been shit for you too.'

Shit was what Violet deserved. If she'd pulled Megan away from that party like she should have done, she'd still be alive. Or if Violet hadn't gone with her to Manchester and brought her *Bad News* along, it might not have happened.

Violet changes the subject. She tells Adam about her flat, her cleaning jobs and her book blog. It's uncomfortable, talking about her life, but at least it keeps the focus away from Megan. She doesn't quite get around to telling Adam about the care home/building sale plan.

Rude to keep talking about herself for too long anyway.

'I'd love to read your blog – what's it called?' Adam ignores the more difficult parts of Violet's verbal memoir.

'It's @BookWorm88'. Violet tells Adam how to find it, touched that he cares enough to ask. 'I shall miss my huge stash of books though. Most of them are piled up in storage.'

'Good thing we're off to the library tomorrow then, isn't it?' Adam grins and he looks so much like his childhood self for a second that Violet wants to cry. Again. Even the nicest memories have sharp edges.

'I'm looking forward to it. Libraries are like little pockets of heaven for me. But Mrs Robson from upstairs told me she works there, and I don't mind admitting that she scares the crap out of me a tiny bit.'

Adam laughs, pulling the elastic band from his hair before gathering up all of his loose strands and fastening it back up again. 'Mrs Robson is a treasure. Pain in the arse – yes. Nosy old bag – check. But her heart's in the right place and she likes me, so I'll protect you.'

Violet stiffens and her jaw pulls tight. 'I don't need protecting.'

Adam pauses halfway through putting on his jacket. 'No,' he says. 'No. I don't suppose you ever did.'

The air in the space between them thickens.

Violet tries to press pause on her internal remote, but the batteries must be running low as it doesn't respond. She's treated to a replay of the year nine playground on her first day back at school after it happened. The whispers, the giggles and the taunts. Adam was the only one who had her back and the one who had the least obligation to do so.

She'd pushed him away. And then she kept pushing. It was far easier to wheedle her way in with the cool kids than to look Adam in the eye each day. They'd been curious about Violet in the end after what she did, and they didn't try to stop her drinking or causing mayhem in the village. The worse she played up, the more they cheered her on. Then when she paired up with Megan, she became the envy of the group and the rush became an addiction.

Violet manages a weak smile. 'I think when it comes to Mrs Robson, I might make an exception.'

CHAPTER 13

Violet

ANXIETY STARTS TO TRICKLE through Violet's veins as soon as she and Adam reach the village. Sweat trickles down the back of her neck and her hands start to tremble. She tries to slow her breathing as her mind fills with fog.

Be more Anne, she reminds herself.

'You okay?' Adam slows next to Violet, placing a gentle hand on her shoulder.

Violet ignores the rushing of her heart in her ears. 'Fine – just, you know. Feels strange still, being back.'

Adam presses his lips together and nods, picking up his pace again to keep up with Violet.

'Wow. The library looks amazing.' Violet's heart lifts as she turns the corner after the Lowerstone bakery. Many of the buildings in the village are tired and worn, shadows of their former selves. But the library looks as inviting as a warm hug. The windows gleam in the sunshine and flowers of every shade and colour sit in neat and tidy plant pots lining the walls.

'That will be Mrs Robson. She might be a battle-axe but she's pure gold when it comes to the library,' Adam says.

Violet inhales deeply as they walk through the automatic doors. She feasts on the smell of books and the citrus Glade plug-in.

The shelves are laid out the same as they used to be, but there's an added 'coffee shop' in the corner that consists of a table and chairs and coffee machine.

Sitting at the table is a woman with a shaved head and a *Made in Brighton* tattoo on her neck. She's engrossed in a book. Violet cranes her neck to see the title but the woman is holding it too flat.

'Claire,' Adam calls over to her.

Claire looks up from her book and her face breaks into a smile. She shakes Violet's hand and kisses both of Adam's cheeks. A million bangles clang against each other as she moves. She's a living wind chime.

'Tell me about your mum,' Claire says once introductions are done with and they're all sitting down.

'She has schizophrenia. And depression. And she has problems with her mobility after an accident she had a long time ago. She injured her spine.' Violet keeps her eyes on the table. She can feel Adam's gaze on her. 'I've been away for a long time and I've never cared for anyone before. It may sound strange, but we don't know each other that well.'

Claire nods, unfazed. 'Must be tough. Caring for family can be tricky regardless of how close you are. Is there anything you're particularly struggling with?'

Violet takes a breath. 'All of it to be honest. I'm useless at personal care, knowing the right things to say … And then there's the financial stuff like Mum's disability benefits and my Carer's Allowance and all the forms I have to fill in.'

Claire sits up straighter when she gets to the part about the forms. 'Now that, I can help with. I've filled in more forms that I can count. Did you bring them with you?'

Violet reaches for her bag and pulls out a wad of paper. 'Yep.'

'Fab. I'll go through the questions with you, but you'll also have to dig out any doctor's letters. Might be worth chasing up any reports from healthcare professionals and taking them with you to her face–to–face assessment. There are so many hoops to squeeze through, and they don't make it easy, so the more medical evidence you have, the better.'

Violet shuffles in her seat and the plastic squeaks. It's strange that her mum has to be subjected to scrutiny from a bunch of strangers to prove she needs support if they'll have access to her medical records anyway. It sounds cruel and undignified.

Claire talks her through the sections of the form, advising her to fill out each question as if it's Glenys' worst day. 'Care needs nearly always vary,' she says, shaking her head. 'So many people need support with things some days that they can manage on their own on others. But if you don't put it on the form, your mum will risk losing her benefit or having it reduced.'

Violet's mind is clogged with information and she sits in the quiet for a moment, letting it all float around. 'Thank you for helping me with this. I honestly wouldn't have known where to start.' She feels herself blushing.

Saying thank you feels hard. It means you've let someone do something for you, that you've let them in and Claire's a stranger.

'Pleasure.' Claire smiles, salutes, and twists the piercing below her bottom lip. 'I wish I'd had someone to walk me through it when I helped my husband with his. We had to learn the hard way. Months of appeals, it was an absolute pile of shit. In the meantime, we had barely any money coming in. My husband, Abbas, and I were both nurses. It's how we met. Then he got ill and had to give up work. It wasn't long before things got worse and I had to leave work to look after him. We've got a little one, Jayden. He's only five. Couldn't expect them both to cope on their own with things as they were.'

'That must have been tough,' Violet says. She can't even imagine caring for her mum at the same time as a small child.

'It was. It is,' Claire amends. 'Abbas was diagnosed with multiple mental health conditions and it took every ounce of strength we had to get through those early days. This was hard work too.' She points at the forms in Violet's hands. 'Those applications are difficult enough as it is, but when you're asking for financial support for mental health problems, it gets a whole lot trickier. You can't see the illness with your eyes, see. People seem to want proof. Scans, X-rays, or it's not real.' Claire's hands are shaking as she puts down her coffee. 'If those assessors could spend one afternoon in our house, they'd have all the evidence they need.'

Adam squeezes Claire's hand before getting out of his seat. 'Thanks again for doing this. I'll leave you two to chat. I'm going to see if there are any new grisly crime books to fall asleep with.'

'He's heard all this before from me.' Claire gives a lukewarm grin after he's left the table. 'He's used to me dancing around on my soapbox.'

'Adam told me you really helped him with his dad's paperwork. He said he'd have been lost without you.'

'It was nothing.' Claire wafts her hand away, making her bangles chime even louder than before. 'His case was fairly straightforward. Must be hard for Adam though, it sounds as if he's lost so much, and I know he really enjoyed his job before he had to give it up. I understand what that feels like.'

Violet's palms sting, and she realises she's digging her fingernails into them.

'Carers lose more than just their wages,' Claire carries on. 'I felt as though I'd lost who I was. I lost friends too. Some of them just didn't get it; lots of people with mental health conditions can work and manage okay without support at home, so I think they thought we should both just get on with it, you know?' Claire's eyes mist up. 'Other people just drifted away after a while. I kept having to turn down invites – Abbas did too. After a while, everyone just stopped asking.'

'That must be lonely.' Violet thinks about her bedsit in Manchester, the one she never invited anyone into. She always had people to go out with and she still managed to feel alone in the crowd. Perhaps she should have tried harder to allow people in, let them closer.

But letting people in isn't that simple when you've been told all your life that you're *Bad News*; there's too much risk of it rubbing onto others.

'It is lonely, yes. But I've got Abbas. And my Jayden. They're all I need.' Claire sits up straight and shakes out a smile that lights up her face. 'We're lucky to have each other.'

Violet and Claire keep talking until Claire's phone bleeps. 'I'm so sorry, I've kept you here for ages.' Violet bites her lip, remembering what Adam had said about Claire not being able to get out for very long at a time.

'It's fine. It was all right actually – just having a chat.' A blush appears across Claire's cheeks.

'Thank you for sharing your story with me,' says Violet. 'And for helping me with the forms – it means a lot.'

'Just popping outside for a fag – then maybe we could get some refills. Us carers need our caffeine.' Claire winks.

Violet wanders over to the bookshelf that Adam's hovering next to. His head's buried in a book and Violet grins when he doesn't notice she's there. She turns towards the rows of novels and inspects the titles, deep in thought. How many other people found themselves in Claire's position, or Violet's? How many are thrown into a new life without warning, one with benefit forms and lost jobs? She thinks about Adam and his dad, and Claire and her husband. There are bound to be others in the village like Violet and her mum with no other family nearby.

'Maybe you should start a club,' Violet mutters.

Adam jumps. 'Didn't see you there. A club for what?'

'Never mind,' Violet says. Daft idea. People are probably stressed and busy enough and she's only been in the village five minutes – hardly enough time to start making suggestions, especially as she's not staying any longer than she has to.

'Grab some books if you like. Stick them on my account for now. Just make sure you bring them back – Mrs Robson's a stickler for late fines.'

Violet grabs just three books, marvelling at herself for her restraint, and the two of them line up at the library reception. The woman at the front of the queue is handing a pile of paperbacks to Mrs Robson who is perched behind the desk, looking over her glasses like the most clichéd librarian there ever was.

'The returns machine ain't working,' the woman says. She's hunching her shoulders as if she's bracing herself for a telling off.

The woman was right to prepare herself, Violet decides, as Mrs Robson launches into a long speech about other customers having to wait for books and how it upsets the order of things in the library. And didn't she *know* how easy it is to renew books online? There really is no excuse nowadays.

'Now *that*,' Mrs Robson says after the woman has left, 'is why I put the *out of order* sign on the returns machine. People don't care about bringing the books late because they just pay the fine and they know the machine won't tell them off. Well, *I* will.'

Violet places a hand on Adam's forearm and leans towards him as Mrs Robson checks their books out. 'I think I've had an idea,' she whispers. Once they have their books tucked back under their arms, Violet leads Adam back to the table and sits down just as Claire turns up again, coffee in hand, bringing a cloud of nicotine with her.

Can Violet just say it? Blurt it out, even though she has no business getting involved in a community she once tore apart. Adam might think she's being needy. Claire might think she's a weirdo or a stalker; someone who doesn't know their boundaries when they first meet people. This is why she doesn't make proper friends – it's complicated and exhausting. Imaginary friends are far easier. Anne Shirley, Elizabeth Bennet, Jessica Wakefield. Violet never has to worry about what they might think of her or what harm she might end up causing them.

Oh, *shut up,* Violet. Just say it. Tell them your idea. What's the worst that can happen?

'It's probably a daft idea,' Violet blurts out. Her mouth dries up and the rest of her words get stuck inside.

'That's okay, just say it.' Claire glances at Adam before leaning towards Violet with a big smile. 'If it's a shit one, we'll tell you, and if it's golden, you'll never know until you tell it to someone.'

'Why don't you start up a group – a support group for carers in the village?'

'A carers' group,' Adam says, leaning an elbow on the table and resting his chin on his fist. 'That could be fun.'

'Carers and the people they look after – if they wanted to be involved. It might bring people together, give everyone something positive to focus on. People can support each other with carer stuff like the things you and Claire helped me with today. Help each other with appointments and forms, give people a space to talk to others who get what they're going through. You could meet once a week or something in one of your houses, or even here, if you're allowed to.'

'Sounds bloody brilliant. Sign me up,' says Claire, banging on the table, making a man in the horror section jump out of his heavily tanned skin.

'Something like that would've been great when Dad first moved in.' Adam gazes out of the window. Violet can almost see the memories dancing across his face. 'I didn't know where to start, and I'm sure there are plenty more in the same situation. There are carers' support groups around, but the only ones I've seen are in the bigger towns. Villages like Lowerstone get forgotten. We could probably open it up to the surrounding villages too.'

Violet's nerves begin to stir inside her belly. What does she think she's doing? Walking into the village was hard enough and sitting here with just two people is a stretch for her. Organising something for a whole group of people in a village that hates her feels like the ultimate act of self-destruction.

But this could be her chance to do something good for Lowerstone. She can never make up for what happened all those years ago, but this might at least be a start.

'I'm sure Dad would love it,' says Adam.

'And I'll ask Abbas,' says Claire. 'He might want to come along sometimes when he's feeling up to it.'

'Maybe Mrs Robson could pop a poster up in the library – spread the word from in here? You ask her, Adam, she likes you, and someone could ask them to do the same in the village shops,' Violet says.

'What sort of poster?' Mrs Robson appears behind Violet's shoulder. 'I require seven days' notice before putting anything on the board.' She glances over at the large notice board on the wall by the reception desk. It's empty except for a sign dated two years ago, informing the village that the community centre was closing.

Violet stays quiet whilst Adam fills Mrs R in on their plans for the carers' group.

'I'm happy to put a poster up and spread the word,' Mrs Robson says in a benevolent voice. 'I'm not a carer, obviously, but I'm very happy to be present at the planning meetings, should anyone actually turn up.'

'I don't really think …' Violet begins.

'You'll need someone to write the minutes, after all. And I have so much experience with running the Neighbourhood Watch group all these years. I'd be an invaluable asset, but no need to thank me. I'm happy to do it.'

Violet opens her mouth and closes it again when she pictures Mrs Robson sitting in her flat each week with the kettle on, waiting for Neighbourhood Watch members who never turn up. She may not be a carer, but she's clearly desperate to be involved in something. 'That would be great. Thank you,' she finds herself saying, ignoring Adam's sudden coughing beside her.

'Oh, here we go. Another person who'd be more than happy to help with the practicalities. Look, there she is.' Mrs Robson points towards the historical fiction shelf. 'Chrissie? Over here.' She looks at Violet and lowers her voice, but not very much. 'That's Chrissie Goode. Her husband's dead now, but she cared for him before that, so I expect that will be enough to get her into your care club?'

Violet fights the urge to laugh. Mrs Robson is blunter than a pair of safety scissors.

'Come and have a chat with this lot, Chrissie,' Mrs Robson says. 'They've got something that might keep you busy. You know a lot about being a carer and you've lots of time on your hands now, don't you, now that you're … well, you know.' Mrs Robson turns to face the table and hides her mouth from Chrissie with a cupped hand. 'She'll be a great help to your group. Plenty of time, probably lonely, ideal really.' Her whisper is far louder than she seems to think it is.

Violet wants to crawl inside her own T-shirt until her head is cocooned inside the purple viscose. Anything other than seeing the pain or embarrassment in the eyes of her beloved former English teacher. She braves a look at Chrissie's face.

Chrissie's mouth twitches as she pulls out a seat and sits next to Violet. 'Thank you,' she says to Mrs Robson in a grave voice. 'I'm at your disposal, obviously. I mean, what else could a grieving widow possibly have to do?'

'Exactly, love. Exactly. Just as I thought.' Mrs Robson sniffs with satisfaction and pats Chrissie on the back before walking back to her desk.

Chrissie snorts and the whole table erupts in giggles. 'That bloody woman.' She dabs at her eyes with a tissue she's pulled from her handbag. 'Now. Tell me what she's on about – I'm intrigued.'

Violet explains. This time she's sure of her words. When she sees the joy on Chrissie's face as she listens to the plan, Violet feels a flicker of pride.

Time to start righting those wrongs.

As soon as Violet gets back to the flat, she goes straight to her room and pulls out two of her favourite throws from her boxes along with a selection of cushions. She drapes them over the armchair and the sofa in the living room. Opening the boxes has released a plethora of smells from her scented candles. Violet chooses four of them and lines them up on the sideboard before lighting two of them.

If it smells like home, maybe it could be, even if only for a little while.

Glenys' nose wrinkles when she enters the living room. 'What's that smell? It's getting right down my throat, I can barely bloody breathe. And what's with all the cushions? Where the hell am I meant to sit?'

Violet just smiles and opens her laptop.

@BookWorm88

I have some lovely new reads to show you that I picked up from the village library (see photos). I actually made some new friends whilst I was there. Do you still use your local library? What experiences have you had during your visits?

Today, I did something new. I asked somebody for help. Twice. It felt good.

#SupportLibraries #NewReads #books #askforhelp

CHAPTER 14

Tammy

TAMMY KNOCKS ON THE door to Violet's flat. It's the first time she's ever knocked on someone else's door – there was never any need to when Mum was around. Would Violet be happy to see her? She might be angry, it's still early. Are people allowed to knock on people's doors so soon after breakfast? The hallway is quiet and Tammy's tummy flutters. She closes her eyes and starts to hum 'We are the Champions' by Queen. Singing always chases the quiet away and helps her feel braver.

Violet has a bowl of cereal in her hand when she opens the door. Her smile has lots of light in it, so it feels safe enough for Tammy to stop making her music.

'It's you. Thank goodness.' Violet looks out into the hallway over Tammy's shoulder before making her voice into a whisper. 'I thought you were Mrs Robson. I'm fairly certain she wouldn't approve of me sitting in my dressing gown at half past ten on a Wednesday morning.'

Tammy stares and takes a step backwards.

'You can come in,' says Violet.

Tammy looks back over her shoulder. 'I don't have to.'

'Of course, you don't have to. But if you want to, you'd be welcome.'

'I do. Want to, I mean. I just meant I don't have to if you don't want me in your flat, causing all sorts of bother.'

Violet laughs. 'That sounds like something Mrs Robson would say. Please come in, I'll put the kettle on, and you can help me sort my life out.'

Violet's living room looks like it should be in a film with ghosts in it. Everything looks old and posh, but it feels cold and sad.

'You can sit down if you like. What would you like to drink?'

Tammy stays silent as she sits at the dining table and peers through the open door of the kitchen.

'Tea? Coffee? Cold drink?'

Lots of choices, it's hard to decide. 'If I said coffee, would you let me?' Tammy looks closely at Violet. Mum never let Tammy have caffeine – said it sent her too bonkers.

'Sure, no problem.' Violet shrugs.

Whilst Violet is making the drinks, Tammy looks at every inch of the room. That way she'll always remember it if she's never allowed back in again.

'What are your plans for today?' Violet asks as she plonks Tammy's drink on the table next to her.

Tammy chews on her thumbnail. 'I don't make plans. They can never really happen.'

Violet looks like she's waiting for Tammy to say more, but the coffee is so delicious, Tammy can't remember what her next words were going to be.

A tractor rumbles past and the glass vibrates against the panes as Violet sits down.

'I'm sorry again about your mum,' Violet says. 'I don't feel like I said it properly the other day. I just want you to know you can talk about it if you ever want to.'

Tammy's stomach sinks fast like it does when you fall over. Her brain changes from light to dark like someone's pressed a button in her head. It's what happens often when she thinks about Mum without a warning. Her knees bash the underside of the table as she shuffles forward, clutching her mug in one fist and clenching the other.

'Only two people were at the funeral. Me and a man I didn't know. I had to walk to the church on my own, and I'm not supposed to go further than the shop without someone with me. Why didn't more people care that she was dead? It isn't fair.' Tammy thumps the table, sending her coffee flying in every direction including Violet's laptop. Her cheeks feel hot and it's tricky to see through her tears, even with her glasses on.

Violet jumps up and lays a gentle hand against Tammy's closed fist. 'I'm sorry. You're right – that's not fair.'

Tammy lowers herself back into the chair, not taking her eyes away from the table. She puts her head in her hands and blinks hard, partly so the grainy picture of Mum in her mind looks clearer, and partly so it goes away completely.

Violet puts an arm around Tammy's shoulders.

Tammy's shoulders let the crying out and it feels much better – a bit like when you sit on the loo in the morning when you're bursting for a wee. It just needs to get out, that's all. Crying is the same. 'She's gone.' Tammy gulps. 'She was supposed to get milk. Two pints, semi-skimmed, green top.'

'Do you have someone else who normally comes to your flat to see you?'

'Just Mrs Robson when she wants to tell me off. No one else.'

'But has anyone else apart from your mum ever … looked after you? Supported you? Helped you with your flat?'

'No. I've lived in lots of different flats. Mum said I didn't need any help from anyone else because I had her.'

Sometimes people came to see Tammy when she was younger after she and Mum moved out of Dad's house. It was because Mum had stopped sending her to school. Learning at home with Mum made more sense, she said, especially because they had to keep moving. Mum used to get all wound up when the people were coming round. She'd tidy and tidy and remind Tammy about all the things she wasn't supposed to say, but Tammy liked it when they visited because they always asked Tammy questions and expected her to know the answers like she was a real person.

Violet takes her hand away from Tammy's shoulder and opens her laptop. She slides it between them so they can both see the screen. 'I have a lot to sort out in my life at the moment. I expect you do too?'

Tammy nods.

'So how about we make a list together for both of us? Things we want, things we need to do, and stuff we need to remember?'

It takes a while. Tammy hasn't ever used a computer before and the letters are all in different places and not in alphabetical order. She just writes the words of things she wants to do, and Violet arranges them into groups.

By the time lunchtime rolls around, Tammy's 'beautifully formatted list' (as Violet calls it) has been pulled from the printer and popped on the table in front of them.

1. A big food shop
2. Buy new clothes (mine have all grown)
3. Go to the cinema (I've never been to one)

'What are you going to put on yours?' Tammy leans an elbow on the table, resting her chin on her fist.

Violet's face looks like a blank screen.

'What things do you want most?' asks Tammy, trying to help her out a bit.

Violet closes her eyes for so long, Tammy starts to wonder if she's fallen asleep.

'To make things right. To help people. And to one day become a journalist.' Violet's dreams fall out of her mouth.

Tammy thinks there's more in there. 'Don't you want to find love?' she asks, peering over her glasses.

'Sure,' Violet says, shrugging. She finishes typing, prints off her list and closes the laptop before calling out to her mum.

Tammy looks at Violet's list. Whilst Violet is looking at her mum's closed door, Tammy swipes it from the printer, folds it up and hides it in her pocket. She wants to remember the things that Violet wants the most, that way, she might be able to help her one day, just like Violet had helped Tammy with her shopping and the electric meter.

Violet's mum is called Glenys and Violet says she doesn't want to come out of her room. Violet makes lunch and takes some in to her mum before tucking into some Happy Shopper hotdogs with Tammy.

Tammy asks for another coffee.

Violet says she can help herself.

'But M–mum doesn't let me use the kettle.' Tammy swallows as she follows Violet into the kitchen.

'Haven't you ever made a hot drink before?' Violet's voice is soft, like a blanket. 'I'm sure your mum had a good reason for not wanting you to use a kettle, but I think you're ready to now. Want me to show you how?'

Tammy nods.

Violet gives Tammy a step-by-step lesson on how to make a hot drink safely. Turns out Tammy can make wonderful coffee. Her tummy goes nice and warm and her eyes feel teary again when she takes her first sip.

'How about we go for your food shop?' Violet suggests.

After calling the bank a few days ago, Violet had managed to get a new card and pin for Tammy, so she'll be able to buy what she needs.

'From the village?' Tammy's throat tightens and her heart beats faster.

'I'll take you to Tesco. It's only a couple of miles away in Lewes. I'll be with you the whole time.' Violet pats Tammy's shoulder.

'I'm not supposed to go further than the shop in the village.' Tammy folds her arms. 'Mum said.'

Violet breathes out like she's blowing out birthday candles. 'Okay. I'm sure there's a good reason why your mum didn't want you going out. But you have your own flat now, and access to your own money – maybe it's time for you to practise doing things for yourself. And I'll be with you the whole time,' she repeats.

By the time Tammy is standing next to Violet's car, her fear has been swapped for excitement. She hasn't been in many cars since it was just her and Mum. She's just about to climb in when she hears a voice behind her.

'Violet – oh, you're on your way out.' The voice sounds disappointed and it belongs to a lady with a pink cardigan and lots of wrinkles on her face. She's holding a see-through box with cakes in it.

The woman is someone called Chrissie and Violet asks her if she wants to go to the shops with them.

Tammy closes her eyes, trying to make Chrissie say no. She's not supposed to speak to strangers, and she wants it to just be her and Violet.

A minute later, Chrissie and Tammy are sitting next to each other in the back of Violet's car.

'I'm sorry to gate-crash.' Chrissie smiles across at Tammy.

Tammy points through the front window of the car. 'I don't think it will be a problem – the gate's missing.'

Chrissie opens her mouth and closes it again before nodding. 'I don't get out of the village very often. The bus takes ages, and I can't leave my dog for too long. Kind of you both to let me come along.'

'What's your dog called?' Tammy feels bad for wishing Chrissie wasn't coming; she has a nice smile and anyone who cares about leaving their dog alone for too long can't be that bad.

'Luna.' Chrissie seems to choke on the name and her eyes bubble up with tears. 'She keeps me company. I lost my husband a few months ago.'

Poor woman. Had her husband seriously been missing all this time? 'Did you look everywhere?'

Chrissie's eyes go wide, and she bites her bottom lip.

'Tammy,' Violet says in a warning type of voice from the front seat.

A funny snorting sound comes from Chrissie. 'He died. We really should just say the word, shouldn't we? You're so right. He's not missing. He's dead.' She stops laughing.

'I'm sorry,' Tammy says. She's seen people say this on the telly when people die even when it isn't their fault.

'So am I.' Chrissie pulls a tissue from her bag and wipes her eyes.

'My mum died too.' Tammy says it without crying and it feels okay. Sad, but okay. Chrissie seems like another safe place to leave her words.

Tesco is the biggest shop Tammy has ever seen. The lights are bright, the music is loud, and the people are all in a hurry.

'You okay?' Chrissie hands Tammy a basket. 'You hold onto this and focus on what you want to put in it. Don't worry about everything happening around you – you'll get used to it.'

Violet zips from shelf to shelf, steering her trolley like a race car. Chrissie told her she'd stay with Tammy so Violet can do her mum's shopping and she seems to be taking it very seriously.

After half an hour of traipsing up and down the freezer aisles of Tesco, Tammy's shiny new bank card doesn't work in the little machine. It says *declined*.

'But Mum said this is where my money is kept. On my card.' Tammy's head goes foggy and she screws up her forehead, trying to concentrate.

Violet's face goes all red and sweaty and she whips out her wallet.

'It's fine.' Chrissie puts her hand over Violet's hand that's holding the wallet. 'It's sorted.' She gets a bank card out of her own bag and puts it in the machine before winking at Tammy. 'Happens to us all sometimes. Bloody technology.'

Tammy decides that next to her mum and Violet, Chrissie is the nicest person she's ever met. Perhaps she could be Tammy's second ever friend.

CHAPTER 15

Violet

AFTER ARRIVING BACK FROM Tesco, Violet makes a cuppa for the three of them in Tammy's flat whilst Tammy unpacks her shopping.

'I still don't know why my money wasn't on my card,' says Tammy.

Violet picks up her phone and helps Tammy phone the bank. Turns out Tammy's benefits had been stopped due to an unreturned form. They'd tried to call the number they had for her, but no one had answered.

'Do you have a phone?' Violet asks.

Tammy's hands bunch themselves into fists. 'It's in the drawer by my bed. Mum said I was only ever allowed to call her on it, and I wasn't ever to answer it unless it was her number. Sometimes I ring her just so I can listen to her voice on the answering machine.'

Violet glances at Chrissie.

'I'm sure she had an excellent reason for saying that at the time,' Violet says. 'But how about I pop my number in it too, just for when you might need anything?'

'And mine – just in case.' Chrissie gives Tammy a big smile.

'Do you have any letters about your benefits anywhere?' Violet asks.

'Don't remember. Mum puts my letters in that drawer.' Tammy shrugs and points to the kitchen units.

The drawer is so full, it's tricky to open properly. Violet wrenches it open and starts to rummage. The form is buried under several unopened letters, a photograph of a smartly dressed lady with wavy brown hair, and Tammy's birth certificate.

'That's Mum,' Tammy says in a quiet voice, pointing at the photo.

The birth certificate says Tammy was born in Brighton General Hospital and her mum's name was Lydia Raynott. Her father's name is Edward Raynott.

Perhaps Tammy's dad might be able to help her when she has to move out. Violet could ask Tammy if they're in touch or if she knows where he is. But some matters need to be handled with care, and things often end badly when Violet gets involved.

She should leave well alone.

It's just hard to stop the questions whirring around in her mind. Why does it feel as though Lydia had wanted Tammy to be hidden away and not allowed to learn how to do things for herself?

Violet's phone bleeps and she groans when she looks at the screen.

'It's Mum. I haven't got long, she needs me home. Will you be okay till later? I'll pop back and help you fill out your form when I've got Mum sorted.'

'I'll be fine – your mum needs you. Can you please help me later with the form? My spelling is so bad, and I don't want them to take away my money.'

'You go, love.' Chrissie pats Violet's arm. 'Tammy and I will fill her form out. We'll catch up later.' She looks at Tammy. 'That okay with you? You'll be doing me a favour – I love a bit of admin.'

Tammy smiles. 'I don't know what admin is, but yes please, Chrissie. Thank you both for helping me. I've never had a friend before. And now I have two. It feels even better than it looks on TV.'

'Where have you been?' Glenys is sitting at the dining table when Violet gets back from Tammy's flat. Her words have jagged edges.

'I took Tammy shopping – remember? I got us a few bits too. Stocked the fridge up. I did call you when I dropped them off, but you didn't answer. I thought you were napping.' Violet pulls out a chair and sits down opposite her mum, flinching when she sees the pinched lines on her face and the steely blue of her eyes.

'Well, I wasn't,' Glenys snaps. 'I was having a lie down and I got stuck. Happens a lot, only your sister usually bothers to help me back up again.'

'I was just upstairs but I hurried back as I soon as I got your message.' Violet can hear the defensiveness in her own voice, but she already carries enough guilt inside her. Any extra helpings of the stuff can damn well be turned into anger and spat back out again. She's doing her best.

Glenys looks down at the placemat in front of her. 'I wanted you to come back to me because you wanted to. To try harder. To care what I was doing.'

'Oh, Mum.' Violet's hand hovers over her mum's before settling on top of it.

Glenys snatches her hand back and holds it under the table. 'But you seem to care more about that bloody girl upstairs who you've known a whole five minutes.'

'I'm sorry,' Violet whispers. 'I do care – I'm trying to. I just don't know how.'

The drip from the kitchen tap echoes around the room. Another thing Violet needs to sort before the house is valued.

'I spent all those years looking after you. Patching you up, kissing it better.' Glenys stares through the window as if she can see the past through it.

Violet remembers the time she fell out of a tree in the woods. Adam had run to fetch her mum and Glenys had come running, first aid kit in hand and a worried smile on her face. She'd scooped Violet up and instantly made it all better with her soft words, squidgy arms and her signature smell of Elnette.

Now the soft words are gone. Glenys' arms are stiff, and her hair sits flat on her head, no volumising hairspray in sight.

'You've never known how to care.' Glenys' eyes glaze over. Her voice has a singsong, dreamy quality that freezes the air in Violet's chest. She lifts a stiff hand to a section of her own hair and twirls it around her fingers. 'You might be fooling yourself, running around after all the neighbours, but you don't fool me. Bet you haven't told any of them yet they have to move out. Thought not,' she adds when her eyes flicker back to Violet's face. 'No heart, that's your problem. You've always been bad news. Took away everything dear to me and pissed off as soon as you could without a single fucking thought.'

And just like that, the flimsy walls of Violet's new life turn to rubble.

CHAPTER 16

Violet

VIOLET STUMBLES OUT OF the front door of Malvern House and keeps walking. She doesn't know where she's going, and she can only see a foot in front of her thanks to the deluge of rain and her own tears.

Goosepimples prick her arms and she shivers; her wet clothes are clinging to her body.

A car trundles past. A cat meows from behind a garden wall. The world going on as normal around Violet just like it had that day, not even bothering to pause when Violet lost her mother for the first time of many.

The shops are on her left by the pond where fat raindrops are making ripples on the surface.

She takes a right turn, still pretending to herself she doesn't know where she's going. The gate to the park is slick with rain and it screeches as it opens. The swings are swaying in the wind and the flat bottom end of the slide is flooded. Violet sits on the bench, letting the wetness seep through her already drenched cotton trousers.

It's been such a long time since she was in this park. Last

time she'd been fifteen. She and Megan had been sitting in the sandpit – *ironically* of course. Violet had her back to the old and crumbling manor house in the corner of the park. If she'd been sitting on the other side, she might have seen, she might have been able to help.

She might not be sitting here now on a soaking wet bench, remembering the day her mum jumped off a three-storey building.

Silence enters the park as the wind stills and the rain slows. Violet stands, her wet clothes clinging on as tightly as the guilt and grief. She runs from the park, away from those moving pictures that follow her anyway. The police officers walking towards the sandpit that day. Their faces. The look that flickered between them before they spoke. And then afterwards, Jodie pushing Violet out of the way whenever she tried to help her mum. *I'll do it. I'll do it.* It had been a year since what happened with Dad. It was another three years until Violet could bear it no more and left after months of retreating into bottles of neon-coloured alcopops and painting the village with every shade of them.

She'd already been *Bad News* for her dad. It had spread to her mum, her sister and then every person who crossed her path. It wasn't always as dramatic as what happened with Kirsty's mum or Megan. Sometimes it was little things like when she got friendly with the guy across the hall at Harper's Court and then his bike got stolen. Or when that new girl started at work and as soon as they began eating lunch together, the girl developed a stomach ulcer.

Coincidence, many would say. Violet knows better.

And that's why she needs to get the hell away from here before she starts messing things up again for everyone.

The living room's empty when Violet arrives back at Malvern House. She pokes her head around her mum's bedroom door. Glenys has her eyes closed and her snoring echoes around the room. She's obviously not that devastated about their altercation, Violet decides. She closes the door quietly behind her and tiptoes to the table, opening her laptop as she sits down.

Jenny has sent her a Facebook message.

Hi Violet,

Hope you're doing okay and having fun. Miss your face! I hope you find your way back to us when you've finished your adventures, the place isn't the same without you. The new guy never smiles. Also, the pile of books I've kept by for you in the cleaning cupboard is getting out of control. If you'd like to send me your address, I can send some of them to you? The domestic team keeps threatening to give them to a charity shop. Please come back soon!

XXX

Violet closes the laptop, but not before a tear falls on the keyboard. She closes her eyes and sees her old office. She smells the coffee and the furniture polish. She hears the excited chatter and the constant buzz of phone alerts. She misses the natters in the cleaning cupboard and the feeling of being part of a team, even from the outer edges. She misses the life she'd managed to build for herself.

Violet grabs her handbag from the back of the dining chair and takes out the crumpled eviction letters. She pops them inside envelopes from the sideboard drawer and writes the tenants' names on them one by one. She was kidding herself thinking she could rebuild her life and make amends for her past. Her place is back in Manchester, far away from those she has caused pain.

She opens the Malvern House folder and looks again at the to-do list. She needs to get back to focussing on the sale of the building; putting it off is doing no one any good.

The leaflet for the residential home stares back at her from the middle of the folder. Violet types the number into her phone and presses call.

'There must be some mistake,' a young voice says on the other end of the line. 'Glenys' name isn't on the waiting list yet. Would you perhaps like to come for another visit? We can get another form filled out for you.'

Yes, yes, they would. Violet makes an appointment for the following week.

Time to start facing the future.

Just as Anne would say: 'I don't know what's around the bend, but I'm going to believe that the best does.'

Next, she scrolls to the number for Mullens' Estate Agents. She may be in two minds about giving the tenants their letters, but she has a plan. Everyone will be at the care club meeting on Thursday evening in the library, a perfect time to get the building evaluated. No need to sign on any dotted line, but at least she'll have made a start, and she'll know what she's up against.

She gets straight through to Michael Mullens himself and makes an appointment for six forty-five on Thursday.

No more dwelling on the past. Onwards and upwards.

An off-key rendition of 'Sweet Child of Mine' makes its way through the flat just before four heavy taps at the door.

'Hi, Tammy.' Violet finds herself smiling for the first time in hours. 'Do you want to c—'

'It's Mrs Robson,' Tammy says, walking straight through the door. 'I'm worried she might be dying.'

'Dying?' Violet's chest constricts and she picks up her phone again, ready to dial 999. 'Is she upstairs in her flat – what's happened?'

Tammy nods. 'She's in her flat. She keeps coughing and sneezing. I knocked on her door and she told me to keep away or I'd catch my death like she had. Something about walking home from the library in the rain.'

Violet lets out a breath and puts her phone back in her pocket. 'Sounds like a cold. Nothing to worry about, I'm sure. I'll go and check on her.'

Tammy starts humming again. 'Mum died when she was walking home. She already had the milk. She caught her death too.'

Violet squeezes Tammy's bony shoulder. 'I'm sure this isn't the same. Put the kettle on, have a seat, and I'll be back in a minute.' She leaves the door on the latch and rushes up the stairs before knocking on Mrs Robson's door.

'What now? If that's you again, with your shouting and your tuneless singing, I swear to you, I will get onto the council again, and you'll be out of here before ...' The shouting comes from behind her door.

'Mrs Robson, it's Violet. Tammy was worried about you. She thought you might be ill.'

Silence followed by a sneeze. 'I am ill. It's only a cold, though. Nothing some *peace and quiet* wouldn't heal.'

Violet takes the hint and leaves.

'Nothing to worry about,' she reassures Tammy once she's back in her mum's flat. 'She just needs some rest.'

'Chicken soup.' Tammy stares towards the kitchen. 'We need to make her some chicken soup. It's what my mum did for me when I sneezed or coughed. I'll make it if you can show me how.' She pulls at strands of her long blonde hair and winds them around her fingers as her eyes fill with tears. 'Please help me – she's in there all on her own and no one should be alone when they're poorly. She doesn't have anyone else to make it for her.'

Violet swallows the sudden lump in her throat. Mrs Robson has so clearly tried to make life difficult for Tammy and all Tammy cares about is helping Mrs Robson to feel better.

'No,' Violet says as she dries up a mug from the draining rack. 'I don't suppose she does. That would be a lovely idea.' She drops the tea towel on the side and rushes towards Tammy. It makes her jump a bit. Then Tammy hugs her back and those pesky tears start to leak out.

'Do you need some soup too?' Tammy asks.

'No.' Violet laughs and wipes her eyes with a tissue from her cardigan pocket. 'I've just got to sort my life out, that's all. It's in a bit of a mess right now.'

When it's almost twelve, Violet shows Tammy where the saucepan is and how to turn on the hob. She gets out the can of soup and a tin opener.

Tammy takes a step backwards. 'Can't. Not allowed.'

Violet shows Tammy how to use the tin opener before placing it gently into her shaking hands. 'You can do this. You only learned how to make coffee a few days ago and now you're a pro.' Violet smiles.

Tammy eventually gets the can open with no disasters, transfers the contents to the pan and stirs it on the hob until it's done.

Violet knocks three times on Mrs Robson's door after deciding it's probably safer for Tammy to hold the bowl with both hands.

Mrs Robson answers the door in her dressing gown. Her eyes are streaming and her nose is a shiny shade of red.

'What are you doing at my door again?' she demands, looking at Tammy as if she's holding a bucket of manure rather than a bowl of Heinz chicken soup.

'You're poorly,' Tammy states. 'This will make you better.'

Mrs Robson stares at Tammy. She moves her gaze from Tammy to Violet. 'I suppose you put her up to this?'

'She helped me with the tin opener but I did the rest.' Tammy beams with pride. 'I made the soup.'

Mrs Robson takes the bowl from Tammy and sniffs it before screwing up her face. 'Hmm. Pretty sure a factory made it.' She gives Tammy the smallest of nods and closes the door in their faces.

'Told you she'd like it,' Tammy says.

Later in the evening when Tammy's back in her flat and Violet and her mum have finished eating a silent dinner, Violet grabs the eviction letters and stuffs them back into her handbag. Tammy's selfless actions, Adam's willingness to help and Mrs

Robson's obvious loneliness can't be ignored. She can't put this on them now. She has plenty of time to try and make things work with Mum. And if she really, truly can't, at least she'll have time to help her neighbours as much as she can before asking them to pack up their lives and move on.

A notification pops up on Violet's phone whilst she's clearing the table. It's a comment on her blog from @ACroft88.

Love your blog! So great to have you back in the village.

Adam ☺ x

Violet's heart squeezes with pleasure. It's a sweet gesture from Adam to make her feel more comfortable being back here. But that's just Adam, he's always been thoughtful.

CHAPTER 17

Violet

'DO YOU THINK THAT'S enough seats?' Adam is standing in the middle of the library looking around the circle of mismatched chairs from the office in preparation for the first care club meeting.

Violet smiles as she watches his constant manoeuvring of the furniture and the checking of his watch. Last week's blog comment from @ACroft88 keeps reading itself over and over in her mind. *Great to have you back in the village.* She shakes herself. Far more important things to be focussing on right now.

'I'm sure that will be plenty of seats,' Violet says to Adam. 'I'm so sorry, but I'll have to slip out for some of the meeting – there's something I have to do for Mum.'

'How many people are coming?' Bill pipes up from his seat by the slushie machine. Mrs Robson is sitting next to him, pen in hand and wads of paper resting on the table. Her nose is still red from her cold, but she's looking brighter. She's already written the date and a list of people already there: herself, Violet, Adam and Bill.

'We had a lot of interest from people in the library after I put up my notice,' Mrs Robson says, pushing her glasses higher across the bridge of her nose. 'Quite a few from the surrounding villages too.'

'Tammy will be along soon too, she's just finishing her housework. I need to pop out for a bit, something I've got to do for Mum, but I'll be back before the end.'

Mrs Robson lets out a loud *hmpf*. 'Your mother not coming?'

'No – couldn't quite convince her to come with me. Perhaps another time.'

Adam gives Violet's shoulder a gentle squeeze. 'I'm sure she will when she's got used to having you around again. She's lucky to have you.' His eyes pull Violet almost entirely inside them. So strange, the way they look the same as when he was a teenager but with all that extra warmth and confidence. Looking into them feels like gazing through a lens that spans the three decades she's known him.

Tammy shows up clutching a piece of crumpled paper. She has a pen balanced behind her ear and her glasses are wonkier than ever. She gives everyone a shy wave and sits in the corner, humming something that sounds a lot like 'What's Love Got to Do with It'.

Claire arrives, holding a wriggly, curly-haired little boy in her arms, followed by a man dressed in black with a nervous smile. 'This is my husband, Abbas,' she says. 'And this is Jayden.' She puts the little boy down and he runs over to the children's bookshelf.

Abbas walks to a seat near reception and sits down without looking at anyone. He studies the swirls on the carpet. 'I won't always be able to come along but today's a good day. It's nice to see you all,' he says, shuffling in his chair and fiddling with the hole in the knee of his baggy jeans.

Claire winks at him and they share a smile full of unsaid words.

Chrissie is next through the door, followed by several faces Violet hasn't seen before. Lots of them don't seem to recognise each other. When Violet lived here last, everyone knew everyone. Perhaps that's what happens when villages lose their pubs and their community spaces.

A bead of sweat trickles down Violet's back and her stomach starts to spin. Far more people than she expected. Probably a good thing she's got to duck out soon.

Adam cracks open a window, letting cool air into the stuffy space. 'Thank you for coming, everyone. I want to start by thanking the person who came up with this idea in the first place.'

Heat rushes to Violet's face. Adam had tried to get her to chair the meeting, and she told him, she *told* him she'd never be able to do it, she doesn't want any attention. None of this is for her, she won't be around very long, it's all for them.

'So, a big thank you to one of my oldest friends, Violet Strong.' He smiles at her before carrying on. 'I thought we could start with introductions. Perhaps we could go around the room, say our names if we feel comfortable enough and give one reason why we'd like to be involved with the care club?'

There's a collective head nod and a seat-shuffle and people look uncertainly at each other.

Violet's mouth is dry, and her words come out as a croak. She forces her shoulders back down and tries to slow her breathing. Public speaking has always terrified her and the group of fifteen or so people sat around her is intimidating. Some of them might have lived here long enough to remember what she did.

'I'll go first. I'm Violet. I wanted to start the care club because I'm a brand-new carer and I'm not very good at it. I'm way out of my depth.'

Every pair of eyes in the room shoots towards Violet. Her heart stops hammering and her muscles unwind. Honesty neutralises the nerves. 'I've been a carer for about five minutes,' she carries on. 'I have no idea what I'm doing and without Adam and Claire's help the other week, I'd have lost the plot.'

Bill chuckles and everyone else nods along except Mrs Robson who is scribbling away on her minutes.

'I want to be a better carer for my mum. And I want to be involved in a project that means something to me. And I thought if I felt that way, then others might do too.'

All that can be heard is the hum of the air con and the scratching of Mrs Robson's pencil.

'I think it's wonderful,' Chrissie says. 'About time something positive happened in the village.'

'We've lost so much.' Claire nods in agreement. 'No clubs or socials since the community centre shut and we can't even go to the pub anymore. This is just what we need – something to bring us together.'

'We could organise some day trips,' Bill says. 'Lots of carers and the people they look after struggle to get out. If people in the village could help with lifts or an extra pair of hands when we reach out to them, it might make things easier. We can make sure everyone has the chance to be included.'

Abbas clears his throat and offers to start a WhatsApp group. 'That way, if anyone needs something from the shop or an errand doing when they can't get out, they can send out an

SOS message and people can help if they can. I'll pitch in on my good days. I know what it's like not to be able to get out of the house, and if it helps someone else – well, then it will be worth the effort.'

Mrs Robson stands up with a clipboard. 'I have an important point to make,' she announces. 'If we want to apply for funding to help with trips out, or perhaps provide emergency supplies for carers who are waiting for benefit payments, we ought to register with the local council. I have a contact, someone I know through the library. I'll set up a meeting for you, Violet.'

Violet stiffens. Why her? Why is she being brought into this – this is not Violet's group. 'Great. And thank you. You've been such a huge help,' she says instead.

'Well, quite,' she says, with her nose pointing slightly higher in the air than usual. 'I'm also sorry to have cancelled the Neighbourhood Watch meeting this week but preparing for this meeting was probably a more effective use of my time. For this week only of course,' she adds in a rush. 'You will all still be welcome at my house at the usual time next week.'

The group groan may be in their heads, but Violet can still hear it. She glances at her watch. It's six forty, just the right time to slip back to Malvern House for half an hour.

She subtly throws Adam an apologetic wave and creeps out of the library door before rushing up the hill, feeling the pull in the back of her calves as she approaches the top before arriving at Malvern House. A gleaming BMW is parked on the driveway.

'Michael Mullens,' the man says as he gets out of his car

and holds his hand out towards her. He has fair hair, speckled with grey, and pale green eyes that look familiar. Perhaps she recognises him from his website.

'Violet.' Violet shakes his clammy hand, and he squeezes it a bit too hard.

Violet unlocks the main door and lets him into the hallway. 'How long will it take, do you think?' She pictures Mrs R, Tammy, Bill, and Adam all tucking into tea and biscuits at care club, completely oblivious to what Violet's up to.

Michael Mullens looks at the briefcase in his hand. 'Well, I need to take a look at the building and the grounds, and then perhaps we can sit down and take a look at fees and what our agency can do for you?'

'Lovely. Let's start on the top floor.' Violet rushes up the stairs, hoping he will hurry too. She really wants him out of the way.

'None of the tenants are in this evening,' she says as she unlocks Tammy's door with the spare key.

'They know I'm here though – you've got their permission I presume?' Michael narrows his eyes at Violet, making her feel like she should be taking up less space.

'Of course.' She throws Michael a professional smile and gestures for him to enter the flat in front of her.

The minutes tick past as he scrutinises every corner of the flat. He peers at the vinyl on Tammy's hi-fi, and Violet starts to feel nauseous. It isn't right, not really, that a stranger's in her flat without her knowledge, even if it's better for her not to know.

'The other two flats; number two and three are pretty much

the same as this. My mum's flat is a little bit bigger with an extra bedroom. I'll show you that one next, then I'll give you a tour of the garden.' Violet just about stops short of dragging him out of Tammy's flat and back down the stairs.

Glenys refuses to speak to or look at Michael whilst he checks out the downstairs, and Violet tries to get him from room to room as quickly as possible.

'This is where you might want to focus most of your efforts if you want to increase the market value,' Michael says when they reach the gardens. He points at the front wall of the house. 'You'll need the upstairs windows repainting, you'll probably want to get those tiles repaired, the back garden could do with a bit of landscaping, and you really do need to get a decent gate put in.'

'What would the valuation be roughly without doing any of that?' Violet glances at the time on her phone. Five past seven. The meeting at the library will be rounding up soon.

Michael gives her a figure that sends her heart down a helter-skelter. It's not nearly enough to pay off the mortgage and the fees for Glenys' care.

'At least I know what will need doing. Thank you for coming.' Violet sticks her hand out towards Michael and a flash of irritation flickers across his face.

'We haven't discussed anything yet – fees, photos, what we can do for you.'

'Perhaps we could do that another day, I need a little time to think things through,' Violet says. The man really does have the meanest eyes.

She walks him back to his car before legging it back to the library and slipping into a seat on the back row.

The library has even more people in it than before and they are talking about how difficult it can sometimes be for carers when the people they are caring for don't want to leave the house, or don't feel able to.

'It is really hard.' Claire takes hold of Abbas' hand. 'But it's important not to force people to go out before they're ready.'

Adam nods. 'It takes a lot of patience, but it's worth the wait. Anyone else got any caring tips they'd like to share with everyone?'

'I've got one.' Abbas keeps his gaze at the floor and speaks quietly. 'I can be a bit … grouchy on my bad days. And it makes it harder when I know it's making Claire feel like she's walking on eggshells around me. I want her to remember that it's her house too and she shouldn't have to change who she is or what she says because of me.'

'Thanks, Abbas, that's another good thing for us all to think about. This has been fantastic.' Adam's eyes are bright and his smile is taking up the whole room. 'Anyone got any ideas for names for the care club?'

People shout out suggestions, many of them terrible.

'Helping Hands,' Tammy says. She hums a tune around her words as she folds the piece of paper in her hand into an aeroplane, and Violet realises how well she's coped with being in a room full of strangers for so long. 'It's what everyone is doing – being a helping hand.'

'Bloody love it.' Claire slaps the arm of her chair before wincing and shaking her fingers.

After a unanimous *yes* vote, Mrs Robson adds the new name to the minutes and Tammy's grin stretches all the way across her face.

'Did you want to add something, Chrissie?' asks Adam. Chrissie looks deep in thought. 'I'd quite like to read to people, perhaps, whilst their carers have a little break? Or just have cups of tea with people when they need a natter – I make a great cuppa.'

'That would be amazing, thank you,' says Adam. 'We'll be flexible about where to hold the meetings. If people can't get out for any reason as is often the case with us carers, we can all meet at their house if they'd like. We'll take it week by week and stay in touch on the WhatsApp group.'

After everyone's made plans for the week ahead and decided who's doing what before the next meeting, people start to relax and chat about their lives as Mrs R and Chrissie start making the coffees.

'Thank you for coming tonight,' Adam murmurs in Violet's ear. 'I know this stuff's hard for you, but it means a lot that you're here – especially as all this was your idea.'

Violet turns her head around to answer him. His face is closer than she thought, and her tummy does that annoying flippy thing. Then she pictures Michael Mullens traipsing through Adam's flat without him knowing, and her tummy feels a different kind of sick. Adam has gone out of his way to help her since she came back, and this is how Violet is repaying him. She really is *Bad News*.

@Bookworm1908

An uplifting read today. **The Pendulum** by JR Taylor (pictured).

A community comes together to save a clock factory from

closing, and in doing so, uncovers a secret that changes the life of the village forever.

A must-read, I highly recommend.

What are some of your favourite reads about village communities?

#books #reading #blogging

CHAPTER 18

Violet

'YOU CAN'T SURELY WANT to just sit and stare out the window all day.' Violet is sitting in the living room with Glenys, desperately trying to coax her to come for a post-breakfast walk. 'It's gorgeous outside. I've been here a whole month and we haven't been out together yet. We can take your wheelchair, go for a spin around the village, have a drink by the lake – whatever you fancy.' She tries to keep her voice casual, remembering something Adam and Claire had said at the meeting about not forcing the issue of going out before people are ready.

Violet of all people knows what that feels like – she still gets a tummy flutter at the thought of walking through Lowerstone.

'Not today, thank you.' Glenys sits up straighter in her armchair, her mouth setting itself into a stiff line.

'How about I put the telly on? Or you can have a look at one of my library books?' Anything to stop her sitting and staring into space all day, it can't be good for anyone.

'You can bring me one of your books. The one with the man on the front who looks like Colin Firth.'

If Violet didn't know better, she might be convinced that Glenys' eyes are glinting.

'Well, hurry up and give it here then. And don't let me keep you. It's a nice day, like you said. No point spending it in this shithole.'

Violet has a sudden urge to kiss the top of her mum's head before she leaves. What might she do if she did? Instead, she grabs her handbag and places the book and her mum's mobile phone next to Glenys and heads to the front door. 'Give me a call if you need anything. I'll be back at lunch.'

Glenys doesn't answer, but she does move her hand in something that could be loosely described as a wave. At least it's an acknowledgement, some progress at last.

Violet makes her way up the stairs and knocks on Tammy's door. The two of them have some clothes shopping to do.

It takes twenty-four minutes to drive into Brighton and almost as long to find a parking space that ends up being miles from the shops. Tammy has sung along tunelessly with the radio with the enthusiasm of a *X-Factor* contestant on a bloopers reel until Violet's ears are close to bleeding.

By the time they reach the high street, Tammy is huffing and puffing with exertion and keeps stopping to watch people. 'What's he doing?' She points to a man sitting up in a sleeping bag in the doorway of a boarded-up shop.

'I expect he's just woken up. Lots of people have to sleep on the streets because they don't have anywhere to live,' Violet explains in a quiet voice, trying to disguise her shock at the lack of experience Tammy seems to have with the outside world.

She has to more or less pull Tammy into Primark to break

her stare at the man in the doorway. Her face is still scrunched up by the time they've reached the women's clothing section. 'But *why* doesn't that man have somewhere to live? It's not fair that he has to sleep outside when I have a bed and a Manchester City duvet.'

Violet hangs the T-shirt she'd just picked up back on the rail and turns to face Tammy. 'You are absolutely right. It's not fair. There are lots of things in this world that are not fair. All we can do is try our best to make things a little better for other people. Like you did for Mrs R with the soup when she was poorly.'

Tammy nods and picks up the same T-shirt Violet had just put back. Then she collects a pair of jeans from a shelf without looking at the size. Violet follows her around the shop as she scoops up a thick jumper and a pair of fluorescent orange swimming shorts.

'Perhaps it might be a good idea to think about what clothes would go with what. Get some matching things,' Violet suggests.

Tammy's brow creases and she starts walking towards the till. 'Come on,' she says. 'I can't hold all this for much longer, it's getting heavy.'

Violet picks up her pace to catch up. 'You really should try them on before you pay for them. Isn't that what you normally do?'

Tammy looks down at the bundle of clothes in her arms. 'Mum usually brings them home with her. I've never seen them in shops before.'

Violet tries her best not to let her mouth fall wide open. 'I'll show you where the changing rooms are. You just need to go behind the curtain, put the clothes on and see if they feel comfortable.'

Two older teenagers are standing by the shelves that hold the jeans. They look familiar. Violet glances at the extended holes in their earlobes and their matching grey tracksuits and remembers that she's seen them both twice before – once at the Jobcentre and once in the village.

The girl catches Violet looking and mutters something to the lad who then turns around to face her. They fix their eyes on Tammy and storm towards her, barging into her from both sides as they pass. Tammy's armful of clothes falls to the floor.

'Hey!' Violet yells. 'Watch what you're doing and help her pick all that back up.'

The teenagers grin at each other before swaggering towards her and putting their hoods up.

The shop assistant appears next to Violet. 'Is there a problem?' he asks.

A tall, skinny figure runs from the far side of the shop towards the exit. He's holding several pairs of jeans and stuffing them under his hoody.

An alarm blares across the shop floor. The shop assistant runs out of the shop and past the window, shouting at him to stop, telling him that he's seen his face and will call the police.

The two youths next to Violet share another grin, lurch for the shelf behind her and grab a few pairs of jeans for themselves before sprinting out of the door and running past the window in the opposite direction.

'See? *They* didn't try them on first,' says Tammy.

★

'You fancy having lunch with Mum and me?' Violet asks Tammy once they're climbing out of the car back at Malvern House. 'It would be nice for you both to meet each other properly.'

Tammy's face lights up with a smile. 'Yes, please.'

'Mum, Tammy's staying for lunch,' Violet says once they're through the door. She keeps her voice bright and confident, remembering some advice Abbas had given at the Helping Hands meeting. No more walking on her mother's ancient eggshells. This is Violet's home too, at least for now.

'Not jam. Fed up with jam.' Glenys looks up from her book and gives Tammy the smallest of nods.

Violet guides Tammy past Glenys and towards the kitchen, praying and crossing all of her fingers that Glenys doesn't mention the sale of the building.

'Right. Do you want to pop the bread in the toaster and I'll put the beans on?' Violet opens the cupboard and pulls out two tins.

Tammy pales and takes a step back. 'Mum says toasters are too dangerous for me – she said I should always wait for her.'

Violet looks at Tammy's long blonde hair and pictures her in a tall tower, hidden from the world and all possible danger. 'I'll show you. It's easy-peasy. You're more than capable.'

After a successful team effort, Violet, Tammy and Glenys sit at the table and tuck into their lunch. Glenys is quiet to begin with but she doesn't throw her food on the floor or inform Violet that she's the worst daughter that ever lived.

Progress.

'That place called whilst you were out – Rossendale,' Glenys mumbles. 'They had to cancel our visit. They said to call them back to rearrange.'

Heat travels up Violet's neck and she knows without looking that blotches are appearing on it. 'No need to worry about that now. I'll sort it later.' She glances at Tammy who is thankfully tucking into her grub, oblivious.

'And don't forget to call up about the windows – they'll need sorting before—'

'All right, Mum. Later, eh?' Violet's words are too sharp, and Tammy stops chewing to stare at her.

Once they've finished clearing the plates away, Tammy rushes back into the kitchen to make everyone a coffee.

Tammy's clearly able to do so much more than her mum gave her credit for. Why has she been kept so hidden away from all of life outside of *Coronation Street* and old vinyl? It feels wrong that she hasn't been given a chance to learn to do things for herself or to get out and make friends. Violet knows what it's like to be all alone; she hides inside books rather than records and TV soaps, but at least her alone-ness has been voluntary.

Violet opens her laptop and types in the name she remembers seeing on Tammy's birth certificate. If she could track down Tammy's dad, she might find some answers. Tammy might have other family who could help her, then Violet won't feel such gut-wrenching guilt when they sell the house.

'Do you know anyone else who lives in Lowerstone or nearby? Do you ever see anything of your dad?' Violet swallows, hoping she hasn't walked her tongue a step too far.

Tammy keeps her back to Violet and doesn't answer.

She either didn't hear or doesn't want to answer. Violet looks at the results her laptop has brought up for Edward Raynott. According to Google, a local brewery in Brighton is owned by someone with the same name. No others appear on

Facebook from the UK, just a profile of someone who matches the photo of the brewery owner. Violet's always fancied a visit to a brewery.

Violet squints at the man, searching for a resemblance to Tammy whilst concocting a plan. Once Tammy has a place to go and someone to support her, Violet can move forward with the sale of the building. Finding Tammy's dad feels like the natural first step. It's what Jenny would do – track Edward down and try to find out the real story.

You'd make such a good journalist. Jenny's words echo inside Violet's mind. Good journalists hear both sides of the story and care enough to get to the truth.

If Violet can find the truth, it might set her *and* Tammy free.

CHAPTER 19

Tammy

TAMMY FEELS LIKE SHE could run around and around and around without stopping when she arrives back in her flat. Mum would say it's because she drank coffee.

Before Violet asked about Dad, Tammy had been enjoying going to new places like the shops and the library. Places that weren't her flat but were still safe. And her flat feels even safer now that she knows how to look after it. It smells like washing-up liquid and there's lots more room to put your feet. It's even better than it used to be after Mum had cleaned. It feels more like a real home now someone has been in it who isn't Tammy and isn't her mum.

The urge to run and shout is not because of the coffee or because of the extra room in her flat. It's because of those pictures in her mind again. *Him* and the inside of the cupboard at the old house they all lived in before Dad went very far, far away. The smell of car polish and the dust from the old coats on the hooks. It was quiet in there. Always so quiet, but only after the yelling and the bad noises from the other side of the cupboard door stopped.

Violet made it all come back into her head, and now it won't leave. It feels like running would be the only way to spill it out again.

She's been outside and further than the shop with Violet more than once without Mum now – she'd even been outside the village. What's to stop her going out on her own? She's already wearing her new trainers and jogging bottoms from Primark. They fit just right, so they won't slip off her when she runs. She puts her key in her pocket and ventures out into the hallway, slamming the door to her flat behind her with a satisfying clunk.

She runs downstairs, along the garden path, and all the way down the road. She runs past the village shops, her long hair whipping behind her in the wind like a cape. She's just like Supergirl.

Across the road from the pond is a gate that leads to a big field. Tammy goes through it and runs and runs across the field, faster and faster until she reaches the railings around the swings, the slide and the roundabout inside them. She's seen parks like this before. Mum only took her a few times when she was little; she said that parks are full of danger.

Tammy's heart pounds hard like a drum. She hasn't run this far in a long time, but there's also something else that's making it happen; those two people sitting on the swings. They're the people from the clothes shop who took the jeans without trying them on.

In *Coronation Street* and other TV programmes, people always chat to people they see out and about. Could she just say hello and start talking? She's already made friends with Violet and now Chrissie too. She's already decided that next to Violet, Chrissie is her favourite person in the world. Perhaps she could make more and more friends and they might all be as nice as Violet and Chrissie. Tammy could be a person that lots of people say hi to when she walks through the village. Mum had been wrong about the kettle, the toaster and the cooker so she was probably wrong about people being dangerous too.

'Are you wearing your new jeans today?' Tammy asks them when she gets close to the swings. 'They look nice. My friend said you forgot to pay for them.'

The boy and the girl stare at Tammy and then look at each other before laughing and laughing.

'I remember you. You shit yourself and dropped all your clothes when we came near you. Your face!' the boy shrieks. 'Did Primark tell you to come and get us?'

Tammy stands very still.

'He's kidding.' The girl looks sideways at the boy. 'We didn't mean to knock everything out of your hands. We just needed a distraction. It was nothing personal, you were just *there*. You helped us, if anything.' She takes a stick of chewing gum from her pocket and waves it in front of Tammy's face.

'No thank you. I'm not allowed,' Tammy says.

The boy and the girl laugh even louder this time. They must think Tammy is very funny. She likes making people laugh. If people laugh, it means they're happy.

The girl twists her lip ring. 'What's your name?'

'Tammy.'

'Tammy.' The boy sounds like he's practising saying the word. 'Tammy. I think you should be our friend. Specially as we're almost neighbours. You live in the village, right?'

'Yes, at the top of the building at the top of the road in

front of the woods.' Tammy closes her mouth, but it's too late, she's said it. Mum always said never to tell people where she lives, *just in case*.

'Nice. We should hang out – maybe get the bus into town. You got money?' he asks.

'Stop it.' The girl reaches over and touches his arm. 'Don't.'

Maybe the girl wants him to herself. She might not want Tammy hanging around.

'Nah, this will be good.' The boy grins and puts his hand over the side of the girl's face before kissing her on the mouth.

It makes Tammy's tummy feel funny.

'Ready to go?' he asks as he jumps up from the swing.

Tammy nods. She's not sure if she is, but she can't think of anything else she could do to get more ready. She follows her two new friends out of the park and waits by a post with a sign on the top before getting on a bus for the first time since she was little. They take Tammy's money to pay their fares and then race up the stairs. Tammy takes a huge breath in and sits on a rickety seat on the top deck.

She's ready for yet another adventure.

CHAPTER 20

Violet

'MUM, YOU'LL ROAST IF you wear that today, it's nearly July and it's way too hot to wear wool from head to toe. We're going to see Rossendale this afternoon, remember – that residential home? You'll want to be comfortable.' Violet is helping Glenys pull her clothes from the wardrobe after a rather successful shower.

Glenys had been in good spirits and even hummed a tune whilst Violet rinsed the shampoo from her hair. They talked about Violet's first day at school and how she'd come home with a lunchbox full of daisies she'd picked for her mum. Violet had no idea Glenys remembered any of that stuff.

But now they're back in Glenys' room, it's as if someone has turned the dimmer switch. Glenys' mouth has turned downwards, and her shoulders are drooping like weeping willow branches. The previous twenty minutes might as well not have happened, and the last thing Violet needs today is for Glenys to dig her heels in and take ages to get dressed. Violet's meeting Joanna from the council in half an hour about registering Helping Hands in order to get some funding for day trips for the carers.

'Don't tell me what to wear,' Glenys snaps. 'I tell *you* what to wear. You're my daughter. Not that you ever listened, walking around showing your shoulders and far too much of your legs.' She looks Violet up and down. 'Not much has changed. Except of course nowadays there's a little more of you to show.'

Glenys' words turn to ice inside Violet. She's had weeks to adjust to her sharp tongue and grouchy moods, but sometimes the arrows find holes in her defences. Her mum knows just where to aim them.

'Don't think I didn't know what you were up to all those years ago.' For someone who struggles with talking when she's feeling low, she's certainly finding plenty of words to use now. 'Sneaking out at all hours with your skirt halfway up your arse, coming back three sheets to the wind, thinking I didn't notice.'

She *didn't* notice. She never said a thing, not once.

'If your father could have seen you, he'd have been spitting in his grave.'

'Spinning.' Why she needs to correct that of all things, Violet has no idea.

'Whatever.' Glenys shrugs. She removes one hand from her walking frame and grabs the hem of Violet's vest top, pulling herself closer until her face is inches from hers. 'You shouldn't have taken it with you that day. You should have left it at home. Your fault. Your fault and you don't even care.'

Violet steps back as if she's been slapped.

Glenys loses her grip on Violet's top and sways.

Violet leans forward, arms outstretched, and everything slows down. Glenys' shoulders graze Violet's fingertips before slipping past them and Violet dives forward and onto her knees just in time to cushion Glenys' fall to the floor.

Glenys' face pales even further and her drawn-out groan makes Violet's insides curdle.

'Mum. Mum. Talk to me. Are you okay? Where does it hurt?' Violet was aiming for calm and reassuring, but each word comes out shriller than the last.

Glenys wriggles on Violet's lap and manages to sit up. 'Nothing broken,' Glenys whispers. Her hands are shaking, and Violet can feel her body trembling.

'Just sit for a minute, don't try to move too quickly.' Violet takes hold of Glenys' hand. 'I've got you.'

Beads of sweat swim down Violet's back. The air is thick with heat.

'I think I'll be able to get up now,' Glenys murmurs. Her hands are still shaking.

Violet leans over and pulls the walking frame closer and between them, she and Glenys manage to stand back up, although Glenys' legs are even more wobbly than usual.

'Let's get you to the bed. You can have a little rest and I'll grab you some water.' Violet rushes to the kitchen and back.

Glenys sips her drink and nods at Violet before shuffling back on her bed. She still looks as white as the duvet she's lying on.

Violet can't leave her yet, not whilst she's so shaken up. She's left her phone in the living room and Glenys' radio alarm has been unplugged, so she has no idea what time it is. She'll sit with Glenys until she's calmer and hopefully she can still make it in time to meet Joanna from the council.

'How are you feeling? Any pain? Dizziness?'

Glenys shakes her head.

Violet's phone is ringing, she can hear it vibrating on the living-room table.

'You go if you need to. I'm fine now.' Glenys squeezes Violet's hand and the gesture brings a lump to her throat. 'I don't want to go to see that Rossendale, though. Not today.'

'Well, only if you're sure you're okay … I'll grab your phone so it's next to you if you need me.'

Back in the living room, Violet's phone tells her she's already five minutes late to meet Joanna and the missed call was from an unknown number. After her appointment with Joanna, she'll need to cancel Rossendale.

She flies out the door, wishing she'd stopped to gulp some water by the time she's halfway down the hill. Her legs feel wobbly from before and the pictures have started, the old ones she keeps locked away.

Damn Glenys for dredging up a past that Violet's spent eighteen years trying to put behind her.

The memories start with the sirens, always. Then the smell of paint. The lurch in the pit of her stomach. She keeps running.

She reaches the village shops on unsteady legs. It's hard to keep making them move forward. Her lungs have shrunk, and she can't fit enough air into them at once and even though she knows it's time to slow her breathing down, she can't. She's seen that first flickering flame in her mind; she can smell the acrid scent of smoke.

Violet stumbles behind the pharmacy and leans her back against the wall, bending over to catch her breath. She closes her eyes, counts backwards from twenty, tries to imagine each of her muscles unfurling. So many tips for dealing with panic attacks, all of them she'd read on Instagram, none of them shared by people she knows in real life – because not a single soul knows she suffers from them.

By the time Violet has pulled herself out of the fog, she's almost half an hour late to meet Joanna.

Mrs Robson is the only person in the library. The table in the 'coffee shop' is empty.

'Joanna left about ten minutes ago. She looked rather cross. You were supposed to be meeting her – I would have taken the meeting myself had I not been working.'

Shit.

Mrs Robson takes off her glasses and stares at Violet with steely eyes. 'I didn't set that meeting up for you not to bother showing up.'

Double shit.

'I tried my best to get here. It was a tricky morning.' Violet's shoulders sag as a wave of exhaustion hits.

'Causing trouble in the village again. Heard you were back, Violet Wrong.' A smug voice makes its way over Violet's shoulder from behind her. She knows who it belongs to even without turning around. It's Kirsty Waters' friend and Adam's ex-wife, Kelly. The two of them used to hound Violet all the way back to Lowerstone on the school bus after what happened. 'I'm surprised you can even show your face around here, let alone upsetting poor old Mrs R whilst you're at it.'

Violet chances a look over her shoulder. Kelly looks exactly the same, just with extra highlights and a few new lines beside her eyes and her pouted lips. She's wearing a floaty white dress, devoid of a single blemish.

Violet's hand starts shaking. Not again. She grips the edge of the reception desk as the room wobbles.

'Violet is doing something wonderful for the community.' Mrs Robson leans across the desk and puts her glasses back on, glaring over the top of them at Kelly. 'If anyone has upset me, it's you. Do you have *any* idea how late back that book is?' She points at the paperback in Kelly's hand. 'I have a list of names as long as my arm of people who are waiting to borrow it.' She tuts as she takes the book from Kelly. 'Anything else you need – no? Well, off you go then before I make you pay those fines,' Mrs Robson adds.

Kelly scampers from the library, her cheeks as crimson as Mrs R's lipstick.

Violet's mouth twitches and she suppresses a victory dance. 'Thank you for saying that. And I'm sorry for not making it in time for the meeting. I think perhaps that side of things should be all yours from now on. I don't seem to be making a very good job of it.'

Mrs Robson sniffs as she puts the book on the returns shelf. She peers at Violet when she turns back around. 'You look dreadful. Look at the state of you.'

Violet goes to make a 'cheers very much' quip but it gets stuck in her tight throat. No matter how hard she swallows, she can't stop the tears from rolling down her face.

'Right. Kettle's out the back. Come through.' Mrs Robson opens the wooden gate by reception so Violet can follow her out into the tiny kitchen.

Mrs Robson gets the cups ready and pulls a little carton of milk from the fridge. 'Don't worry about people like Kelly – and if you're worried about me finding out, you don't need to. I know what happened in Lowerstone when you were young. People talk.'

They certainly do.

'But I think you're brave – coming back. It can't have been easy. And the only Violet I'm bothered about is the one I see in front of me – the one who looks out for people. And this Helping Hands Club is going to help a lot of people. Too many around here don't have anyone to talk to.'

Violet watches Mrs Robson as she squeezes the teabag hard with her spoon. The tea is going far darker than she usually drinks it, but Mrs R isn't stopping, she's just staring at it. Violet will drink her tea however it comes, probably best not to mention it.

'What about you?' Violet asks softy. 'Do you have family nearby?'

Mrs R shakes her head. 'My family were from Kent – most of them are dead or we don't speak. I didn't know anyone around here when I first moved to Lowerstone except my husband and his family.'

'That must have been hard, leaving your family behind and starting again in a new place.'

'It was.' Mrs Robson sips her tea and grimaces. She stands up straighter. 'But within a fortnight I knew everyone in the village. People were always in and out of each other's homes, sharing sugar and cups of tea. It's just not like that anymore.' She shakes her head. 'Nowadays, no one wants to stop and talk, and we all have to hold our handbags closer when we walk past each other on the street. After my husband … went, none of his family really bothered coming around anymore either. So, it's just me.' She picks her cup back up and downs the rest of her tea.

Violet resists the urge to hug her stiff shoulders. She wonders if the rumours she's heard from Claire are true – whether Mrs R's husband did die or if there was indeed a secretary and another country involved. Violet decides not to ask; it's none of her business.

'The village just isn't what it used to be. Not enough jobs, not enough for the youngsters to do.'

Violet's jaw clenches as a wave of nausea hits. She knows whose fault it was that the village began to gradually collapse all those years ago.

Hers.

'Don't let your tea go cold, I don't make drinks in here for just anyone, you know.' Mrs Robson points to Violet's cup. 'None of us can change the past. But you're doing something to help change the future, and that's what matters.'

CHAPTER 21

Violet

AS SOON AS VIOLET reaches the top of the hill, she can hear an engine running from the driveway of Malvern House. A marked police car is parked next to Pat-the-Fiat. Its doors open and Violet hears the loud humming of a Cher song she can't remember the name of. Violet only knows one person who hums like that and she hurries towards the car, her heart pounding. Tammy coming home in a police car can't be a good thing.

As Violet walks up the driveway, she watches Tammy climb out of the car and stand next to a uniformed police officer.

'That's her. That's Violet.' Tammy points at her. She doesn't say hello or grant Violet any eye contact, she just gets her keys out from her pocket and lets herself into the building with no explanation.

'Could we perhaps have a word?' the officer asks. He introduces himself as PC Jenkins and flashes Violet his badge.

'Yes, that would be good, please. Has something happened with Tammy?'

'She said it's you who looks after her,' says PC Jenkins.

Violet's cheeks tingle with heat. 'Well, yes. But not in any official capacity – I've been trying my best to be there, but it's been a little tricky, what with …'

The police officer looks down at the device in his hand. 'Tammy was caught shoplifting in Brighton. She walked out of Marks and Spencer's with several items of unpaid-for clothing under her jumper.'

Several areas of Violet's mind light up after a sharp intake of breath. 'Oh, Tammy.' She pictures her new friend being marched out of a shop in handcuffs, and swallows hard, clasping her hands together. 'Please believe me, she's not a criminal, she wouldn't have understood what she was doing.'

Had she, though? Violet's taken Tammy shopping before, and she knows that things have to be paid for. Something feels off.

'It's partly my fault for taking her clothes shopping the other day,' Violet adds.

PC Jenkins looks at her with a raised eyebrow.

'Tammy has a learning disability,' she carries on. 'And I know this sounds odd, but I think it may have been the first time Tammy had been in a clothes shop. She didn't seem to have a clue how it all worked – and whilst we were in there, there were people nicking pairs of jeans.'

Tammy must have got confused. Violet's fault for taking her. For being *Bad News*. This is what happens when Violet gets involved.

'I had a chat with her in the back office of the shop. The store manager soon realised that Tammy might not be aware of the consequences of her actions and agreed not to take things further, so I've let her off with a warning.'

'Thank you.' Violet gives him her most grateful smile.

'There was one main reason for my concern.' PC Jenkins' face straightens. 'When I looked at the CCTV, Tammy didn't appear to be alone. She seemed to be with a couple of other known shoplifters. When we asked her about it, she denied knowing anything about them – but they were very clearly sending each other signals across the shop floor.'

'I don't think that's possible.' Violet slowly turns all the information over in her mind. 'Tammy doesn't really have any sort of social circle.'

'If you don't mind me saying, that makes it even more important to be vigilant about who she may be hanging out with. Some people prey on those who are isolated and vulnerable.'

By the time Violet gets back into the building, Tammy has locked her door.

'I'm having a lie down.' Tammy's voice travels through the door after Violet knocks.

'I just want to check you're okay. The police officer was worried about you. *I'm* worried about you,' Violet adds.

Silence reigns for several seconds, and then she hears movement before Tammy's door is pulled open.

'Thank you for letting me in. I promise I've not come to … oh, Tammy.' Violet's hands fly up to her mouth as she surveys the scene in front of her.

Three dirty plates are strewn across the floor. Food-encrusted cutlery sits on the coffee table which is now stained in several places with bolognese sauce. The sofa is covered with empty crisp packets and chocolate wrappers.

'Why did you eat three bowls of the bolognese – it must

be all gone already. Were you hungry? And where did you get all of those crisps and chocolate bars from?'

Tammy looks down at her feet. 'I forgot to wash up. I'll do it now – I know how to,' she adds.

'I know you do. You've been doing so well, that's why I don't understand what's happened today.' Violet stops talking when something catches her eye. Hanging out from the top of the bin in the corner is an empty vodka bottle. Violet crosses the room in three long strides and pulls it out. 'Did you drink this?'

Tammy shrugs and Violet thinks quickly. She's not Tammy's parent and even if she was, Tammy's an adult. What gives Violet the right to lecture her about her alcohol consumption? Somehow though, she just can't picture Tammy drinking a whole bottle of vodka since the last time Violet watched Tammy empty her bin. She looks closely at her. Tammy's eyes are bloodshot, and she looks pale and clammy.

'Why don't you sit down for a few minutes,' Violet says. 'I'll get you a glass of water – you look dreadful.'

As Tammy sits down on the sofa, Violet walks to the sink and fills a glass with water. The stale stench of fag-ash reaches her nose seconds before she notices the pile of dog-ends heaped onto an upturned saucepan lid.

She takes the water to Tammy and crouches next to her as she gulps it down.

'Who else has been in here? I know you don't smoke cigarettes. I'm not sure that you drink vodka either,' Violet says in her gentlest voice.

'No one. And I do now.' Tammy still won't meet Violet's eyes and she's shivering.

Violet plucks Tammy's dressing gown from the end of her bed and wraps it around her.

'I think there were other people here. And I think they were the same people who made you take the clothes from that shop. I know this has been such a difficult time for you since your mum—'

'They didn't make me,' Tammy blurts out. She shuffles around on the sofa until she's lying down, looking up at the ceiling.

'I get that the High Street is new to you – and that perhaps you aren't used to some of the ways people can be. But it's really important *never* to take things from shops without paying. It's wrong, and it's stealing. And other people shouldn't ask you to do it for them either.'

'I know w–what those rules are,' Tammy says. 'But they are different for some people, aren't they?'

'How do you mean?'

'Like, for people who don't have money with them – they're allowed to take things out of the shop as long as they don't let other people in the shop see. It's because they might get jealous that they have to pay, so it's the nicer thing to hide it until you're far away.'

'I don't know who has told you that, but they are very wrong. If you take something without paying for it, it's stealing, and you can end up in a lot of trouble. And no one's allowed to make you steal for them.'

'But it wasn't their fault.' Tammy's eyes fill with tears. 'They have no food, and they needed more clothes. They were nice to me. I just w–wanted to be a good friend.'

Tammy lets Violet give her a hug.

'I think you should have a little sleep. I'd like to make a phone call about maybe getting you some support, someone to help you. You happy for me to do that?'

Tammy murmurs her agreement, moments before her eyes close.

It takes Violet twenty minutes to get through to the council – then she's passed to several departments before she's able to report her concerns about Tammy. Someone will come and assess her, but it won't happen straight away because she's not in immediate danger.

Violet waits until Tammy has dozed off before returning downstairs, the *Operation Sell Malvern House* to-do list floating around her mind.

Violet will keep trying her best to help Tammy until she has some proper support in place. She wants all the tenants to be okay and it's important that they have somewhere to go after the building's sold, but she can't keep taking her eye off the end goal. Her mum needs to be somewhere that's right for her, somewhere she can get the care she needs. Violet's care skills are so far from perfect and everyone deserves to be looked after properly by people who know what they're doing – Violet will call the residential home again.

There's no answer from Rossendale when she calls to rearrange her mum's appointment yet again, and she hates speaking to answering machines. Instead, she spends the next hour pulling up the weeds from the driveway and cleaning the ground-floor windowpanes. She needs to smarten the place up a bit, create a good impression for when the next estate agents come to valuate. *Three valuations, and go with the middle one,* Jodie's instructions said.

The rest of the evening is spent looking again at flats for the other tenants to rent in Lowerstone and the neighbouring villages. Violet's heart inches higher when she sees the perfect apartment near the park for only a little more rent than the tenants are currently paying.

It's on the ground floor, so it would be perfect for Adam and Bill.

Or for Mrs R.

Or for Tammy.

One flat available in the whole area – how is it fair for just one household to have somewhere to move to that isn't miles away?

Violet should have told them all right at the start. She's in too deep now. What would they think if they knew what she was planning all along?

She's not the Anne Shirley who brings life and joy to Green Gables, or the one who aced her exams and made the whole town proud when she returned to teach their children. She's the Anne who accidently dyed her hair green, who smashed a slate over someone's head and got her best friend drunk. Anne the Screw-up. Violet the Vile.

@BookWorm1908

Have you ever found yourself in the middle of two impossible choices? Miranda Pardon in **Five Days After Autumn** by Jenna Colton is in exactly the same position. She's tortured by her past mistakes and seems destined to keep repeating them until she ends up alone, despite wanting nothing more than to make everyone around her happy – anyone relate?

A wonderful read, very sad at times, but beautifully written. I highly recommend.

What books have you read about people making difficult decisions? Any favourites?

#books #decisions #regrets #whatwouldyoudo?

CHAPTER 22

Violet

VIOLET IS RUNNING LATE and the traffic on the outskirts of Brighton is gridlocked. Her mum is sitting tight-lipped in the passenger seat after an hour of Violet coaxing her inside Pat-the-Fiat for the first time since she arrived two months ago.

'Can you remember everything we spoke about, Mum?'

Silence.

'Just answer their questions as well as you can. Tell them how hard you find things on your most difficult days. I've got all your paperwork from the hospital and the doctors so everything you tell them will be backed up.' Violet glances at Glenys before checking her mirrors and changing lanes, squinting in the August sun. 'It's just one morning. One morning, and you'll get your money sorted – you won't have to do this again for at least a couple of years.'

More silence and Glenys' hands are shaking. Violet doesn't blame her – who wants to spend hours spewing out personal stuff to a stranger with a tick sheet? Or be prodded around by people who are trying to see whether or not you're on the fiddle? Claire was right when she'd said the process was cruel, it's clearly rattled Glenys this morning and they haven't even reached the building yet. It just feels like such unnecessary stress for people who are having to manage so much already, for those with health conditions, and for their carers.

All the disabled parking spaces at Shaftsbury House are taken. Violet parks Pat on the far side of the packed car park and retrieves her mum's walking frame from the boot. As Glenys struggles across the tarmac, Violet already feels self-conscious. She can feel the assessors' eyes at the window. *Oh, look. Managed to get out of the car and walk all this way without even needing a disabled bay.*

It's a tall, unwelcoming building that blocks out the sun. A grab-rail runs the length of the path, right up to the revolving entrance that leads into the crammed waiting room. Thick, sticky silence is punctuated only by coughs, groans and fidgeting bottoms on squeaky seats.

The queue to the Perspex-encased reception is long and littered with walking frames, crooked sticks and nervous faces.

Not everyone's burdens are visible, lots are inside. Trapped. Unseen.

The chairs sit all around the outside of the waiting room, all different sizes, some with low backs and higher ones too. All designed to catch people out, to see if their sitting abilities match the answers on their forms. A middle-aged man lowers himself to sit and one of the Perspex-covered people reaches over and tick-checks his form. What had he put down about sitting? What sort of chair and for how long at a time? How long is he allowed to sit there without shuffling around before he becomes a liar in their eyes? So many pairs of eyes in the room, all of them staring yet not seeing.

'Glenys. Glenys Strong,' Violet says when they're at the front of the queue and it's clear her mum isn't going to say anything.

The people behind the screen stare back as if they're at an animal park. *A close-up of the benefit scroungers. Round up, round up, everybody. Claimants being fed in a few minutes. Come and have a nose at their natural behaviours.*

'Do you have your form and identification?'

Glenys nods and holds her hand out towards Violet who has all the paperwork in her handbag. Should she have done that? Would that go against her? *It has been noted that Mrs Strong can, in fact, move her head. Therefore, she is deemed fit for work in a role where nodding would be a principal aspect of her role. PIP benefit denied.*

'Please could you sign here, Mrs Strong.' One of the receptionists hands Glenys a pen and exchanges meaningful glances with the others in the glass box when she takes it.

Shit, she can sign her name? Get this woman a job in admin at once.

Violet can hear what their eyes are saying. They're almost shouting it in people's faces. Letting them know about their complete lack of worth or usefulness. Did they know what people thought of them? What a waste of tax-payer's well-earned money, the bunch of fakers. Violet takes a deep breath as she and Glenys sit down. She watches a young girl as she hurries to the exit, fighting to take back her breath from the panic that stole it.

In the corner sits an elderly lady, slumped on her chair with pronounced scoliosis. Did she have a Claire or an Adam to advise her about the forms? Violet catches the woman's eye, and she smiles back at her. Her heartrate returns to normal just in time before Glenys' name is blasted across the waiting room for every pair of ears to hear.

There's not much to look at in the interview room. Just a pair of disapproving glasses sitting low on a suspicious, twitching nose. The nose belongs to the assessor who is sitting behind a desk that holds an ancient computer, a pencil and yet another bundle of forms.

'Don't be nervous,' the woman barks. 'Just relax and be as honest as possible. We're not here to catch you out, it's just a standard process. Everyone has to go through it, there are some chancers out there after all. I'm not implying that you're one of them, of course.'

Glenys scowls at the woman.

Violet wishes she could tap her heels together like Dorothy in *The Wizard of Oz* and just disappear.

'So how did you get here this morning?' the woman asks with a bright smile. Too bright. Far too many teeth.

Uuum ... Teleported? Apparated?

'By car. She's called Pat.' Glenys' voice comes out all gravelly.

'Uh-huh.' *Gotcha.* 'So driving isn't a problem then?'

'I drove her, actually,' Violet interjects.

The beaky nose is already scribble-scribing away with her squeaky-scratchy pencil.

'Erm – did you hear me?' Violet leans around the computer screen that seems to have been angled in front of her, shutting her out of the conversation.

'I'd just like to hear from your mum, if that's okay. It's not you who's being assessed.' Polite, frosty, dismissive words.

Glenys is slumped in the chair, a faraway look on her face, the one that always comes out when she's feeling especially stressed.

'How do you manage day to day – personal hygiene,

cooking, housework?' The woman peers at Violet's mum. 'I see you've just been able to take off your own cardigan?'

Glenys is staring at the *in case of fire* notice. Violet wonders if she's going to manage to say anything at all. 'Fine. All fine.' She doesn't even blink.

'She doesn't mean fine. She isn't fine.' Violet's words sound shriller than a car alarm. If Glenys doesn't get her PIP reinstated, Violet won't qualify for Carer's Allowance. And if she can't work because she's looking after her mum, what on earth are they supposed to live on?

'Miss Strong, I'm going to have to ask you to allow your mother to speak for herself. It says on the application that she's perfectly able to.'

Violet closes her eyes.

Claire had warned her this might happen. *Carers and advocates get shouted down and ignored all the time,* she'd said. *Tell them every struggle, every detail. How things are on a bad day. Leave no stone unturned.* Her voice coaches Violet from inside her mind and joins in with a more familiar mantra.

Be more Anne.

'Mum's having a bad day today.' Violet stands up so that she's on full view again. 'So, I'm afraid you're going to have to listen to me.'

This carer will *not* be silenced. Not today.

'Just getting out of the house is a struggle for Mum, and having to come here today is one of the toughest things she's had to do in a while. That's why she's so shaken up and won't talk. So, I will have to tell you instead.' Violet runs through the list of every obstacle her mum faces every day. 'Mum has days when her depression holds her to her chair and doesn't let her speak. There's chaos and voices in her mind caused by her schizophrenia, and she suffers daily with pain and stiffness from the injury to her hips and lower back …' Violet pauses for breath.

The woman is tap-tapping away on her keyboard, trying to keep up. Her face is blank, not an expression in sight, she probably hears this stuff every day. But for the first time, Violet sees – really sees this time – what life is like day to day for her mum. She's been so busy focussing on her own guilt, her own *poor me* thoughts, she hasn't once allowed herself to view things through Glenys' slightly scratched lenses.

'She's had to battle so much.' Violet finds herself whispering. She looks at her mum and manages a smile. 'She can be a cantankerous old bat, but I don't know if I could cope with everything life has thrown at her and keep on going.'

Glenys' mouth twitches and she looks directly at the assessor for the first time. 'She's right. Everything she just said. So, shove that up your—'

'You'll get a decision within thirty working days,' says the woman.

Glenys and Violet just about make it into the car park before Violet surrenders to a fit of giggles. 'What were you going to tell her to shove? And where? My goodness, Mum. That definitely wasn't on the list of things we'd prepared to say.'

By the time they reach Pat's passenger door, Glenys is shuddering, her shoulders are going up and down and a strange noise is coming from her.

Violet whips around in front so she can see her face.

Glenys is laughing. Proper, actual laughter is rattling her slender body. Violet can't help but join in, even though nothing is really that funny. Perhaps it's the relief from getting through the tense appointment, or maybe it's the sudden narrowing of the chasm between them. Whatever it is, Glenys' face has tears rolling down it and she's clutching onto Violet's arm to keep herself upright.

Both Violet and Glenys are still chuckling when Pat reaches the outskirts of Brighton.

'You did a good job in there,' Glenys says in a gap between songs on Radio Sussex. 'It would've been worse without you.'

It's the first time Violet has ever heard her mum say thank you.

'I'm so tired.' Glenys' eyes are beginning to droop. She and Violet have just finished their dinner in the living room in companionable silence.

'Have a little read on the sofa. I'll make us a cuppa.' Violet doesn't want her mum to fall asleep, not just yet. Not when they've spent the last few hours since Glenys' PIP appointment in a rare afternoon of harmony. She might well wake up far away again and the precious moments of having her mum back will be lost.

By the time she returns from the kitchen, Glenys is holding her book open on her lap and her eyes are closed.

'Mum?' Violet places the mug down on the coffee table beside her.

'Still awake.' Glenys' words are slightly slurred. 'You could read to me instead.'

Violet perches next to her and picks up the book.

'Not that one.'

'Which one?' Violet's confused.

'You know which one. *Our* book. Our Anne.'

Violet's chest fills with warmth. She remembers the nights of reading together by the fire. *One more page, Mummy.* Mum retelling Violet's favourite scenes as she tucked her in at night. They both knew *Anne of Green Gables* back to front and inside out by the time Violet was eleven. They used to spend hours together with their books before everything went so horribly wrong.

'My only copy of that is back at ho— back in Manchester,' Violet says. 'And given my old bedroom doesn't exist any- more, I doubt my old book stash is still lurking around.'

'That one is,' Glenys murmurs. 'Kept it. It's in my bedside cabinet. Couldn't throw it away. It's *our* book. Our Anne.'

And sure enough when Violet goes to look, there it is. Violet's throat tightens as she strokes the dog-eared cover with her thumb. A tear lands on one of Anne Shirley's red braids, the same shade as her own.

A contented smile stretches across Glenys' face as Violet starts to read, transporting them both all the way to Avonlea. All the way to happier times, happier places.

Glenys starts to snore, but Violet carries on and on, smiling to herself when she still pictures Gilbert Blythe as Adam. Her Adam. Same hair, same face, same smile. Same ridiculous butterflies in Violet's tummy.

Three loud knocks on the door drag Violet back from Green Gables. She jumps up and opens it.

'I need chicken soup,' Tammy wipes her brow with her forearm as she enters the room.

'I'm sick. Really sick.' Drama oozes from Tammy's voice.

'Poor thing. I'll grab you a paracetamol. And I've got a tin of soup you can take back up with you.'

Tammy blinks as if Violet's just slapped her. 'But I'm sick. Someone has to make it for me – like we did for Mrs Robson. Like Mum did for me.'

Violet glances at Glenys, still asleep on the sofa, and nods. 'Won't be long, Mum,' she says in a low voice.

No answer. Violet grabs her keys and her phone. She's almost certain she hears Glenys mutter something under her breath before she closes the door but when she looks back, her mum's eyes are closed.

Tammy's skin is hot to touch and her eyes are bloodshot. Violet tucks her up on the sofa with a dressing gown and heats the soup through. She sits by Tammy and watches the second half of *Coronation Street* before slinking back downstairs.

'Oh, it's you.' Glenys is awake and her voice has all its starch back in it. Her eyes have hardened, and she won't look at Violet.

Who else did she think it would be – Jodie? Does Glenys still wish Jodie were there instead of Violet?

'I'm going to bed,' Glenys snaps as she pulls herself up with her frame and makes her way to her bedroom without a backwards glance. 'You might as well go back upstairs again. Wouldn't want your new friend to be left on her own.'

It had been wonderful having her mum back for a few hours. Claire warned her about how hard this part of caring can be. She'd told Violet how quickly Abbas' moods can change, and that it doesn't take much for a good day to turn into a bad one.

Well, it was lovely while it lasted. All good things come to an end. Violet should know that by now.

CHAPTER 23

Tammy

TAMMY IS FREEZING. SHE'S in bed and she can't stop shivering, even with her Manchester City duvet and an extra duvet on top of her. How is her skin staying so hot when her insides are so cold? Her nose feels too full to let much air through it and her throat feels like it's been stung with nettles. She'd fallen into a whole load of them once, just after they left Dad's house for the last time.

Her ears make a buzzing sound all of their own. She rolls over and leans on her other side. The noise isn't coming from inside. It's the door buzzer.

She floats towards the intercom by her door; her legs have disappeared. Tammy can't feel anything, only her scratchy throat and chattering jaw. It takes effort just to lift the receiver. 'Hello?'

Silence. Followed by a strange crackling.

Goosebumps prick up on the backs of Tammy's arms. She knows that sound, it happens in all the spooky films. The sound of ghosts when they're recorded.

A blurry picture fills her mind. The wall by the intercom

is wobbling around and funny lights and shapes move around in Tammy's eyes. She blinks them away and concentrates instead on the blurry picture until it's clearer than what's in front of her.

A face. Twinkling blue eyes and a mouth that's moving as it makes silent words.

Mum's face.

Mum's words.

Tammy's heartbeat is everywhere, all over her body. Pounding in her arms, her feet, her ears. She closes her eyes and peers at her mum's red lips. What's she saying?

I'm outside.

Tammy drops the receiver. She fumbles with the door handle and moves down the stairs. She's still floating like she's in a dream. She's not, but how is this possible?

'There's a lot you don't know about the world, and a lot you don't need to know,' Mum always said. Maybe this is something she just doesn't know about. People come back from heaven.

I'm outside.

Tammy opens the heavy door to Malvern House and stands on the doorstep. The shivering is out of control and none of her bones will stay still. It makes it hard to walk.

Keep going.

It's getting dark outside, and it's cold. So cold. Tammy blinks hard as she crunches across the gravel. She walks through the gap in the wall and onto the pavement and then she sees her.

A figure at the bottom of the hill. Just a blurred blob from this far away but it's her. Tammy just needs to get closer.

She keeps moving. Past the shop, past the bakers. She stops outside the boarded-up pub. No sign of Mum. Where is she?

Tammy turns towards the park, following the flicker in the corner of her eye. The park is covered in a thick fog. Or is it just her blurry eyes?

Tammy's through the park gate. She's going the right way; she keeps glimpsing it through the fog. Mum's hat. She'd been wearing it that day when she went to the shop. And there's her brown handbag.

Almost there.

Tammy stumbles towards the sandpit.

Mum turns around. Her face glows, and she opens her arms. 'My girl. My one and only.' Same old smile, same old clothes she had on last time.

No more shaking or shivering. Gliding forwards into Mum's arms takes no effort at all. Her arms are so solid. So real. Tammy buries her head in the crook of her mum's neck, inhaling the sweetness of her perfume. The tears fall.

'Everything's all right. You're safe now, Mummy's here.' Mum's finger strokes Tammy's face, taking a tear with it. 'It's just you and me. It's always been just you and me.'

The shivering's back. The whooshing in Tammy's ears gets louder and everything goes dark.

Every part of Tammy's body aches. It's the first thing she notices when she wakes up. She's warmer than before and wrapped up in something thick and soft. Something tickles her ear.

'Thirty-nine point two. At least it's coming down.' A male voice.

Tammy tries to open her eyes. They're heavy and it's so bright.

'That's good. I called 111. They said to call back if her temperature doesn't come down. Oh, and we need to take the duvet away. Too many layers make it worse apparently.' Violet's voice.

Tammy's shoulders relax. Violet's voice sounds like music. She grips the edge of her duvet and pulls it tighter. The warmth feels so good after all that shivering.

Then the warmth is wrenched away. A cold draught wraps itself around Tammy. She opens her eyes, properly this time.

Three faces loom over her. Violet, Adam, Chrissie.

Mum is nowhere to be seen.

'Well, hello, young lady. You're awake.' Chrissie crouches down and takes hold of Tammy's hand. 'How are you feeling? You gave us all a fright, wandering around the village in your PJs and nothing on your feet.'

Tammy peers over the top of Chrissie's head. They're in her flat. 'M-mum. She was here. Well, not here, but outside. With me.' The wobble in her voice is probably from all that shivering. Why can't she stop? 'Where's Mum now? What's going on?'

Violet, Adam, and Chrissie all take turns to look at each other and pull worried faces.

'Chrissie found you in the park. She was out for a walk with Luna,' Violet carries on. 'And she saw you in a crumpled heap in the sandpit. You're not very well, I think you may have flu.'

Tammy swallows. It hurts.

'You were talking, but you couldn't seem to hear what I was saying,' Chrissie says. 'I couldn't just leave you on the cold ground, so I put out an SOS on the WhatsApp group and Adam and Violet came and carried you home between them.'

Violet pulls a strand of hair away from Tammy's face. 'I'm so sorry. I think because you're poorly, you were seeing things that weren't there. It's what happens when you get such a high temperature, you can get confused.'

Tammy pushes Violet's hand away and sits up. The duvet is at the bottom of her bed. She grabs it and lies back down, pulling it up to her chin.

'We really need to keep that duvet off you,' says Violet. 'Can we take her temperature again?'

Another poke in the ear.

'Thirty-eight point one. Still high but much better,' Adam says.

'I guess you can keep the duvet.' Violet's chewing on her own bottom lip.

'I know I can. It's not up to you.' Tammy's jaw is tight, like it needs oiling. 'You're not my mum.'

Violet's face goes paler and she looks at the floor. Tammy shouldn't be talking to her like that. She shouldn't be angry with Violet. But it's like Violet chased Mum away.

'Death is a strange old thing.' Chrissie puts a warm hand on Tammy's shoulder, making it relax beneath her touch. 'I see glimpses of Fred sometimes. And I hear his voice. I know he's gone, but perhaps he finds little ways to say hi. I'm sure your mum would like to do the same. There are lots of things in life we'll never know for sure.'

Tammy puts a clammy hand on top of Chrissie's. 'Please can you stay with me?'

'Of course I will, love.'

'I can stay if you need to get home,' says Violet.

'It's fine. You get back – your mum might need you. And same for you and your dad, Adam. Tammy and I will be fine, just the two of us.'

'Just the two of us,' whispers Tammy as she falls all the way back to sleep.

CHAPTER 24

Violet

THE VILLAGE IS GENTLY rumbling to life. The birds have been awake for hours when the shop shutters clatter open, and so has Violet. Her legs are numb and tingly from sitting on the bench, waiting to buy the coffee she'd run out of.

Chrissie has updated the WhatsApp group to let everyone know that Tammy slept well and is doing much better.

Thank goodness Adam had been there to help last night too. He'd been so calm and brilliant with Tammy as he'd strode purposefully towards Malvern House, helping Violet carry her home. Tammy's stricken face is still imprinted on Violet's mind. What would have happened if Chrissie hadn't found her in the park? She could have been there all night with no one to help her.

Tammy needs more. Deserves more. What if she has to leave the village when the building sells because there's nowhere else for her to go? Who will look out for her then?

There's only one thing for it. Violet slips her phone from her pocket and scrolls to the number she'd saved in her contacts. Edward Raynott's brewery.

The phone goes to voicemail. *Damn.* Violet buys her coffee and makes her way back to Malvern House, deep in thought and searching for other ways to track down some of Tammy's family.

She almost bumps headlong into a jogger as she walks around the corner by the phone box, and her heart does a double flip. Adam.

'You're mad, running in this heat,' Violet teases.

'What are you doing out so early – Glenys having a lie-in?'

'Coffee emergency. I'm on way back to her now.'

'I'll walk back with you.' Adam lifts the hem of his T-shirt and mops the sweat from his brow, giving Violet a glimpse of his torso.

'Thank you for helping with Tammy last night. Couldn't have done it without you.' Violet forces herself to look away. 'Goodness knows what would have happened if she'd been left on her own.'

'Does she not have any family at all?'

'I've been trying to find that out. She's a little cagey about it and I don't like to push her too much with questions.'

'Maybe she has good reason to be. Perhaps they're not good people.' Adam slows his pace.

'Possibly. But I'm not sure if her mum has made her fearful of them. It seems like she wanted to keep Tammy hidden away – almost like she didn't want to share. I thought it would be wise to try and track them down and sus them out myself. I think I might have found her father – Edward Raynott. He owns a brewery in Brighton. Tried to call but it went to voicemail.'

Adam shakes out his shoulders and a grin lights up his face. 'I have an idea.'

★

'Are you sure you don't want to come to Brighton with Adam and I?' Violet asks Glenys as they eat their breakfast.

Adam had already planned to take Bill there for the day. It's going to be a scorcher and he's packed his people carrier up with beach chairs, a windbreak and plenty of snacks. Lots of room for Glenys' wheelchair next to Bill's. They should all go, he'd said. Then they could pop to the brewery on the way home and see if they can speak to Edward Raynott in person.

'No thank you,' Glenys says stiffly as she tucks into her breakfast.

'But Adam and his dad are our neighbours. It might be nice to spend some time with them. And you always used to get on so well with Bill.' Violet bites her mouth closed. Stupid thing to say. They'd got on well *before*.

'They won't want me there.' Glenys pushes her plate away, half a slice of toast untouched.

A knock at the door makes Glenys flinch.

Adam and Bill. Two huge smiles and a boatload of energy between them. Violet had never noticed how alike they look until now, although Bill's eyes have the edge on levels of twinkling.

'I'm really sorry – Mum doesn't feel up to it, and I can't really leave her on her own,' Violet says. Disappointment leaks into her voice.

'Erm, I can speak for myself, thanks very much,' Glenys shouts through the door with surprising force. 'I will come – just let me finish my tea.'

'Mrs Strong, you are looking wonderful this morning. Your carriage awaits.' Adam gives a ridiculously low bow towards Glenys when she eventually makes it through the front door, and he gestures towards the window. 'Look at that sunshine – you must've put a word in for us to get decent weather on a Saturday.'

The lines around Glenys' mouth soften. She's trying not to smile. 'I'll need to sit in the front. I get car sick,' she says.

Violet heaves Glenys' wheelchair into the boot of the car. Glenys manages fine with her frame around the house but walking around Brighton would result in an excessive amount of pain afterwards. Twenty minutes later, they are trundling along the coast road; Adam and Glenys in the front of the car and Bill and Violet in the back.

'He's over the moon to have you back,' Bill whispers, nodding towards the back of Adam's head.

Violet's heart beats harder as so many emotions jostle inside of it. How could Bill bear to be in the same car as her, let alone be so kind and smiley? She'd taken someone dearest to him. She plays his words again in her head. *Over the moon to have you back.*

Great to have you back in the village.

Adam genuinely does seem to want her around, and Bill doesn't seem to bear any ill will towards her. Perhaps the people who need to forgive Violet the most are the remaining two people inside of this car.

Thanks to Bill's blue badge, Adam's able to park near the seafront. Other drivers in the car park glance at their car, looking away when they see Adam pulling the wheelchairs out, satisfied they're worthy of a disabled bay.

Glenys says nothing as they slowly move down the path towards the pebbles, and she remains silent for the first half-hour of sitting on the beach, but Violet doesn't mind the quiet. Bill and Adam are silent too and the hush of the group makes it easier for her to relax as she listens to the slosh of the sea against the base of the pier, the sound of waves against stones and the shouts of children as they paddle in the water. Jangly music from amusement arcades and the rides on the pier crackles enticingly.

Violet pulls off her sandals and wiggles her toes, every part of her unwinding as the wind whips her hair from her face. She's missed this over the years, the taste of salt on her lips and the collective smell of sun cream, cigarettes, and fresh doughnuts.

'Fancy a paddle, anyone?' Adam pulls off his trainers.

'Not for me, son. You two young-uns go in. Glenys and I can have a nice catch-up.'

Glenys purses her lips and stares at the pier.

'Not sure about leaving those two alone. I wouldn't wish Mum on anyone when she's in a bad mood,' Violet says in a low voice once she and Adam reach the water's edge.

'It'll do them both good to spend time together. They always used to get on and they're neighbours after all.'

Violet dips a toe in the water. The sudden chill is a good distraction from old memories and the mental picture of Bill's notice of eviction letter in the pocket of her handbag. Neighbours for now at least.

'Come on. You can get in faster than that,' Adam teases. He overtakes her, taking huge strides into the sea until the water is higher than his knees, the waves lapping against the bottom of his rolled-up shorts.

'It's the pebbles.' Violet knows she sounds whiny. 'They hurt my feet. It's okay for you, with your posh swimming shoes.

And I only said I'd paddle; I'm not going all the way in with these clothes on.'

Adam grins. Violet knows the look, it's the same one he always got when they were kids and he was about to dare her to do something. She never backed down, not once. And neither did he.

'I guess I'll just have to carry you in, then.' Adam scoops her up and moves deeper into the sea, pretending to drop her into the waves.

Uncontrollable laughter wells up inside Violet – the shock of being swept up and hovered over the water whilst fully clothed, mixing with the reckless thrill of being played with and teased. No one had done that for so many years. No one had been close enough.

Adam's very close. His arms all around her, her shoulder against his bare chest.

She braves a peek up at him and his face mirrors her own laughter. The crinkles around his eyes are deep as he narrows them against the glare of the sun. The same sun that's bringing out those gleaming flecks of burnt orange inside the pale green of his eyes.

Adam shifts his gaze towards her face and catches her looking. The laughter disappears from his face.

That mouth. So close to Violet's. So …

The world flies backwards and Violet's insides plummet downwards half a second before the rest of her follows. She gasps as the freezing water envelops her and her lungs fill with water. Panic grips her and she clasps hard onto something flesh-like, possibly an arm or a leg as she flails about, trying to flip herself over and swim.

The water disappears as she's heaved up from the sea. Violet coughs and coughs, blinking the water from her stinging eyes. She's being held again by a very red-faced Adam.

'Shit. Didn't mean to drop you – that wave knocked me off balance. You okay?' He looks as if he can't decide whether to laugh or cry now that Violet's eyes are open. 'I'm so sorry.'

Laughter erupts from Violet. She's more than okay. Her clothes are stuck to her, there's seaweed stuck around her ankles and she's shivering in the sunlight.

And she hasn't felt this okay for a very long time.

'Oh, shit. Your clothes – you're soaked. I'm so sorry,' he repeats. His eyes flicker over her and he looks away, his face a deeper shade of red.

Violet looks down at herself, bits of her poking out at all angles courtesy of her clinging, pale and now very see-through, dripping dress. She scrambles out of Adam's arms and stands in the sea, wincing as her feet meet the sharp stones. 'I forgive you,' she says, still laughing. 'But don't think I've forgotten, and I *will* get you back one day.' She cups both hands under the water and flicks it towards him. It's rather ineffective as he's already soaking wet, but she does watch the droplets as they land on his chest and trickle down his torso.

'I don't doubt it for a second. You never were one to let things slide.' Adam smiles. He takes Violet's hand as she stumbles back to the shore and they tiptoe back up the beach.

Bill and Glenys are deep in conversation. Glenys is laughing. Real, actual laughter.

It's as if she's been swapped with a long-ago version of herself. Violet can't stop staring.

Adam reaches down and pulls a towel from his bag, discreetly passing it to Violet.

'Oh, hello. Nice paddle, both of you?' Glenys turns back towards Bill without even a glance at Violet's wet clothes.

'See,' Adam murmurs in Violet's ear. 'Told you a day out was a good idea.'

CHAPTER 25

Violet

AFTER A COUPLE OF hours of drying out on the beach, followed by a walk along Brighton Pier and a surprisingly competitive game on some slot machines between Glenys and Adam, it's decided that a fish and chip lunch is in order.

The Groove café is light and bright and full of people, but Bill spots an empty table by the jukebox and makes a beeline for it.

To anyone else in the restaurant, she realises, they probably look like a family. The F word holds too many emotions for Violet. Guilt, longing. Unworthiness.

But family should mean other things too. Fun, Love. Laughter.

As Anne says: 'Life is worth living, as long as there's a laugh in it.'

'Do you two fancy staying a bit longer for a coffee whilst Violet and I go for a little walk around?' Adam wipes his mouth after they've finished eating.

'We'll be fine.' Bill smiles. 'We'll have a gossip about you two.'

Glenys has slumped a little and is staring hard at a picture on the wall of a 1960s Brighton street. She doesn't look up at Violet or say goodbye.

'I'm not sure if I should ...'

'They'll be fine.' Adam takes her hand as they walk out of the door. 'Dad will call me if there's a problem. They're adults. Just because we're their carers, doesn't mean we're in charge.'

Adam's words play on repeat in Violet's mind as they wander up the road. He's been doing this a lot longer than Violet; he knows what he's talking about.

'How do you do that, though – be a carer, but remember you're not the one in charge? I can't ever seem to get the balance right.'

'Practice.' Adam grins. He points to a street sign. 'Here we are – is that the road we're looking for? Raynott's brewery should be down here on the left.'

The brewery is less impressive on the outside than it looked on the website. Peeling paint on the walls, a rusty sign and windows crusted with salt and dirt.

Violet's heart speeds up when a woman buzzes them into reception.

Edward Raynott is all smiles and neat, straw-coloured hair. 'Are you here for a tour or to place an order?' Professional, friendly, calm. It's only when Violet peers closer she can see the bloodshot eyes and the dark circles beneath them.

'We're here about Lydia Raynott,' Violet says in a low voice.

Edward's face pales, making his freckles stand out. He glances at the woman on reception.

'We'll just be in the office.' He beckons Violet and Adam to follow him up a draughty corridor and into a drab room that reeks of hops.

'Are you journalists?' he asks, wheeling chairs towards them both. 'I don't know how much help I'll be. I hadn't seen her for nearly nineteen years before she died, although I did make it to the funeral. You do know we were divorced?'

Violet looks at Adam. 'We're not journalists.' She introduces herself and Adam and describes them both as just *locals*. 'It's not just Lydia we're here about. It's about your daughter, Tammy.'

'She's not mine. Tamara's not my daughter.' Edward's words come out in such a rush; Violet barely had time to finish her sentence.

'I thought she was,' he slows his words down. 'Right until just after she was born. Then she left with the baby, and presumably *him*. The actual father. Never heard from her after that, except through lawyers.'

The yeast smell from the brewery is thickening in Violet's throat and the whir of the fan is vibrating in her ears. 'I'm sorry. I don't mean to drag up your past or pry into your personal life. We're neighbours of hers. We're just trying to help …*Tamara* to track down her family after losing her mum. She doesn't remember any grandparents …'

'Lydia was estranged from her parents. They weren't good people.'

'Ah. And I don't like to ask, but it seems there hasn't been a father around for many years. Do you know who he is or where we might find him?' Violet shifts about in her seat on the itchy material.

Edward cracks his knuckles and Adam winces.

'I'm afraid I have no idea. She wouldn't tell me, and none of her friends seemed to know anything either. She just disappeared. And that was that.' He shrugs.

Adam clears his throat. 'Is there anything else you could tell us about her? Where she worked? Places she liked to go?'

Edward shakes his head. 'Sorry. She was a waitress all the time I knew her, though. She loved it – never wanted to do anything else. She didn't seem bothered by the crap tips and the aching feet. She just loved people.'

Violet thinks back to what Tammy had said about the two of them only having each other. Something big must have happened for her to want to hide her daughter away from the world, especially if she was the people-person Edward's describing.

'Thank you for speaking with us.' Violet holds out an awkward hand for him to shake. 'And sorry again if we brought up difficult memories.'

'Well, that's not much to go on,' Adam says on the way back to the café. 'All we know really is that Tammy's mum used to be a waitress – and that Edward Raynott isn't her father.'

'It's something. And thank you for coming with me – it's been quite a day.'

Adam's dimple comes out as he smiles. 'It sure has. First of many, I hope.'

CHAPTER 26

Tammy

TAMMY SWITCHES THE HOOVER off and smiles at her tidy flat. The social worker will be here soon, and she wants the place to look nice.

'Are you sure you don't want me to help?' Violet is watching Tammy from the sofa. 'It's only been a week since you were laid up with the flu.'

'I'm fine, I'm all better, and I like doing it.'

Violet keeps looking at Tammy like she wants to say something else. 'Did your mum used to go to work?' she asks after Tammy's finished putting the hoover away.

'At night, she did. Three times a week,' Tammy says. 'She got people their drinks and they gave her money.'

'Do you know what the place was called – where she worked?'

Tammy wrinkles her nose and tries to remember. 'She just called it work. She said, I'm going to work, bye. And then she left. She said it was near the pier, though.'

'Did she have to wear a special uniform?'

'Yes. Green with a black stripe across the top. From here to here.' She demonstrates with her hand.

The door buzzer blares.

Tammy looks at Violet unsure of what to do.

'Go on — you answer it. It's your flat,' Violet says. 'Just because I help you sometimes, it doesn't mean I'm in charge.'

Tammy's tummy flutters when she hears the man's voice in the intercom. What will he think when he sees her? Will he be pleased with how well she's been doing or angry about all the trouble she's caused with the shoplifting and letting those people into her flat? Mum always said if Tammy didn't behave or if she did anything dangerous, someone from Social Services might take her away.

'I'm doing very well,' Tammy says when the man with a *Steve* badge walks through the door.

'That's good, Tammy.' Steve sticks out his hand and smiles. 'Today's really just about having a chat so I can see if you need any extra help. Is it okay if I sit?' He points to the space on the sofa next to Violet.

'I'm Violet.' Violet and Steve shake hands.

He has thin blond hair and funny glasses. He opens his briefcase and asks Tammy how she's been.

'I can make coffee. Violet showed me how.' Tammy leaps up and puts the kettle on.

'Tammy's been working really hard to improve her independence and living skills,' Violet says.

Steve and Violet talk in quiet voices whilst Tammy pours the kettle. Steve isn't quite managing to be quiet enough because Tammy can still hear him.

'So, Tammy's been improving?' he asks. 'I assumed because we were called that she's actually in need of more support?'

Tammy puts the drinks down on the coffee table a bit too hard and one of them spills over the side of the cup.

'It's been a tricky time for Tammy. Lots of changes,' says Violet.

Between them, Tammy and Violet tell Steve about all that's been going on. Tammy lets him know about how she ran out of electric and couldn't watch *Coronation Street*, and he sits forward.

Tammy's tears sting her eyes when she talks about Mum. 'I miss her. It was just her and me. Mum and me against the world, she used to say.'

Violet starts talking about the shoplifting and Tammy looks at the carpet, wishing her face would stop burning.

Steve pulls out lots of pages of questions. Most of them have four possible answers for Tammy to choose from so that he can *assess Tammy's level of need*. It's a bit like playing *Who Wants to Be a Millionaire?* but less fun. Some of the questions are a bit tricky to answer, so she just picks 'D' for those ones.

When the last question has been asked, Steve gathers his papers into a briefcase and heaves himself up off the sofa.

'We'll be in touch,' he says. 'I'll see what I can do about arranging some support, but it probably won't be for some time as you don't appear to be in too much of a crisis. I'll pop you on the waiting list and keep you posted.'

Tammy looks down at the floor. No words want to come out of her.

Violet follows Steve out of the door, leaving it a tiny bit open.

Tammy tiptoes across the room and presses her ear next to the gap in the doorway.

Violet is talking in a low voice. 'It's been a long time since she's had any help from anyone except her mum and there seems to be a few things that don't quite add up about Tammy's past. I'm aware she has learning difficulties, but she seems to have made so much progress in terms of what she can do for herself in such a short space of time. I'm beginning to wonder if she was so dependent and needed support because she'd never been shown how to do things. When I took her shopping, it appeared as if she'd never been to the shops before, so it seems like she's barely been outside since she was a child.'

Steve frowns. 'Mmm. I'll pass that on to any support workers she may get allocated. Okay?'

Tammy probably shouldn't be listening. They're whispering now. But if they're saying things about her, she should be allowed to hear what they're saying. She catches words like *vulnerable* and *taking advantage*.

'I'll be in touch.' Steve's face looks softer when he says goodbye.

'And in the meantime, I'll try and keep an eye and make sure she doesn't let any more strangers into her flat,' Violet says.

Tammy won't be doing that; she's learned her lesson. Not everyone you meet can be your friend but thank goodness for friends like Violet.

CHAPTER 27

Tammy

TAMMY IS FLOATING. EVERYTHING weighs less than usual. She'd had a bath earlier, and the feel of the warm wind drying her still-damp hair as it blows behind her fills her with energy. Like she can do anything. The stress of her meeting with Steve yesterday has lifted off her and drifted up to the white puffy clouds.

She skips along the pavement beside Chrissie. Chrissie is taking her to the library so she can help Tammy learn how to read a bit better.

'Not *better*,' Chrissie says when Tammy brings it up as they walk past the park. 'Just more joyfully. Reading for pleasure instead of achievement is the point. We just need to find out what you like.'

'How many books will I be allowed to take out of the library?' Tammy asks when they get close to the red doors of the small brick building.

'Six at a time. But we still have to carry them home.'

Last time Tammy was in a library she was seven. She and Mum had been soaked through from the rain and they had two small suitcases with them. Mum kept crying and making phone calls until they had somewhere to stay. Tammy had read *Hairy Maclary from Donaldson's Dairy* nine times until she knew it word for word. She'd always been a good reader even though she hardly ever went to school.

This library has the same smell as the last one. There are lots of windows and armchairs beside the shelves. She heads for the books in the boxes beside the beanbags, but Chrissie points her towards the shelf next to the boxes. It says *Young Adult* on a sign at the top.

'You might like these ones,' Chrissie says. 'Choose any you like, and we can take your ID to Mrs R at the desk and get your library card.' Chrissie's voice is turned up at the edges and her tone has changed; it's like she's singing the words. She says it's because libraries are her happy places.

Two other ladies have just come in. They look like women from adverts or the shiny front covers of the magazines Tammy's mum used to buy. They keep whispering to each other and giggling.

'Hello, Kirsty,' Chrissie says to one of them when they get closer. She doesn't sound like she's singing now. Her words sound like they'd rather not come out at all. Chrissie walks off towards the desk where Mrs Robson is standing.

Tammy runs her finger along the spines of the books. *Sweet Valley High, Twilight, The Hunger Games*. She pulls one from the shelf and starts to read the back of it. She can't concentrate on the words. All she can hear are the ones coming from the two ladies – they think they're whispering in their inside voices but they're not doing a very good job.

'Can't believe Violet came back to the village,' one of them says. 'How can she show her face around here after what she did?'

'Lowerstone hasn't been the same since,' the other one says. 'Never recovered from the fire. All those people out of work. And her own father – bet Violet's mum can't even look at her. And that's not even counting what she did to your Adam's poor mum.'

'He's not my Adam anymore.'

'No, but he might be if his mum was still around. He might not have been lumbered with his dad. Still can't believe he chose him over you, not when there are so many nice nursing homes. My nan's one even has a hairdresser's.'

Violet has been telling Tammy she needs to mix more with people. That she'd spent too much time on her own and that life isn't always like *Coronation Street*. After what happened with those two shoplifters and now what these women are saying about Violet, perhaps lots of people are worth staying away from. Maybe her mum had been right after all. *People are trouble.*

'Well, one thing's for sure. Violet *Wrong* has a lot to answer for. And I'm sure one day, she will,' the woman with the red top on says. She picks up a book and Tammy turns back to the shelf in front of her before the ladies catch her staring. Violet's always telling her it's rude to stare.

Tammy picks up three books without looking at them and walks over to Chrissie. 'I'm glad Violet still shows her face around the village. I like it,' she says.

Chrissie looks at the two ladies and then back at Tammy. She squeezes Tammy's hand, and it feels nice. Only her mum has ever done that. She misses her mum's cuddles. Chrissie looks sad now, though. Tammy needs to find a way to bring back her smile and her sing-songy voice.

She also needs to make sure Violet doesn't have to answer for anything, like those people just said. It doesn't sound like it would be a nice thing. Tammy files away the words she heard so she can write them down when she gets home. Then she can maybe ask some questions of her own. Mrs Robson says that Lowerstone is a village and in villages, *people talk*. Surely people talk wherever they live, but perhaps some people might talk to Tammy – tell her what happened a long time ago. *Fire. Village out of work. Adam's mum. Violet's dad.*

Tammy waits until they've lugged their library books home and had lunch with Violet and Glenys. Then she says she's going up to her flat. Which isn't a lie – she does go up there, but just to get a pen and pencil from the kitchen drawer.

She tiptoes back down the stairs and closes the heavy front door quietly behind her. She doesn't want Violet or Chrissie to come with her – she needs to do this on her own.

The pharmacy has a huge queue outside of it. Tammy tries the bakery first.

'Sorry, love. Only lived here a few months. Don't know anyone called Violet.' The man is smiley and although he doesn't say any words that can be written in Tammy's reporter's (as elsewhere) notebook, he does give her a custard doughnut that he says needs using. Not everyone should be kept away from, especially not ones with baked goods that smell like heaven.

'I'm investigating a story,' Tammy says when she gets to the pharmacy. She's heard people who work for newspapers say that sort of thing a lot on TV. 'I'm looking into what happened with,' she has a look at the list she'd written down, so she doesn't forget anything, 'Violet, the fire, Violet's mum, Adam's dad and lots of people not going to work.'

The woman behind the counter is sorting out the packets of tablets on the shelf behind the counter. She has grey hair and a face that looks like it's been glaring at someone for most of its life.

'I'm afraid we don't talk to journalists in here. Patient confidentiality. If it's gossip you're after, I suggest you try the corner shop.'

Her voice matches her face, Tammy decides.

She tries something a little different in the corner shop. The woman in there looks a lot more fun, and she's wearing a T-shirt that says: *I bet you thought this would say something funny.*

'The lady in the pharmacy told me you're the best person to speak to for local gossip. It's to help Violet Strong – I'm here to clear her name.' Tammy stands up straight. Saying things like that makes her feel taller.

The woman in the T-shirt looks around the empty shop and at the door. 'You've come to the right place,' she says with a nod. 'I went to school with Violet. She didn't deserve what happened to her. Or how people treated her – bloody nasty they were, and she was only a kid.'

The woman behind the counter talks for a long time as Tammy scribbles in her notebook.

'Turned out afterwards, the insurance on the factory wasn't quite the ticket. The place never reopened. Half the village worked there, and it caused mayhem for a long time. After a while we lost the pub, then the community centre, some of the shops. No one had any money, see? So, people gave Violet and her family a hard time. As if she didn't have enough to deal with after losing her dad. And she was a kid. *A kid*, for goodness' sake. She may have caused a bit of trouble for a couple of years after that, but who could blame her, poor cow? I certainly didn't. She did put a brick through the window of the phone box, mind you, and I wasn't impressed with that. It was the only way I could call my boyfriend without my parents earwigging,' she adds when Tammy keeps scribbling.

Tammy crosses out the last couple of sentences. 'You've been very helpful.' She puts on her serious voice.

As soon as Tammy's back in her flat she copies out her notes into a report and makes it as neat as possible. She'll read it out at the next Helping Hands meeting this afternoon and soon all the village would know that what happened wasn't Violet's fault. Especially if it's true that *people talk*.

Maybe then, people will stop saying mean things about her friend Violet in libraries.

Chrissie's living room is overflowing with people and lots of them have to sit on the floor. Apparently, word has got around in the village since the last Helping Hands meeting, and now half of Lowerstone want to be in the club.

Tammy is wedged between Adam and Chrissie. Even though her legs shake every time she thinks about reading her report, this meeting doesn't feel as scary as the first one. She knows lots of people this time. A whole room of humans who want to help each other. She's been especially excited about this meeting because Adam had asked Violet to be in charge and Violet had said yes, if I must, but then smiled like she was secretly happy about it.

'I wanted to start by saying a huge thank you to everyone who signed up to the Helping Hands WhatsApp group.' Violet is sitting in the middle of the room holding a clipboard and her whole face is a smile. 'So many people have told me how helpful it's been already.'

'Ah, tell me about it,' says a woman Tammy hasn't seen before. 'Someone gave my son and me a lift to the clinic the other day when our taxi didn't turn up. We'd have missed it if it hadn't been for their kindness and we'd had to wait over a year for that appointment.'

One by one, people tell the group about how they'd been helped since the last meeting and everyone claps and smiles at each other. One lady says she's thankful to have made some new friends and she can't believe how kind people have been.

Tammy remembers what Violet told her about kind people: *There's probably more of them than we realise.*

'A couple of other things to mention.' Violet glances down at her clipboard. 'It might be an idea to do some fundraising. After chatting with some of you over the past few weeks and from looking at the WhatsApp group, I've realised just how many financial problems come up for carers and the people they look after – especially when there are issues with waiting for benefit payments. I'd like us to put together some emergency parcels for people who need them. Basic food and toiletries, cleaning products, that kind of thing.'

Everyone nods and tells Violet she's right and that it's a good idea. Then they all shout out ideas for ways to make money whilst Violet writes them down.

Beside Tammy, Adam isn't saying anything. He is watching Violet in that way people sometimes do in films, right before they kiss each other. It reminds Tammy of the number two on Violet's wish list. *True love.* It was really Tammy's wish for

Violet, but she'd still written it down, so it has to count for something.

'I have one other thing to run past you all,' Violet says. 'I have a blog – only a small one and it's mostly about books I'm reading. I was thinking about maybe starting another one for the Helping Hands Club? Any of us could add a post to it – a personal story, a poem …'

Chrissie stands up slowly and clears her throat. 'You could always combine your two ideas.'

Violet stares at Chrissie with questions in her eyes.

'How about instead of a blog, we could start up a village paper – a gazette for the locals? You were so good at running the school paper. You could put it online to start with and ask for donations from readers, then any money it makes can go towards the group's emergency fund.'

Violet leans forward in her seat so fast, her thick braids of hair swing around from behind her shoulders. 'Chrissie, you're a genius.'

Everyone claps and cheers, and Violet's eyes go all shiny. 'I think this will be good for all of us. It's something we can do that's not just about caring or needing to be cared for.'

'We could interview people from Lowerstone,' Bill says. 'So many stories are hidden away in our village, and that way, we can make sure everyone has the chance to be included.'

Abbas clears his throat and offers to write a piece about his mental health journey. 'Not sure it would be any good; I've never really written about it before, but I can give it a go. And if it helps someone else – well, then it will be worth the effort.' He shrugs.

Mrs Robson stands up. 'I have something to add.' She

casts a beady eye around the room to check everyone's looking at her. 'We could get local businesses on board to advertise with us once we've established it. I can think of a few who might be willing to pay a small fee.' She says lots of names. 'Not all of them are good at answering emails or returning calls, so we might need to pay them a visit in person – perhaps with biscuits.'

'That's fantastic,' Violet says. 'In the meantime, there's nothing to stop us planning our first online issues – we can send out paper copies once we have the funds.'

'And I guess we can print a few sneaky ones off in the library for those who can't wait and don't have internet access,' Mrs Robson says.

'Anyone got any ideas for names?' Violet asks.

'Let's keep it simple. The *Lowerstone Gazette*,' says Adam.

'Sounds good to me,' says Bill.

After a big *yes* vote, Violet writes down the name for the paper. Adam is still watching her with a soppy smile that makes Tammy want to giggle.

'Anyone else got ideas about what they'd like to do?' Violet asks. 'Anything you'd like to write about? There are plenty of other things to do for people who don't want to write. We'll need designs, artwork, someone to liaise with the local companies. Once we have paper copies, we'll need people to distribute them too.'

People all speak at once. Some throw forward article ideas and others volunteer for positions. Mrs Robson wants to be in charge of dealing with the businesses and Claire says she's good at doodling and is happy to come up with some designs.

'What about you, Chrissie?' Violet asks.

'I'm not quite sure.' Chrissie frowns. 'I want to help others in some way – offer a listening ear perhaps?'

'A problem page,' Claire yells from the back. 'You could be the agony aunt of Lowerstone.'

Chrissie opens her mouth, and for a minute, it looks as if she's going to say no. Tammy wouldn't blame her at all – other people's problems are sometimes really tricky, especially the ones people phone up about on *This Morning.*

'Okay.' A smile spreads across Chrissie's face. 'I'll do it – if you think I'm up to it.'

'We'll leave a box in the library for people to post their questions in,' Mrs Robson says. 'Safer that way. Best not give out Chrissie's name and address or people might start hounding her for advice. She'll have to think of an alias.'

'Those of you who want to write articles, I'll give you my email address so you can ping across your ideas,' Violet says.

'I've already written something very important that would be good for everyone in the village to know about. I was going to ask if I could read it today.' Tammy's heart is doing a weird dance inside her chest and her neck feels all sweaty.

'Excellent, Tammy. Go for it.' Violet's eyes are sparkly and her whole face is smiling.

Tammy hopes the smile is still there when she's finished reading.

CHAPTER 28

Violet

VIOLET WATCHES TAMMY PULL a crumpled piece of paper from the pocket of her jeans.

'The Factory Fire: An Investigation,' Tammy reads.

People often talk about cutting atmospheres with knives. Violet thinks a sledgehammer would be required to bludgeon its way through this one. The eyes of every person in the room flicker towards every other person's. Except Violet's. No one looks her way. If they did, they would see the sudden quiver in her hand and the lack of blood in her face. All of it has drained to her now-numb legs.

Tammy carries on after her dramatic pause. 'The fire took place at S.J. Strong's Paint Factory in the winter of 2003. Two people sadly died and a few more were injured. It happened on a Saturday, which was lucky, otherwise more staff would have been working.'

Not so lucky for the ones who were there.

Violet closes her eyes. She has to, she can't risk seeing Bill's or Adam's faces. Her stomach sloshes one way and then the other. She can't be sick, not here. And the path to the bathroom from where Violet is sitting is not an easy one to negotiate right now.

'It's wonderful that you've written something, Tammy, but I'm not sure if people need to hear any more. I'll help you find something else to write about.' Violet's trying to keep the smile on her face, but it's hard when her whole body is trembling.

'I'm sorry.' Tammy's face pales, and her eyes fill with tears that look giant behind her glasses. 'I didn't mean to upset anyone. I only wrote it so people would stop saying mean things about you, Violet.'

Violet holds her breath to calm her heart rate. 'It's okay. I'll tell everyone what happened. It's time I faced up to it.'

It was a freezing cold day two weeks before Christmas, but then it always was draughty at Malvern House. Violet pulled her Girls Aloud duvet from her bed to the sofa and huddled under it, gripping tight to her Gameboy Advance.

'I can hear you playing *BattleJar* under there.' Jodie's sharp voice pierced its way through Violet's makeshift fortress against the world. 'Mum said you're not allowed on your Gameboy until you've tidied your room.'

Violet turned the volume up on her game. Some things just weren't worth replying to.

'I know why you're glued to that thing,' Jodie carried on. 'You actually think you can beat my score. Good luck with that, I'm on level *nine*.'

Cowbag. Violet glanced at the top of her screen. *Level four.* 'Yeah, well, so am I nearly.'

An arm appeared under the duvet. Five fingers adorned with

chipped black nail polish came hurtling towards her Gameboy, trying to scoop it out of Violet's hand.

'Let me see, then.'

'No.' Violet tightened her grip and shoved her knee in the air.

'Ow!' Then a crash followed by, 'Mum! Violet just *attacked* me.'

As soon as Violet heard footsteps on the stairs, she peeled the duvet away and sat up, staring hard at her screen. 'No idea what she's talking about, I'm just sitting here playing my game.'

'Honestly, you two.' Violet's mum stomped over to the sofa and loomed over both sisters. 'Anyone would think you were four and seven, not fourteen and seventeen. This is exactly why I'm having second thoughts about the caravan this year.'

The Gameboy bleeped. Violet had five points to go and she'd be at level five. She pressed the left button to aim and fire. Almost there. That smug smile needed wiping off Jodie's face.

'Will you get your head *out* of that thing?' Mum's voice was as tired as her face was pale. She'd been up late, arguing with Violet's dad about the caravan, Violet had heard every word.

The Strong family spent every Christmas in Dorset, it was a tradition. Only this year, Mum didn't want to go. She'd been in one of her *moods* for weeks. Pacing the house at night, sleeping all day and forgetting to take off her dressing gown when she went to buy bread.

Dad had sorted it all out before he went to work that morning. He'd pulled Mum in for a hug in the kitchen and kissed her hair. 'We'll do whatever you like this Christmas. If you want to stay at home, then at home we shall stay. I just want you to get better, love.' He'd caught Violet watching and winked at her over the top of Mum's head.

That was how Dad was; he was a sorter-outer. A peace keeper. One look at his gentle smile always made Violet feel safe. No matter how bitchy her sister was being or how all over the place Mum was, Dad was the rock.

'Look after your mum today,' he'd whispered after walking out of the kitchen. 'I've got to pop into the factory.'

'Urgh. It's Saturday. Why do you have to go to work?' A groan had fallen out of Violet. A whole day on her own with Moody Mum and Jodie.

'You know what it's like this time of year,' he said.

Violet did know. Dad owned a paint factory right out at the edge of the village – nearly everyone in Lowerstone seemed to work there. People always bought paint right after Christmas so they could decorate in the new year when the walls looked bare, bereft of their tinsel. It meant the factory had to have extra supplies ready for the shops.

Adam's mum once told Violet that everyone liked working for her dad, because he always got stuck in and helped, even though he was the boss.

'Okay,' Violet murmured. 'I'll look after Mum. Just as long as you're home tomorrow.'

'I will be,' Dad had promised, before kissing Violet's head and walking out of the front door.

That was three hours ago, and Violet had already managed to upset her mum and her sister.

'Sorry, Mum.' Her finger hovered over the off button, but then it bleeped again. *You have reached level five.* 'Yessss!'

Violet's mum rested a hand on her hip and her shoulders sagged forward as if someone had let some of the air out of her. 'Your dad's forgotten his lunch. Violet, you can come with me to take it down to him. I'll take ours as well and we can eat it together whilst he's on his break.'

Violet looked down at her screen. Another couple of hours and she might get to level six. 'Can't I just stay here?'

'Nope. I'm not leaving you two on your own to scream and fight.'

'Why can't Jodie go?' Violet muttered as she got up and started looking around the room for her charger. If she was going, she was at least taking it with her. It was in the sideboard drawer. She shoved it in her mini rucksack along with the Gameboy and followed her mum out of the door.

Most of Violet's sulking melted away when she saw her dad's face light up.

'What a lovely surprise,' he said, taking the lunchbox from Mum's hand. He let Violet play on her game whilst they ate lunch. *Just this once.*

The battery was low, so she'd plugged it in and sat on the office floor next to the socket with her back against the wall as Mum and Dad went back and forth again about where to spend Christmas.

All Violet wanted was to get to level six.

Every eye from the Helping Hands Club is focussed on Violet. The silence is full of held breaths.

'It spread so quickly because of all the paint chemicals,' Violet carries on. 'If it had happened during the week, half the estate might have been killed.'

Violet's memories are eighteen years old now, but their edges are just as sharp. They cut through her defences as if they're made of paper.

The coffin at the front of the church. The hushed whispers. Mum staring forwards; not speaking, not hearing, not seeing.

She'd almost got to level six by the time Mum said they had to leave. She sulked about having to turn the game off. She ripped the wire free from the Nintendo.

This is the exact second of her life she revisits every night in her dreams and several times during the waking hours of each day. Just one glance back at the wall was all it would have taken. She'd have remembered to unplug the charger.

Another funeral had taken place the same week as Dad's. Adam's mum had been working in the storeroom next door. A faulty fire alarm and late insurance payments meant the factory was never rebuilt. Jobs lost. Lives lost. Families torn apart, Violet's and theirs.

Ripples that can still be felt in the village to this day, all because of one thing a young girl forgot to do in one split second.

'I'm so sorry for what happened.' Violet's voice breaks as she gets to the end of her account. 'I know I can never make amends for it, but ever since I've moved back, I've been trying my very best to do what I can to give something back to the village.'

Tammy jumps back up again. 'I just need to finish saying my bit.' She looks around the room to check she has everyone's attention. 'From my investigations and interviews, I have concluded that Violet was not to blame.' She says it with authority, as if she's in a courtroom drama. 'She did not know her charger was faulty; it was an accident. Not only that, but she was a child at the time. Just fourteen years old. Therefore, her name is clear of all charges.'

The room is thick with silence.

Tammy starts using her normal voice again. 'I didn't mean

to upset you, Violet. I just want people to stop saying mean things. So that everyone else knows it's not your fault.'

'I wish my mum agreed with you,' Violet whispers.

Glenys had always been what people in the village called 'eccentric', even back then. She often needed whole days in bed and for those days, Dad always tried extra hard to show Violet and Jodie how cherished they both were, wrapping them up in a soft blanket of love. When he'd gone, the blanket was ripped away and buried alongside him.

The remnants of Glenys were sparse afterwards. Her struggles from before were magnified a hundred-fold. She couldn't seem to see Violet, even on the rare occasions Jodie had allowed Violet anywhere near her.

Tammy sits back down. Adam stands up, mumbling to people that he needs to get past with Bill and his wheelchair. Violet doesn't look up at them until they are leaving through the door, but she can see tension in the bunched-up muscles of Adam's back. It's too much — of course it is. Violet was stupid to think they could put the past aside for long.

'Thank you.' Violet pulls Tammy into a hug after most of the Helping Hands members have disappeared. 'It was a lovely thing to do. I don't think it needs to go in the *Gazette* — it's enough that you believe in me.'

'Not just her,' Mrs Robson says from over her shoulder. 'We all do.'

Several arms are slung around Violet all at once. They belong to Chrissie, Claire and Mrs Robson. Abbas gives her a thumbs-up from the sofa.

Violet still has bridges to mend. But at least now she has people to keep her afloat whilst she patches the holes.

CHAPTER 29

Violet

SLEEP CAN BE A stubborn thing, and tonight it's remaining far away from Violet's reach, refusing to budge. Violet rolls one way and then the other, tangling her feet in the duvet and trying to *force stop* her brain now that her past has tumbled out in front of everyone.

Every time she closes her eyes, she sees the flames, the fire engine. Even when she opens them, she can still hear her mum's scream, the sobs from Bill as they stood helplessly around the ambulance. All those buried memories, clawing their way to the surface of Violet's mind.

She tries to focus on the hugs from the group after the Helping Hands meeting, on the reassuring words of comfort from her new friends. But she keeps seeing the stoop of Adam's shoulders as he left the room. It must have been excruciating for him and Bill to have to listen to all that in front of everyone – what had Violet been thinking? She should have taken Tammy aside quietly and explained that it wasn't the time or the place.

As the dawn chorus sounds, Violet falls into feverish dreams about her dad, Adam's mum, and Lydia Raynott, who turns out to be Liz McDonald from *Coronation Street*.

Violet wakes up exhausted and shaky, and the morning passes in a haze as she goes through the motions of breakfast and getting Glenys ready for the day. Lunchtime comes and goes, and Glenys retires to her room for an afternoon nap. Violet feels like doing the same as she clears away the plates. Her mind is spending so much of its time back *then*, and the day is just slipping away.

A message pings on her phone from the kitchen worktop, pulling her back to the present day. *Adam.*

Carers' cuppa at the library? Emergency caffeine and moan time. Claire and I already here. Thought you might like to join. X

One kiss. Not that it matters, she's just relieved he's still speaking to her after last night and it's good of them to invite her.

Claire and Adam are sitting in the library with their hands around steaming cups when Violet arrives. She owes a huge apology to Adam about everything being dragged up at yesterday's meeting; she needs to address the elephant in the library before it stomps all over them. Adam's been such a support to Violet since she arrived back and the last thing she wants is to cause more hurt between them, but then she sees Claire's face up close.

'Just had to get out of the house.' Claire has red, puffy eyes. 'Abbas is having another bad day, and I've tried to help. Tried everything. But I keep saying the wrong things and making it worse. I'm so fucking tired.' Some of her drink sloshes out of the top of her cup and pools across the table.

'I expect you've helped more than you know,' says Adam. 'Not easy trying to be there twenty-four-seven for someone, especially when it's someone you love. It can stretch both people to their limits.'

'And you should see the state of my house,' Claire says. 'I didn't have time to clear up last night. Or the night before. Stupid really, I'm home almost all the time and still can't manage to keep it clean. And it's Jayden I feel sorry for. He doesn't understand why his dad gets confused or distant. Abbas tries so hard not to let him see but it's impossible to keep it up all of the time.'

After so many years of shying away from friendships, Violet had forgotten this feeling of shared pain. Listening to the wobble in Claire's voice breaks Violet's heart into pieces. Claire's becoming a real friend, and Violet wishes she could hold some of the hurt for her for a while.

'And what about you?' Violet takes a gulp of her coffee. 'It can't be easy for you either.'

Claire grabs a tissue from her pocket and dabs under her eyes before the tears have a chance to fall. 'It's not. I've barely stopped crying each night this week and I've got no energy at all. What must that be like for Jayden? Doc's put me on happy pills. He says it's common for carers to suffer from depression. But of course, that's made me feel even guiltier – I'm supposed to be the strong one – what happens to us all if I fold up like a bloody deckchair?'

Violet takes a breath. She's used to being a listener, but she's not usually good at finding the right words to say. She places her hand gently over Claire's. 'You are strong. One of the strongest I've ever met. Depression isn't a sign of weakness, and neither is seeking help. What would you say to Abbas, or my mum for that matter, if they were struggling or having a bad day – would you think they were being weak?'

''Course not.' Claire blows her nose. 'But they have a diagnosis. They're under the mental health team. It's different. I'm supposed to be the carer – the one holding everything together.'

'And you're doing a great job,' Adam interjects. 'Jayden's well cared for and happy. And I've seen the way Abbas looks at you – he adores you. Give yourself some credit. Caring is hard work. None of us will get it right all the time. There's no perfect art to caring – all we can do is our best.'

'I'm just so tired of being tired. I hate seeing Abbas going through it. And sometimes,' she pauses, 'sometimes I would just love to say *yes* when my friends from my old work invite me out for drinks or for dinner. I have to say no so often, most of them have stopped asking. I can tell they don't understand, especially the ones who have met Abbas on a good day.'

'Do you have any other family nearby?'

'Nah. Me and my mum don't get on and I don't speak to my sisters. I usually see my nan a lot but she's poorly herself at the moment – she's just moved into a nursing home. Now it's just me.'

Claire's words take Violet back to Mrs Robson's a couple of weeks ago: *Now it's just me.*

'I'm sure he's just as tired too. Probably needs a few hours away from me just as much. Chrissie's sitting with him. They're watching reruns of *Deal or No Deal*.' Claire manages a weak smile. 'It's nice to get out and catch up with you two.'

'Thanks for the invite.' Violet pops her cup back into the

coffee machine without leaving her seat. 'It's my first time out of the house as well today. Mum didn't want to go out and I spent half the morning on the phone chasing up her PIP decision. She got it, thank goodness, and thanks to you two for all your help.'

'That's great.' Adam smiles.

'How's things with Tammy?' Adam looks at Violet. 'Have you made any more progress with finding her dad?'

'No, but there is one thing: Tammy told me her mum worked as a waitress near Brighton Pier and she always wore a green uniform with a black stripe.'

'I doubt there are that many establishments around there with the same uniform,' says Claire. 'We could go and check them all out – see if we can find someone who worked with Lydia. They might know something about Tammy's dad.'

'Sounds like a plan.' Adam glances at his phone. 'I need to get back for Dad, but perhaps if we could pop a message on the WhatsApp group, we could ask people to cover us for an afternoon one day soon?'

Violet pulls out her phone. 'Good idea. Might be a bit tricky to find three people to stand in on the same day, though. And I can't leave Mum with someone she doesn't know well.' She types a message to the group.

'I'm sure plenty of people would be happy to help. Sounds like a fun adventure – quite fancy myself as a PI. A young, good-looking one, obviously not the jaded, old silver-haired ones like on TV.' He puts his arms in the air before stretching them out in front of him, a big grin on his face.

'An adventure?' Mrs Robson is right behind them, straightening a notice on the wall about a boot fair that happened two months ago. 'What kind of adventure?'

Violet opens her mouth to say that they're just looking for someone, but Claire blurts out the whole story.

'See if people can help you on a Thursday. I close early on Thursdays, and even luckier for you, I know Brighton like the backs of both my hands.' Mrs Robson's eyes gleam over the top of her glasses.

'What did you go and tell her all that for?' Violet whispers once Mrs Robson's back is turned. 'I don't even know if we can go yet.'

Violet's phone bleeps with a message from the Helping Hands group chat.

Chrissie: I can help next Thursday. No need for anyone else. I'll be around for Bill, Abbas, and Glenys. You leave it to me – I have a plan. X

The next Thursday afternoon turns out to be a hot one. Violet, Adam, Claire, and Mrs Robson step out of Pat-the-Fiat, shielding their eyes from the sun. They cross the car park and walk towards Brighton promenade, singing silly songs as if they're on holiday.

Violet and Adam say goodbye to Claire and Mrs Robson as they part ways towards their allotted ends of the seafront near Brighton Pier. They decided it would be easier to split up so they could check more places.

'Probably would've been easier to call all the eateries first,' Violet says after they've been into three restaurants: two with black uniforms and one with none. None of the staff had heard of Lydia or of a café where staff wear black and green uniforms.

'Maybe. But people are less willing to talk over the phone.

At least we've got Lydia's photo with us to show them once we hit the right place. Can't do that over the phone,' says Adam.

'*If* we hit the right place.' Despondency hits Violet as she glances at the text on her phone to see that Claire and Mrs Robson haven't had much luck either. 'She may not have even worked this close; it might have been further into town.'

'Then we'll search there too.' Adam injects his regular supply of cheeriness into his voice and Violet bats away a flash of irritation.

'The staff don't seem to like us asking questions in some of these places. The girls in that burger bar looked at me like I was a slice of trodden-in gherkin from the floor.'

'Fuck 'em,' Adam says in an easy voice that's sympathy-free. Not a platitude in sight.

'Fuck who?' Mrs Robson appears around the corner of the high street, Claire panting behind her. Violet has never heard her swear and it makes her snort.

'Rude people in cafés,' Violet explains. 'And we've had no joy with the green uniforms.'

'Us neither and we've finished our list,' Mrs Robson says.

The four of them stand on the pavement, facing each other in a deflated circle.

'Well, that's that, then,' Violet mumbles. 'Only two coffee shops to go, and they're both chains – I'm fairly sure neither of their staff wear green uniforms.'

They each give a cursory look inside as they pass the two remaining places, and it was just as Violet thought: no green to be seen.

'Never mind, love.' Claire links her arm through Violet's as they turn to walk back. 'We'll come back another day. Try some of the surrounding areas.'

'And in the meantime, let's focus on getting that first *Gazette* issue done.' Mrs R gives Violet's other arm a squeeze before letting go of it.

Violet swallows. She's still getting used to people being so supportive and having others around to pick her up when she's starting to sink. It's strange to have people in her life who know anything about what's important to her. All those years of thinking of things she wanted to write about, the stories she wanted to share with the world. Now she has the chance to, if only for her little corner of the planet. Claire's right, she still has other ways to make a difference, even if it takes a little longer to help Tammy find her family.

'Thank you.' Violet envelops her in a bear hug she isn't expecting and feels Claire's shoulder muscles stiffen as she clears her throat.

'Sorry.' Violet releases her from her grip and shakes her limbs. Claire isn't a hugger. Noted. Should have asked first.

'It's not that,' Claire says, staring in front of her. 'I think we might have found what we've been looking for.' She points over the road towards a woman with long blonde hair, standing under some scaffolding and sucking on a cigarette. Behind her is a blue door with a neon sign that's sporting a tall dancing pole, a pair of stilettos and two long legs. The woman flicks her cigarette onto the pavement and grinds the heel of her shoe over it. She's wearing a green uniform with a thick black stripe across the top.

'You think Tammy's mum was a lap dancer?' Adam says, too loudly.

The woman in the green uniform glances over at them and frowns – probably because they're all staring at her – before opening the stiletto-adorned door and slamming it behind her.

'No – I mean, I doubt the lap dancers wear uniforms like that, they're not very, erm, exotic. But perhaps the bar staff do?' Claire says.

An open-topped bus trundles past leaving a fog of fumes in its wake.

'We'd better hurry up if we're going in there. I've taken my chops out of the freezer and they'll need putting in the oven soon,' Mrs Robson says. She takes a step towards the kerb and presses the button to cross the road.

Claire shrugs and follows close behind as Adam and Violet stare at each other open mouthed before joining them.

The stiletto-adorned door opens onto a staircase that leads to a basement. It's poorly lit and the smell of damp carpet hits the back of Violet's throat as she gingerly climbs down the steep steps, hanging onto a splintery handrail whilst following the sound of a nineties' R&B track.

'I was expecting it to be a little more – well, a little more glamorous.' Mrs Robson sounds disappointed when they reach a small, square lounge area, framed with padded benches and mismatched bar stools. In the corner of the room is a mirrored staging area with a pole in the middle of it.

'Where do you think the bar is? And why is no one else in here?' Claire whispers. She peers suspiciously at the upholstery on one of the stools before nodding and perching on the edge of it.

The door behind the staging area swings open, and in walks the blonde-haired woman they'd seen outside.

'It's a fiver entrance fee for each of you. Includes a free drink,' she adds through a mouthful of chewing gum.

'Oh, we're not staying,' Violet explains. 'We're looking for someone who may have worked here – Lydia Raynott?'

The woman shakes her head. 'Can't help you. It's my first week – one of the dancers would know, most of 'em have worked here for ages. You can't just sit and wait for free though; this place costs money.'

The four of them swap glances. Adam reaches into his pocket and pulls out two banknotes. 'I've got fifteen on me?'

'And I'll pay the other five.' Mrs Robson reaches for her handbag and Violet's mouth falls open.

'You don't have to do that,' Violet says.

'I know we don't.' Mrs Robson pats her hand. 'But this is for Tammy. Besides – I've always wanted to know what happens in these places.'

They all sit down as the waitress in black and green takes their drinks order before disappearing behind the stage. Her presence is replaced by a tall woman with a snake tattoo all the way around her hips and a pink tasselled bra that reminds Violet of Mrs Robson's sofa. The woman clasps the side of the pole and slowly sways her hips before taking an elegant leap up it and hanging upside down.

Mrs Robson lets out an audible gasp and she and Claire whisper to each other about how *bendy* the dancer is, and how they miss the days when they might have been able to do that.

Violet watches, mesmerised, as the woman slides down by her ankles and effortlessly stands back up again before spinning clockwise, the back of one knee hooked around the pole. It's strangely relaxing, watching someone else's gymnastic feats.

The dancer pulls out an impressive finishing move as the song fades out and Claire, Mrs Robson, Adam and Violet burst into applause. She climbs down from the stage and walks towards them with a grin on her face. 'Who's going first, then?'

She wriggles into the space between Adam and Mrs Robson on the bench. 'For a lap dance,' she says when no one answers.

'That's not quite why we're here,' Adam says. 'We're looking for someone.'

The woman's eyes narrow. 'You police – undercover? Because they usually still have a dance.'

'We're not police.'

'HMRC? Because I can assure you every dancer here is up to date with their self-assessments.' She glances towards the door behind the stage.

'We're looking for someone who used to work here,' Violet interjects. 'A woman called Lydia Raynott. We think she might have been a waitress.'

The woman screws up her eyes for a moment before shaking her head. 'Nope. Doesn't ring a bell.' She stands back up and shuffles past Adam's knees. 'I've been here three years and never heard of her – but then most people don't use their real names in here. It's that type of place.' She gives them a small smile and takes a couple of steps away towards the stage.

'Wait,' Violet calls out. 'I have a photo.'

The woman stops and walks back as Violet rummages about in her bag. She pulls out the picture of Lydia and waves it in front of her.

A flicker of recognition crawls across her face. 'You promise you're not cops?' she asks. Her voice has softened.

'Promise,' Violet says.

'That's Louisa. Louisa Crewe. And I know that's her real name because I picked up a prescription for her once when she was the only waitress working and it was heaving.'

Violet looks around the small, bare room. It's difficult to imagine it ever being heaving, but it is only ten to five.

'She's not in any trouble, is she?' Faint lines appear on the woman's forehead. 'She was lovely she was, we missed her when she stopped coming in, but that's normal here. People come, people go.' She shrugs.

'I'm so sorry to have to tell you this whilst you're at work. I'm afraid … *Louisa* has died. She had a heart attack.' Violet's voice trembles.

The woman's face crumples. 'Shit. Oh, poor Louisa. That's awful. The other girls will be gutted.'

'When did you last see her?' Adam asks.

'About two months ago. There was something, now I think about it …'

All four lean in towards her as the music builds behind them.

'Last time I saw her, she'd been drinking on shift – lots of us do, the dancers and the waitresses, but it was unusual for her. She was crying in the loos and her make-up was everywhere – all down her face. She said she didn't know why we were all so nice to her – that she didn't deserve it. I told her not to be so stupid – that she's a lovely woman – and she told me I wouldn't be saying that if I knew what a mess she'd made of her life.'

'What had she done?' Mrs Robson asks, leaning so far forward Violet's worried she might fall off her bar stool.

'Dunno. She stopped talking after that and I like to mind my business. Most of us have got secrets, haven't we?'

Violet feels herself shrink under a gaze that feels like it's just for her. 'Thank you so much for your help,' she says, holding out her arm to shake the woman's hand. Her mind keeps wrapping itself around the name she'd given them. Louisa Crewe. She knows that name; she's seen it written down somewhere. If Lydia was receiving prescriptions under it, she must have changed it somehow from Lydia – that must be why she's been so untraceable.

Perhaps now they have a name, Violet can make some progress and help Tammy get one step closer to finding a family of her own.

CHAPTER 30

Tammy

TAMMY FEELS STRANGE SITTING in Violet's flat when Violet isn't there. Chrissie is about to prepare a picnic in the garden for the people in the Helping Hands Club who are the ones being cared for, but Tammy's sure it's mostly so the carers can go out and have fun for a change.

Glenys is sitting on the sofa next to her and pretending to read a book so that no one speaks to her.

Bill and Abbas are in the armchairs talking about rugby, little Jayden is looking at a picture book on Abbas' lap and Chrissie's hovering in the middle of the room taking orders for drinks.

'I'll help make them,' Tammy says, jumping up from the sofa. She follows Chrissie into the kitchen.

'I don't think I ever said a proper thank you for looking after me when I was ill that night,' Tammy says as Chrissie pulls the milk from the fridge. 'So I'm writing a thank you poem about it, and I'm going to ask Violet if I can put it in the *Gazette* – if that's all right with you.'

Chrissie smiles. 'Of course, lovey. Thank you. You gave us quite a fright when you were poorly.'

Tammy's chest goes tight. She keeps picturing Mum, holding her hands out towards her in the park. It was so real.

'Thank you.' Tammy fills the kettle. 'You and Violet have done so many nice things.'

Chrissie pats Tammy on the arm. 'You're welcome. I'm pleased you and Violet have each other.'

Tammy's hand wobbles as she dips a spoon in the coffee jar. 'I just don't understand why she's so nice to me. She's a busy lady but she always tries to help, just like you do.'

'Because that's what friends do. They help each other out.' Chrissie passes the sugar bowl to Tammy. 'There doesn't have to be another reason.'

Tammy wants to do some more nice things for Violet. She takes the tray of drinks through to the living room and thinks hard as she sets it down on the table. 'I have an idea,' she says to Chrissie when she follows with the biscuits. 'Shall we save the picnic and have one later with the others – it can be a thank you present for the carers? I'll help make some more food.'

'Sounds great. I'd be well up for that,' says Abbas from behind Tammy's shoulder. 'It's been a rubbish week in our house and I've probably been a nightmare to look after. Claire deserves a treat.'

'Lovely. Count me in.' Bill's eyes twinkle from the sofa.

Even Glenys looks up from her book and gives Tammy the tiniest of nods.

'A dinner party in the garden.' Tammy feels herself light up from the inside. It will be just like on *Come Dine with Me*, only without looking through Violet's underwear drawers whilst talking to a camera.

They only have a couple of hours to pull it together, and

the challenge feels rather thrilling to Tammy. Between them, they chop, peel, and cook.

Glenys takes over the potato salad and won't let another person near it. But when Chrissie tastes it and tells her it's delicious, Glenys smiles and it's a real one that uses her eyes as well as her mouth.

'Violet and the others are going to love this,' Chrissie whispers in Tammy's ear as they take the plates into the garden. 'You're a good friend. Violet's lucky to have you.'

The joy inside Tammy's tummy grows so big, she's worried it might burst.

CHAPTER 31

Violet

PAT-THE-FIAT PULLS INTO THE driveway of Malvern House and spits out all four of her passengers.

Violet hobbles towards the front door, cursing herself for wearing her least-comfy pumps without socks to trek around Brighton in.

The door opens and Tammy is standing behind it, an excited grin taking over her face.

'We've got a surprise for you,' she says. 'For all of you. Come this way,' she adds, grandly gesturing towards the door to Glenys' flat.

The flat is empty and quiet. Violet and the others follow Tammy into the kitchen and out through the back door into the garden.

A huge banner made from an old bedsheet is tied to a tree. Large letters spell out in felt-tip pen: *To our carers. Thank you for all you do.*

The garden table has been covered with a tablecloth and a vase of fresh flowers sits in the middle. Platters of food cover every spare inch of the surface and there are bottles of wine at each end.

All of Glenys' dining chairs plus a few that look like they're from Adam and Bill's flat are crammed around the table, half of them already occupied.

Tammy pulls a party popper from her pocket and covers everyone at the table with brightly coloured streamers.

'I popped to the shop,' says Chrissie. 'But I did absolutely nothing else. All the cooking, the preparing, the banner – that was all this lot.'

Abbas gets up from his seat and walks over to Claire, taking both her hands in his. 'I'm sorry about earlier. I know I can be hard work sometimes. I – we – just wanted you all to know you're appreciated.'

Claire's eyes mist over, and she shakes her head, laughing. 'It's true. You are a pain in the arse. But I'm glad you're feeling better. And I'm glad you put cheese and pineapple into the mix,' she adds, nodding towards the table.

'I know it's your favourite.' Abbas keeps his eyes on Claire's.

Bill clears his throat and inches himself up from his seat, gripping on to the table. He slowly picks up a spoon and clinks it against his glass. 'And I just wanted to say how wonderful my son is. It's not been the easiest of times for him. He's made some of the biggest sacrifices anyone could make so he could take care of his old man. His mum would be so proud of him.'

An ache forms in Violet's chest as she watches the look that passes between them.

A cloud of silence hovers over the garden as everyone avoids looking at Glenys. Everyone except Violet. Her eyes had swung hopefully towards her mum the second Bill sat down.

Glenys is watching the branch of a tree as it swings in the wind. She looks peaceful but shows no interest in joining the conversation.

'Thank you for helping me, Violet.' Tammy takes a swig of her drink before wiping her mouth on the back of her sleeve. 'I think you're the best carer. I'm not your family and you still help me, even though no one told you to.'

Violet tries to push aside the picture in her head of Tammy's eviction letter, still stuffed inside the front pocket of her handbag.

'Your mum made the coleslaw – and the potato salad,' Chrissie whispers in Violet's ear when she sits down. 'She's tired herself out so she might not say very much, but she does care. She wanted to help even when it took her so long to chop the potatoes. She wouldn't stop or sit down until it was done.'

'Thank you.' Violet lays a hand over Chrissie's. 'And thank you for overseeing all of this, it means a lot. And not just to me.' She smiles across at Claire and Abbas as they whisper to each other, laughing over a shared joke.

By the time the food has been eaten and the wine has gone, the sun has melted into fire-coloured fingers behind the dancing branches of the trees. A welcome breeze cools Violet's warm skin as she gathers the plates from the table. Eyes are drooping and people start to trickle off home with smiles and thank yous.

Violet helps her mum settle down to bed and put the plates into the sink.

Now everyone has headed home, she can't wait any longer – she opens her laptop on the dining table and types 'Louisa Crewe' into Google and Facebook. Turns out there are a few Louisa Crewes, but only one with a Facebook profile with

Brighton listed as a hometown. The profile photo is of a sunset and the account is private so there's no way to know for sure. There are listings of previous waitressing jobs in her 'about' section though.

Violet runs to her handbag, gets out her phone and scrolls to Jenny J's number, hearing the echo of Jenny's words in her ears. *If you ever need anything.*

Jenny sounds thrilled to hear from her and not at all perturbed to be called out of hours. ''Course I'll help. Easy-peasy when you know the right things to search.' Jenny's assured, clipped tones remind Violet just how efficient she is at her job. 'Stay on the line and I'll see if I can get a match for a man connected to Louisa Crewe, nee Lydia Raynott from Brighton.'

'Thank you. I really appreciate it.' Violet stays quiet and listens to the tap-tap of the keys on Jenny's computer.

'Ah. Louisa Crewe, previously Lydia Raynott, former employee of The Dairy Bar. Her credit check links to a man she used to live with called Michael Mullens. People often change their name to hide from an ex, so if you do make contact with him, please be careful.'

Michael Mullens.

Could it be?

Violet thanks Jenny as soon as she can make her voice work again and hangs up before going back to her laptop and opening Facebook.

Michael Mullens.

She clicks on the first profile picture she sees, and it looms large on the screen. Dark hair speckled with grey. Wide eyes and a narrow nose, and he's wearing sports clothes and an energetic smile. Occupation: Estate Agent.

Something smashes to the floor behind Violet.

'Close it. It's Dad. Can't see it – not allowed. I'm not allowed to look.' Tammy's a living statue, pale and still, with one arm frozen in front of her face, blocking her view from the screen. A pile of glass that was once a tumbler from Glenys' cupboard, sits on the floor beside her.

Violet's limbs shake from the shock of the noise and she digs deep to find her voice. 'What are you doing here? I thought everyone had gone.'

'I've been sitting in your garden, listening to the birds. I like it out there, the flowers are pretty. I'm sorry, I didn't know you wanted me to go home.'

'It's fine. I didn't want you to leave, I just didn't realise you were here.'

Tammy's eyes are peering at the laptop through the gap in the crook of her elbow. Violet can't read the expression on her face. Something between wonder and shock.

'Don't move. I'll get a dustpan and brush. Can't have you cutting your foot again.' Violet gets up from her seat.

'You need to close it,' Tammy repeats. She's shaking.

Violet shuts the laptop. 'Why aren't you allowed to look at your dad?' she uses her gentlest voice.

Tammy shrugs. 'Mum said I wasn't allowed.' She lowers her arm to her side, noticeably more relaxed now the screen is no longer visible. She doesn't say anything else, just that she's tired and needs to go to bed.

Violet sits at the table in the lamplight for a long time after Tammy has gone. Lydia may have had good reasons for hiding Tammy away from Michael – she looked frightened enough when his photo was shining from the screen. But there had been something else there too, a longing? And Lydia seems to have kept Tammy from doing a lot of things aside from seeing her dad.

From what Violet can piece together, Lydia appears to have been pathologically controlling. She'd kept Tammy away from everyone in the world, not allowed her to learn how to look after herself and made her completely dependent on her mum for everything. Michael might not have done anything wrong. He might be thrilled to be reunited with Tammy and she might be just as happy to have him back in her life.

Violet clicks onto Michael's email address and composes a message. Perhaps if she finds a way to get to sus out Michael a little more, it will be easier to decide what to do about reuniting him and Tammy. She won't do it unless she's as convinced as she can be that he's a safe person. She hadn't warmed to him last time, but she'd been anxious about getting the valuation over with.

Hello Michael,

Many thanks for coming to value Malvern House a few weeks ago. I would like to request a second appointment to discuss our options. Please could you let me know when you might be available?

Many thanks,
Violet Strong.

She presses *send* and then stares at the notifications screen for ten minutes before logging off. Violet has thrown out the hook.

All she needs now is a bite.

CHAPTER 32

Violet

VIOLET STEPS OUT OF Malvern House with Tammy, Mrs Robson, Adam, and Bill. The agenda for the next Helping Hands meeting is attached to the clipboard under her arm. Now she's somehow become chair, an agenda feels like something safe to cling to. It's still scary speaking to a whole room of people. The meeting is at Claire's house this evening.

'Your mum not coming?' says Bill.

'Not today.' Violet had tried her best. Glenys has been distant again today and she barely said two words at dinner time. Their relationship still feels like a never-ending game of snakes and ladders.

By the time they arrive, Claire's living room is crammed with smiling, eager faces and fold-up chairs that cover every inch of carpet. Chrissie is sitting in the corner with a ball of wool and knitting needles in her hand. No sign of Abbas, but he's probably in his room.

Violet glances at her clipboard and clears her throat, watching as the Helping Hands crew wind up their conversations and swallow their mouthfuls of Jammy Dodgers.

'Thank you all for coming back and for all the ideas and articles some of you have sent for the *Gazette*,' Violet says. 'We're opening the meeting with something very special this week.' She smiles at Tammy. 'We have a poetry reading from our very own Tammy Raynott.'

Everyone claps and cheers as a blushing Tammy stands up and makes her way to the front of the room. She's spent most of the week with Chrissie, practising her writing. She refused to show Violet the poem she'd written, though. She'd wanted it to be a surprise.

Tammy stammers the first couple of lines and then stops, tears filling her eyes. Violet swallows the urge to take over.

'Come on, Tammy,' Claire shouts from the back.

'You've got this,' calls Adam.

Words begin to flow from the page to Tammy's mouth to Violet's ears. Beautiful, touching words about friendship and learning to live a life that's bigger than her living room. It's as if Tammy's true self, her thoughts, her longings, are squeezing themselves out into the world through the gaps in each line. She says things about Violet and Chrissie that make Violet's heart grow bigger. Tears prick her eyes as she watches Tammy.

The young woman who taught her how to be a friend.

Mrs Robson gets up from her seat and pats Tammy on the back and almost everybody in the room wipes their eyes as she sits back down.

After taking a moment to breathe, Violet walks over to where Tammy is sitting and pulls her into a hug. 'That was the nicest thing anyone's ever said about me,' she whispers, before straightening herself up, clearing her throat and sitting back in her seat. 'Has anyone got anything else they'd like to share?'

'I've come up with a few designs for the logo for the *Gazette*. And some drawings to showcase – only if there are any spare pages, obviously,' Claire adds as she flushes pink.

Adam gasps as he peers at the pages Claire has laid out on the table and the sound is echoed by every person in the room as a collective gaze falls on Claire's drawings.

'These are incredible,' Violet whispers, awestruck by the refined details. One of the pictures is of Lowerstone Park. The focus of the drawing is a little boy in the sandpit. Jayden. He's concentrating on the sandcastle he's building, and his tongue is poking out at the corner, he's completely at peace. Violet waits for the sickening flashes of sandpit-related memories. A cloak of sadness covers her, but this time there are holes so she can breathe.

She peers at the drawing without looking away. Violet's making new memories in Lowerstone now; memories that help make those painful ones just a little more bearable.

Claire's other work is just as impressive. Sketches of the village in black and white, and one of them is drawn as it looked in 1950.

'These are most definitely going in – people will want copies of the paper just to see these,' Violet tells a blushing Claire. 'How on earth have you found the time with everything you've got on?'

'I've been doing it whenever Jayden's watching cartoons and Abbas is napping. Never thought I'd have time to go back to my art – but it helps me switch off – I've been able to sleep properly in the daytime which I couldn't do before. I've even been less of a grumpy bitch all week – so thanks for giving me the push to do it – my family will thank you for it too,' she says with a grin.

It feels like the first issue is coming together, especially when Chrissie reads out some of the problem page questions she's already received from the box in the library. They range from the mundane to the screamingly funny. She reads her gentle and wisdom-soaked answers, and everyone gives her a round of applause.

'Thanks, everyone.' She looks pleased. 'It's been so nice to be able to help people again — it's kept me busy.'

Footsteps sound from behind the living-room door. It creaks open and Abbas walks through it, breaking the silence with a cough.

'I've written down some stuff,' he mutters, running a hand through his dark, curly hair. 'Some of the shit I've gone through in my head this week. Things that have helped me, that kind of thing.'

'That's wonderful.' Violet finds her voice. 'Please don't feel like you have to read it out if you'd rather not.'

'I want to.' Abbas rushes his words out. 'I need people to hear, and it might help other people who feel as crappy as I do.'

Abbas' hands start to shake as he holds his piece of paper up in front of him. The room holds its breath.

Violet struggles to understand the first few words due to Abbas' nervous stammering. She closes her eyes and focuses on his voice. As he relaxes, the sentences become clearer and images come easily into Violet's mind that make his words come alive. He speaks about the early experiences of his diagnosis. The horrors of his thoughts over the past two weeks and the battles he and Claire have faced together.

Lots of glistening eyes can be seen around the room and everyone claps loud and hard.

'Thank you for sharing something so personal,' Violet says. 'You've written it beautifully and from the heart. You have a real talent.'

One after the other, people read out their offerings for the first issue and by the end of the meeting, Violet feels like weeping with joy. So many skills from one village. They have enough great quality content to fill two bumper issues. Now they just need to get cracking with getting some businesses on board so they can get future issues into print as well as online.

'We need to start thinking about the party.' Claire grins from the back of the room.

'Party?' says Violet.

'Yep. If we're launching a fab new *Gazette* for the whole village to read, we're not doing it without a bang. A launch party.'

Adam turns his head towards Mrs Robson. 'Do you think we could use the library?'

Mrs Robson clears her throat and slides her glasses further up the bridge of her nose. 'I might have a better idea. I'll have to ask, of course, but I'm sure if we agree to give the place a clean-up and a lick of paint, we might be allowed to have it in the community centre. It's been boarded up for so long now – if we could get it reopened, the village will have a community space again – one we could use for the Helping Hands, for *Gazette* meetings – and it will give the kids of the village somewhere to have their birthday parties.'

'It would be lovely to see the centre open again,' Chrissie says. 'The locals really miss it, and it wouldn't cost much to do it up – we can use some of the money we make from the paper. Be good for us to give something back to the village, a way to thank everyone for their support with Helping Hands.'

'We could make it a joint party – the reopening of the community centre and the launch of the *Gazette*. We can invite the whole village.' Claire's eyes are shining.

A room full of smiles. Violet would like to keep them all in a bottle and carry them everywhere she goes.

CHAPTER 33

Tammy

TAMMY CAN TELL THAT the Helping Hands meeting is about to finish because they are all making plans for next week's one. Excitement starts swimming around in her tummy because as soon as the meeting's over, Chrissie's taking Tammy to the cinema. Going to the cinema is on Tammy's wish list. Afterwards, she'll be able to tick off everything on it and make a whole new one.

As everyone stands up and picks up their handbags, Chrissie leans towards Tammy. 'Ready to go and see *Little Women*?'

Tammy has no idea what *Little Women* is, but Violet says it's based on one of her favourite books. It was Violet's idea that Chrissie and Tammy should go to the cinema tonight, but she said she wouldn't come because she's too busy. She went red and looked at the carpet when she said it, so she knows Violet's up to something.

Tammy says goodbye to everyone and follows Chrissie out of the building. They're getting the bus to the cinema, and a taxi back because it will be dark by the time the film is over.

'I haven't been to the cinema before,' Tammy says, speeding up to keep up with Chrissie as she rushes towards the village.

'What, never?' Chrissie slows besides her, and Tammy links her arm through her new friend's elbow. 'Well, we'll have to make this an evening to remember. We'll order the largest box of popcorn.'

The cinema is even better than Tammy thought it would be. She'd seen them on the telly, but she had no idea how spongy the seats would be or that the whole room would smell so delicious. She keeps pulling the seat down next to her, loving the way it pops straight back up again. She only stops when she realises Chrissie is giving her a look that reminds Tammy she used to be a teacher.

'Do you think Violet liked my poem? Did you like my poem?'

Chrissie smiles so much that her eyes water. 'It was beautiful. And I know Violet felt the same. She looked so happy.'

'Good. I like making Violet happy.'

Tammy's still thinking about making Violet happy when the film starts. She puts her hand over the pocket of her jeans; she can still feel Violet's wish list in there. She thinks again about Adam and the way he kept giving Violet all those funny smiles all the way through the meeting. An idea pokes its way into her head. Another thing Chrissie might be able to help with. She leans back towards Chrissie.

'Just watch the film.' Chrissie says it in a loud whisper but she's laughing a little bit too. 'Tell me afterwards.'

Tammy sits back in her seat and watches the adventures of Beth, Meg, Jo, and Amy. They make her laugh and then they make her cry. A lot.

Chrissie cries too and between them, they use up all the tissues in her handbag.

Tammy's tears aren't just for the characters. They're there for the first film she's watched with another person since Mum died. She takes hold of Chrissie's hand and gives it a squeeze.

As soon as the lights come back on, Tammy takes Violet's wish list out of her pocket and peeks at it.

1. To help other people
2. True love
3. A job in journalism

Tammy knows how she's going to help with number two so that can be the one she starts with. She's seen enough episodes of *First Dates* to know how that stuff works. On the way home in the taxi, she makes a list in her head of the things she'll need from the shop. Adam will be easy to contact, he only lives downstairs.

All the right ingredients are there. Tammy just needs to put them all together and see if they make *True Love*.

CHAPTER 34

Violet

A SLEEK BMW PULLS up in the driveway next to Pat-the-Fiat.

Violet's been keeping watch at the window for the last forty minutes. Michael Mullens from Mullens' Estate Agents is late. Not a good start if this was a real second appointment.

It's a relief he's turned up at all this evening – Violet made sure that Tammy would be out of the way with Chrissie. There's no way she wants Michael to know where his daughter lives and the shock would be too much for Tammy if she were to bump into him on the stairs.

Violet's had a ball of nervous energy rolling around in her tummy ever since Michael emailed back, saying he only had evening slots available for the next few weeks. It's the perfect opportunity to sus him out more, but she can't let slip that she knows Tammy – he has to believe he's there because she wants him to sell the house.

Jenny's words ring loud in her head. *Be careful.*

Violet opens the main front door and ushers Michael inside Glenys' flat before anyone else in the building sees him. He's wearing a flashier suit than last time.

'Nice to be back,' says Michael as he steps inside.

Violet shakes his hand again. It's sweaty, and he holds on for a few seconds too long. He stands still as if he's waiting for Violet to say more, and he doesn't take his eyes off her, even for a second. It's unnerving.

The homely smell of cookies she'd baked earlier moves from comforting to sickening and the buzz from the fridge seems to rise in pitch and volume as if a hundred people are having a party in her eardrums.

'Okay to set up here?' Michael sits himself down on the sofa and pulls a laptop from his briefcase. He leans forward, giving Violet a closer look at his mean eyes. Which, Violet realises, look just like Tammy's. Or they would without the meanness.

'Of course. Mum's having a sleep – she's not really up to dealing with the house sale, so I'm overseeing things.' Violet sits down and keeps her voice light, bright and devoid of suspicion.

Hopefully.

'I'm glad you were able to fit us in.'

'I'm glad too.' His pout becomes a smirk, and he narrows his eyes before looking Violet up and down in a way that makes Violet want to scrub her skin clean.

'So, you said you wanted to move forward with the sale in your email,' he says, pulling a laptop from his bag. 'Shall I start by talking you through the process and our rates before I take another look around?'

'Erm, yes please. The rates would be good – and the, er, the process. I probably won't be able to show you much right now, I haven't had the chance to do any of the things we discussed.'

Irritation flashes across Michael's face. 'I noticed as soon as I drove in. Guess we'll stick with the original valuation then I can talk you through what we might be able to do for you.'

'I'll make us a drink – what would you like? Tea? Coffee? And I've made cookies.' Violet's hoping her baking skills might be good enough to help Michael lower his guard.

Michael strokes the minuscule amount of stubble on his chin. 'Could do with something stronger now. Perhaps we could do that after the boring stuff.'

She pretends not to hear him. 'Two coffees, then,' she says brightly as she walks off towards the kitchen. She watches him out of the corner of her eye as she makes the drinks. He's sitting up straight and scrolling through his phone, frown lines bunched up tight.

She uses the time to slow her breathing and to compose some sensible questions that might help her find out what she needs to without giving too much away.

Violet pours the coffee and plops his down on the table in front of him along with a plate of cookies. 'Have you always lived around here?' She aims for a casual tone as she swoops into the armchair.

'Lived in Brighton all my life.'

She nods and make patterns with the froth on the top of her drink with her tiny spoon.

'What about you?' he asks. 'You sound local.'

'Same,' she says without missing a beat. 'Born and bred.'

Michael sips his drink and grimaces. 'You forgot the sugar.' He pulls his smile back out again. Or presumably what he thinks is his smile.

'You been an estate agent for long?'

'I've always worked in property.' He bats his hand away from himself. 'Bigwig stuff – I won't bore you with it.'

Violet jumps up, walks to the window and pulls at the curtain. 'Just to let you know that all carpets and curtains will be included in the sale. These are practically antiques.'

'I'm not sure if that's much of a selling point,' he smirks.

'I know,' Violet says in an even voice. His smarmy smiles and wandering eyes are making her nauseous. She's going to have to take the plunge and speed things up before his coffee ends up over his comb-over. All she really needs to know is whether he might want his daughter back in his life. She needs to move this along as quickly as possible. The last thing anyone needs is for Michael to still be here when Tammy gets back from the cinema. 'So – is your agency a family business?'

'Not really. It's just me.'

'Ah. No one to hand the reins to when you ...' Violet breaks off. Perhaps asking Michael what's going to happen to his business when he dies is not the best way to go.

Michael gives Violet a long stare. 'Running a business alone means it has my full focus. No children, no family distractions.'

'So, you like being single?'

'Mmm.' He nods. 'I lived with a woman a long time ago. Bit of a psycho.' He taps the side of his head with his index finger. 'Used to turn up every now and again like a bad smell,' he sniggers. 'What about you – anyone in your life?'

'Not yet,' Violet says sweetly. She thinks of Tammy at the cinema watching *Little Women* with Chrissie. She balls her hands into fists.

Michael chuckles. 'Enough talk of families. When would you like me to draw up the paperwork?'

'Whereabouts in Brighton did you say you lived now?' she blurts out.

Michael wiggles his eyebrows. 'I didn't.'

Violet forces out a laugh. 'Sorry – I thought I remember you saying.'

'I live in West Street, near the old ice rink. Some nice places around there, quite a few of them are on our books. If you're looking for somewhere to move into, I have some great properties available.'

'Thank you. I'm not sure what my plans are at the moment. I'm just focussing on selling this place first. Perhaps we'd better get on with talking about your rates and the house-selling process. I've got to be up early tomorrow.' She gives him a regretful smile.

'Yep. Let's do it.' Michael leans his laptop towards Violet and runs through slide after slide about what Mullens' Estate Agents might be able to do for Malvern House.

Violet knows where he lives. He'd denied Tammy's existence, so it seems unlikely that he'd be the right person to help her. Violet doesn't like him one bit; the man gives her the creeps, and she won't rush into trying to reunite the two of them without giving it some serious thought and perhaps some more digging.

'Right – well, thank you for coming,' she manages once Michael's spiel has wound down. 'I appreciate you taking the time to talk me through everything. There's lots to think about, so I'll need some time to mull it all over. I'll be in touch.' Violet walks him to the door and freezes when Adam's door opens at the exact same time.

'Oh. Hello.' Adam looks surprised and then covers

it with a friendly smile. His eyes flicker towards the ID badge around Michael's neck. 'I was just popping over to have a chat. I can come back if this is a bad …'

'Not at all. Mr Mullens was just leaving.' Violet keeps her voice as sweet as she can as she ushers Michael out of the main door.

Bloody great timing, Violet.

'I hope you don't mind me just turning up,' Adam says as he closes the door behind him.

'Not at all. Mum's just gone to bed.' As soon as the words are out, she blushes. Adam and Violet haven't been alone together since their afternoon traipsing around cafés in Brighton when there'd been definite flirting.

'Didn't interrupt anything, I hope?' Adam does a weird half-grin.

'Not at all.' Violet can't think clearly, she's still nervous and jumpy from Michael's visit.

'I thought he might be an estate agent.'

'No – not an estate agent exactly.' Violet's heart thumps hard as the blood rushes to her cheeks. She can't have Adam guessing about the house sale – not just yet.

An engine starts up from the driveway outside and Adam glances through the window. 'Weird that he wears a badge with *Mullens' Estate Agents* written all over it.'

Violet's breath catches in her throat. Now could be the time to come clean about the house. Adam deserves to know what the plan has been, even if it hurts him.

But.

'When I say he's not an estate agent, I just mean he's not

my estate agent. He was just doing some cold calling, drumming up some business. Apparently, Lowerstone is tipped to become quite the up-and-coming area.' Violet hates herself more with every word as she sits down. She could have just told the truth – at least most of it – that she's sure Michael is Tammy's dad. But she hadn't known that last time Michael was here evaluating the building. She'd panicked. It'll look even weirder if she tells him now, and she might let it slip that she'd invited him before to view and value the building for real.

Adam nods and the faint lines on his forehead smooth out. 'I haven't seen much of you on your own lately. We've not had much of a chance to chat properly.' He plonks himself on the sofa next to Violet. He has a piece of paper in his hand. 'I wanted to run an article by you for the *Gazette*. I know you said to email you, but this is something close to my heart and I wanted to show you in person.'

He's wearing one of those T-shirts with extra-soft material, the type that makes Violet want to cuddle up against it. Violet nods and makes encouraging noises, trying not to stare at the stubble on Adam's jaw. He smells of Davidoff and freshly baked bread.

The article's about the dog rescue home on the outskirts of the village. Adam used to work there before he had to give it up to look after Bill. It's a place still close to his heart and they're struggling for funding.

'I thought if I could write a piece about what they do, various animals who have been helped and perhaps interview some of the staff, more people might consider supporting it – or maybe even rescue a dog themselves. We could go and visit the centre together if you like?'

Violet pictures Adam at the rescue centre playing with abandoned puppies and it makes her face tingle with heat.

'Lovely idea,' she says. 'I'd love to come along.'

Adam smiles. 'Great. Anyway, enough about that. Are you okay? You look like you've got a lot on your mind.'

If only he knew.

'It's Tammy. I've been wondering if I'm doing the right thing by searching for her father. She seems so alone in the world now her mum's gone and she's still quite vulnerable. But I can't know for sure that he's someone who should be in her life.'

'He might be a proper wrong'un. Lydia probably kept Tammy away from him for a good reason. Besides, Tammy's not alone, she has you, Chrissie, and all of us from the Helping Hands Club.'

'Mmm.' Violet stiffens. She should tell him the real reason why Tammy might need her family one day soon. She wants to stick around in Lowerstone for longer now if she can, just the thought of leaving her new friends and the Helping Hands lot makes her heart hurt, but she can't guarantee she'll be able to stay for the long term. Glenys is still up and down with Violet – so much of the past still swims between them. If she does have to go into residential care, the building will still need to be sold and Tammy, Adam, Bill, and Mrs Robson will all be without a home. But maybe she shouldn't tell him that, not when nothing is definite, it would cause unnecessary stress.

Violet curls her feet up underneath her on the sofa. 'It does seem as if Lydia had some issues of her own. It sounds like she was pretty controlling towards Tammy – wouldn't let her do anything, go anywhere or meet anyone. It could be something to do with her dad, but it might not be – it might have been her own fears.'

Adam nods and shifts around towards Violet, placing his arm over the back of the sofa.

'But is it really my decision to make?' Violet carries on. 'If I do find her dad, but then I don't tell her about it, I'm being as controlling as Lydia.'

'And if you reunite them and he's dangerous, it might put her at risk,' says Adam.

'Exactly.' Violet's head is pounding from going back and forth. It feels good to share it with someone.

'Do some more digging and then decide when you've got all the facts. Whatever you decide will be because you think it's best for Tammy. Trust your instinct.'

'That,' says Violet, 'is very helpful.' A real smile cracks its way onto her face for the first time in hours. 'Thank you. You always were good with problem solving. Broken tree houses, den design issues, forgot to do my homework – you always had creative solutions.'

Adam inches closer. His fingers graze the edge of Violet's shoulder. 'I think you'll find your den-making skills were far more superior. And starting up the Helping Hands Club for the village was pretty creative. I guess we're both good at problem solving. We make a good team.'

'I think so too,' Violet says in a light voice.

Adam strokes Violet shoulder with his thumb without taking his eyes away from hers as he moves closer towards Violet.

'Violet, can you get me a glass of water please?' Glenys yells from her room. 'I think I might need a wee as well, could you get my frame for me?'

'Sorry.' Heat floods Violet's face.

'It's fine. Go and sort your mum out. I'd better get going. I'll let you know when I've arranged a visit with the rescue centre,' he adds when Violet doesn't answer.

'Err, yes. Thanks. That would be great,' Violet babbles. 'Coming, Mum!' She bellows so loud that Adam jumps beside her.

He picks up his article, mumbles goodbye and scarpers from the room, barely giving her a second glance, let alone a smile.

Maybe Violet shouldn't have spent so long going on about Tammy. Adam had come over to talk about the dog rescue centre, and she'd just wittered on about her own stuff. Violet's clearly still got a lot to learn about friendship. Or he'd put two and two together about Michael's visit and the sale of the building. She tries to quieten her mind as she gets up to help Glenys.

Perhaps, just like Anne Shirley, Violet just needs to stop her imagination from running away with her.

CHAPTER 35

Violet

IT'S NOW BEEN TWO days since Adam popped round, and Violet hasn't heard any more from him about the visit to the dog centre.

She decides to distract herself by trying to recreate last night's episode of the *Great British Bake Off*. After traipsing to the shop and back in the pouring rain, she arranges the ingredients for gingerbread on the kitchen worktop and coaxes Glenys up from her armchair.

'If I must,' Glenys mumbles when Violet slides her the mixing bowl.

Within five minutes, Violet manages to drop flour down the front of her own top. Glenys chuckles, and Violet flicks a teaspoon of it at her.

A grin makes its way across Glenys' face as she scoops up a fistful of flour and throws it over Violet.

The rare moment of silliness makes Violet's heart swell. The day no longer feels wet and miserable, but cosy and warm. Before long, Glenys' kitchen looks as if it's been swept up by a tornado, *Wizard of Oz* style. Flour covers the worktops, the floor and almost every square inch of Violet's black top and jogging bottoms.

By the time the flat starts to smell of slightly singed gingerbread, Glenys is tucked up with a blanket and napping on the sofa, exhausted from all the fun. Violet's pleased she's found something the two of them can enjoy doing together, especially if it means they can have delicious treats to taste afterwards. Though judging from the aroma, it might take a few goes before they reach a status of deliciousness. Perhaps baking, like caring, is not a perfect art.

Violet takes the decidedly well-cooked creations out of the oven, thinking about preparing something for dinner, when there's a knock at the door. She's already pulling down the door handle when she remembers she's covered in flour.

'You need to come to my flat.' Tammy's rubbing her hands together in the doorway. 'Come on – you need to be quick before he leaves.'

'Before who leaves?' Violet asks as she's rushed up the stairs and through Tammy's front door. She can't have been letting those troublemakers back into her flat, could she?

Violet stops moving when she sees who's on Tammy's sofa.

'Come and sit down.' Tammy guides Violet across the room and signals towards the chair opposite Adam. The coffee table is in the middle and it's covered with several tea towels.

'I didn't have any tablecloths,' Tammy explains.

On top of the tea towels are three mugs of coffee, and a jam jar filled with water and dandelions from the back garden. The sticker is still on the jar: *Raspberry*, from the corner shop.

'I'm glad you were both able to make it today,' Tammy says in a serious voice.

Adam glances at Violet and gives her a grin that makes her tummy flip.

'Right. You both stay there. I'll get your beans on toast. That's what your starter is.' Tammy curtsies before walking to the kitchen worktop and returning with two plates balanced precariously on each hand. 'Whose was the beans on toast?' she asks.

'Oh. Mine, please,' Violet says. 'And erm, this is very lovely of you, but what's the occasion? Has something happened?' Violet darts her eyes towards Tammy and waits for her to say she's been in trouble again – perhaps she's invited Adam over and made food to soften the blow.

'Here you go.' Tammy places the plates down. They're piled high with slightly burned toast and beans. 'Enjoy. Your main will be chicken soup. I'll leave your bowls on the worktop for now.'

Violet gives Tammy a small smile and takes a bite of the toast.

'This is delicious. Thanks for the invite.' Another grin from Adam who shrugs his shoulders when Violet looks his way. He clearly has no clue what this is all about either.

'No need to worry, neither of you will have to stay long. There are only a few questions for Violet to ask. I've written them down for her.' Tammy retrieves a bit of paper from her pocket.

It takes Violet several seconds to realise what Tammy is reading out, and when she does, her stomach plummets towards the floor so hard, she's surprised it can't be heard bouncing off the lino.

'Tammy – is this – do you think this is a date?' she asks, mortified.

Tammy beams and nods her head. 'Thank you, Adam, for coming,' she says. 'I am helping Violet with her number two.'

Adam's mouth twitches and Violet sinks lower into the sofa.

'Number two on Violet's *to-do* list,' Tammy flattens the paper out on the table, 'is to *find true love.*'

Oh, kill me now. Violet digs her nails into the cushion.

Tammy carries on. 'She's working on her other tasks. Because Violet has been very busy, I wanted to help. She's done lots of work on her list already – all she needs now is love.'

Silence fills every inch of the room. The walls themselves might burst apart with the pressure of containing it until Tammy starts to hum *Sweet Child O' Mine.*

'It's not how it sounds,' Violet bursts out. Her cheeks feel like they've been inside an oven on gas mark six. 'I had no idea Tammy was going to do this.'

'No. Violet's right,' Tammy pipes up. 'It was a surprise. Something to say thank you for all the help she's given me. And yesterday, she was miserable all day and kept staring at her phone. People do that when they're waiting for someone to call. But you never did, Adam, did you?'

'That's fine, we don't need to talk anymore about that. The beans on toast was delicious. Thank you,' Violet says brightly to Tammy as she hands her plate back to her.

'But you haven't had your main yet – your soup is waiting.' Tammy looks dismayed. 'And you still have to ask the questions.'

'Tammy, this was a very kind thing for you to do,' Violet says. 'But I don't really think—'

'I'm sorry.' Tammy's face is going pale. 'I didn't mean to be … inappropriate. Or waste your time. It's just that you've been such a good friend and I want to be one too.'

'Maybe you could just start the questions,' Adam says with a light voice. 'I'd be more than happy to answer them.'

Violet swallows and clears her throat. 'Fair enough.' She looks down at the piece of paper Tammy has given her before reading aloud. 'If you married Violet, would you rather stay at Malvern House or would you want her to move away with you and live in a bigger house?'

'That's a very good question.' Adam smiles at Tammy, and Violet's shoulders relax. At least he's willing to play along.

'Well, answer it carefully,' Tammy says. 'Your answer is very important for our decision.'

A smile tugs at the corner of Violet's mouth and she looks away from Adam's face.

'I think that's something we'd have to discuss a bit closer to the wedding,' Adam says in a serious voice.

'Number two,' Violet says, warming to the list of questions in front of her written in Tammy's scrawled handwriting. 'Would Violet be given lots of time off to visit Tammy?' A chuckle sits at the back of her throat and she has to swallow it down before she can trust herself to speak. 'Marriage isn't supposed to be like a job, Tammy – when people get married, they don't have to ask for "time off". They shouldn't have to, anyway.'

'That being said, I would absolutely make sure that Violet has plenty of time to spend with you,' Adam says.

Tammy gives him a satisfied nod.

'And last question – would you make sure that Violet stays as happy as possible for the rest of her life?' Violet's voice cracks towards the end of the sentence and it's all she can do not to throw her arms around Tammy's shoulders and weep.

'I would never marry anyone I didn't intend to make happy,' Adam says. He looks at Violet and the silly grin disappears from his face.

'Well – I think we're onto a winner – what do you think, Violet? Do you like the man I found you?' Tammy spins around.

Violet places a gentle hand on Tammy's shoulder. 'You did well. Thank you. But I don't think I need any man to be happy. Not when I have a friend like you.'

Adam gets up and collects the bowls of soup from the worktop. 'We can still eat this lovely soup, though – no point letting it all go to waste.'

The three of them sit and eat until all the plates and bowls are empty. They're so busy laughing and chatting, Violet doesn't even taste the food. All she can think about is how good it feels to be joking around with Adam. No awkwardness, no barrier now that Tammy has smashed her way through the ice.

'Thank you for going along with this,' Violet leans over and whispers to Adam when Tammy gets up to stack the plates in the sink.

Adam places a hand over Violet's. His skin is warm and he smells of Persil. 'Who says I was playing along? Best date I've had in a long time.'

Violet turns her face towards him. 'I just … I've been feeling bad for the last couple of weeks. About saying all those things at that meeting about the fire. I know it can't have been easy for you or your dad to hear.'

'It wasn't.' Adam's hair flops across his face as he shakes his head. Loads of his hair has fallen loose from his topknot and Violet wants to run her hands through it. 'It was horrific for everyone back then. For you and your family, and for me and mine. It was a tragic accident, but that's exactly what it was – an accident. I've never blamed you, not once. Not then, not now.' He runs his thumb lightly across the inside of her wrist, sending goosebumps up her arms. 'Thanks for a lovely evening, Tammy. Violet and I are going to head off.'

Tammy beams and waves them down the stairs from her doorway.

Adam lingers in the downstairs hallway.

'I need you to give me two days,' he murmurs to Violet. 'I'm going to pop a message on the WhatsApp group – see if someone can be around for Dad and your mum on Tuesday evening. There's somewhere special I want to take you.' Adam pulls Violet so close she can feel his heart beating through his shirt.

'Sounds good,' she mutters into his shoulder.

Adam kisses her on the forehead, steps backwards and walks into his flat without saying another word.

@BookWorm1908

Today, I've been reading **Anne's House of Dreams.** It's a classic and I've read it a million times before but that's because it's the most wonderful thing in the world that Anne and Gilbert end up together happily ever after, even with the odds stacked against them. Not many people end up with their very first love, though they are rarely forgotten.
I've never forgotten mine.

What are your favourite books about first loves? Are any of them classics?

#Love #FirstLove #AnneShirley #ClassicBooks

CHAPTER 36

Tammy

'I'M READY TO GET a job,' Tammy announces as soon as Chrissie opens the front door to her bungalow.

It's been two days since she organised Adam and Violet's date and she's been looking for something else to focus on.

'You'd best come in then.' Chrissie gives Tammy a big grin and doesn't even mention that it's eight o'clock in the morning or that Tammy had forgotten to call first to say she was dropping in.

Tammy had only realised how early it was when she saw Chrissie's fluffy dressing gown that makes her look like a deliciously squidgy marshmallow. She couldn't stay in bed any longer this morning, she'd been awake all night.

Thinking.

Day dreaming, but in the dark.

All these things she can do now, that she couldn't before – except that she *could*, she just hadn't known it. What else might be out there that she can do, but doesn't know it yet? If the last few months is anything to go by, the only way to find out is to try.

Kettle, toaster, shopping, cooking.

Making friends.

'My writing's getting better – especially after all that help you've been giving me. I want to do my exams; the ones I would have done if I'd kept going to school.'

Chrissie starts looking around her living room and peeking over her glasses, behind the sofa, beside the armchair.

'Did you hear me?' Tammy asks. 'What have you lost?'

'My handbag. Ah.' Chrissie reaches under her table and plucks her bag from the floor. 'I need it because you and I are going into Brighton. First stop, the Adult Education Centre, then we can have a look around for places that are hiring. You, my dear, are more than ready for the big wide world.'

Excitement stirs Tammy's belly as she runs along next to Chrissie on the way to the bus stop. Chrissie is the wisest woman she's ever met – even wiser than Rita Sullivan in *Coronation Street*.

The bus ride is an exhilarating one. They sit on the top deck with the windows open, and the salty air comes billowing through as the bus picks up speed on the coastal road. Tammy's eyes soak up the blue of the sea and the flecks of sunshine as they wink at her from the waves. She's got this, they say. And they're right, she has.

Tammy and Chrissie get off the bus by the pier. Twenty-five minutes later, they are sitting in an office filling out admission forms for an adult literacy and maths class for the following term.

'Thank you.' Tammy slips her hand into Chrissie's soft, leathery one as they walk back up the road. 'Knowing that you believe I can do something, helps me believe it for myself. I think I …' She stops when she sees the sign in the neon-pink-framed window across the road.

Apprentice Wanted, Part-time

'I've always wanted to go on *The Apprentice*,' Tammy says. She feels out of breath, even though they've only just started walking. 'Have you seen it, that thing on the telly where they all have to—'

'I don't think that's what they're after in there,' Chrissie laughs. 'That's a hairdresser. They want someone to work in there whilst they learn how to be one.'

'I want to go in.'

'I didn't know you wanted to be a hairdresser – we can keep looking around, you don't have to go for the first job you see.'

Tammy thinks about all those people, chatting away under hairdryers and telling their stories while their hair changes colour or goes all curly.

'I want this one. Wait here, I'm going in – I can do this on my own.'

As the bell dings on her way in, Tammy puts on her best smile without even trying. Somehow, she knows she's opening the door to a brand-new adventure.

By the time she reaches the front desk, she seems to have forgotten how to talk. The woman behind the counter has bright purple lips and glitter on her cheeks. She's chewing gum and staring at Tammy, asking questions with her eyebrows instead of her mouth.

'The sign outside says you want someone to be an apprentice?' Tammy manages to get the words out slowly, one at a time as her heart pounds harder.

The woman looks her up and down. 'Julie does, yeah. Julie!' she yells across to a tall lady who has very bright trousers on and a hairdryer in her hand.

'Hang on.' Julie puts the hairdryer on a hook by the mirror and walks towards them. She smiles at Tammy and it helps her words come back.

'Mmm,' Julie says, after Tammy's told her why she's there. She frowns and looks at the clock. 'We're short today, actually. Our other girl's called in sick. The aprons need rinsing and we're fully booked. If you can stick around now and do some hair-washing and tea-making, I can give you a week's trial. How does that sound?'

Terrifying. Strangers are coming and going through the door. The purple-lipped woman is still staring at her and the smell of hairspray is getting right down her throat.

Tammy turns and looks through the front windows. 'My friend's waiting outside – I'm not sure if I can …'

Chrissie is pushing the door open. The bell dings. She's walking towards them.

'Of course I don't mind. I've got shopping to do anyway. I'll come and meet you when you've finished,' Chrissie says once Tammy has stammered her way through the situation.

The first hour is the worst one. Tammy puts the aprons in the washing machine on the wrong setting and some of them are ruined. She manages to trip up a customer with her broom when she sweeps up Mrs Johnson's trimmings, and she almost burns a lady's scalp when she washes her hair.

The woman with the purple lips is called Jade and she says to Tammy, 'You've never had a job before, have you?'

Tammy doesn't want to lie, and she also doesn't want to

say no because she has a feeling it will make Jade's smirk even bigger.

'I'd just go home if I were you. Julie won't want you back after today – you're wasting your time.'

Tears sting the backs of Tammy's eyes. She runs to the kitchen to put the kettle on for the next customer before pulling off her glasses and wiping her face.

Jade's right. Tammy shouldn't be here. She's not the sort of person to have a job. Mum would have a fit. Tammy belongs at home where it's safe. She takes her phone out of her pocket and holds it close to her face so she can find Chrissie's number.

'No, I will not come and get you.' Chrissie uses her firm but gentle teacher voice when Tammy's finished telling her what happened. 'You're bound to make mistakes, that's how we learn. But I know you can do it. You just need to show *yourself* that you can.'

The door dings. The next customer is here. Tammy covers her shoulders with one of the non-ruined aprons and washes her hair gently. This time she knows how to get the water temperature just right and how to rinse out the shampoo without getting it in the customer's eyes.

After she's brought the lady her drink and sat her down in front of a mirror, the lady takes a sip and says, 'That's the best cuppa I've had all day. And it was so lovely talking to you. Did you say your name was Tammy? Next time I come in I'm going to ask for you again.'

Tammy sees the smile land across her own face in the mirror. She stands up straighter. 'Yes, that's right. I'm Tammy.'

And she's never been prouder to be herself.

CHAPTER 37

Violet

CHRISSIE ARRIVES AT MALVERN House armed with cake and a crossword book for her and Glenys. 'Don't look so nervous,' she says to Violet, chuckling. 'Your mum and I will be fine, just go and have a wonderful time with that lovely man. Doesn't seem five minutes since you two were whispering to each other at the back of my English class. Oh, you do look a picture,' she adds with a smile.

Violet allows herself a last glance in the mirror. She hasn't had time to straighten her hair, so it's still in her usual thick braids, but she's pulled on her favourite purple T-shirt dress and applied a light dust of bronzer across her freckled cheeks.

Adam's waiting on the doorstep with the smile of a child who's excited to show off something he's made.

The sun's low in the sky and the air is fresh from a day of rain. Violet carries the blanket Adam had instructed her to bring, along with a bucket-load of nerves, as she follows Adam around the side of the building, through the back garden of Malvern House and up the footpath towards the woods.

Neither speak until they reach the lake.

Adam places a gentle arm around her waist and whispers into her ear. 'Close your eyes.'

Violet laughs as Adam guides her across the bridge, giddy from the heat of his hand on her hip.

'We're on the other side. The ground is uneven from now on, but I'll try not to let you trip.'

'Wow, thanks.' Violet surprises herself with how normal her voice sounds when her heart feels like she's swallowed a whole packet of caffeine pills. 'Is it muddy? These are my only trainers, you know.'

'No. It's been so warm this evening, everything's dried out. Lucky for us.'

Sticks crack beneath Violet's feet and the smell of lavender and earth tickles her nose.

Adam takes his arm away from her. 'You can look now.'

'Ohh.' Violet lets out a long breath. Directly in front of her is a perfectly constructed den, nestled beneath her favourite childhood climbing tree. Several blankets have been draped over sticks that have been placed inside the bushes surrounding it, and fairy lights twinkle from the tree trunk.

Violet walks forward and crouches down, peeking inside. A large blanket covers the ground. In the middle is a picnic basket, a bottle of wine and two glasses. Tea lights and torches in the corners give the den the cosiest glow imaginable.

Adam was always a perfectionist when it came to building dens. When they were kids, it used to take them a whole afternoon to get one just right.

Adam gives Violet a mock bow and gestures for her to go inside. 'I hope it lives up to my past attempts.' He climbs in after

Violet and sits on the other side of the picnic basket. 'I started building it the morning after the dinner date Tammy put on for us. I'm impressed it's still here and hasn't been demolished by the kids from the village – that's what usually happens.'

'You still build dens?' Violet smiles at Adam's blushing face.

'Not regularly. Just when I'm feeling nostalgic.'

Violet thinks back to her recent tree climb with the matching trip down memory lane. 'This was a lovely thing to do. It looks beautiful. Thank you.'

Adam pours the wine, and they clink glasses, looking each other full in the eyes for the first time since leaving the grounds of Malvern House. Violet suspects her cheeks are as flushed as Adam's are and her hand trembles as she lifts her drink to her lips.

'Now, this is something we never had in our old dens.' Adam laughs and waves his glass in the air.

'Just as well. We were a little young for rosé.' Violet pictures the last time she and Adam sat inside a den together, clumsy hands and nervous words. Not much feels different if she's honest.

They both fall silent. The birdsong around them gets louder.

'Made up for it after, though, eh?' Adam chuckles but it sounds hollow. He stops and fiddles with a tea light that's flickered off.

Violet goes cold. 'I'm not proud of how I acted back then. Drinking, acting up. I didn't know how else to cope.'

'I know, I'm sorry, I didn't mean to drag it all up. You were just a kid.'

Even the birds are silent now. All that can be heard is the swish of the wind in the branches above.

'I just hated losing you.' Adam stretches his legs out in front of him. 'You were my best friend. I needed you, especially after Mum.'

Violet opens her eyes wider to stave off the tears. 'I thought I was the last person you'd want hanging around. I still don't know how you can stand to be near me.'

A frustrated growl rumbles from Adam and he sits up, both hands balled into fists. 'I've told you this before, but you never seem to hear what I'm saying. It wasn't your fault. I didn't blame you then and I don't blame you now.'

Violet picks at the loose skin around her fingernails. 'Everyone else did.'

'They didn't. They really didn't. It was an accident; how could you have known? And who would blame a child for that?'

Violet shrugs. 'Lots of people did. Everyone at school. Mum said half the village were against us and Jodie definitely thought it was all my fault.'

'It wasn't everyone at school. Maybe a couple of them, but they were kids too. And yes, the village gossiped about it; people were in shock. But most people wanted to help, they felt awful for you and your family. You always get the dickheads who wants to stick the boot in but that doesn't mean everyone was against you.'

Violet's arms are chilly. She wraps her blanket tightly around herself. 'Mum thinks it was my fault. She always will.'

'Your mum wasn't well. She still isn't. I'm sure Glenys doesn't believe that deep down, and your sister was so young. She was grieving and had the sudden responsibility of taking care of your mum.'

Violet closes her eyes and holds a breath inside her as the memories flood her mind.

'I want to believe what you're saying, I really do. I've carried this stuff for so long. I keep remembering your face the first time you saw me after it happened. So much shock and hurt – it haunted me. I looked into your eyes and saw hate.'

'I hated what happened. Hated that I lost Mum, that you lost your dad. And I hated that my best friend didn't want to be anywhere near me. But I've never hated you.' Adam wipes his eye with a corner of his sleeve and points to a back corner of the den. 'Do you think it's still there?'

'What?' Violet says before it registers.

The diary.

'Shall we have a look?' Adam grabs a spoon and a knife from the picnic basket and starts hacking away at the ground.

'I buried it again – the year after we wrote in it together for the last time,' Violet mumbles as Adam pulls a mud-caked book from the earth.

'That's funny. So did I.' Adam carefully opens the diary and turns the pages before handing it to Violet. The ink is faded but still readable. 'I wrote it when I was eighteen – the New Year's Eve after you left, I dug it up and found your sorry note. I didn't think you'd ever get to read my reply, but I guess it felt important to write it anyway.'

Dear Violet,

I wish you'd said this to me instead of burying your apology in the ground. I could have told you that there was no need for sorry – that it wasn't your fault, what happened.

Now you're gone and I've lost the only girl I've ever loved. No one will ever take your place.

Be happy.
Adam. X

Violet picks up the picnic basket that's sitting between them and moves it to the other side, shuffling into the gap next to Adam. He puts an arm around her and pulls her close, until their thighs are touching.

'Thank you,' she whispers. A tear trickles down her face, followed by another. 'I tried to tell you, I tried to say sorry the night before I went away. The night we …'

Adam brushes the tears away from Violet's cheek with his thumb and Violet realises they're mirrored by his own. She hooks both hands around his neck and leans her face on Adam's shoulder. His arms pull tight around her waist and they fall sideways until they are lying down, chest to chest, their hearts thumping close together.

They lie still for a long time, holding each other's memories between them.

Adam pulls back to rub his eyes again with the inside of his elbow. 'I'm glad we talked,' he murmurs. His face is inches from Violet's. 'I've been wanting to clear all that up for a long time. Amongst other things.'

'Me too.' Violet hears the wobble in her own whispered voice. She can't take her gaze away from Adam. In the warm glow of the den, the burned orange flecks glint amongst the green of his eyes. He looks down at her mouth and she inches closer.

In the seconds before their lips meet, another kiss plays itself in the back of Violet's mind. A kiss of two thirteen-year-olds, the accidental clashing of teeth and nervous giggles. It had been the happiest moment of Violet's teens.

Violet starts to chuckle.

'What's so funny?' Adam says. Their mouths are so close their lips brush against each other as he speaks.

'I was just remembering the first time we did this.'

'Mmm, me too. I'm still just as terrified.' A deep chuckle comes from his throat.

'Don't be.' Violet's had enough of the sweet torture of waiting. She wriggles against him, covering his mouth with her own.

It's like switching on an ignition. Adam returns her kiss urgently, deeply. He pulls the bands out of Violet's red braids and runs his fingers through her hair. She pulls off his jumper and runs her hands under his T-shirt, feeling the warm skin of his chest beneath her touch.

Every inch between them closes as they pull each other closer. Violet can't tell where she ends and Adam begins, the last nineteen years stretching between them from their first kiss until now. Every now and again, Violet pauses to look at his face to make sure it's really Adam in her arms. It's as if time is playing tricks on her and nothing has changed since last time. Nothing exists except two far-apart moments bending to meet with a kiss.

'You've no idea how much I've thought about this moment,' Adam says in a low voice between kisses. His lips brush her neck, her collar bone, her shoulder. 'I obsessed about you enough back then. I had no idea how crazy you'd still be making me all these years later.'

Violet nuzzles her nose against the soft skin of Adam's neck, savouring the subtle scent of his aftershave. 'I never stopped thinking about you. Every New Year's Eve text I got from you just dented my heart a little more and knowing you were married ...' Violet cringes at herself. Why bring that up now? 'Stupid really after all that time. What did I expect, that you'd stay single for life?'

The kiss had happened about six months before the fire. They hadn't mentioned it in the days afterwards, just played in the lake and the trees as usual, too embarrassed to bring it up in case the other one regretted it. Nothing is scarier to a thirteen-year-old than rejection.

'I missed you so much back then. I hated seeing how crazy you were getting with Megan and the others.'

'I wish you'd said something.' Even at sixteen, Violet's chest hurt whenever she passed Adam in the street. It made her cling all the more to the alcohol. She went from one year eleven boy to the next, blocking out the pain and the longing. Whoever said teenagers can't know what it is to be in love never met someone like Adam. A first love is a punch to the gut. It leaves a scar that has something to say for itself in every subsequent relationship.

You never forget your first love.

'I wish I had too. But life happened how it happened. Can't change it now.' Adam laces his fingers through Violet's, and she snuggles back against him. 'What matters is where we are now.'

'Mmm. I like it here.' Violet smiles before kissing his earlobe. She shuffles to the opening of the den, looking out at the patches of lake visible between the tree and taking in a gulp of fresh air.

Adam sits behind her, curling his arms around her waist and supporting her back with his chest as she leans against him. 'Me too. It's always been our place. Maybe we could get back in the habit of regular den-making?'

An alarm begins to sound deep within Violet. She tries to push it away, so the sound grows fainter. She can't stay in Lowerstone forever — if things progress as she'd planned on her arrival, then Adam won't be living in the building in front of these woods for very much longer either.

Tell him.

Adam's fingers draw slow circles on the inside of Violet's thighs, and he plants soft kisses on the nape of her neck.

Plans change. If she can find a way to get through to her mum, or a way to stay, Adam never needs to know.

CHAPTER 38

Violet

VIOLET CAN'T STOP SMILING as she collects the empty dinner plates from the garden table after a cheerful meal with Glenys. Ever since her den-date with Adam three days ago, she's been sleeping better than she has in years, and now every ray of sunshine feels like it was formed especially for her.

'You sure you don't want to come to the Helping Hands meeting at the community centre, Mum?'

The council had got back to Mrs Robson promptly about the community centre. They were more than happy for the Helping Hands gang to reopen it, as long as they covered the cost of cleaning and decorating.

Violet and Adam had visited the dog rescue centre the morning after their den-date. Whilst they were interviewing the staff for the *Gazette*, a customer who owns a garden centre in Upper Dorking overheard. Half an hour later, he left the centre with a receipt for six-months'-worth of advertising and a tiny chihuahua called Dave. The Helping Hands gang decided to put the money towards getting the community centre opened for the village and tonight will be their first meeting inside it.

'We're giving the place a lick of paint, sprucing it up for the launch party. Adam and Bill are coming,' Violet adds with a grin. Adam and Bill have been over for lunch for two days in a row and Violet has never seen Glenys laugh as much as she does when they're about.

'I've got one of my headaches. But I might come next time.' Glenys looks Violet in the eye and smiles. She means it.

After Violet has settled her mum, she meets her entourage of Malvern House residents by the fountain and they make their way together down to the village, collecting Chrissie and Claire on their way.

Adam takes hold of Violet's hand and gives it a squeeze whilst they wait for Mrs Robson to unlock the door with the rather rusty key she'd collected from the council office.

'Did the date work, then? Did I help you find true love?' Tammy whispers, not very quietly to Violet.

Violet hangs back and lets everyone else go in front of her.

'You know what?' Violet grins at Tammy. 'You definitely helped. Thank you. The date was a wonderful idea.' She pulls Tammy in for a hug. 'I heard your trial at the salon's going well?' Violet doesn't want to lose Tammy or move away from her – not ever. Tammy has become a true friend and watching her build a life for herself over the past few months has been incredible.

'It's been brilliant so far.' Tammy's grin is stretched so wide, it looks like it might snap in half.

Violet's stomach churns with a slew of conflicted emotions as she follows Tammy through the grimy green door into the hall. After weeks of stressing about how to get the tenants sorted so Violet can sell the building and get Glenys settled in a nursing home, it's now the thing she dreads the most. How can she go back to Manchester now, back to a nameless life? If things could just stay as they are, it wouldn't be the worst thing.

But for that, she needs to get Glenys on board, and Violet sticking around probably isn't a train her mum wants to get on.

Violet's breath catches in her chest as the memories bump up against each other the second she enters the hall. End-of-term discos, children's parties, and local plays. Jumble sales, Christmas fayres. Things that happened *before*.

The parquet floor and heavy velvet curtains are thick with dust and Violet sneezes three times as she opens the windows. The edges of the room are littered with empty cans and crisp packets and that musty smell will take some getting rid of. They'll need to do some serious cleaning between them before they can crack open the paint pots.

'I have excellent news,' Violet says as she hands out sponges, buckets and bin bags from the cupboard at the side of the hall. 'I've put together all the pieces we went over last week, and our first online issue is ready to go live tomorrow.'

Whoops and whistles echo around the hall and Claire balances her phone on a windowsill, pressing play on her list of nineties' hits that blast their way into everyone's ears as they scrub, mop and dust.

There's something satisfying about washing away the years of dirt and neglect. The cleaner the hall gets, the lighter Violet feels. It's as if she's scrubbing away the past and rinsing the memories, replacing them with something shiny and fresh.

An hour later, when they stop for a tea break, Violet places the printout of the first *Gazette* issue in the middle of the room on the now-clean floor.

Claire blushes again as everyone raves about the logo she designed.

'I've put a poster up in the library with the web address,' says Mrs Robson. 'And people have been told how to sign up to have the *Gazette* emailed to them each week. I've also printed off a few copies for people to pick up from reception if they don't have any computer access. Though of course, it will be wonderful to have it printed on a larger scale so that everyone in the village can read our articles and be connected to the paper.'

'I have something for the next issue.' Bill speaks quietly from his chair as he pulls a sheet of paper from his pocket; he's struggling with his speech today. Adam reads Bill's piece out loud for him after Bill whispers something in his ear. It's an interview Bill had undertaken during the week with an older friend of his who has lived in the village since he was evacuated as a child at the beginning of the war. It's a fascinating story, vivid and poignant, and Violet closes her eyes as Adam reads it, viewing the village through the eyes of a different time.

'Thank you, Bill. That's fabulous. Is your friend happy for his story to be in the paper?'

'He signed the form.' Bill manages a nod and a smile. 'I knew you'd ask. Glad you like it. It was nice talking to him. Haven't seen him since my health started playing up.'

'That's wonderful. And Chrissie has collected enough questions for the problem page for the next six issues … Oh, so sorry, please excuse me for a sec.' Violet's phone is buzzing with a call from Jenny. She steps away from the group and walks to the back of the hall.

'Not looking good for Mr Mullens,' Jenny says. 'I did a background check on him after speaking to you the other day. He's got several previous convictions for GBH over the last ten years. My guess would be he may not have treated Lydia well. Probably why she changed her name and why she's kept Tammy away.'

'Thank you, Jenny.' Violet's been mulling over what to say to Tammy about her dad ever since she's known for sure who he is. This information has pushed her much further towards not telling her. It feels too risky.

'How are things going?'

Violet finds herself telling her all about the *Gazette*.

'You sound happy,' Jenny says. 'I always knew you had it in you to work for a newspaper – sounds like the perfect experience for you. And I'm sorry it's bad news about Michael. From what it sounds like, Tammy is lucky to have you and your Helping Hands Club around her – perhaps she's not that alone after all.'

Jenny's words echo around Violet's mind long after she's hung up the phone. Violet may not be able to help Tammy with her blood relatives, but she can do her best to make sure she and the others stick by her.

That's what families do.

CHAPTER 39

Tammy

TAMMY'S FLAT FILLS WITH sunshine as she opens the curtains to a new day. Through the window she can see that Violet and Mrs Robson are just about to get into Violet's car.

Tammy can't hear what Violet is saying or see her face from where she is, but she can tell by the tune in her voice that she's happy. Tammy likes making Violet happy. So far, all of Tammy's plans to make Violet happy have worked. The date she set up helped Violet find her true love. Her investigation into the factory fire helped her to know that people didn't blame her.

Tammy does remember one more thing that Violet said. *I wish my mum could see it that way.*

Perhaps Tammy's investigation is incomplete. When she has all the facts, maybe Violet will be happier to put the report in the paper. She picks up her reporter's notebook and pencil from the top of the fridge and squidges her feet into her slippers before running down the stairs, two at a time, to Violet's flat. Tammy doesn't know how long Violet will be out for and she might be cross if she catches Tammy in her flat when she's not there.

Glenys might not answer. Tammy knocks extra loudly in case she's asleep. No sound comes from the other side of the door, even when Tammy presses her ear up against it.

It could take Violet's mum a while to get up, so Tammy busies herself with singing 'Take on Me'. She's just got to the second chorus by the time the door opens, and Glenys is standing on the other side of it.

'You call that singing?' One of Glenys' eyebrows is higher than the other. Perhaps she's not a fan of A-ha.

'Yes. I like singing. You don't have to be good at something to enjoy it. Can I come into your flat, please?'

Violet once said Tammy needs to get better at reading people and that it would come with practice. Tammy thinks she must be getting better already because she can tell that Glenys wants to say no.

'I'll make the coffees – I'm good at them – and I promise to leave as soon as you say you don't want me there anymore,' says Tammy.

It works. Glenys still doesn't smile but she nods and pulls the door wider open so that Tammy can get through.

Tammy walks straight to the kettle, fills it with water and switches it on. She opens her notebook and turns to face Glenys. She's lowering herself into an armchair.

Tammy needs to ask her questions carefully this time. It was one thing speaking to those people in the shops, but it wasn't their husband who had died.

'I'm sorry your husband died in a fire. It must have been awful. Do you think it was Violet's fault? Most people don't think so, but Violet thinks you do. Could you tell me your side of the story, please?' Tammy uses her politest voice.

Glenys is blinking so fast it's a wonder her eyelashes aren't falling off and flying around the room.

'In your own time,' Tammy adds when Glenys doesn't answer. On TV, it's what people say when they want people to hurry up, but they need to say it nicely.

'I thought you were making us a coffee?' Glenys stares at the carpet.

Tammy's pouring the milk into the cups when she hears Glenys' frame creaking behind her.

Glenys' words are quiet, almost a whisper. 'I keep trying to tell her the truth, but the words never seem to come out. What happened wasn't Violet's fault. It was mine.'

CHAPTER 40

Violet

VIOLET KNOWS SOMETHING'S WRONG the second she gets through the door. Her mum's sitting at one end of her dining table and Tammy's perched on the other side. Both have tear-stained faces and Tammy is scribbling something in her notebook.

'What's happened?' Violet hangs her handbag over the back of a dining chair and sits down.

'I need to …' Glenys breaks off, leaning her elbows on the table in front of her and covering her face with her hands.

'Your mum needs to tell you something,' says Tammy as she stares at Glenys.

Violet's chest tightens around her thumping heart.

'I will. I … will. Not here though. Violet, I want you to take me to your dad.'

Blood pulses loudly in Violet's ears.

'I want you to take me to where he's buried. I think that will be the best place for me to tell you.' Glenys' mouth is set in a determined line and her words pick up strength as they fall from her lips.

'I'll be in my flat if you need me.' Tammy picks up her notebook, hugs Violet and walks over to Glenys.

Glenys' shoulders stiffen as Tammy approaches her. 'I don't deserve your hugs. Not until I've told Violet the truth.'

Violet unfolds Glenys' wheelchair with shaking hands and the two of them venture into the afternoon chill. The road to the village is foggy and thick with silence.

Neither of them speak until they reach the gate to the churchyard. Violet's chest feels tight and full of air as her mind races through scenario after scenario of what Glenys might be about to tell her. The tall iron gate is cold beneath Violet's fingertips and it creaks as she pushes it open.

'Take me straight to him. No stopping.' Glenys' voice wobbles. 'I've not been in here for sixteen years.'

Three paths point in different directions between the neat lawns. Violet manoeuvres Glenys' chair onto the first one, her gaze falling on the back left corner of the churchyard.

She still remembers exactly where it is.

It starts to rain. Violet's heart picks up some extra beats. She's forced herself to face a lot of things lately but her grief for her dad is something she's barely locked eyes with. She hadn't allowed herself the luxury of mourning when her father was so cruelly ripped away. The grief belonged to her mum and to Jodie. They wore it tightly around themselves and there hadn't been a corner left for Violet to grab hold onto.

'Stop.' Glenys raises a hand. Her voice cracks. 'I need a minute. You go first. Go and see him. Speak to him.'

Violet swallows and nudges the wheelchair brake on with her foot. 'If you're sure.'

Glenys nods. Her face is pale and her mouth quivers. 'I'll catch up.'

Violet makes her way slowly down the rest of the path until she reaches the headstone.

Steven Strong. Beloved husband and father. Loved by all.

Violet moves closer. She reaches out and grazes the top of the headstone with her fingertips.

'Hi, Dad,' she says, feeling foolish. 'Sorry it's been so long.' She doesn't know what else to say so she gives up with words and closes her eyes instead. She pictures his face when he used to get home from work. He used to scoop Violet up and lift her high in the air, even when she was way too big to be picked up. He was always laughing, even when Mum was in one of her moods.

The raindrops are getting bigger and they keep splashing across Dad's name. Violet pulls up the zip on her jacket and walks back to her mum. 'You ready?'

'Yes.'

Glenys stands up from her chair as soon as they stop. She hooks one hand inside the crook of Violet's elbow, and they take small steps across the grass. Once they're just a few feet away, Glenys lets go and shuffles ahead until she's in touching distance of the headstone.

Glenys' shoulders heave but she doesn't allow her sobs to get in the way of what she needs to say to her husband. Her gnarly knuckles turn white from gripping tightly to the top of the headstone.

Violet listens. Perhaps her dad is listening too; Violet hopes he is.

'I'm sorry, Violet. I'm so, so sorry.' Glenys turns to face

Violet with water pouring in all directions from her eyes like a badly drawn cartoon.

Glenys traces the engraved letters of *Steven* with her fingers before turning back again to face Violet straight-on. 'I've carried this guilt for a long time. If I'd been braver and spoken up earlier, perhaps you'd have dragged a lighter load through your life.'

'What are you talking about?'

'The fire. Those Gameboy Advances you and Jodie both had.'

Violet's stomach twists, the way it always does whenever she thinks about the charger cable that ruined so many lives.

'The wire for Jodie's got ruined,' Glenys carries on. 'Jodie's, not yours. It split because I rolled my chair over it by accident and I put it in a drawer out of the way.'

The leafy branches in front of Violet become a blur. She places her hand against the nearest tree trunk, fighting to stay upright.

'An hour after I put it away, Jodie was pestering for me for her charger and I didn't have the energy for an argument. I gave her yours instead. I forgot about it after that – my memory wasn't always good back then, still isn't, really. You must have found the charger in the drawer and thought it was yours. You wouldn't have seen the split in the wire, it was tiny. After the fire, I remembered but I could never get the words out. It wouldn't have brought your dad back and it wouldn't have brought Marian back. So, I said nothing. The guilt ate away at me every day. Every time I looked at you, I thought about what I'd done.'

It's more words than her mum has ever said before at once and each one of them churns around in Violet's mind as she stares at her dad's gravestone.

'I know I pushed you away, Violet. I couldn't look you in the face. I always thought you blamed me.'

A car rumbles past the wall of the cemetery. A bird starts singing from the oak tree beside them.

Violet puts one arm around her mum and then the other, and then they are holding onto each other. Both crying. All those years of guilt. The wasted years of blame and separation.

'We can't change the past, Mum.' Violet pulls her arms away and collects the tears from under her eyes with her fingers.

'No. But I want to try and make the present a bit better. I want to be a proper mum to you. I'm not very good at it – I never was – but I want to try.'

Violet thinks of the nights by the fire as Glenys plaited her hair and read her stories. 'You were good at it for lots of the time. We all just lost our way when we lost Dad.'

'I'm glad you came back.' Glenys' voice breaks again. 'I'm sorry I told you I didn't want you here, it was a lie. A wicked, nasty one. I thought you'd leave, and I'd be protecting you from me.'

'I thought you hated me.'

Glenys' face crumples. 'Never. I've never hated you. Only myself. Seeing you again after all those years ... I was terrified of ruining things for you for a second time. I wanted you to leave, to go back to the life you'd built for yourself without me. That way, you stood a chance at being happy.'

The rain stops. It's like someone's turned the tap off.

It's as if the life is returning to Violet's soul after too many years of keeping it still. Like an arm that's been slept on awkwardly, the numbness turns to a tingling before the blood starts flowing freely once again. Seeing the love in her mum's eyes, knowing that it had always been there despite being buried beneath so much guilt and grief; it's almost too much to hold inside Violet's heart.

Violet searches for her own anger. It must be there somewhere. Her mum's actions had allowed Violet to think everything that happened with Dad was her own fault. All those years of making decisions based on the belief she was *Bad News*. That she didn't deserve a fuller life. If the anger is in there, it's hiding right now, cloaked by the knowledge that her mum has lived with this ever since and by the overwhelming relief that Violet wasn't to blame.

In order to truly move forward with Glenys, honesty needs to be a two-way street. It's Violet's turn to tell the truth.

She looks for the right words to place inside the silence. 'Coming back here was one of the hardest things I've ever done. At the time, I thought the best thing to do was to get the building sold as quickly as possible, get you into residential care and then leave the village. I didn't think you and I would get the chance to get to know each other again.'

A tear trickles down Glenys' cheek.

'And I didn't expect to make friends here, real friends,' Violet carries on. 'If we sell Malvern House, some of those friends will have nowhere to go and they'll have to leave the village. I don't want to leave. I want to stay. And I want *you* to stay instead of moving into Rossendale. I've been wanting to tell you for weeks, but I was too afraid of your answer. So, what do you think?'

Glenys stands up as straight as she can, linking her arm back through Violet's. 'That,' she says, 'is the best idea you've had since you came back home.'

CHAPTER 41

Tammy

TAMMY'S THROAT FEELS LIKE something has been tied around it and pulled into a tight knot. Her eyes are filling with tears and if she can't swallow in the next two seconds, a huge sob will probably fall out. Which is weird because she's not sad, not even a little bit.

It's those flowers, making her want to cry. Or it's Violet's face as she holds them out towards her. No one has ever given Tammy flowers before, not even her mum.

'They're only from the garden,' Violet says. She's wearing a stripy pinafore and her eyes are red and puffy. 'I just wanted to say thank you. And you can keep the vase – Mum's got way too many of them crammed into her cupboard.'

The flowers smell like earth and sunshine with a dash of honey. They are purple and yellow and red. Tammy takes the vase from Violet and puts the flowers on her coffee table. Tammy's flat is transformed. Love now lives there with her and it's in the shape of several dozen petals.

'You've normally rushed to the kettle to make me a cuppa

by now.' Violet's laughing and Tammy wonders how long she's been staring at the flowers.

'Do you want a coffee?' Tammy rubs her hands together. Making a drink for Violet and herself and sitting and *Having a Natter* as Violet calls it is the happiest part of Tammy's day.

As soon as the two of them are perched on the sofa, mugs in hands, Violet starts saying thank you again.

'Speaking to my mum about the fire was incredibly brave – she's not always the easiest person to talk to.'

Tammy remembers how pale Violet's face had gone whilst she'd said her mum needed to speak to her. 'Sorry if I made things worse,' she mumbles. 'I didn't mean to upset anyone.'

'You didn't.' Violet leans forward and squeezes Tammy's hand. 'You helped my mum and me to have a conversation we'd been needing to have for eighteen years. I'll always be grateful for that. You gave me back my mum.'

The tight-throat-and-tears-thing is back again. Tammy had never realised before that so many happy things could make you want to cry.

'And how is your true love?' Tammy asks. A giggle falls out and she wishes she could cram it back inside where it came from. Giggling makes her sound like a child. Like a baby.

Violet's mouth moves into a smile that's so big, it takes over her whole face. 'He's great. We're great. More than great. I'm just so grateful we've been given a second chance with each other. Guess I've got you to thank for that as well.'

Tammy takes a gulp of her drink.

'I was only thirteen the first time Adam kissed me. We kept laughing and bumping teeth, but it was still wonderful. I just can't believe we've got a second chance after all these years.'

Tammy wonders if she'll ever meet someone she can fall in love with. She hopes when she does, it will be someone who could also fall in love with her. And what are the chances of that for most people? It all sounds very complicated.

Violet's eyes are all twinkly and shiny by the time she's finished her drink and she keeps fidgeting. Maybe Tammy made her coffee too strong.

'Right. I'll be off.' Violet puts her mug down. 'I'm meeting Adam this evening. In our den,' she adds with a giggle that sounds every bit as childish as Tammy's had. Maybe it *is* okay to be an adult and still giggle sometimes.

Tammy waves Violet down the stairs, thanking her again for the pretty flowers. It's not until after she's rinsed the cups that she sees it – Violet's pretty handbag with the purple hearts on the front. She's left it behind. Tammy picks it up, meaning to hang it on one of her coat hooks until she next sees Violet. She heaves it upwards, only it's lighter than it looks, and it swings forward. The corner of it catches on some of the flowers, toppling the vase to one side. Tammy drops the bag and catches the vase with both hands just in time. She straightens the flowers, relieved they aren't ruined and that none of the water was spilled on the floor.

Other things have fallen instead, out of Violet's bag. Three brown envelopes with Violet's loopy writing on the front. One is addressed to Adam and Bill, one to Mrs Robson and one to Tammy. Tammy bets they're invitations to the launch party – Violet must have forgotten to give them out. Tammy gathers them up, grabs her keys and runs down the stairs to the bottom of the building. She slides Bill and Adam's letter under their door before running back up and doing the same for Mrs Robson.

Once she's got her breath back, she plonks herself down on her bed, rips open the envelope that's addressed to her, and pulls out the letter.

Chrissie always tells Tammy that if ever she's confused by what she's reading, she should go back and read it again. Tammy keeps starting from the beginning until she begins to understand.

Then she reads it over and over until she feels sick.

CHAPTER 42

Violet

'DO YOU WANT ANY help getting ready for bed, Mum?' asks Violet.

'I'll be fine. I had my shower this morning and I'm more than capable of getting my nightie on. You got somewhere you need to be?' Glenys' face teeters between amusement and suspicion.

Violet glances down at the trainers she'd surreptitiously slid her feet into whilst her mum was watching TV. They look a little strange with her ankle-length lilac sundress, but there are times in life when a person likes to dress up and be practical at the same time. Sandals don't mix well with the wild woods of Lowerstone.

'Just wanted some fresh air,' Violet begins. She sees the twinkle in her mum's eye. She's not fooled. 'And I'm meeting Adam.' Glenys is usually tucked up in bed by now, but she'd asked for hot chocolate and plonked herself down on the sofa.

'Ah.' Glenys grins. 'You can always invite him here. This is your home too; you don't have to sneak off into the woods every night like a couple of teenagers.'

Violet's face flushes pink. 'Would you rather I stayed until you're in bed?'

'No. It's been a long day. Lots to think about. Think I'd like to sit here and have some time in the quiet.'

It's a cool September evening and Violet pulls her oversized cardigan tightly around her carefully chosen sundress as she makes her way through the back garden and across the path that leads to the woods. She crosses the bridge and arrives at the den. No blankets, no tea lights, and no Adam, but she is a couple of minutes early.

Crawling into a den made of branches and bracken whilst trying to keep your best dress clean is no easy feat, but somehow Violet manages to get inside without a scrape. She pulls her phone from her pocket and checks her make-up in it as butterflies bat their wings a little harder against the inside of her tummy.

The anticipation of seeing Adam, the care she'd taken with getting ready and spritzing herself with her favourite perfume, has made her feel fourteen years old again and it's exhilarating.

According to her phone, he's over a minute late. Not at all like meticulous Adam. Perhaps he's been spending extra time getting ready too. Violet leans back against the huge tree trunk in the centre of the den and closes her eyes, allowing herself to replay the encounter that had taken place between herself and Adam the last time she'd been sitting in that exact spot.

It certainly passes the time. Except now he's ten minutes late. The pitter patter of Violet's heart moves to an altogether less satisfying *thunk* and sits a little lower in her chest. His text had definitely said: *eight thirty in the usual place.* Followed by six kisses and a wink emoji. Violet knows this because she's read it so many times it's imprinted itself onto the inside of her eyelids.

Violet scrolls to the message and hits reply.

Keeping the den warm for you. Where are you?

Violet waits. No buzzing, no notifications. Just an empty, taunting screen showing nothing but the minutes marching past.

Perhaps something's happened to Bill. He could be having a bad night; he might have had a fall. And here's Violet, selfishly getting impatient. She pops her phone into her pocket and crawls backwards out of the den, caring a lot less this time about snagged hems or muddied knees.

The closer she gets to Malvern House, the faster she runs and the more convinced she is that something terrible has happened. The sweet honeysuckle air now feels thick and sickly in her chest and her feet keep tripping on the uneven ground.

By the time she's through the main door, Violet is gasping for breath.

She raps hard on the door to Adam's flat and then worries she'll wake Bill. Adam may have just forgotten to meet her. Even as the thought enters her mind, she knows it's not true.

No answer. Silence.

Something's happened, Violet just knows. Her hands shake as she knocks again. They've either gone out or neither of them can get to the door. Her mind swirls with a hundred different scenarios, each one more dire than the last. Then the door clicks from the other side.

Violet steps back, trembling with adrenaline. Thank goodness.

It's not Adam pulling the door open. It's a shorter man with white hair and an even whiter face.

'Hi, Bill.' Violet's voice is all breath and wheeziness. Perhaps it's just as well Adam didn't answer. At least this way she might have time to compose herself. She smooths her hair and attempts to soak up the sweat from her brow with the back of her hand. 'Is Adam around?'

The usual twinkle is absent from Bill's eyes and his mouth is so straight it looks like it's been drawn onto his face with a ruler.

A prickle of guilt creeps through Violet. It takes Bill such a long time to get to the door on a bad day. Adam would have answered it if he'd been around – she shouldn't have knocked so impatiently. 'If he's ill or in bed I can come back tomorrow. I'm sorry for disturbing you.'

Bill stares at her, his face unchanging. 'He's here,' he says eventually. 'He's not ill and he's not in bed. I just don't think he wants to see you.'

Violet should be used to being punched in the gut by rejection. Weirdly though, it's not something you can ever seem to build up a tolerance towards. She's still trying to make sense of Bill's words when a voice from behind him helps the air to climb back into her lungs.

'It's okay, Dad. I'll come to the door.'

The relief is short-lived. Adam looks angrier than his father. Bill shrugs before turning and walking slowly away from the doorway.

'I've been waiting in the woods like a Disney princess. Or like Aragog from *Harry Potter*,' Violet whispers. Adam and his dad have probably had a row. No point making him feel worse about standing her up; she knows what it's like to be mid-conflict with the person you're caring for.

Adam's eyes narrow and the corner of his mouth curls up into something resembling a snarl. It's definitely not a smile.

'I thought you'd changed. I thought you'd gone back to the sweet, kind, funny person you were before the fire. Turns out you're still the selfish teenager who'd rather do your own thing and turn your back on everyone.'

Each word stings like a sharp slap on wet skin.

'I haven't turned my back on anyone. It's *you* who didn't turn up. And why are you dredging up the past again? You promised you didn't hold it against me.' Violet fights to keep the tremble from her voice. She sounds like a child and she hates it. 'You made me think you'd forgiven me. You said ...'

'I know what I said.' Adam's eyes are dark and empty. 'But things change. You of all people should know that.'

His words ricochet off every corner of Violet's mind as the peephole in the slammed door arrives just inches from her face.

Violet's mind is numb as she walks back across the threshold to her mum's flat. She feels nothing as she changes into her pjs and climbs between the sheets of her bed. But she lies there, still and awake until the birds strike up their majestic Tuesday morning dawn chorus. Each file in the cabinet of her mind is opened, checked and cross-referenced. Adam has every reason in the world to hate her.

If it wasn't for the fire, he'd still have his mum and he'd probably still have his wife. Is that what this is about? Is he still pining? He'd said he'd moved on from the breakdown of his marriage, but maybe striking things up with Violet has opened old wounds.

The hurt and the guilt circle around, stirred up by her thoughts. They bump up against each other and split apart like oil and water before churning themselves into something else. Something far easier to deal with.

Anger.

Turns out rage sleeping is not an easy thing to achieve and Violet slithers from her bed with a brain full of fog. Her legs wobble beneath her as she drags herself towards the kettle, the toaster, and a new day.

This new day would be Adam-free. Her phone remains agonisingly devoid of notifications and she's certainly not going back over there to grovel, not after his shitty behaviour last night, standing her up and then being off without explaining why.

Old Violet would have stayed in bed stress-eating chocolate and crying over the pages of a soppy love story. Or she'd have packed her bags and got on the nearest train. But despite what Adam said, life is different now – Violet's different. She might be carrying a deep ache that's threatening to pull her inside out and back again, but she has other things to think about now and the life she's building here matters. Not just to her, but to other people too. No more running when things go wrong.

'Morning, Mum.' Violet smiles as she slides into Glenys' room armed with a mug of coffee. She sets it down on the bedside table and perches on the edge of the bed.

Glenys reaches for Violet's hand and gives it an unexpected squeeze. 'Boy trouble?'

Violet would have given anything as a teenager for her mum to embarrass her by asking about boy trouble. Better late than never.

'How did you know?'

'You were home early, your eyes are red, and you haven't taken off your mascara. It's halfway down your face.'

'Okay, Nancy Drew, you've got me,' Violet manages. 'But I'm not talking about him today. I'm not even thinking about him. I'm going to the library to help Mrs Robson sort the print copies for the *Gazette* and then maybe you and I can have lunch in the garden and I'll read the rest of *Anne of Green Gables* to you.'

Glenys smiles. 'Sounds like a good day to reach for Anne. I'm in.'

Violet helps Glenys shower and get ready in no time, marvelling at how much easier it feels than it had all those months ago. Afterwards, she makes her way to the library, pretending to herself she doesn't want to bump into Adam in the hallway on the way out of the building.

She doesn't.

And neither does he shout from his window for her to come back as she walks down the path. Not that she'd been hoping he would.

The library's closed. It shouldn't be, and there's no sign on the door explaining why it's locked. Violet makes her way around the side of the building and peeks through the window. None of the lights are on and the reception desk is empty. The books have only each other to whisper to.

Mrs Robson isn't answering her phone. For the second time in less than twenty-four hours, Violet is plagued with panic about something awful happening to one of her neighbours. She pictures Mrs Robson lying on her kitchen floor all alone in a puddle of tea with a broken china cup beside her.

She rushes past the village shops as she hurries to get back up the hill that leads home, but as she passes the pharmacy a flash of brown catches her eye from the bench by the pond.

It's a brown cardigan and it's sitting around the arms of Mrs Robson.

Mrs Robson's body is sitting on the bench, but her mind looks as if it's gone for a long walk, maybe a two-week cruise. She doesn't answer Violet when she calls out. Her eyes don't as much as flicker away from the patch of grass she's staring at beside her sensibly-clad feet.

Violet sits down next to her, clearing her throat and nudging her from her reverie.

'I've just been to the library,' she says. 'Terrible service. They let me go way over my lending amount and then forgot to fine me for taking my books back late.'

Still nothing.

'I'm sorry.' A sob falls from Mrs Robson and her shoulders begin to heave. 'Ridiculous getting in this state at my age, people have to move all the time. It's just that there's nowhere else in the village to rent – I've checked – and I don't want to have to start all over again somewhere else. I can't leave the library.' Tears are coursing down her face.

Violet places an arm around Mrs Robson. 'I honestly don't know what you're talking about. Who told you that you had to move? Has Mum said something? Because she gets confused sometimes, or wound up and she says things she doesn't m—'

'It was you. *You* told me.' Mrs Robson frowns as she dives into her handbag, retrieving a brown envelope with her name scrawled across the front.

Oh shit. Oh shit. Shit, shit, and more shit.

A ball of dread wrapped in realisation teeters over the summit of Violet's mind. She can do nothing but watch and wait as it cascades over the edge, hitting every bump on the way down until it lands squarely in the middle of her consciousnesses.

Poor Mrs Robson thinks she has to move out because she's seen Violet's letter. Which means so have Adam and Bill. That explains their behaviour last night. Even worse, Tammy's probably seen hers too. Violet remembers the bag she'd had with her when she took Tammy's flowers up to her flat. How she'd poked the letters inside it all those weeks ago before she knew for sure if she'd be shredding them or posting them through letterboxes.

She should've bought a shredder.

'Mrs R, we have to get back to Malvern House. I need to see Tammy right *now*. I'll explain on the way, but I promise you don't need to go anywhere. It was all a huge mistake. A misunderstanding.'

Violet continues to gabble all the way up the hill until they arrive on the doorstep, drenched in sweat and huffing and puffing like a cartoon steam train.

She runs up the stairs, two at a time. Tammy's door is ajar. Violet pushes it open and steps inside.

Tammy has gone. Her coat and trainers are missing, and her phone charger isn't by its usual socket. Perched against the vase of flowers Violet had given her is an envelope with Violet's name scrawled across it.

'No!' The shout comes from deep within Violet and she slaps her hands across her eyes as Mrs Robson appears behind her.

She forces herself to pick it up. Mrs R puts a gentle hand on Violet's shoulder as she opens the envelope with shaking hands.

To Violet,

Thank you for your flowers and for helping me with so many things, especially teaching me how to make coffee and to put electric on my card. Thank you for being my first ever friend and for teaching me how to be one back. I tried as hard as I could.

I'm sorry I did lots of things wrong. I let those people into the building and stole from that shop, and I was too loud sometimes, so I understand why you want me to leave. My key is on the coffee table.

I will never forget you.

Love from Tammy. Xxx

CHAPTER 43

Violet

VIOLET AND MRS ROBSON are back in the village as quickly as they'd left it, both of them calling Tammy's name into the warm summer breeze.

'Sorry, not seen her,' says the pharmacist, the baker, and the cashier in the sweet shop.

'Nope,' says the teenagers near the skate ramp in the park.

No one can be seen around the lake and the only people in the woods are dog walkers.

'She might have gone to see someone. Adam? Your mum? She may have gone to Chrissie's place, or Claire's,' Mrs Robson says.

Claire and Abbas haven't seen her, and Chrissie isn't answering her phone or doorbell.

Glenys is fast asleep.

That only leaves Adam and Bill.

Adam answers on the first knock, the frown lines on his face deepening when he sees Violet on the other side of his door.

Violet swallows the hurt. This isn't about her and it isn't about Adam. The only important thing right now is that they find Tammy.

'Tammy's gone. She's read the same letter I'm guessing you've had – the one about the building being sold. They weren't supposed to be given out; they must have fallen out of my bag and she found them. All her stuff's gone – I'm so worried something might happen to her – she's not used to being out in the world by herself – where would she even go?' Violet's voice cracks.

Adam's red puffy eyes soften. 'I've not seen her – I haven't seen her leave and I've been sitting near the window most of the morning. Maybe she left last night?'

'Oh shit, that's even worse.' Violet covers her eyes with her hands. 'I need to call her social worker. Probably the police as well – she has nowhere to go, barely any money and she's only just begun learning how to look after herself. Anything could happen to her out there.' Hot tears burn in Violet's eyes. 'And it's all my fault. If I hadn't written those letters …'

'Hush, now. You weren't to know this was going to happen.' Mrs Robson puts an arm around Violet's shoulders.

Violet braves a glance back at Adam, hoping to see Mrs R's compassion reflected in him.

Adam's eyes have turned steely again and he turns his head away. 'You'd better come in,' he mumbles. 'I'll get us a cup of tea. Violet can make her phone calls and then we'll come up with some plans to help.'

Mrs R suggests to Violet that she could post a photo of Tammy on her Facebook and ask everyone from the WhatsApp group to share it on their pages. All Violet can think about is that she doesn't have a single photo of Tammy and neither has she seen one in Tammy's flat.

How is it possible for someone to reach the age of nineteen

and still not have your photograph as part of another person's album? To have no goofy school photos on a wall or silly selfies anywhere on the internet?

Violet should have taken photos of her. Why hadn't she captured the moment when Tammy had baked her first cake or gone on her first adult shopping trip?

After Violet's dad died, no one took photos of her either. And even after she left home, she always avoided group snaps. She doubts there are more than one or two pictures out there in the universe that show Violet as any older than fourteen.

Perhaps Violet and Tammy are more alike than she'd realised. No wonder they were so drawn to each other.

Violet's phone rings as soon as she walks into Adam's kitchen. It's Chrissie. 'She's with me. Thought I'd better let you know in case you'd seen her note. She turned up at my house first thing this morning in a bit of a state, poor love. I'd have phoned before but I ended up going on the bus with her to work. I told her to take the day off, but she wanted to keep busy.'

'Thank God. And thanks for letting me know.' Violet's fingers shake as she hangs up.

Despite the huge relief of knowing Tammy's safe, the ache of hurting her spreads through Violet as the others talk around her.

When Mrs Robson gets up to leave, Violet hangs back by the door. She waits until Adam is the only person left in the room. 'Can we talk?'

Adam chews his bottom lip before nodding slowly. 'I don't know what more there is to say, but okay.'

'I typed those letters weeks ago,' she says quietly. 'I was in an impossible situation. Mum didn't want me here and I had no clue how to look after her. It was Jodie's plan to sell up and pay for Mum's residential care.'

'And now?'

'Now, I don't want to go anywhere. Mum and I are learning how to be mother and daughter again. Even though there are so many difficult memories, I love being in Lowerstone because it's home. I've got the Helping Hands Club to think about, and you guys. All of you,' she adds in a hurry. 'I'm happier than I've ever been. I had no one in my life before coming back here, not really.'

'Not even a mention of me or *us* in that little speech.' Adam looks Violet in the eye for the first time since she stepped into his flat this morning.

Violet swallows hard. Crying seems futile. 'I didn't think there was any point. I can see just by looking at you that your feelings have changed.'

Adam takes a step forward, and for a moment Violet thinks she's got through to him, that he's going to take back the anger and the hurt and then they can start again.

'You didn't even tell me what you were planning. When did you decide you weren't kicking us out after all – before or after you kissed me?'

The silence is heavy with the weight of regret and unspoken words.

'I can't go through this again.' Adam pushes his hair away from his eyes. 'The woman I was married to just dropped me and ran without a hint of what she'd been planning. Do you know how shit that feels? To know that someone's been planning to leave but hadn't thought to mention it?'

'I'm so sorry,' Violet whispers.

'And where would it have left Dad and me? It's difficult to find affordable lets around here that will take tenants on housing benefit and even harder to find places on the ground floor. Don't you think it would have been fairer to give us plenty of warning? And as for what happened between us last week – I just can't get my head around us getting as close as we have without you telling me the truth – even if you had changed your mind by then.' Adam paces up and down in front of the fireplace.

'I just wanted to forget the past. I didn't want to unsettle you or Bill unnecessarily until I had to, and by the time I knew I wouldn't need to, there didn't seem much point in saying anything.'

'Maybe I could get past it if it was just once, but it's not the first time you've done this.' Adam lowers his voice. 'I've never forgotten waking up after we'd spent the night together to find that you'd left without a word. I might have been eighteen years old, but I never got over that, *never*.' He opens the door to his flat and stands aside so that Violet can walk through it. 'I never stopped wanting you in my life, not once. I thought about you all the time, even when things were good with Kelly. I always wondered what could have been. My mind went straight there every single bloody New Year's Eve.'

'The messages.' Violet always forgot how to breathe whenever a New Year's text from Adam popped up. 'I know I should have been honest. I really am sorry.'

Adam unfolds his arms and lets out a breath. 'Having you back in my arms last week was incredible.' A crack appears in his voice. 'And I wish I could get past this …'

Three heavy knocks from the main door makes Violet jump.

Adam steps into the hallway as Violet swings the door open.

If she could shut it again, she would, but Michael Mullens' foot is in the way.

'Violet.' Michael puts one hand on the doorframe and leans over the threshold, breathing cheese-and-onion-crisp breath all over Violet. 'I was in the area and thought I'd pop back to go through that paperwork for the house? I could take some pictures of the outside while I'm here too – the light's quite good right now.'

Bloody great. Violet grits her teeth before risking a sideways glace at Adam.

Adam's ears are bright red and he's staring at the parquet floor.

'Not a good time, Michael. Sorry.' Violet closes the door as far as she's able to without trapping Michael's fingers. Much as she'd like to.

'Yup. Clearly not your estate agent. Check.' Adam's voice is as sharp as the splinters in Violet's chest. 'You know what? I don't think I'm ready to trust anyone again, not you and not now. I'm done.'

Michael's foot and fingers disappear from the doorframe and the front door slams shut. Adam's door follows a second later.

Glenys is fast asleep on the sofa when Violet lets herself into the flat. She sits at the table and gets her phone out. Getting through to Tammy needs to be her priority right now; she hasn't been answering all morning. She might have it on silent at work.

It isn't easy after all that drama to focus on typing a text to Tammy. Violet tries to wrap up Adam's words and put them in a box at the back of her mind. Only they don't all fit, and some of them keep squeezing back out.

After half an hour of wrestling with words, tears, and prickles of guilt, she has a screen full of sentences that she hopes and prays Tammy will read.

'Please, Tammy,' she whispers as she presses send. 'Please forgive me.'

Violet hates herself for the mess she's caused. She has so many sorries inside her, she's surprised they're not falling out all over the table.

CHAPTER 44

Tammy

THE CUTTING EDGE IS only five minutes' walk from the bus stop. Chrissie's walking the whole way with Tammy because she can't stop shaking.

'Are you sure you'll be okay to be at work today? I can speak to your boss for you – explain you've had a difficult morning?' Chrissie says.

Tammy wants to curl up under a duvet and cry until she has no tears left. Chrissie has told Tammy she can sleep on her sofa for as long as she needs to. But she can't expect to stay at Chrissie's forever and this job could be all she has now.

'I'll be fine.' Her throat feels tight when she speaks.

'Please call me if you need anything today.' Chrissie gives Tammy's arm a squeeze when they arrive at the door of the hairdresser's. 'I'll have a chat with Violet too – I really do think there's been some sort of misunderstanding.'

'No. I know what the letter said. Thank you for helping me this morning.' Tammy kisses Chrissie's soft cheek before taking a deep breath and stretching her mouth into a smile.

Music from Radio Sussex is blaring through the shop when

Tammy walks through the door. She's greeted by four of the people who work there. Jade on reception doesn't look at her, but she never does. Julie said Jade is just jealous because everyone prefers Tammy's coffee. She also said that because it's Tammy's first job, she'll need to learn about something called *office politics*.

The door dings just as Tammy is putting the kettle on and Julie calls her back onto the shop floor so she can wash the hair of the first customer of the day.

Tammy puts on her best smile and makes sure she gets the water temperature just right for the lady's scalp. Tammy has three most important jobs. Making drinks, washing hair and then sweeping it up once it's been cut off. She enjoys doing all of these things, but her favourite part is the talking. Julie said she has to be careful not to do that too much in case she tires out the customers but most of them seem to like it.

One lady said that Tammy was the first person to speak to her for a whole week. She thinks that's perhaps why some of them come in. Some people's hair already looks perfectly fine before they've even walked through the door.

Being there is helping. Doing things that other people need her to do. She can be sad about what happened with Violet *and* know she's still going to be okay, both at the same time.

'I've got something for you,' Julie says when Tammy's finished washing Mrs Johnson's hair. 'Pop this in your handbag so you don't lose it.'

Tammy stares at the white envelope. 'What is it?'

'It's this week's wages. You'll get one every week from now on if you like. Your trial's over and the job's yours if you want it.'

Smiles don't only appear on faces, Tammy decides. Some smiles happen right inside your tummy and then get so big, they burst out through your mouth. She throws her arms around Julie and shouts *thank you* in her ear.

Julie jumps. Perhaps it was a bit loud, but she's laughing so she can't be very cross. 'At some point today, we'll give you a try on reception. Be a good chance for you to learn our booking system.'

The morning goes quickly. There are lots of heads to wash, lots of mugs to clean and then fill again. When it's finally time to sit down and eat her packed lunch that Chrissie made her, Tammy's feet are aching. Julie told her you get used to it after a few weeks of being on your feet all the time. She pulls her handbag onto her lap and slips out the white envelope, just to peek at it again. She likes looking at her name on the front, and the amount of money. It makes her feel proud.

All she has to do now is get some practice on the front desk.

'I'm afraid I have far too many bookings to go through,' Jade says when Tammy asks if she can have a go, just for a few minutes. 'Sorry. The website needs updating regularly, or all this falls apart.' She gestures around the room with a sweep of her arm.

She doesn't look very sorry. Tammy glances at the screen. It's strange that the website isn't called The Cutting Edge, it's called Tinder. Must be confusing for some of the customers.

Tammy has to wait all afternoon. As soon as the receptionist walks out of the door, Tammy slips behind the desk. Just as she's looking through the next day's appointments, her phone vibrates in her pocket.

Three missed calls and a message from Violet.

'We're closing. We need to log off and shut the computer down now, love.' Julie's voice sounds like it's coming from a long way away and Tammy's brain is just forming the words to answer her, but it stops halfway because she sees the first words of the message.

Dearest Tammy.

'Tammy? You need to switch it off now. I need to count the till.'

Dearest Tammy. Please get in touch when you've finished work. Call me or come back to Malvern House and knock on my door. I just want to know you're okay. You will always have a home here – that letter was a mistake, and you were never meant to read it. I wrote it when I first moved back in – before I got to know you all. I'm so sorry you thought you had to leave. Xxx

There's too much air in Tammy's chest. It's all stuck in there and won't come out. She grabs her handbag and runs out into the street, forcing out all of her breath into the cooler air of the street. Violet wants her back. Tammy hasn't done anything wrong.

She dashes across the road, ignoring Julie's shouting from behind her. She knows she's being rude, but she *has* to get to the bus station. What if she misses the bus by one tiny second, just because she stopped to talk to Julie?

Her legs start to burn as she runs faster and faster. She keeps picturing Violet's worried face as she reads Tammy's letter. She shouldn't have just left like that, she should have said goodbye properly, checked she'd got things right.

The rush-hour traffic is pootling along beside her. It takes so long to get a good enough gap to cross the road.

Tammy can see the bus station in front of her. She just needs to cut across the traffic. Then she sees it – the bus marked *Lowerstone*. It pulls in next to the stop, making lots of noise. It sounds like it's breathing out as heavily as Tammy is. If she runs, she might just be able to make it.

The bus makes another whooshing sound. It's saying, come on, hurry up.

Tammy runs into the road. Almost there, she's sure it will wait.

It doesn't hurt, not one bit when the white van hits her from the left. You'd think it would, it's ten times bigger than her, probably more. Tammy's flying, higher and higher into the air like she's in one of those gliding dreams. There's a lot of shouting and screaming but it sounds like when you're in the bath or the shower and your ears are full of sloshing water.

It feels like she's in the air for a long time. And then her tummy does that thing it does when you dream that you're falling. Except this time, she keeps falling all the way through the floor and the dream comes screeching to an end.

CHAPTER 45

Violet

VIOLET ALMOST DOESN'T ANSWER her phone as it vibrates on the kitchen worktop. She doesn't recognise the number on the screen, and no one ever calls except those people who like to inform her she's been in a traffic accident and might be entitled to compensation.

But the buzzing is too irritating to ignore; it's like an angry wasp trapped behind a curtain.

She'd guessed the traffic accident part right. She was wrong about who was involved.

Violet's chest fills with shards of jagged ice as a tired voice on the other end of the line tells her he's from the Royal Sussex County Hospital. The intensive care unit is mentioned and Violet grips the edge of the worktop when she hears Tammy's name.

'Can I see her?' Violet's parched throat makes her words come out as a continuous croak.

'Maybe later this evening. No more than two people at a time. But there are some things I need to tell you first.'

Violet listens to a stream of sentences, certain phrases

snagging against the edges of her mind. *Coma, head trauma. We'll just have to wait and see.*

'I'm coming with you,' Glenys says when Violet tells her what's happened. 'You're upset. You shouldn't be on your own.'

Violet's heart squeezes at the concern in her mum's pale eyes. 'But you hate hospitals. You don't even really like being in the car.'

'I'll be fine. We all will. Let's just get through it together.'

Violet nods before picking up her phone and scrolling through her contacts. She puts a message on the Helping Hands WhatsApp, letting them know what happened. Everyone answers except Adam, so she sends him a text before grabbing her keys.

There's still an hour to go before evening visiting hours when Violet and Glenys arrive in the waiting area for ICU.

Glenys convinces Violet to get a coffee and a chocolate bar from the machine and to sit down before her shaky legs give way beneath her.

It's probably the first time she's ever not been able to finish a Crunchie. It's hard to swallow food and cry at the same time. All she can think about is the smile on Tammy's face when Violet had handed her those stupid flowers from the garden. If she hadn't taken them up to her, she wouldn't have left her bag behind with those letters in it.

And Tammy wouldn't be fighting for her life on a cold, hard hospital bed.

Glenys sits quietly beside Violet, saying nothing but squeezing her hand every now and again, following her glances towards the clock on the wall.

The doors to the waiting room swish open to reveal a huddle of humans from Helping Hands.

'I know you said only two at a time. And I'm sure it's your voice she'll want to hear the most,' says Chrissie, rushing forward and taking hold of Violet's hands. 'And we won't all clog up the waiting room, but we wanted you and Tammy to know we're here. We'll be down in the canteen if you need us. We'll keep bringing you coffee – anything you need.'

Adam is standing at the back of the group. 'I can stay in the waiting room with you when Violet goes in if you like, Glenys. I know what she's like when she gets talking. You could be here for a long time.'

Violet can hear the hidden edge beneath his joking tone, and there's sadness hidden inside the cheery smile. She throws him a grateful nod, hoping he knows how much she appreciates him. Glenys hates hospitals and Violet had been dreading leaving her outside the ward on her own. Expecting her to sit by Tammy's bedside might have proved a step too far.

Violet stands when she's finally called in and she braces herself before walking towards the nurses' station.

'There's been no change since we called,' the nurse tells Violet as he ushers her towards Tammy's ward. 'And I should warn you, she's badly bruised. You'll see a lot of bandages and tubes.'

Violet's own breath is stolen from her when she reaches Tammy's bed. A large screen is up in the corner of her bed space showing a slew of observations, numbers, and graphs. The room is full of bleeping and buzzers and floral disinfectant.

Tammy's skin is almost as pale as the bandages wrapped around her arms. The front right section of her hair has been shaved off and a spaghetti junction of tubes are coming at her from all angles.

The nurse lingers long enough to swab Tammy's lips gently with a wet cotton bud. 'Have a seat.' He gives her an encouraging smile. 'Keep talking to her. I'll be over there if you need me.' He points to a desk just a few metres away. 'Tammy's obs are stable and we're keeping a very close eye. Very little can change without an alarm being triggered by that screen there.' He points to the monitor above their heads.

As Violet digests the nurse's words, an alarm sounds from further down the ward. Two of the nurses behind the desk glance at each other before disappearing from sight. A rumble of calm voices can be heard above the machines along with the sound of a trolley being moved. Then the alarm stops, and the normal bleeping patterns of the ward can be heard once again.

What must it be like to spend each day in here, fighting to keep people alive and watching numbers on screens, desperately trying to keep them within the right parameters, and keeping those alarms at bay?

Tammy's hand feels warmer than it looks. Violet keeps hold of it and perches on the plastic chair beside the bed.

Keep talking to her, the nurse had said.

Where have all the words gone?

'I'll make sure that *Coronation Street* is recording for you when I get home,' says Violet, feeling ridiculous. 'Can't have you getting behind whilst you're in here, can we?'

Seeing the lack of change in Tammy's face twists Violet's

stomach into knots. A tear falls from her face onto her own arm and she wipes it away with her forehead rather than letting go of Tammy's hands, even for a second.

This is all Violet's fault.

A quiet cough makes Violet jump.

Adam is standing there with a book and an awkward smile. 'Your mum said to give you this. It was in her handbag. She said you'd know what to do.'

It's the dog-eared edition of *Anne of Green Gables*. Violet swallows a sob as she takes it from him.

Adam pulls the remaining plastic chair closer to Violet and sits on it.

'You don't have to stay,' she whispers. 'You can go back and wait with Mum. I won't be much longer.'

'Your mum's fine, Chrissie's with her. She told me to come and sit with you. Said she was fed up with my gibber-jabbering.'

Violet raises an eyebrow, highly doubting his words. Adam was hardly one for wittering and it's not a word she's ever heard Glenys use.

Violet looks again at Tammy's sleeping face before diving into the book, knowing straight away which chapter she's searching for. She falters to begin with, self-consciousness leaking into her voice as she trips over sentences. The longer she reads, the more the familiar words dance through the well-worn journeys of her mind and move smoothly to her tongue. She gets lost inside a world where Anne is eaten up with guilt for giving her 'bosom friend' copious amounts of alcohol by mistake instead of raspberry cordial and making her sick.

By the time she remembers that Adam is still watching her,

Violet has read three and a half chapters. She stalls, cutting off mid-sentence as she takes her eyes off the page and allows them to meet Adam's. His face is soft, full of compassion and something else that Violet can't put her finger on.

'I'll go and check on your mum.' Adam wrenches his gaze away from hers. 'I'll be back before you get to the bit where Marilla tells Mrs Barry and Rachel Lynde to fuck off.'

'She never says ...' Violet grins when she sees Adam winking at her. She'd forgotten how much she used to go on about Anne Shirley when they were kids. She'd even convinced Adam to sit through several showings of the TV series during a few of their lazy Saturday mornings.

Adam leaves the ward, closing the door gently behind him.

Violet takes hold of Tammy's hands again and gives them a gentle squeeze. 'You're my Diana Barry,' she whispers. 'Please wake up.'

'I think you should let that Adam boy know how you feel,' Glenys says that night as Violet helps her into bed. 'It's obvious he has his eye on you. You could do much worse,' she adds, eyeing Violet up and down.

'He's hardly a boy anymore.' Violet laughs. 'And he knows how I feel. He's just not interested. I messed up. Best thing I can hope for now is to repair our friendship, but it might take a while.'

'Well, that's not how it looked at the hospital.' Glenys sniffs. 'He was pacing up and down that waiting room, chomping at the bit to get back in that ward with you.'

'He was just worried about Tammy. And looking out for us. He was just being nice – it's what he does.'

'Mmm. Well, it wouldn't hurt to go over and thank him.'

Violet doesn't answer, she just kisses Glenys' soft, leathery cheek and says goodnight.

It's a close, sticky night. As soon as Violet has shut her mum's bedroom door, she rushes to the back door and pulls it open, gulping greedily on the cooler air. Rumbles of thunder grumble in the distance and the night sky flickers to life with a flash of lightning.

She should go and thank Adam.

He was good to them today. It had helped, knowing he was there. A considerable part of her wants to fold herself into his arms, listen to the sound of his comforting words and let her guilt and worries be washed away by the storm.

But that's the part of herself she needs to ignore, at least for now. Tammy is what matters. She prays in her head for the millionth time since her phone rang earlier and makes her way across the hall to Adam and Bill's door.

Adam answers on the second knock, as if he's been waiting just the other side of it.

'Has there been more news?' The soft lines of his forehead bunch up, concern etched inside the gaps.

'No.' Violet can't decide if she's relieved or disappointed that her phone hasn't rung since they left the hospital. She's not sure she could live with herself if Tammy doesn't get better. 'It's my fault she's there.' She wishes she could suck the words back in as soon as they're out. The last thing she should be doing is swimming in self-pity and splashing it all over Adam in the process.

'You weren't to know that was going to happen.' Adam brushes the loose strands of Violet's hair away from her face.

Violet pulls him close and buries her face into his shoulder. 'You had every right to be angry. I just want my friend back.'

'I'm sure she's fighting as hard as she can.'

'I wasn't talking about Tammy. I want her back too, obviously. But I was talking about you.'

Adam tightens his grip around her waist. Raindrops batter the windows and the grumbles of thunder get louder. 'We'll find our way back to being friends,' he says quietly.

Violet peers over Adam's shoulder. 'Where's your dad?'

'Sleeping in my room. He's a light sleeper and heavy rain is much louder in here.' He glances over at the hospital bed in the far corner of the living room. 'Want to eat biscuits and watch old *Dr Who: The Sylvester McCoy Years* in bed, like the old days?'

'We were such geeks,' Violet groans. 'But, yes, let's. I can't *believe* you still have all the old episodes.'

Adam fiddles with the ancient DVD player and grabs a packet of bourbons from the kitchen cupboard.

Sylvester McCoy flickers onto the screen and Violet and Adam spend ten minutes ridiculing the terrible effects. Violet sneaks a peek at Adam's profile. She should feel awkward, sitting side by side in bed with him like this. But instead, she's transported back to a simpler time, and at least for now, it's somewhere she wants to stay.

She stretches out her legs and snuggles further under the duvet. The pillow is the perfect amount of squishy beneath her head and she's toasty-warm. The hum of the TV and the patter of raindrops get further and further away as her eyes grow heavy.

When Violet opens her eyes again it's considerably darker.

The television has been switched off and the storm has passed. All she can hear is Adam's soft breathing. She turns towards him, watching the rise and fall of his chest.

Violet closes her eyes, her mind whizzing around in every direction. Being this close to Adam is comforting but it can't take away the high-definition image of Tammy lying in a hospital bed surrounded by wires.

Keep fighting, Tammy. Don't ever let go.

CHAPTER 46

Violet

IT HURTS VIOLET TO hold Helping Hands meetings without Tammy. There's always a spare seat, regardless of how many Violet pulls out beforehand, and it's impossible not to think about her friend's pale body lying in that bed. Tammy's been in hospital for three weeks and every day the hole she's left in the village feels a little bit bigger.

Today, Violet feels shaky and crushed, like a heavy weight is sitting on her chest. She stays quiet during *share time*, a part of the meeting where anyone gets to vent about anything they've struggled with during the week. It's always better to talk about everything else once everyone's had a chance to unpack. Violet has so much she wants to say, but the words are bound to come wrapped in tears and she hadn't got the energy.

She talks about the *Gazette* instead. 'We've had a wonderful email from someone in the village. A woman has just been reunited with a twin sister she didn't know she had. She's almost eighty and they want to share their story – would anyone like to interview them?'

'I will,' Glenys says, before anyone has a chance to open their mouths.

'Are you sure?' Violet says, not managing to keep the surprise from her voice. Glenys isn't one for making chitchat with strangers. When Violet first arrived, it would have taken the collective powers of the Avengers just to get her mum to leave the house.

Glenys studies the carpet for several seconds before lifting her face to meet Violet's. 'I'm sure. I know a thing or two about tricky family reunions. It's not always easy and getting it right can take time.'

A buzzing from the table distracts Violet. The number on her phone screen slows the blood inside her vessels until she can feel a surge at every pulse point.

'She's awake,' says the voice at the other end. It's all Violet needs to hear.

Less than five minutes later, Violet's sitting alone in Pat, whizzing towards Brighton.

Please be okay.

The hospital is busier than usual, and she keeps getting stuck behind groups of people, dawdling through the corridors armed with magazines and 'Get Well Soon' balloons.

At last, she's pressing the buzzer for ICU. At last, she's inside the ward. And at last, she can see the whites of Tammy's pale blue eyes.

'Violet.' Her voice is croaky, cracked in the middle. But she's speaking, smiling, and she knows who Violet is.

Tammy's hands are warm beneath Violet's. Having them squeeze her back makes the lump in her throat expand to the size of an orange.

'Good morning, you.' Violet smiles through her tears. 'Nice sleep?'

Red rings hug Tammy's eyes, making her face look even paler. 'The nurses said you've been here every day.'

'I wanted to be here when you woke up. How are you feeling?'

'Okay. A bit sore and quite worried,' Tammy adds.

Violet plants a gentle kiss on Tammy's forehead. 'Now, *you* should not be worrying about anything right now except getting stronger and coming back home to us.'

'Home.' Tammy's voice drops to a whisper.

'Yes, home.' Violet pulls her chair closer to the bed. 'Those letters were a mistake. I wrote them a long time ago when I thought I had no choice but to sell the building. Things have changed now, and I want you to stay – if you're happy to. I love having you as my friend and neighbour and I'm so very sorry for causing you so much distress. Everyone's been so worried about you, I've been so worried. The whole village has been rooting for you to get better.'

'I know about the letters,' Tammy says. 'I saw your message. You don't need to be sorry and of course I want to come home and be your neighbour again. You're my best friend.' She grimaces as she moves to sit up. 'I'm worried about the hairdresser's, though – they'll think I don't want to work there anymore. Do they know?'

'Chrissie told them, so don't worry about that.' Violet lays a gentle hand on Tammy's arm. 'They've sent you cards and flowers and they just want you to get well. Your boss said they can't wait to have you back – all their customers have been asking for you.'

A glimmer of pride swims across Tammy's face as she shuffles upwards in her bed. She opens her mouth, and three weeks' worth of talking all comes dancing out.

'I love my new job. And the whole world is such an interesting place,' Tammy says with shining eyes. 'I didn't realise how much I'd been missing out on before I met you. I wouldn't have known how to do any of it if it hadn't been for you. When I got your message, I was on my way to come and say thank you properly, when …' She breaks off and her eyes go a darker shade. She shivers and Violet pulls the blanket up over Tammy's arms.

'Your job sounds amazing. You are amazing. I'm so proud of you and now we just need to concentrate on getting you better,' whispers Violet. 'That's all that matters right now.'

'I thought the world was just this awful, scary place. Mum kept me away from so much. She thought I'd always be in danger if I went outside on my own.'

Laughter bursts out of Violet before she can stop it. 'Well, she wasn't entirely wrong.' She nods towards the monitor above Tammy's bed. 'There is plenty of danger out there. But lots of wonderful things too, and you've shown that you're more than capable of looking after yourself.'

'We really need other people, though, don't we? Even if it's just to show us that we can look after ourselves.' A tiny frown appears on Tammy's face. 'I want you to interview me for the *Gazette*. I want people to know how important they are to each other. There might be other people like me, all on their own with no one to show them that they matter.'

Violet clears the emotion from her throat. 'I will. We'll do it as soon as you're well enough.'

'I feel well enough now.' Tammy groans. 'I've already wasted three weeks lying around. The nurses are going to help me get up and walk around this afternoon and ...' she blushes and lowers her voice, 'do you know my wee is going straight into a tube? How weird is that?'

Violet smiles. 'There's something else you don't know.' She decides to plunge right in. Tammy's been kept from things her whole life. It's time that changed. 'For the past couple of months, I've been searching for your dad. Michael. I was worried about you having no family to turn to. I thought you might need someone else to look out for you once the building was sold.'

Tammy grips the corners of her blankets and her knuckles whiten.

'I found him,' Violet carries on when Tammy doesn't say anything. 'He lives in Brighton. He doesn't know where you are.' She adds, 'And it's completely up to you if you want to see him. I found out some things I didn't like, and I thought it might be best if you didn't, but I was wrong to think it was up to me to make that decision for you. I'm sorry.' Violet looks at Tammy's screen, hoping the numbers on them don't start bleeping out of control; Tammy's still attached to some of the wires.

Tammy shrugs. 'It's okay. That was one thing Mum *was* right about. He's a dangerous man. He never hit me, but he used to hurt Mum all the time.'

'Oh, Tammy.' Violet places her hand over Tammy's clenched fists. 'We don't have to talk about this now. I shouldn't have brought it up, you need to rest.'

'I want to tell you about it.' Tammy closes her eyes. 'He

... he used to put me out of the way when it happened. The cupboard. Said it was the best place for me, but I could still see what he was doing to her.' Tammy's voice cracks. 'I don't remember much else from back then, but I do remember that cupboard. The dark, the cold.' She shivers. 'And the dust made me sneeze. Then when it was over, it was quiet. So quiet.' A tear trickles down Tammy's face.

Violet swallows and blinks fast to clear the water from her eyes. 'I'm so sorry.'

Each revelation from Tammy adds a number to the sum that Violet's been trying to work out ever since they met. It explains why Lydia wanted to keep her so close and so hidden. He'd relentlessly followed them when they first got away. It only stopped once Lydia and Tammy had moved enough times to make their trail turn cold.

It sounds as if Lydia's mental health had suffered afterwards, and that she'd clung on to her daughter for dear life. Tammy should still have been allowed to grow up, though, Violet says fiercely to herself.

'I don't want to see him, I've already decided.' Tammy makes 'ouch' noises as she shifts around towards Violet. 'I have so many things I want to do with my life now. So many good things to think about that have nothing to do with him. And I'm not even scared of him anymore. It's just that whilst you were out looking for my family, you and the rest of the Helping Hands Club *became* my family. I have everything I need back home.'

CHAPTER 47

Violet

VIOLET HAS ONE MORE read through the article she's just written before adding it to the rest of the *Gazette* issue she's put together. It's due out in the morning, which is cutting it fine, but she's been channelling her inner Jenny and making her fingers fly across the keyboard in time for the deadline.

The first half of the piece is Tammy's interview with Violet, scribbled down earlier this evening after Tammy's first ever walk around the ward. She hadn't wanted to wait any longer and she convinced Violet to sit, listen and take notes. The interview led seamlessly into the second part of the article, which was something Violet had been trying to write for weeks but it just hadn't clicked into place before this evening. It's about loneliness, alone-ness, and their effects on communities.

Just as she's finished scheduling the article for 7 a.m the next day, her phone dings with a text.

I can't wait any longer. I need to see you.

Violet's heart thuds harder. She's been pushing Adam to the back of her mind as much as possible since the night she'd slept beside him. So much else has been happening with Tammy and the *Gazette*. It was enough to have him back in her life as a wonderful old friend, she hadn't wanted to push the other stuff, not whilst Tammy was fighting for her life in hospital. And the risk of losing his friendship again feels like a high price to pay for something that might not even work out. But perhaps it's time to talk. To pull out her heart and show Adam what's written on it. Hands shaking, she adds a comment below his.

By the lake in half an hour.

That gives her time to freshen up, and find something to wear that looks half decent, but not too try-hard. She opts for her purple T-shirt dress and shakes her hair free from her usual braids, combing it carefully to avoid the excessive frizziness that usually follows. Her stomach spins with nerves as she dabs on a layer of mascara and a dollop of lip balm. She pops her head around her mum's door to check she's asleep. She is.

It's dark outside, but the sky is well lit by an almost-full moon and a bright array of stars. She pops a mini torch from the sideboard into her pocket for good measure.

She listens for movement on the other side of Adam's door – it will totally ruin any romance if they bump into each other in the hallway rather than at the Lake of Shining Waters.

Silence.

She bolts out of the front door and waits until she's walked around the side of Malvern House and climbed through the fence to the footpath before she gets her phone out.

On my way to the Lake, she texts Adam. At least he'll know the coast is clear if he isn't there already.

A figure is standing on the bridge. Violet takes a long, slow breath before arranging her face into a casual smile. No need to look too keen.

Adam's face glows in the torchlight as he turns around. 'I decided we were overdue a catch-up in our very own woods. We've got a lot to talk about.'

Violet swallows. 'Keeping the sale of the building from you was wrong. And I should never have allowed things to happen between us before telling you the truth – especially after what you've been through. What you've *all* been through.'

Adam takes another step towards Violet. 'I was hurt. Angry. But watching you with Tammy in that hospital – it reminded me who you really are. Someone who cares. Someone who would drop everything for someone else, even if she gets it wrong sometimes. I'm sorry I went off at you about it. I really would like to start again. If that's what you want.'

Violet wanders if Adam can see the slow smile crawling all the way across her face. She looks towards the lake beside them. 'Fancy going in?' She keeps her voice light. In films and books, she's always thinks it's overwhelmingly romantic when lovers swim in lakes. Or any body of water really. And who knows when she'll get another chance?

'It's been a good few years since you and I swam in a lake,' Adam says slowly. Then he starts pulling off his T-shirt. 'Race you.'

Violet is just about to protest about the race, but then she glances at his bare chest and changes her mind. Who is she to argue with the man's challenges? She sprints to the lake, pausing at the edge to peel off her dress, hoping she looks at least a little alluring. Her sleeves get caught around her elbows, suspending her arms above her head, and obscuring most of her face. She keeps trying to wriggle it off, and she stumbles forward until she's suddenly submerged in the freezing water.

'What exactly are you trying to do?' Adam's amused voice travels through the material as soon as her feet find the riverbed and she wrestles herself into a standing position.

'Erm. Trying to seduce you?' Violet mumbles through the wet fabric.

Adam's throaty chuckle makes goosepimples bump up across her skin. Or it could be the freezing-ass water.

Adam steps closer and gently hooks his fingers under the trapped hem of her dress, easing it over her head.

'Well, it's working,' he says.

Violet holds her breath, hoping he's about to kiss her, but then there's a splash and Adam's swimming past her. 'I don't give it away that easy, you know,' he says with a laugh.

Violet grins and dives into the water. She's either a much faster swimmer, or he's going slowly on purpose, but she catches up with him in a matter of seconds and swims onto his back, curling her arms across his chest.

Adam stops swimming and stands up in the water. He takes Violet's hands and gently pushes her away, only to pull her back towards him as he turns around. Then his lips are on hers and his arms are wound tightly around her waist.

After the kiss has broken, Violet leans her chin on Adam's wet shoulder. She peers across at the rest of the lake, watching as the moonlight dances across the water. Perhaps this is as romantic as she'd wished for after all.

'All these years later and you really are my Gilbert Blythe, kissing me under the stars in the Lake of Shining Waters,' she mumbles.

'Oh, my *days*. Some things never change.' Adam laughs and lets go of her. 'And just for that, I'm getting out.' He splashes past her towards the water's edge.

Violet's teeth start to chatter as soon as she stands back up on dry land. Adam pulls her close as they make their way back to the house, their hair dripping particles of the Lake of Shining Waters all over the dusty paths.

She'd like to tell herself that his closeness is enough to stop her thinking about how cold she is but that would be a lie. Her wet feet are slipping around inside her trainers and she's shivering like a tree in a hurricane.

The two of them squelch through the main door and into the hallway. 'So, here we are. Home.' Adam's watching Violet's face, his eyes suddenly serious.

'Indeed. Home,' Violet agrees.

Neither of them speaks. Footsteps sound from above. Probably Mrs Robson walking away from the window after watching them come home. Violet will be fielding plenty of questions tomorrow.

'Dad's sleeping back in the living room,' Adam says pointedly.

Violet takes a step forward. Another creak from a floorboard upstairs. 'Then perhaps we should hurry up and get inside my flat,' Violet murmurs. 'Because Mrs Robson is bound to be down here any second.'

They take it in turns to shower the lake away and dry their hair with fluffy towels before tiptoeing into Violet's room.

As Violet stretches out next to Adam, snuggling close to him in her tiny bed, she searches again for his mouth.

'I'm glad you're sticking around,' Adam murmurs. 'Turns out I'm still the boy who's in love with his very best friend.'

CHAPTER 48

Violet

VIOLET PUSHES THE BRAN Flakes around her bowl, pretending to eat her breakfast whilst ignoring her mum's narrow stare. Her tummy is churning around like a washing machine and she keeps replaying the events of last night over and over, trying to suppress the stupid grin that keeps creeping onto her face.

'I heard you coming back rather late last night,' Glenys says in her pointiest voice. 'And I heard the shower running. *And,*' she pauses for dramatic effect, 'I'm pretty sure I heard a man's voice.'

Violet feels the blood rush to her face and she shoves a huge spoonful of cereal in her mouth, so she doesn't have to answer. Big mistake as she's far too excited to swallow food, especially a mouthful of glorified cardboard. She'd sneaked Adam out of the door just minutes before Glenys got up this morning but there's no way she doesn't know.

The door buzzer blares and Violet forces her food down before picking up.

'It's Claire. You need to hear this.' Claire's voice is drenched with excitement.

Violet buzzes her in and opens the flat door. It's probably something to do with the launch party, it's less than a week away and Claire's had party fever ever since they'd started planning it.

Claire's wearing jogging bottoms and a hoody, but Violet can spy a flash of pyjama top beneath the collar. Jayden is standing at her side in his school uniform, gripping tight to one of Claire's hand's. The other one is holding a half-eaten slice of buttery toast.

'Can't stay long,' she says breathlessly through a mouthful of crumbs. 'Need to get this little one to school, got a bit behind this morning. Wanna know why?' The grin has taken over her face and she keeps shifting her weight from one foot to the other.

'Check *The Lowerstone Gazette*'s Twitter account – your loneliness article has been shared over a thousand times and the number's still climbing. You're going to put the village on the map. And the comments – you really have pulled it out the bag this time. Every business in the area is going to want to advertise with the *Gazette* now. This could mean some serious funding for Helping Hands and for the community centre.'

Violet pulls her phone from her pocket and opens Twitter, selecting the *Gazette's* profile and reeling when she sees the number of notifications. 'I don't even know what to say. It's amazing.'

'Gotta go. We're going to be so late. Just wanted to let you know in person and see your face light up. Totally worth it. Catch you later.' Claire and Jayden rush out of the building as fast as they rushed into it.

Violet flops into the nearest armchair, awestruck. She starts making her way through the notifications, glancing at Glenys, expecting a barrage of questions about what Claire wanted. Glenys is staring out of the window with a blank look on her face, her breakfast untouched.

It's going to be one of *those* days with Mum.

Violet has clicked on only the first five Twitter alerts before the direct message icon on the *Lowerstone Gazette* site flashes up on her laptop. It's from the *Brighton & Hove News*.

Dear Violet,

Our team have just read your article online – the one about the young girl and loneliness. We really loved it; it's just the right flavour for us. Would you be happy for us to reprint it in our paper?

We also have a paid internship opening coming up and we'd like to offer you an interview. Interviews are next Tuesday and Wednesday between 10 a.m. and 2 p.m. Please do let me know which day suits if you're interested. My number is 07775094194.

Tara Tunnock
Editor-in-chief
Brighton & Hove News

Violet pictures herself back in a bustling newspaper office, writing up notes from an exciting interview and eating a pastry from the canteen. A bubble of joy expands in her stomach but she holds it still. There's so much to consider, even if she does get offered the job. She needs to be around for the Helping Hands lot, and there's Mum to think about.

She dials Tara Tunnock's number with shaking fingers.

She answers immediately, sounding pleased to hear Violet's voice.

'I just wanted to let you know I'd be thrilled for your paper to reprint the article. And thank you so much for your interview offer.' Violet lowers her voice as she glances over at Glenys. 'It's a wonderful opportunity, but I'm afraid I have caring responsibilities ...'

'We can be flexible with the interview – we can do it online if necessary. The role will involve some remote working anyway.'

The warmth in the woman's voice pulls at the corners of Violet's mouth and she knows she's grinning like a kid in a chocolate factory.

'Can I have a think and get back to you about the interview?'

'Of course. Just call me back or drop me an email.'

As soon as Violet puts her phone down, Glenys announces that she wants to go back to bed. Exhaustion is written between the lines on her face, the type that hits hard alongside a fresh wave of depression.

Violet helps her to her room, perching on the side of Glenys' bed for a while until she starts snoring softly. Her mum is getting so much better at managing her conditions, but she still has so many bad days. There's no magic wand. How can Violet even think about going back to work? Caring is a full-time job in itself.

Violet's phone continues to buzz as she waits for the kettle to boil and she looks at the latest retweet from @KirstyWaters – *Check out this article. I went to school with the author!*

Smiling, Violet clicks on the link to her article and reads it one last time, starting with Tammy's heart-wrenching interview about what life had been like growing up inside a bubble without anyone from the outside world to talk to. She moves on to read her own reflections, still fresh in her mind from last night.

Studies have shown that in the last ten years, loneliness has risen sharply. Two-fifths of the population are said to be chronically lonely. Research has shown that loneliness is harmful to our health. It is suspected that social isolation carries a risk factor equal to smoking fifteen cigarettes per day and is more dangerous than obesity. Loneliness increases the risk of mortality by twenty-six per cent.

So, why are we all so lonely? Several factors have been identified by researchers, ranging from the hours that employees are working, financial pressures and the over-reliance on technology. Changes in the wider economy have caused many people to move away from their families and their support networks.

Five months ago, I lost everything I'd built up for myself. I started my life again, completely alone, and moved back to the village I grew up in. It took this dramatic change in circumstances to show me I'd been living life lonely for fourteen years. Life lied to me about how being alone was safer, that the bubble around me should never be popped.

I used to think that only widows were lonely. Old people in residential homes with no family to visit them. Then I opened my eyes to the people around me. I found parents working long hours to make ends meet and provide for their children. I met people living in a new country, still getting to grips with a new language. I met people who were grieving for their loved ones with no one to chat to over a cup of tea. People with mental health conditions. Young people with no one to guide them.

A long-standing resident from my village has told me about how it used to be around here. How people used to pop in and out of each other's houses. They swapped sugar and milk and news from the town. They took each other to hospital appointments and if someone wasn't seen in the local shop for a few days – someone noticed.

When a person is kept away from the world for too long, there are consequences. I've watched people come back to life when loneliness is washed off them; when people come together in a community to do something meaningful, something creative, or even something completely ordinary, but they do it together.

If you're lonely, take a small step outside if you're able. Join a group – even seeing a few of the same people once a week can make the biggest difference. And if you know someone else that's lonely, start the group, be the friend, be the difference.

Because life can change in the blink of an eye.

Violet switches off her phone, picks up her keys and walks out of the door. She heads for the lake and plonks herself down on the bench by the water's edge, her own words from her article echoing through her mind.

Violet had been the lonely one when she first arrived in the village. Since then, she's been so busy believing it was everyone else that needed her. Chrissie with her bereavement, Tammy with her sudden dive into a world she knew little about. Each one of those she's been 'helping' has taught Violet how to live again, how to let people in.

Giving up her life up north had felt like too much.

Pat-the-Fiat had practically dragged her down here kicking and screaming. But reconnecting with her mum has brought her more joy than she's ever dared hope for.

Her mum still needs her. She won't pursue the internship. This time, she's more than happy to make the sacrifice.

CHAPTER 49

Tammy

TAMMY'S LEGS SHAKE AS she climbs up to her flat, one hand on the railing and the other held by Violet.

'Thank you for coming to get me from the hospital.' Tammy's voice comes out like a squeak and she doesn't know why. It's being back here again. Last time she was on these stairs she was leaving forever, thinking nobody wanted her to stick around.

'Don't be daft. I've been counting down the days for you to come home. We all have.' Violet throws Tammy's holdall onto the sofa once they're through the door. 'Hope you don't mind, but I've made you up a fresh bed. And the flowers on the side are from everyone at Helping Hands.'

Warmth travels through Tammy's chest, melting some of the tiredness she'd felt on the journey home.

'Sit down, feet up. I'll make a drink,' says Violet.

Tammy has a lot she wants to say. She reaches into the pocket of her hoody and pulls out the list she'd made this morning of all she needs to do.

'Is that a to-do list?' Violet looks delighted.

Tammy nods. 'Can I borrow your computer? I need to fill a form out for the people who put my benefit money in the bank. I have to tell them I'm working part-time, so they send me less money.'

'Working?'

'At the hairdresser's. Julie said I can start back next month if I feel well enough.'

'Next month?' Violet's forehead needs ironing, it's all creased. 'But you've only just come out of hospital. And how will you get to Brighton and back each time?'

Tammy grins. 'I'll be fine. And I'll get the bus. I'll just try not to get hit by one this time.'

'Not funny,' Violet says, but she still laughs.

As soon as they've finished their coffees, Violet disappears, coming back a few minutes later with her laptop. 'Help yourself. Do you need some help with the form?'

Tammy thinks for a moment. 'I'll try and do it myself first. If I get stuck, I'll ask you. Is that okay?'

'More than okay.' Violet plants a kiss on Tammy's forehead. 'I'm proud of you for attempting the form on your own, and I've every faith in you. I'll try to stop jumping in all the time, but I'll always be here if you need help. I'll leave you to it – I said I'd go for a little walk with Adam and Bill this afternoon. I've got my phone switched on.'

After Violet's gone, Tammy lays the laptop on the coffee table and opens it up.

Violet hasn't closed it down properly and the screen is open on her messages. She presses a button, trying to get onto the Google screen so she can find the website with the form. Instead, she accidently opens an email.

Dear Violet,

Thank you for getting back to me. We were disappointed to hear that you're unable to attend the interview for the internship position at the newspaper, but I completely understand that you need to put your caring responsibilities towards your mother first.

Do feel free to get in touch again if your circumstances change.

Many thanks,

Tara Tunnock
Editor-in-chief
Brighton & Hove News

Tammy closes the laptop, feeling guilty for reading something that wasn't supposed to be for her. She opens it again, this time shutting down the email screen and searching for what she needs.

Something keeps tickling her mind, making it hard to focus on her form. It's that message for Violet from the newspaper. Violet always talks about how much she'd love to work for a newspaper; it was on her wish list. It isn't fair that she had to say no to an interview that could change her life. Tammy's already helped with her number two – maybe this is her chance to help with her number one.

Music seeps into her mind, and she gives into it, humming to begin with before belting out the words to Tina Turner's 'Let's Stay Together'. It had been one of her mum's favourite records and it helps her to think.

The idea crawls into Tammy's head and grows until it has enough words to say out loud.

She jumps up from the sofa, probably faster than the nurses at the hospital would like, but she needs to be quick if she wants to speak to Glenys before Violet gets back from her walk.

'What do you want?' Glenys looks like she can smell something horrible when she opens the door. Tammy had been waiting on the other side of it for a long time, watching the main door and willing Violet to stay away.

'I need to speak to you about Violet.'

Glenys' face gets softer and her nose unwrinkles. 'You'd better come in.'

Glenys' flat smells like baking and lavender. Tammy takes a big gulp of the delicious air and sits down at the dining table.

'Violet's been offered an interview. It's for her dream job, I think. And she's turned it down.'

Glenys reaches the table and leans on her frame, lowering herself into the chair beside Tammy. 'Because of me, I'm guessing,' she says once seated.

'Yes. But I have an idea.'

Glenys stays silent whilst Tammy lets all the words from inside of her head out into the air between them.

'It could work,' Glenys says slowly once Tammy pauses for breath. 'But I'll warn you now, I'm a right twat most of the time. I'm not easy to care for.'

'Oh, neither am I.' Tammy waves a hand away from herself. 'None of us are all of the time, that's the whole point. We'd all be pitching in if everyone's up for it. I'll be at the salon for two days a week, so it wouldn't always be me, but Adam and Bill are across the hall, and Chrissie, Claire and Abbas are only down the road. And Mrs Robson's upstairs when she's not at the library.'

'I won't need someone with me all the time anymore.' Glenys wriggles in her seat. 'I've been doing more and more the last few months for myself. I still have bad days but I'm stronger than I was. Having Violet back and going to the Helping Hands meetings – it's helped me to live a bit again. I was just getting through the days for so long. Sleeping, eating, sitting.'

'So, you're in?' asks Tammy.

'I'm in. If everyone else is. Let's start ringing around and see what people say.'

The noise of a key in the lock makes Tammy jump. Violet and Adam are back, carrying big smiles. Glenys gives Tammy a look that's all pointy.

'Violet, can you come up to my flat for a bit. I really need help with that, err, form. It was harder than I thought,' says Tammy.

'And I'll make Adam a drink. Off you go then,' Glenys shoos Violet away.

Tammy looks from Adam's face to Glenys' before leaving with Violet, crossing her fingers as she walks.

It's Violet's time to shine.

Tammy leads Violet into her flat and Violet smiles as she sits down on the sofa. She's probably pleased to be asked to help with the form. Tammy doesn't need to ask for her help so much anymore, and Violet always looks happy when she does.

She shows Violet what she's typed in so far, which is pretty much just her name and date, before adding the address of the salon very slowly, one letter at a time. After they've gone through some of the next bits of the form, Tammy's phone buzzes. She snatches it out of Violet's sight and holds it up close to her face, peering at the screen.

It's Glenys.

Adam, Bill, and the others are up for the new plan.

'Actually, you can go now. I think I've got the hang of it. Go back and spend some more time with Adam.' Tammy winks at Violet over the top of her screen. 'Thanks for helping – couldn't have done it without you.'

CHAPTER 50

Violet

THE COMMUNITY CENTRE IS humming with music when Violet arrives with Glenys.

Tammy's sitting by the coffee machine blowing up balloons. 'You might need to give me a hand with some of these,' she says. 'Mrs R has bought six packets. She's really gone all out on the decorations.' Her eyes are bloodshot with effort.

Mrs Robson is covering several small round tables with sparkling white tablecloths. She's wearing a Christmas jumper with flashing lights, despite the fact September's not quite finished yet.

'What can Mum and I do to help?' Violet asks her.

Mrs Robson looks over at the long table in front of the staging area. It's covered with bowls and platters and packets of food. 'The rolls need buttering, and the crisps need sorting into bowls. We have about an hour to go.' Mrs R tuts as she looks at her watch. 'Adam and Bill should be here by now. They're in charge of drinks.'

Violet stays close to Glenys as they make their way to the table. 'I'm so pleased you're here,' she says to her.

'I bet you are. There are about a thousand rolls here – you'd never get it all done on your own.' Glenys gives Violet one of her rare grins; one that Violet adds to a brightly coloured box in her mind. It's there for her to open on the days her mum's smiles stay locked away.

'I mean it, Mum. I know you find these things difficult when there's lots of people. Means a lot that you came.'

The front door bangs open and a large banner that says, *The Lowerstone Gazette Launch,* edges its way into the hall, followed by Claire and Abbas.

'Where shall we put this?' Claire shouts.

Glenys nudges Violet. 'Here he is.'

Violet follows her mum's gaze towards the entrance. Adam and Bill are walking through it.

Violet's tummy wobbles like it always does when Adam smiles at her the way he is right now as he walks towards her.

'I've brought a little something for when the dancing starts,' he whispers in her ear as he pulls her close. He shows her a play-list on his phone. 'I'm going to hook this up to the speakers later.' The songs are all from the winter of 2002 when Adam and Violet had first shared that first awkward kiss.

As six o'clock approaches, the community centre fills with so many people that Mrs Robson starts muttering about fire regulations.

'The whole village is here,' Claire says in Violet's ear.

Mrs Robson plugs an ancient microphone into a speaker that looks as if it's been in the dusty back cupboard since the day the community centre was built. She blows into it and wiggles it around, wincing when its feedback screeches across the room, bouncing against everyone's eardrums.

'Thank you, everybody, for coming here on this very

important day to celebrate the reopening of the community centre and the launch of,' she pauses as she looks across at Violet, 'the *Lowerstone Gazette.*'

Violet's heart swells as claps and whistles echo around the room.

Mrs Robson's still watching her. 'As soon as I've gone through the fire procedure, I'm going to invite someone up to speak to you about the paper. It's her initiative and I'm sure you'd rather hear about it from her.'

Violet's chest fills with excess air, and most of it gets stuck on the way out of her lungs. Her fingers and toes go numb and tingly. It had been hard enough to begin with, speaking in front of handfuls of people from the village in someone else's living room.

Everyone's here, even Kirsty and Kelly.

Someone squeezes her left hand, seconds before someone grasps her right one.

Chrissie one side, Mum the other. Two smiles. Two pairs of eyes that believe in the person they're looking at.

Violet walks towards Mrs Robson and takes the microphone.

'Hi, everyone.' Even her smile is shaking.

All those faces. Every one of their gazes points towards Violet in a swirling sea of expectant smiles.

Adam gives her a thumbs-up from the drinks table in the corner.

'I arrived back in this village nearly six months ago. I didn't want to come back; there were so many painful memories, and I'm not going to lie, I didn't plan on sticking around any longer than necessary.'

The natural hush of the hall is restored. The only noises

to be heard are from outside of its walls. The two-hourly bus chugging past, the chirping of the birds from the autumn leaves.

'I felt unwanted. Unworthy of a village I'd torn apart many years ago. I would do what needed to be done and get out again. Go back to the life I'd made for myself. The life that had very little room in it for other people. It felt easier that way.' Violet's voice goes hoarse at the end, and Abbas passes her a bottle of water.

'And then I met a few of you. I got to know you, some of you for the first time, and some all over again.' Violet glances at Adam who's wearing her favourite one-sided smile. 'I met people who care for others from the depths of their hearts every single day, even when they're pouring from empty glasses. People who will drop everything in a heartbeat to help out a relative stranger. Some of you have circled through hell and kept going anyway because you hold enough hope inside you that you will make it back out again. It's because of you that we were able to reopen this centre. It's because of all of you that the *Lowerstone Gazette* exists. It's here because so many of you cared enough to lend a helping hand.'

Violet takes a swig of her water. 'This group gave me back my confidence and taught me how to care. You may not know it, but you helped give me back my mum too.'

Glenys rolls her eyes and sticks her middle finger up at Violet, but she's smiling and her eyes brim with tears.

'She loves me really.' Violet grins as the room fills with throaty chuckles. 'So many of you have lent a hand to the carers in our group over the last few months. We wanted to give something back to the village. Going forward, we'll be using some of the money we get from advertising to fund this centre. It will mean that the Helping Hands Club and any other community groups will have a space to meet. This paper means a lot to all of us. I'm so grateful that you've all come to support its launch today and I hope you all enjoy reading it for years to come.' Violet raises her water bottle in the air. 'To the *Lowerstone Gazette*.'

Arms and drinks are raised to the roof as Violet's words are echoed back to her.

Chrissie gets out of her seat and makes her way towards Violet. She takes a piece of paper out of her pocket, plucking the microphone from Violet's hand.

'I had the pleasure of teaching this woman. She had talent back then, bags of it. I know she'd tell you all about everything she messed up when she was younger, the regrets she has about not chasing her dreams sooner. But I'd like to read something she wrote for the last online issue of the *Gazette*.' Chrissie unfolds the paper in her hand and reads the loneliness article that had gone viral last week.

Swirls of pride dance inside Violet as she listens and watches other people listen. Her words matter, they make a difference, even just for a handful of people in a village she dares to call home.

A round of applause breaks out across the hall when Chrissie's finished reading.

'I think we can all agree that these words are important, and that we should keep on looking out for each other. Let's do everything we can to make sure that no one in our village stays lonely for long.' Chrissie finishes with a smile.

More clapping, and Tammy grabs the microphone. 'Hands

up who thought that was good?' She peers around the room, grinning when all the hands shoot up in the air. 'Hands up who thinks Violet should have the job she wants at an even bigger newspaper?'

Confused faces point in different directions and a few uncertain hands go up.

'Violet, you don't have your hand up.' Tammy puts both hands on her hips.

'How did you …?' Violet reaches out to take back the microphone, but Tammy keeps hold of it.

'I have a surprise for you.' Tammy is jigging about on the spot now as if she's about to take off. 'I emailed the nice lady back at *Brighton & Hove News*, and you have an interview.' The grin takes up Tammy's whole face and clearly she's expecting Violet to join her with the jigging.

Violet's heart quickens. It's like a snare drum in there. 'But – how?'

'I saw the emails on your computer when I was doing my form, and thought I'd send the lady an extra one from you, saying you'd changed your mind. The interview's tomorrow morning.'

'Tomorrow?' Violet yells, forgetting she's next to the micro-phone and she makes herself jump along with the rest of the room. She looks across at Mrs Robson by the speaker and makes a turning gesture with her hand. 'Could you please?'

Mrs R nods before leaning over and switching off the mic, giving Violet a chance to take two slow breaths.

Tammy's just trying to do something nice, Violet *knows* this. But she's having to work hard to keep the stress from her voice.

'Tammy, there are so many reasons why I can't do this. I don't even know if I can get there tomorrow. I'd have to get someone to sit with Mum ...'

'Ha! That's where you're wrong. It's an online interview. Tara Tunnock said it would be fine.'

Violet blows out a breath big enough to extinguish a hundred birthday candles. 'But there's a reason I turned down the interview in the first place ...' She cuts herself off when she sees the crowd that's appeared around them.

Glenys clears her throat and leans over her frame. 'I know about the job interview. And I know you turned it down so you can keep caring for me, but there's no need.'

'I'm going to sit with your mum whenever she needs me to, on the days I'm not at work,' says Tammy. 'If you help your mum get up and ready in the mornings, one of us can check on her and help with lunch, and then you'll be back in the evenings. I know how to look after people – you showed me how.'

'And Adam and I are only across the hall if they need anything,' says Bill who's appeared behind Glenys' shoulder. 'I just want you to be happy, as happy as you've made my son by coming back home to the village.'

Adam slips past the group, walks towards Violet and takes her hand in his. 'What do you reckon?'

Violet swallows the mountain of emotion that's wedged inside her. 'It's so incredibly kind of you all. And I appreciate it – truly. That job really would change my life. But I'm just not sure. I can't let you all stop living your lives just so I can follow my dreams.'

Mrs Robson makes a huffing sound. 'Stop living our lives,' she mutters. 'Always so dramatic.' She stands up next to Glenys.

'It's mostly thanks to you, Violet, that we all have each other. You brought us together by founding the Helping Hands Club and we're a family now, whether you like it or not. Caring is what we do. Chrissie and I have already said we can come and sit with your mum whenever you and Tammy are at work. We'll all be company for each other.'

'Please do the interview.' Chrissie smiles through misty eyes. 'Ever since you were a girl and running the school newspaper you've always wanted to write. Don't throw away an opportunity when we're all happy to support you to make it work.'

Violet surrenders to the tears. 'Thank you all so much. You – all of you – have become everything to me, and I'll never forget this. But I still have to get through the interview first.

'Just be Violet Strong,' Glenys says. 'They've already said they love your work, so the interview's probably just to check you're not an absolute twat.'

'Cheers, Mum.' Violet's mouth falls into a grin. 'I'll give it my best shot.'

The opening bars of 'Tubthumping' by Chumbawamba blares out from the speakers.

'Come and have a dance. Enjoy tonight, you've earned it. Blow off some steam and relax before the interview tomorrow.' Adam does a ridiculous robot impression.

'Fine.' Violet laughs and grabs both of Adam's hands as they make their way over to the middle of the community centre where everyone's dancing.

'So, if you get this job, you'll have crossed off two of the three things on your list – for real this time. You have your dream job and you'll still be helping people. What about the other one – your true love? You still saying you don't need a man, or do I need to get Tammy to arrange another date night, this time for all the village bachelors?' Adam chuckles into Violet's ear whilst everyone dances around them.

Violet laughs softly and Adam turns to face her. She catches his gaze and holds it still.

'I'm still saying I don't need a man.'

Adam stares at the glass of bubbly Claire's just handed him.

'I don't need a man. I just want one. And not just anyone.' Violet closes the gap between them and inches her face closer to his.

Adam smiles. 'You want me to write some more questions for him?' he murmurs, watching Violet's lips.

She snakes her arms loosely around his neck. 'No. I only have one question I want to ask him. Will he now admit that he has been and always will be my Gilbert Blythe? Does he know that my heart squeezes tight whenever I'm close to him? Does he know I want to kiss him every day until I die?'

'I think that's way more than one question,' Adam says. He puts his hands on her waist and lowers his mouth until it's almost touching Violet's. 'I think the answers to all those questions is probably *no-but-he-does-now*. And he probably wants to ask you two of the same ones. And he probably wants to kiss you.'

The butterflies inside bat their wings harder. 'Then he probably should.'

Violet washes down her toast and marmalade with a big gulp of coffee. She and Glenys were up early, and they've spent the past twenty minutes talking about last night's launch party. Violet's feet are still throbbing from all the dancing.

'Not long now. Better sit and prepare myself for the interview, and think of at least one impressive thing to say.' Violet can hear the sudden nerves poking out beneath her own chuckle.

The buzzer hums in unison with the knocks on the front door.

Tammy, Mrs R, and Adam are in the hallway. Bill is opening the main door to the building, and Chrissie, Abbas, and Claire are on the other side of it.

'What are you all doing here?' says Violet. 'Do we have a meeting I've forgotten about?'

'We're here for your interview, obviously.' Claire grins. 'Moral support.'

One by one, they all walk around Violet and into the flat. The living room looks tiny with everyone squashed in like that.

'Erm, this is all very kind of you, but usually interviews are solo affairs,' says Violet. 'I can hardly bring you all with me.'

'Well, take your laptop into your bedroom and get on with it,' says Glenys with force.

'We'll be as quiet as mice,' says Claire. 'You won't even know we're here.'

Violet looks around at the watching eyes and feels herself shrink like Alice after sipping the *Drink me* potion.

'You've got this,' Adam whispers.

'I'm so proud of you.' Chrissie's eyes are shining.

'Remember – don't be a twat.' Mum's contribution.

Violet closes her eyes, soaking up the good vibes before walking into her room and opening her laptop. What if she screws it up? All those people outside her door, believing she can do it. How would she tell them?

Dark whispers from old places play quietly at the back of her mind.

This isn't for you, it's for other people. People who deserve it. People who know what they're doing. People who didn't give up on their dreams half a lifetime ago.

Violet looks at the framed photo on her bedside table. It's of all the members of the Helping Hands Club huddled together in front of Malvern House. They'd had it taken for the front cover of the first print issue.

Be more Anne.

You've got this.

Just don't be a twat.

She looks for the link in the email that Tammy had hidden away in a separate folder and clicks on it.

Tara's friendly face fills the screen, and Violet's nerves melt like raspberry ripple ice cream on a sunny day.

She talks about her cleaning job at the *Salford and Manchester Times* and how she'd longed to be part of the stories that zapped from screen to screen. She talks about her book blog and the *Lowerstone Gazette*, and how she's hoping it will help fund support for carers in the area.

Before she knows it, almost an hour has passed and she's wondering how on earth she could have thought she'd have nothing to say.

'Such fantastic experiences.' Tara's face smiles through the screen. 'And we've had a wonderful response from the article you kindly allowed us to reprint.'

When the interview draws to a close, Violet closes her laptop and takes another peek at the photograph by her side.

She opens the door, and the living room falls to an immediate hush.

Violet drinks in the faces of those dear to her and thanks whoever may be up there for second chances.

Everybody needs one.

'Hi, everybody.' She speaks loudly and proudly. 'I have excellent news.'

Before she can say any more, so many pairs of arms wrap themselves around her, Violet feels like she's being hugged by an octopus. She hugs as many people back as she can reach.

Violet has her very own tribe, a brand-new job and a place she's proud to call home.

A person's home is their castle. It doesn't matter how tiny it is, or how messy. The important thing is that the door's wide open for those you care for.

ACKNOWLEDGEMENTS

This book exists because of the help of so many people that if I said everything I would like to, the words would fill the space of another novel.

Hugest thanks to my husband, Patrick, and my children, Jack and Emilie, for being the most supportive family and housemates I could ever ask for, especially during such a difficult year. I also add my sincerest thanks to all my children's teachers, especially Mrs G for providing such fantastic remote learning support during lockdown. Without that, editing this book and meeting my deadlines would have been far trickier.

To my wonderful agent, Sarah Hornsley from The Bent Agency. I will always be grateful to you for taking a chance on me, for believing in my work and for your support and dedication.

So many thanks to Katie Seaman, my fabulous editor. This book is all the richer for your brilliant suggestions and hard work. Thank you for always being honest and kind with your feedback (whilst using humorous analogies!) and for your encouragement and patience. Thank you to Gabriella Nemeth for doing such a wonderful job with the copy edits.

Massive thanks to my wonderful publicist, Lily Capewell, and equally wonderful marketing executive, Becca Joyce, and everyone from the amazing HQ Stories team. Thank you also to Charlotte Mursell for welcoming me into the HQ family.

This story began its life as my dissertation for my creative writing MA, so I would also like to thank all the lecturers on my course at Canterbury Christ Church University, especially my personal tutor and mentor, Peggy Riley. I have been extremely blessed to be a part of such special groups of human beings, such as the wonderful Inklings and you fabulous people at writing group, the brilliant Debuts of 2020 & 2021 who have been such a great support and sounding board during the past year. Thank you to my tribe, The Jesus Misfits, for listening to my rants, stresses and celebrations.

Anstey Harris, you have been a rock throughout the process of writing this story. Thank you for your endless support and cheerleading.

Mum, Dad, and Anita and David, thank you for being the best and most supportive parents and in-laws a person could ever ask for.

Lastly, but very importantly, I want to thank all carers, everywhere. I've had the privilege of working alongside carers in many settings, supporting people with learning disabilities, mental health and additional needs. I'm also a carer for my incredible husband. Thank you, Patrick, for being patient with my very own imperfect art of caring and for teaching me so much. I know from experience how difficult this last year in particular has been for carers and the people we support. I hope this story helps to highlight the challenges faced and that it brings some hope and laughter along for the ride.

Make sure you've read Jessica Ryn's uplifting and life-affirming debut novel

She's not lost. She's just waiting to be found . . .

Dawn Elisabeth Brightside has been running from her past for twenty-two years and two months precisely. So when she's offered a bed in St Jude's Hostel for the Homeless, it means so much more than just a roof over her head.

When St Jude's threatened with closure, Dawn worries that everything is about to crumble around her all over again. But with a little help from her new friends, Dawn is determined to find a way to save this light in the darkness.

And maybe, just maybe, Dawn will finally have a place to call home.

ONE PLACE. MANY STORIES

Bold, innovative and
empowering publishing.

FOLLOW US ON:

@HQStories